I0670278

A DESPERATE CHOICE
A SOPHIE STAR SERIES BOOK SIX

L. J. WEBB

A DESPERATE CHOICE

A Sophie Star Series Book Six

BY L. J. WEBB

Copyright © 2023 by Linda J Webb
Published by L. J. Webb
Longview, WA

Cover by Adebayo S. Oluwatosin

Some of the Bible Stories in this book are paraphrased by the author to move the story along.
Scriptures that are quoted are from the following versions.
King James Version
Or the
New King James Version®
Copyright © 1982 by Thomas Nelson.
Used with permission. All rights reserved.

eBook ISBN **979-8-9888416-2-3**
Paperback ISBN 979-8-9888416-3-0
Library of Congress Control Number: 2023921151

This is a work of fiction. The characters, dialogues, and incidents are a creation of the author's imagination and are not intended to be taken as real. Any similarity to any person, living or dead, is entirely coincidental. Any discrepancies to law enforcement policies or legal processes were made to move the storyline along and were not intended to reflect accurate procedures.

No part of this book may be reproduced, stored in a retrieval system, or transmitted, in any form or by any means electronic, mechanical, photocopying, recording or otherwise without prior written permission.

Do not be deceived: "Bad company ruins good morals." I Corinthians 15:33 (Amplified Bibl

TABLE OF CONTENTS

CHAPTER ONE

TUESDAY

I was the first one to come around. My mind started to rally, and I could feel I was lying on something hard and cold. I was on my side and rolled over on my back. The pain in my ribs brought me out of my stupor quickly. The memory of what happened became fresh in my mind.

I opened my eyes, "Robin," I called out, barely recognizing my voice; it was so raw. He didn't respond. I tried to turn my head; it hurt, but I needed to find my brother. "Robin," I cried out again, with no response. I looked to my left. My brother was lying unconscious on the garage's concrete floor, bleeding. His arm was twisted in a way that made it evident it was broken.

I tried to stand, but my body wouldn't support me. I crawled over to Robin and tapped his face. "Robin, wake up."

Robin opened his eyes but started crying out in pain when he became fully conscious.

"It's ok, Rob, I'm going to take you to a hospital," I used the bumper of the old Jeep behind us and pulled myself up. I bent over to try to breathe through the pain.

I sat on the Jeep's bumper, positioning myself behind my brother. I put my arms under Robin's to try to lift him, but he was in no condition to help. My brother screamed out in pain.

"Rob, listen to me. You have to help me get you on your feet. I know you're in pain. But I have to get you to a hospital."

"I can't, Felix."

"You have to. Now, bend your knees when I put my arms under your armpits. Try to get your feet under you."

It took three tries to get Robin on his feet. I put Robin's good arm around my neck. I practically dragged him to the 1970 Boss Mustang my dad gave me for graduation before he died. Someone had taken it into his shop for repair and never picked it up. Legally, it was considered abandoned. He later heard the man died, but no one came looking for it.

I opened the back passenger door and set Rob down. Then I went to the other side, put my arms under his arms, and slid him in so he could lie down.

I got in the car after shutting both doors and the now empty trunk. The keys were still in the ignition. The garage door was open, so I backed out.

I could hear Rob in the back seat moaning and whimpering. *This is all my fault. Rob never wanted anything to do with this. When Mom died of Covid, Dad fell apart. He started drinking all the time. When the lockdown lifted, Dad had lost his auto repair shop. He no longer cared. He didn't look for a job. We survived by the government unemployment benefits and handouts until those stopped.*

Then, the deferments ended, and we got a letter that we needed to start making house payments again. But there was no money. I returned to my tire shop job, but it wasn't enough to pay for everything. I made partial payments on the house, but then they refused the partial payments. Robin had been going to trade school when everything shut down. The trade school remained closed even after the lockdown lifted. Dad had become ill from all the drinking, and someone had to stay with him. Rob took care of him so I could work.

Dad died a few months later from liver disease brought on by the alcohol. He had a small burial policy. We received a check in the mail. I was making arrangements for his burial when I got a certified letter saying our house would be repossessed unless I paid them $8,722.

I had a choice to make. Use the money to put Dad in a nice coffin, bury him next to Mom, or keep the house. I paid the money to the mortgage company. I had enough left to cremate Dad and asked the funeral home to bury his ashes in my mother's plot with her.

It didn't take long for us to get behind on house payments again, even with the minimum wage job Rob found.

That's when I made the worst decision of my life.

I pulled up at the emergency room door and ran in, looking for someone to help me get Rob inside. The man at the counter grabbed a wheelchair and came out to the car with me. We managed to get Rob into it, and the man pushed him into the emergency room while I parked the car.

I registered my brother and myself at the counter and situated Rob's wheelchair before I sat next to him.

A half-hour later, a triage nurse called Rob's name. I got up and pushed his wheelchair into the triage room. I asked to stay. She saw that I needed treatment, too, so she let me.

The nurse took our blood pressure, temperature, and shined a light in our eyes. I could see her concern that our blood pressure was high. She kept us in triage instead of moving us back out to the waiting room. She put a catheter in our arms to give us fluids through an IV. She continued to check our blood pressure every fifteen minutes.

A phlebotomist came in and drew blood. It looked like Rob had fallen asleep, so I closed my eyes.

I was startled when the nurse returned and started trying to wake Rob.

"Robin, Robin," she said as she patted his face. When he didn't respond, she left the room and came back with an ER doctor. He tried to rouse Robin, even rubbed his chest bone to stir

9

him. When it didn't work, he told the nurse to get an orderly and take my brother for a CT scan.

I started to follow the ER bed he was on, but the nurse told me to go back to the waiting room. I watched until I didn't see him anymore, then rolled the IV out as I left the room.

As I sat there waiting, I wondered if I had changed one thing I had done, would everything be different? Maybe if I hadn't decided to visit Derreck that night. We used to sneak out to see him when our folks went to bed. We weren't allowed around him because he was older and into drugs. He had caused the family a lot of heartache. But we thought he was cool. He never tried to get us to try drugs. I don't know why. But he gave us beer, and we played poker with him and his friends. We usually lost our allowances.

We went to see him a couple of months after Dad passed away. He wasn't strung out like I remembered. He had a nice apartment and seemed to have money in his pocket.

When we walked in, he handed us each a beer, and I asked him if he still did drugs. He said no, but he qualified it with; he only smoked weed now. He never touched the hard stuff.

I asked him why. He said he met a man in rehab. They became friends. His friend had been in and out of rehab several times. But this time, something one of the counselors said stuck in his mind. I asked what it was.

Derreck repeated it to me. 'All of you here have chosen to live a wasted life. Some counselors say now that you are addicted, you are victims. I don't believe that. Don't get me wrong,' he said. 'Right now, you are an addict. But you can free yourself of this bondage the same way you chose to become a drug user. Not by yourself, not right now. But with help and making a choice every day, choosing to get loose of this millstone around your neck.

'There are those who find that strength from God. And to me that is the best way. However, it's up to you. Choose to get better. Don't be a victim of your own making.'

Derreck said the other counselors didn't use that approach. But he and his friend helped each other. They talked about getting out and going into business together. It worked for them. They decided to supply drugs rather than use them.

I told him that was hypocritical and not likely what the counselor intended. But he said somebody would supply the drugs, so why not them? They set up a business plan and figured out a way to keep off the DEA's radar. They committed to each other to stay off the hard stuff. They had an endless supply from a drug lord who moved to Austin from Mexico. The man bought eighty acres just outside the city limits, although Derreck nor his partner had been there.

It had been over an hour since they took my brother, so I went to the counter and asked to see him. The girl at the desk looked up his name and said he was in emergency room 12. She pointed to the door and buzzed me in. I went to look for his room, rolling the IV beside me.

I pushed the curtain back and saw my brother awake on a bed. "Robin, how are you feeling?"

"I hurt, but they give me painkillers through the IV. And they set my arm."

I saw his arm in a black, heavy-duty plastic cast. "Has the doctor told you anything yet?"

"No. Not since he set my arm."

"I'm going to find someone to tell us what's happening."

I went to the nurse's station and asked to see Robin's doctor. The male nurse made a call and told me the doctor would be in shortly.

The nurse and the doctor came in and spoke to us. He said Robin had cracked ribs, a broken arm, and a concussion. Because of the concussion, they wanted to keep him overnight.

Then, the doctor saw I was also in need of treatment. He listened to my chest, then pressed on it. When I cried out, he told the nurse I needed an X-ray.

The nurse put me in a wheelchair and took me to imaging. In fifteen minutes, I was out of there and put in an ER room next to my brother.

The doctor returned an hour later and told me I had two cracked ribs. He said they no longer wrapped cracked ribs, since it made it hard to take a deep breath. There really wasn't much they could do but let them heal. He asked the nurse to keep me there until my blood pressure went down and to put pain medication in my IV.

I asked her to let me know when they sent my brother to a room. I wanted to stay with him.

The male nurse nodded, and I laid back on the ER bed.

Four hours later, they finally took my brother to a room on the third floor. The nurse came and checked my blood pressure. He said I could go to Rob's hospital room, but an orderly had to take me in the wheelchair.

The nurse handed the orderly doctor's written instructions to the head nurse. I was to have one more bag of fluids with pain medication, and then they could remove the catheter.

Once I got to the room, I moved out of the wheelchair and into the reclining chair next to Rob's bed. I watched my brother sleep for a while.

I should have found another way, but Derreck made it sound so easy.... I told him we were having trouble making our house payments. When I told him how much we needed, he laughed.

'I will make that in a couple of days. Look,' he said. 'I can hook you up with my source.'

Robin's eyes got big, and he looked at me. I could tell he wanted nothing to do with it. I told him we didn't want to be drug dealers. Derreck laughed again.

'You don't have to do it as a living. Just do it long enough to get you on your feet. Then, Robin can get back in trade school and you can open your own tire shop.'

I thought about it and asked how it worked. Robin poked me in the ribs. I knew he wanted to leave, but I kept asking questions. I asked Derreck what kind of drugs he was talking about.

Derreck told me he and his partner started with fentanyl, but too many of their customers died from overdoses. After that, they decided to stick with cocaine. He said they built their business on the middle to wealthy clients and vetted new customers. They buy bricks of cocaine from a source they know, who cuts it with only sugar and caffeine. By using the same source every time, they can be sure it's not cut with fentanyl. Their customers knew that and became loyal to them. It was a good business move. He said he could easily clear $75,000 on one brick or Kilo of cocaine, selling it in one-gram baggies. They deliver the product to the customer so no one can lead the police to Derreck's home. The buyers must purchase a minimum amount to make delivery worthwhile, or they won't deal with them.

Derreck was willing to introduce me to his source, but the minimum purchase was four kilos. I told him there was no way I could sell that much. This was a one-time thing. Derreck said he would take two bricks off our hands, but we couldn't tell Luis DeLeon's man.

I knew I needed to convince Robin this was a good idea, so I told Derreck I'd get back to him.

Rob and I argued all the way home. I told him we needed the money to get on our feet. The money would pay for him to return to school, and we would open an auto repair and tire shop when he graduated. He asked me how I planned to sell it. 'Are you going to stand on a street corner?' That was a good question. I wasn't sure. Derreck had managed to find clients. The kids I went to school with were still in college. I could contact the ones I knew had experimented with drugs in high school. I could see if they wanted to earn money by selling it on campus to people they knew.

When we got home, Robin went straight to his room, but I had already made up my mind. I was going to do it. Derreck had said that Luis DeLeon gave 30 days to pay. I'd only have to sell one brick to pay our half. I was going to do this with or without Robin.

Around midnight I called Derreck back. I knew he was up. I told him I was in. He said he would contact and make arrangements with Taco, DeLeon's man he dealt with. He had never actually met DeLeon in person. He said to call him back the following evening.

I waited to call until seven the next night. He said Taco was expecting me the next day at five in the evening and gave me the address. He said that wasn't typically where he picked up his stuff, but it should be fine. I told him I would call him when we got home so he could get the two bricks, he agreed to buy from me.

My head was down, and my eyes closed when the nurse came in to wake Rob again. But I wasn't asleep. My mind was still racing through how we ended up here. I lifted my head.

"How is he?" I asked. She jumped.

"Oh, you startled me. I thought you were asleep. Your brother's blood pressure is going down." She noticed Rob's fluid bag was low and went out to get another one. After she replaced it, she came over to me.

"My notes say this is your second bag. Is that right?"

"Yes."

"Good. I can remove your catheter," she disconnected the tube from the bag and removed the catheter from my arm. She put a bandage over the puncture wound.

As the nurse tended to me, the phlebotomist pushed his cart in. He went over to Rob and found a vein to draw blood.

When the phlebotomist left, I asked him to close the door. I got up and stepped over to see my brother. He had already fallen back to sleep. I patted his head and went back to the recliner.

My mind immediately went back to earlier the night before. *I told Rob I'd go alone to pick up the cocaine, but he said I needed someone to watch my back. It took a while to get to the property. Of the eighty acres DeLeon owned, five acres were enclosed by a ten-foot rock wall with concertina wire at the top. There was an enormous rod iron gate in front.*

We pulled up to a monitor on a brick pillar and pushed the button. We watched guards walking the compound with dogs while we waited.

'Yes,' a man's voice came out of the speaker, but no face on the monitor.

'We have an appointment with Taco.'

'Your name?'

'Felix and Rob Wynne.'

The gate opened on its own, and one of the guards held up his hand, indicating for us to stop. He walked the dog around the car and waved us on. We had no idea what he was searching for. A bomb?

We parked and walked to a large one-level stucco home with a terracotta tile roof. When we approached the door, another guard opened it before we knocked.

A guard walked us through the entry on a Mexican-patterned tile floor. The walls were in yellow-orange shades, and a half-round entry table was set against the wall. It held a bronze sculpture of a man breaking a bronco. It looked expensive.

I don't know what I was expecting. Maybe a stereotypical pockmarked fat man from the 'sixties' mob movies. But we walked into a huge, great room impeccably designed. Standing there was a handsome man taller than me with tanned skin, black hair styled short, and brown eyes. He wore khaki pants with a guayabera shirt in a medium blue with two stripes of dark blue embroidery running down the front.

He had a cigar and offered one to each of us, which we declined. While we waited for him to light his cigar, I could feel the cool breeze from four ceiling fans moving the air conditioning around us.

The man didn't introduce himself. I figured it was Taco.

The man asked if we were Derreck Wynne's cousins and if it was true this was a one-time purchase. I said yes to both questions. The man explained he was doing this as a favor. But he wanted to be clear about what would happen if we did not pay on time. 'That means 30 days. Not 30 days and one hour, or 31 days, but 30 days,' he said, then paused. 'I will break a bone for each hour you are late, and when all your bones are broken, I will start cutting off parts of your body. Since you are not regular customers, your price is $125k for four kilos.'

I indicated I understood, and he sent us out with one of the guards, who loaded our trunk with the four bricks.

As soon as we cleared the gate, I turned the air conditioner on full blast. I was sweating through my shirt.

Rob looked at me. 'Felix, we are in over our heads. We will never be able to sell this coke. And I don't think that man was someone named Taco. I think that was DeLeon.'

'No. No way the big guy would meet with us. Besides, we only have to sell two bricks," I said. "Derreck will sell the rest."

I was trying to be positive but was just as scared as he was. We didn't speak the rest of the way home. Rob pushed the garage door opener, and I pulled into the garage next to the old Jeep, Rob and I were restoring.

I got out of the car. Rob grabbed the remote to close the door, but before he did, someone pulled up. The rest happened fast. Two large men in black masks swooped down and beat us mercilessly. They never said what they wanted or why they were doing it. When Rob fell to the floor unconscious, that man moved over to the trunk of my car and opened it with the crowbar he used to beat Rob. I didn't see what happened from there because the man beating me put me out with the last punch.

I had just put the pieces together. No one knew about this but Derreck, his partner, and Taco or Luis DeLeon, if Rob was right. There would be no reason for DeLeon to steal his drugs. He could have simply refused to sell them to us.

That only left Derreck and his partner. My dad always said he was no good. He stole from every family member to keep feeding his drug habit before he got clean. Why would he do it? He had his own stash of drugs to sell. We were family.

The more I thought about it, the angrier I got. I didn't care that the sun hadn't risen yet. I was going to find out if he did this. And why.

CHAPTER TWO

WEDNESDAY

I pulled out my cell phone from my back pocket. The face was cracked. It must have happened when I hit the concrete on the garage floor. I dialed Derreck. The phone rang and rang. I thought it was going to voicemail when he picked up but didn't say anything.

"Derreck?" I heard an "oomph" on the other end. "Wake up, Derreck. I need to talk to you." I could hear the sounds of someone pushing themselves up from a lying position.

"Who is this?"

"This is Felix..."

"What time is it?"

I looked at my watch, "It's 5:20."

"What are you doing calling me at this hour?"

"Who did you tell, Dereck?"

"Tell what?'

"About the pickup last night."

"No one. What's going on?"

"What's going on is Rob is in the hospital, and I was in the emergency room."

"What?! What happened?"

"Someone followed us from the address you gave me and stole the bricks. You were the only one who knew about it."

"Are you accusing me of something?"

"Who else? Who did you tell?"

Derreck's demeanor changed, "Honest, Felix, I'd never do that to you. How could you think I would do that?"

"Rob's in a bad way. Somebody knew. THINK!"

"Ok, you called Tuesday early evening..."

"It was seven."

"Ok, seven. You know my cousin Willy on my mom's side. He comes over a couple nights a week, and we play poker. He sells a lot of product for us. He brought over a couple of big dudes he met at the bar. They wanted to play cards. Not long into it, they started asking how they would get their hands on drugs to sell. Big mouth Willy started yapping. I shut him up. No way was I going to sell to these guys.

"Then you called. I walked across the room to discretely grab my gun from my desk and slipped it in the back of my pants. I gave you the address and time, and then we hung up."

"They must have heard you."

"Even if they heard the address, they didn't know what you were going there for."

"They figured it out. What did they look like."

"Gideon was a big dude. Dante was about my size, maybe a little taller. Both were bulked up."

"What are their last names?"

"I have no idea. I never met them before."

"Would Willy know?"

"I doubt it. He just met them that night. They said they were from Dallas."

"It had to be them. I have to get it back. You'll help me, right? You owe for two of the bricks," I said.

"What are you talking about. This is your mess. Until that product is in my hands, I don't own it. When you're in business, you take the losses with the profits. This is on you."

I was stunned by the response. "You won't help me get it back?"

"No. First of all, we will never find them, and these guys are trouble. I don't do trouble anymore. I'm sorry, Felix, but you wanted to take the risk," Derreck hung up.

I sat looking at my phone for a long time. My insides were churning, and I was angry. Angry at Derreck for washing his hands of me when I needed him. Angry at myself for being so stupid, and if I thought God would have cared, I'd be mad at Him too.

I'll find these thugs myself and get back the cocaine. It can't be that hard to find someone.

I was getting sicker and sicker, stewing about it. I realized there was no way out for me. The situation was impossible. I decided to turn on the TV to stop my mind from racing. I was clicking through the channels when the nurse returned to wake Rob and take his blood pressure. After putting it on mute, I put the remote down and stood by Rob. I wanted to talk to him.

The nurse shook Rob, his eyes opened, but it startled him, and he was disoriented. He jerked his body and then cried out in pain. I turned his head to look at me.

"Robby, it's me, Felix. You're in the hospital. Calm down. You'll be fine."

"Felix?"

"Yeah, it's me, buddy," he calmed down. The nurse shone a light in his eyes to check the pupils but decided to wait to take his blood pressure. She felt it would be artificially high and said she'd be back. I sat on the edge of Rob's bed.

"How are you feeling, Rob?"

"What happened? Why are we here?" He looked at Felix and noticed his injuries for the first time. "Are you alright?"

"I'm fine. We'll talk about it tomorrow. Go back to sleep." I could see his eyes were closing as we spoke.

I went back to the recliner and unmuted the TV. Two people were sitting on an elaborately decorated set. I was ready to change the channel when I heard the woman mid-sentence.

"...I had made a horrible mess of my life. Made one big mistake after another. I didn't see a way out. But God saw through the mess I had made and put me on the path to salvation. When I finally heard the gospel preached at a small Pentecostal Church, I knew it was what I had been looking for my whole life. Jesus changed me from the inside. But He didn't just care about my soul. He also helped me to make things right in my life."

"Thank you for sharing your testimony with us. Is there anything else you want to say before we pray for our audience?" The male host asked.

"I worked with a minister's wife, and when she heard I got saved, she asked for my forgiveness. She said she used to pray for me but quit because she thought it was impossible for me to be saved.

"I say that because there may be someone listening, thinking no way she messed up her life the way I did. Trust me, if the Lord saved me, there is hope for you."

At that point, the nurse returned to take Rob's blood pressure. I muted the TV and watched them pray with the sound off. When the nurse left, the show was over. But I couldn't help but wonder if God could do that for me. I didn't know what her messed up life was about, but I was sure it had nothing to do with drugs. *I don't think God helps people like me.* Even though I was certain of that, a strange calmness came over me, and I closed my eyes and fell asleep.

The phlebotomist's cart woke me. I looked at my watch and saw that I had slept four hours. I looked over at Rob to see he was awake too.

I headed to the bathroom while the man took blood from my brother's arm. He was rolling the cart out when I walked in.

"Felix, were those guys there to steal the cocaine?"

"Lower your voice. Yeah, they took it all. At first, I thought Derreck betrayed us and sent them, but it wasn't him, at least not on purpose. Willy met these guys at the bar, then took them to Derreck's to play poker. They started asking about finding a supplier. Derreck shut them down. He said he had a bad feeling about them. That was about the time I called, and he gave me the address and time. The guys must have figured out what was going on and waited at the address, then followed us home.

"But don't worry, I will get it back."

"No. Felix, we could never win a fight with them...unless you want us to become murderers now, too."

I lowered my head. He was right. How deep into this pit was I willing to fall.

"We'll figure another way. You said Dad had a safe deposit box at the bank. Maybe he has money in there. We can sell your Mustang and the old Jeep. I'm sure we can come up with sixty thousand dollars in thirty days," Robby said. I didn't reply right away. "Felix, I don't need to go to school. I'll get a job, too. We'll get back on our feet. I don't want to be a drug dealer."

"It's not that, Rob. We owe $125 thousand, not half of it."

"No, Derreck was going to take half."

"He said he never took possession, so he doesn't owe us a dime and won't help."

"Dad always said he was no good," Rob said; he looked up at me. "What are we going to do?"

"I've got to find those guys and get it back."

The doctor came in hours later and said he wanted Rob to stay another night for observation. Fortunately, we still had state insurance. I told Rob I was going to go home and get cleaned up.

"I'll be back tonight and stay with you."

I pulled into the driveway; the garage door was still open. Blood was on the floor. I got out of the car and grabbed a bucket of sand we kept to absorb oil from the old Jeep that leaked. I spread sand over the blood to soak up what it could. Then, I closed the garage door. I figured I'd clean it up in a couple of days.

I unlocked the door and walked into the kitchen. First, I grabbed the cereal, the chocolate syrup, a bowl, and a spoon. I set them on the table, then reached into the refrigerator and grabbed the milk.

I poured the Cheerios into the bowl, poured chocolate syrup over them, then scooped a spoonful of sugar from the bowl on the table and sprinkled it on. Then I poured milk over it all and ate. When the Cheerios were gone, I still had milk, so I poured in more and ate that, too.

I headed to the shower, changed, and then grabbed my laptop. I had no idea why. Without last names, I had nothing to search for.

CHAPTER THREE

*"S*ophie, if you don't hurry, we will miss the boat. Literally," Houston hollered.

"Did you put doggie diapers in the bag with our stuff?"

"Yes, dear," Houston said.

Sophie came out of the room in a sleeveless white top, blue short pants, and deck shoes.

"Houston, you will be too hot in those jeans. Go put on a pair of walking shorts. Stick the jeans in the bag with my sweater."

"Yes, dear," he said in a jokingly sarcastic way.

"Don't dear me," Sophie snarked.

Houston grabbed all their gear and headed to the SUV. Emmett had left hours ago. He said he had to help Jared prepare the yacht they were renting and help haul all the supplies on board.

"I should have gone with Emmett to help get things ready."

"Houston, he told you he had plenty of help," she put a hand on his cheek. "You don't have to prove yourself to anyone. They know you're a good man."

"That's not it, sweetheart. I was always taught you never come after the work is done or leave before the cleanup is finished."

"And we will pass on that work ethic to our children. But really, it's all right."

Houston parked in the marina's parking lot next to CJ's SUV. The parking lot was almost full.

"Do a lot of people get on their boats on the fourth of July, Sophie," Houston said.

"They do. We had only done it a couple of times before I left," she put a leash on Bully, and Houston grabbed their bags.

"Lizzy told me they do it now every other year. The other year, they volunteered at the church's food booth. They all take turns in the booth or outside on the grill. Lizzy says it's great fun. And when they are not in the booth, they watch the kids and check out the art booths and the entertainment."

"I wouldn't mind volunteering for the fundraiser," Houston said.

"Me either."

CJ was on the pier when he spotted Houston.

"You timed it perfectly, showing up after all the work is done," CJ teased.

Houston gave Sophie a look. "He's kidding, Houston."

"Sorry, buddy. I was given bad advice," Houston replied and slapped CJ on the back in greeting.

"Well, the least you can do is carry on the last box, Houston."

Liam came up behind them on the dock, next to a woman Sophie recognized. She took Cherysh Chandler's place as the interview host of Good Morning Austin. Cher was now an anchor for the show. Sophie couldn't remember her name, but she knew the woman interviewed Ricky and Liam last week on the show.

"Hey, guys. This is Wynter White, she..."

"The host of Good Morning Austin. I recognize her, Liam," Sophie said, extending her hand. "I'm Sophie Star Townsend, and this is my husband, Houston, and..." Sophie patted Bully's head, who was sitting next to her, "this is Bully."

"Oh, yes, Liam mentioned you," Wynter said. "You're bringing a dog aboard a yacht?"

"He's a service dog," Liam said, trying to cover up the rudeness in how Wynter said it.

CJ saw his wife lugging a bag, Jett, and Coco on a leash. He ran to meet her at the top of the pier. He grabbed the shoulder bag she was lugging and Jett and headed to the yacht.

Wynter noticed and commented under her breath, "another dog?" Liam heard, hoping no one else did.

Houston stepped aside to let Liam and his date head up the ramp first. Then he supported Sophie's arm as they headed up. Bully walked up behind them.

Then Houston turned to reach out to Lizzy to help her onto the boat. Ricky and his date stepped up behind them. Sophie noticed the pretty woman with him, figuring it must be Deanna. She smiled at them as they made their way on board. Ricky introduced them.

"Deanna, this is Lizzy, my sister, her husband CJ, and their son Jett," he turned to Sophie. "And this is my other sister, Sophie, and her husband Houston."

"I'm so happy to meet you all. Ricky talks about you all the time," Deanna said.

Sophie laughed, "I hope not."

"It's all good, I assure you," Deanna smiled.

As they moved from the ramp, Sophie noticed Wes and Lady Be stepping onto the pier. She pointed them out to Houston. He headed down the ramp and up the pier to help pack their things onto the boat. He greeted them and saw the rest of the family coming up behind them, including Scarlett and Bridget.

Lawson came from the Bow of the yacht. When he saw her, he put an arm around her.

"Hello, Sophie, how's my patient," Lawson smiled.

"I'm great, Lawson. I'm so happy you were off so you could come."

"I'm on call for emergencies, but I'll call a water taxi if they call me in."

"Did you bring your lovely girlfriend I've heard so much about?" Sophie asked.

"She wanted to come, but her family had plans to go out of town for the holiday."

"I can't wait to meet her."

"You will like her," Lawson said.

"How long have you been here?"

"I came early to help."

"Please don't tell Houston. He wanted to come, but I told him Jared had plenty of help. He's already upset with me because he saw CJ here helping."

Lawson laughed, "I get it. No one wants to be thought of as a slacker." Lawson saw Houston lugging bags and chairs for Wes' family and headed there to help him.

As Jared backed the yacht away from the pier, the men set up additional deck chairs and TV trays. They were careful to make an easy flow for people to move around. Carmen Whiteing insisted her caterers supply all the food for the trip. The ladies were sorting through them, making sure anything that needed to be refrigerated ended up there.

The teens and kids took their backpacks and extra deck chairs to the top deck. China carried Jett up with her. Bully and Coco followed to spend time with the *cool kids*.

It took a while for everyone to be seated after saying hello. Sienna invited her cousin on her mother's side, Veronica Sutton. She had moved back from Seattle, where she finished her degree in Marine Biology. Veronica had that gorgeous girl next door look about her. Long, light brown hair, brown eyes, and a good figure. She was shorter than Sienna and had the same bubbly personality as her cousin.

Chantel, Rayne, and Piper sat with Sophie on one of the padded benches surrounding the deck. Xander, Blaze, Dex, Cade, CJ, Lawson, Jean-Paul, and Houston were standing along the railing talking. Ricky and Liam were sitting together with their dates, enjoying themselves.

The Scotts, Youngs, Diazs, Wes, and Lady Be were all sitting in the center of the deck with Emmett. Jared was still piloting the yacht.

Wynter started asking Liam questions about his family. Being a TV host, she recognized a number of famous people on the boat. Liam got the feeling she was going to use this outing as a way to promote her career. It would be quite a coup to secure interviews with celebrities of this caliber who don't usually do them.

"I'm going to go mingle, Liam," she said. He took her hand.

"Wynter, this is not a business trip. Please don't start interrogating my family."

She sat back down, "Look, Liam, I know what I'm doing, and I haven't been in one place with this many famous people. Carmen Whiteing, Scarlett Ryan, Blaze Walsh Cornish. This is an opportunity I can't pass up."

Wynter wiggled out of his hold and headed for Scarlett Ryan. Scarlett was sitting with Sienna, Veronica, and Lizzy. The guests had been moving around, enjoying being with all their family in one place. Wynter walked up on their conversation.

"...it is tragic, Scarlett, but Houston and Sophie got Teresa and Kato justice for their father's murder."

The women looked up when Wynter stepped into their space.

"Hello, I don't think Liam introduced us yet. I'm Wynter White. I'm a host on Good Morning Austin."

"How nice to meet you, Wynter," Sienna said.

"Dat is a lovely name," Scarlett said. Even with all the tutoring from the linguistic specialists Lady Be provided, Scarlett's accent came through occasionally. Everyone loved it. Brigett took to the tutoring and seldom slipped.

"Didn't you interview Liam and Ricky on your show?" Lizzy asked.

"Yes. That is how we met. This is our first date. And you are the vice president's daughter, right?" Wynter asked, turning to Sienna.

"Yes."

Veronica spoke up, "Well, you would be hard-pressed to find a nicer guy than Liam to date."

Wynter turned to Scarlett. "I really enjoyed your last movie, Scarlett. I notice you don't do many interviews. Is there a reason for that?"

"My sester and I want to 'ave as normal a life as we can outside of my wahrk. I want Bridget to avoid getting poehlled into de lifestyle dat surrounds de industry.

"It's mahre important to me to be kend and carin'. De traits ooehr families and friends can mirror for 'er."

"How long are you in town?" Wynter pressed.

Lizzy was getting uncomfortable with the prying. Scarlett kept her schedule a secret to keep the paparazzi away. She decided to distract Wynter.

"Sophie," Lizzy hollered. Sophie looked up and saw that Lizzy was calling her. She excused herself and walked over to her.

"Sophie, did Liam introduce his date to you?" Lizzy asked.

Sophie knew this tactic, "Yes. Wynter White, right? Let me take you around and introduce you to the rest of the family." Sophie could see that Wynter was annoyed at being dismissed, but she got up.

Jett was having a good time, but he was getting cranky. He threw his hat over the railing and started crying because he wanted it back. China picked him up and went to the deck railing above the lower deck, where his parents were.

"Lizzy," she hollered. Lizzy looked up. "Jett tossed his hat over the side, and now he's crying because he wants it back."

Lizzy turned to her companions, "He needs a nap." She started to get up, but CJ heard and told her he'd take care of him.

Veronica saw Liam sitting alone while Sophie introduced Wynter to the rest of the family. She headed over to say hello.

"Hi, Liam," Veronica said as she sat in the empty seat.

"Ronnie, hi. Are you here on vacation?"

"No, I'm back. I graduated in May," Veronica said.

"Congratulations. What was your major?"

"Marine Biology."

Liam leaned forward, "That's cool. Do you have a job waiting?"

"No. I'm applying to go out with an exploration team. I haven't been accepted yet. For now, I'll get a local job and keep applying."

"That sounds fascinating. Is there a certain area of exploration you want to specialize in?"

"Yes, I want to examine the health of the coral reefs worldwide," she lowered her head. "But you have to make a name for yourself to be invited on one of the boats."

"You will, you're smart. You'll get there."

"I'm going to save all my money because if you can contribute to the cost of the expeditions, you will more likely get invited."

"Yeah, I'm sure. Or you could run your own exploration."

"Yeah, like that will happen," she laughed. Liam had known her for many years. But what seemed like the first time, he noticed how pretty she was.

Sophie and Wynter made the rounds and made it back to Liam. Ronnie looked up.

"Oh, I'm sorry, did I take your seat?"

"Yes," Wynter said. Ronnie stood up to leave with Sophie.

"Ronnie," Liam said. She turned. "We'll catch up later." Liam smiled, and when Wynter turned to sit, he mouthed 'sorry' to Sophie.

"Who was that?" Wynter asked.

"Veronica is Sienna's cousin. I know you were introduced."

"Oh, yeah. She wasn't memorable."

Liam stared at her, shocked at her lack of graciousness and self-awareness. He turned to watch Ronnie intermingle and laugh with other family members.

"Sophie introduced me around. What I don't get is the deference everyone gives her. As far as I can tell, she is the least famous of the group," Wynter said.

"You have no idea who she is or what she has done. There are a thousand reasons why she is so loved. But the most recent is that we had no idea where she was for the last nine years. She showed up a few months ago. We are all so grateful she is back."

"Sophie disappeared?" Wynter asked.

"It's a long story. This isn't the place to get into it," Liam shut down the conversation. He didn't want her to find a way to use the information for her own benefit.

The young people from the upper deck came down in a group. Drew asked Aunt Carmen if they could get lunch.

"I'll help you. Go on down to the galley," Carmen said as she stood.

"I'll go with you," Anna said. Zoey and Ruby volunteered too.

The commotion from the group woke Jett. He stood in the small, padded playpen he'd been sleeping in and said, "Rue."

Drew looked over, "I see you, buddy," and lifted him from the playpen. "Pee-yew, air pollution," Drew held him away. Jett put his little hand to Drew's nose and pinched it when he said Pee-yew.

"Stop it, Drew, you know how to change a diaper," China said.

"Not one of these," he responded.

"I'll do it," China said, grabbing the diaper bag before taking Jett to one of the cabins.

"Ina," Jett kept saying, patting her face when she took him. "Eat, eat."

"Yes, Jett. I will feed you as soon as we change your air pollution, ok."

"K," Jett said as he pinched his own nose this time.

Jared had anchored the yacht a couple of hours ago. He sat down next to his brother. "Jared, I thought you would bring your new friend?"

"Nina had commitments with her own family. I'll bring her to the next BBQ," Jared assured him. "She is a fascinating woman."

"She better be. You have been talking about her for weeks. And based on what you said, she could be a model."

"Nina actually paid her way through college by modeling," Jared paused. "You know Houston and Sophie are building a house in the gated community?"

"Yeah, Dad told me."

"He wants our construction company to build it."

"I thought you and Dad turned that side of the business over to your project manager."

"We did. Our men mainly work with Walter Hutchinson's crew on the company Dad formed with him and Tom Curtin. But Walter has his own jobs and crew. We pull our men when we need a job done."

"So, you and Dad are going to have your crew do it?"

"Yeah. Dad and I only use our crew to build on our properties. I'll manage it. Besides, it's for Sophie."

"I'm so glad they are planning to make Austin their base," David paused. "I'm thinking of asking Sienna and Teresa if Kato can live with us while she's in Dallas at culinary school. He could have anxiety about being away from his sister. Being with Drew could help with that. They are as close as brothers."

"I know Drew would be happy about that," Jared commented.

"Anna and I would too. We love Teresa and Kato."

As the evening progressed and the sun started moving toward the horizon, you could hear the music beginning to play at the park. They could see the lines at the food booths get longer, and people were laying out blankets for the families to sit on the grass and watch the fireworks.

Sophie and Lizzy were collecting empty paper plates from dinner and taking them into the galley to put in the garbage. Scarlett came up behind them with hands full of empty plates.

"Do you mind ahpenin dat garbage bag fahr me?" she asked.

"Back to real life, huh, Scarlett?" Lizzy joked with her.

"De best part. I lahve being with all of you. It's such foehn," Scarlett paused. "Sahphie, I hoped I'd be able to be 'ere when you 'ave yooehr baby, but Chantel is due at de same time."

Sophie hugged her, "Of course, you need to stay with her. I want to be there, but I'm sure I won't be able to fly by then."

"Sahphie, we missed you so moehch. Rayne told oehs a little about what you ded fahr de trafficked wahmen. I'm 'ere fahr a few days. Will you spend time wit me and tell me how dat all came abooeht?"

"Of course, Scarlett. But I would much rather hear about you. Are you happy with your choice to follow Carmen into an acting career?"

"I lahve it, but I feel it 'as no 'umanitarian value. I want my life to matter."

"Scarlett, you work with Carmen's and Lady Be's charities. Helping orphaned children and those aged out of the system and onto the streets is very important."

"I know it is. But when I heard dat over a thousand wahmen were rescued frahm 'uman traffickin' by you and yooehr team... It makes me want my life to make a difference," Scarlett lowered her head.

Sophie directed her to the couch in the galley while Lizzy made sure no one came in so they could have a private conversation.

"Scarlett, God has a plan for your life. Your job gives you access to people the rest of us might never meet. You can make a difference wherever you are. Pray about what direction the Lord wants your energies to be directed. Jesus won't let your talent or desire to make your life make a difference go to waste. He gave you both your talent and your desire for a reason. The Bible says in Proverbs 18:16. 'A man's gift will make room for him and bring him before great men.'"

They were interrupted when Wynter tried to come into the galley. She had noticed Scarlett heading that way and wanted to talk to her.

"Wynter," Lizzy said louder than necessary, "are you having a good time?"

Scarlett hugged Sophie and whispered. "I always dank de Lord for brengin' you all into my and Briget's life. Please fend time fahr me."

"I will."

Wynter worked her way in and headed for Scarlett. "Scarlett, would you be willing to come onto my show for an interview?"

"I'm so sahrry, Wynter, but my schedule is foehll. Excuse me while I go back to my family."

Wynter watched her leave, then commented, "Well...isn't she full of herself."

"Excuse me," Sophie said.

"Scarlett Ryan has let her celebrity go to her head. She has no time for the little people anymore."

"You know, Wynter. People might think you were credible if you had any idea what you were talking about and did your research. Scarlett spends most of her time and money helping orphanages, so the children are happy and have a proper education."

"Then she should be happy for people like me who could get publicity for her charities."

"She is not looking for publicity for her good works. She is looking to make life better for the children," Lizzy said.

"What about you, Sophie? I've been told you have done some interesting things. You're not a celebrity, but people may be interested," Wynter said.

Lizzy was incensed. "If you had any idea..."

Sophie interrupted her. "Wynter, I'm afraid my life would bore your viewers. Let's go back out to the deck."

As they headed back on deck, they heard Lawson's cell ring. They knew it had to be an emergency because no one else had their cell phones on.

"Hello," Lawson said. He listened for a moment, then said, "I'll be right there."

"What's happened?" Emmett asked.

"A little girl is in heart failure. I need to get back."

"I've already called one of the boat taxis," David said.

"While we wait. Let's take a moment to pray for her," Anna said. Everyone stopped and prayed together.

The boat taxi picked Lawson up to take him to the pier. Another taxi would meet him and take him to the hospital.

Wynter plopped down on her chair next to Liam, who was busy laughing with his friends and didn't notice.

"Liam," Wynter poked him. Liam turned to her.

"Wynter, I didn't notice you came back."

"Yeah, well, why should you be any different from the rest of your friends," she chided.

"What are you talking about?"

"No one will talk to me. I know some big names are here, but I'm a celebrity too," she pouted.

"Wynter, there is not one of my family that would not speak to you like a friend. But you are trying to drum up business for yourself. That doesn't work with my family. If they wanted publicity, all they would have to do is make one call.

"They come here to be with family and friends. You could have become a friend. Instead, you put on an air of your own celebrity and tried to get a scoop and distanced them. You have no one to blame but yourself."

Wynter didn't reply. She sat back in the seat and said, "I need a drink."

"I'll get it for you. Do you want sweet tea or lemonade?"

"No, I need a real drink with alcohol."

"Wynter, have you seen anyone here with an alcoholic beverage?"

"I didn't notice."

"I told you I didn't drink."

"Yeah, but I knew some big names were coming. No way they don't drink alcohol."

"I hate to break it to you, but no one on this boat drinks. If you want me to get you something else, I'd be happy to."

"Lemonade then," Wynter relented.

Veronica was close by and heard. "I'll get it for you, Wynter."

"Thank you," Wynter said, then turned to Liam. "What's her name again?"

Dusk was fast approaching, time for each family to migrate and sit together for the fireworks. The young people grabbed cushions and sat in the middle of the deck. CJ pulled out Jett's little camper chair and set it on the deck next to China, placing him in it.

Bully came and lay down next to Sophie. Coco lied down by Jett.

Houston took Sophie's hand, "I'm excited for the ultrasound tomorrow." He kissed the palm of her hand and held it to his chest.

"Me too. I know you will love our child, whether a boy or a girl. But are you hoping for a boy?"

"Sophie, no. I want whoever the Lord blesses us with. And we already know it's a girl," he winked at her. "I was hoping our home would be ready, but realistically, it isn't going to happen."

"The cottage is big enough for the three of us until it is," she patted his face and smiled.

CHAPTER FOUR

I had no idea where to start looking for the thugs who beat us up and stole the cocaine. I called Willy to see if he had the last names of the guys he took to his cousin's house.

He didn't, but he said he met them at the tavern down the street from Derreck's. He was willing to go down there and see if anyone knew them. I told him I'd go with him.

We spent hours talking to patrons of the tavern. They either had no idea who we were talking about or didn't know their last names. The barkeep was more helpful. He said he had heard them talking, said they were from Dallas, and asked if he knew anyone who sold drugs. The barkeep didn't say anything but pointed them to Willy. Which is why the guys approached him and bought him a drink.

I was going around in circles, getting nowhere. I had promised Rob I'd be there to meet up with the doctor when he returned that afternoon. I thanked Willy for trying to help, leaving him at the tavern, and drove to the hospital.

Robby was looking better when I got there. He was awake watching TV.

"Felix, did you know that some birds mate for life? Cool, huh."

"Yeah, penguins too. How are you feeling?" I asked.

"I'm better. Penguins are birds too."

"Oh. I never realized that. Has the doctor come back today?"

"Not yet."

"Good," I dragged over the padded wooden chair and sat beside Rob. The other bed in the room was still empty. "I called Willy to see if he knew the last names of the thugs that stole our product. He didn't, so we went to the tavern where he met them. The barkeep said he heard they were from Dallas."

"How does that lead them to us?"

"They asked the barkeep if he knew someone who sold drugs. He directed them to Willy. Willy made offhand remarks about his cousin, Derreck. Willy said he was headed to a poker game, so they asked to join him. When they heard my call with Derreck, they took the chance we were picking up drugs."

"So, they laid in wait."

"Yes."

"Felix, we can't go after these guys; they'll kill us. I already told you that."

"Rob, we have no way to pay back DeLeon. We can check out Dad's safe deposit box at the bank, but I can't imagine much is there."

"Without their names, how do you expect to go after the cocaine?" Rob asked.

"We could hire a detective."

"A detective? And just what do you plan to say to a detective? We bought cocaine, and some dudes stole it from us, and we want you to find it. Are you nuts? They will turn us into the cops."

"Maybe I won't say they stole our drugs. I could just say I need to locate the two men," I argued.

Rob started to respond, but the doctor and his scribe came in.

"Mr. Wynne, how are you feeling today?"

"Better."

"Good, Good. I'd like to do another CT scan to make sure the swelling in your brain has gone down." The doctor shined his penlight into Rob's eyes, moving it quickly to see how the pupils reacted. He looked at the chart and saw that his blood platelets were still low, and his blood pressure was still a little high.

"I'd like you to stay one more night for observation, Mr. Wynne," The doctor said. Rob looked at me.

"Are you worried about something, doctor?" I asked.

"I'll know more after the CT scan."

"Ok, doctor, if you think he should stay," I turned to Rob. "Right, Rob?"

"Yeah, ok."

After the doctor left, I moved the wooden chair out of the way and scooted the recliner closer to the bed. I could see out the window, and the way Rob's bed was placed, he could too.

"It's the fourth today, Felix, I miss Mom and Dad. We always went to the park and bought dinner from the food booths," Rob looked out the window toward the park. We saw the first firework burst into a thousand pieces of white sparkles that zigzag back down to earth.

"Me too, Rob," I whispered as we watched the fireworks.

When it was over, I noticed Rob had fallen asleep. I patted his arm. "Maybe next year, brother."

THURSDAY

After Lawson performed surgery on the two-year-old girl for heart failure, her father collapsed in the waiting room. Lawson worked on him in the ICU, waiting for his surgical team to return. He did the angiogram himself, inserted the die, and waited for the images to appear.

Lawson spotted the blocked artery and performed the carotid endarterectomy while he had the patient on the table.

Lawson spent the night in his office, checking on the man every few hours.

Lawson hated leaving his friends last night. He loved his job, but his family and friends made him genuinely happy. And now that he could be around Sophie without feeling the pain of her rejection, he was happy to have their friendship restored.

He couldn't tell Sophie this, but his new girlfriend, Anita, is like her. Intelligent, funny, and challenged him to get out of his routine. Being single for so long made him set in his ways.

Lawson cleaned up and went to the pediatric ward to check on his little patient. Her mother was asleep in the recliner next to her.

A nurse followed Lawson in with the chart. He watched the monitors for a minute, leaned into the crib, and whispered her name to wake her up. Her mother sat up, startled.

"Is everything alright, doctor?" She said, frightened.

"Yes, I'm here to check on Candy," the little girl smiled at him. "Hello, Candy, you look pretty today."

"Preddy," she mimicked.

Lawson placed his stethoscope on her chest. She reached up and patted his face, saying, "preddy." Lawson laughed. He rolled her on her side, placed the stethoscope on her back, and listened again.

Lawson turned to the nurse to check the chart for the last blood test results. The tests showed improvement.

He looked up at Mrs. Hull. "Odett, at this point, your daughter is responding as expected. I would like to keep her here for four or five days."

"But she's getting better, right?" Odett asked.

"Yes, her tests show what I would expect at this point."

"How's my husband?"

"I kept an eye on him through the night. He should be fine. I'll have him move to the third floor this afternoon. Candy should sleep quite a bit in the next few days, so don't be afraid to leave her and see your husband. If he feels up to it, he can come down in a wheelchair and sit with her for a while. He should be able to go home tomorrow."

Odett stood and came around the bed and gave Lawson a quick hug. "Yesterday was the worst day of my life. I thought I was going to lose my husband and my daughter. Thank you, Doctor Lawson."

"I wish I could take credit, but God intervened for your daughter. It was touch and go for a while."

Lawson smiled, returned the chart to the nurse, and checked on his other patient.

I woke up first and headed to the bathroom to freshen up. A nurse gave me a patient packet with a toothbrush and toothpaste.

When I left the bathroom, Rob was awake, and a nurse was taking his vitals. The phlebotomist was waiting at the door to take his blood.

The day nurse who took vitals was young and pretty, and I could see Rob staring at her. She smiled at him and made small talk while she took his temperature.

I moved the recliner back, grabbed the padded wooden chair, and sat down. After the guy took his blood, I whispered to Rob.

"Why don't you ask her out?"

"Who?"

"The cute nurse."

"No way she would go out with a loser like me," he said, moving his head away.

"Rob, since when do you think you're a loser."

He turned to me, "Look at us. We are in the hospital because we got beat up by thugs who stole drugs from us that we intended to sell. In my book, that makes me a loser."

I thought about what he said, or more to the point, what I had done to my brother. He never wanted this. He wanted to be a mechanic. I did this to him. Now, it was up to me to get us out. How, was the question.

"I'll call your breakfast into the kitchen. What do you want? When it comes, I'll go to the cafeteria and eat."

"I want the pancakes and scrambled eggs…sausage too."

"You know that's like turkey sausage or something," I told him.

"I don't mind."

When his food came, I headed downstairs and grabbed the same thing. The sausage wasn't half bad. I couldn't get our situation out of my mind. I'd need help tracking these guys down. Rob thinks it's crazy to hire a detective, but I don't have a choice. On the other hand, I wasn't sure how I would pay for it.

Houston had asked Emmett to watch Bully while he took Sophie for the ultrasound. He knocked on his sliding glass door and saw him coming.

"Good morning, Houston. Heading out soon?"

"We are supposed to, but Sophie seems to be in snail mode."

Emmett laughed, "Son, you have need of patience. You have to go with the flow when your wife is pregnant."

"Thanks, Emmett. That sounds like good advice. Are you sure Bully won't be in the way?"

"No. Jared and I are headed over to mark the boundaries for your foundation today. Bully can come with us."

"Would it be possible to get a remote for the gate so I can show Sophie later?"

"Of course, come in. Let me get one from my office." Emmett grabbed a remote and handed it to Houston.

"Thanks, Emmett. I can hardly wait to see the house go up." Houston headed back to the cottage.

Sophie was at the door waiting. "Now, who is holding up the train," she said, teasing him.

Lawson was in Mr. Hull's room in the ICU. He checked his vitals and listened to the blood flow using his stethoscope.

"Mr. Hull, your arteries sound good, but I want to keep you one more night. The stress you were under brought on by your daughter's condition can cause other issues."

"How is she, Doctor?"

"Candy is responding well. I will be keeping an eye on her for a few more days."

"Odett said I could see her when you move me upstairs."

"Yes. But I want you in a wheelchair."

"Will I be able to hold her?"

"Mr. Hull, your daughter is hooked to monitors and an IV. But you can lower the crib's side and get close to her."

"Thank you, Doctor. I was told we were blessed to be in Austin when this happened. They say you are the best pediatric heart surgeon in the US."

"Mr. Hull, you have a lovely daughter, and I am happy I was able to help her."

Lawson left the room and went to the nurse's station.

"Mr. Hull can be moved to the third floor as soon as you have an orderly available."

"I'll call it in now, Dr. Cornett."

Sophie was thumbing through a magazine while waiting for her name to be called. Houston put his hand over hers.

"Sweetheart, are you nervous? You aren't even looking at the pages," Houston said. She turned to him. He could see it in her eyes.

"What if something is wrong. I lost our first baby."

"*We* lost her. But there is no reason to be concerned. Dr. Banerjee has analyzed your blood and hasn't seen anything to be concerned about."

"I know. I just want to see for myself."

"We will, in a few minutes…" he started to say more, but a receptionist appeared and called her name. He kissed her cheek and helped her up.

After the doctor rubbed the gel on Sophie's abdomen, he ran the transducer probe back and forth. The doctor turned the screen so Houston and Sophie could watch as an image started to show. Houston took her hand.

"Alright, let's see what we have here. Do you want to know the sex of the baby?"

Sophie looked up at Houston, he smiled, "yes."

The image was becoming clear. "Oh," the doctor said.

Sophie began to panic, "Is something wrong?"

"No, no. It's not that. Let me keep checking. Give me a minute."

Houston squeezed her hand, trying to control his own fear. He whispered in her ear, "It's all right, sweetheart. Our baby is fine."

The doctor kept moving the probe further around the side of her belly. Going back and forth. Then he smiled.

"Congratulations. I don't know how I missed it, but it appears you will be having twins." There was no response. The doctor looked over at their shocked faces. Then smiles and laughter came.

"Twins, Doctor? Are you sure?" Houston asked.

"Yes, look here," the doctor ran the probe to the side of her belly. "See," he pointed, "that is another foot. This baby is hiding behind his or her twin."

"Can you determine the sex?" Houston asked.

"Of the one in front. Yes. You have a little girl. We will have to wait for the twin to move to determine the sex of the other one. I'll do another ultrasound in a few weeks. But now that I know you are having twins, I want to see you at least twice a month."

"Are you worried something will go wrong, Dr. Banerjee?" Sophie asked.

"No. But I was there after you drowned in the ocean, and I know how close to death you came. I don't want to take any chances. I'll keep a close eye on you."

Dr. Banerjee handed Sophie paper towels to wipe off the gel. "Make an appointment for two weeks before you go, and I will send orders for a blood draw downstairs. Please do it before you leave the hospital," the doctor printed out the image and gave it to them, then got up to leave. He hesitated at the door. "I have a vested interest in your pregnancy. I wasn't sure...," he paused. "I admired what you and your team did for our country."

Houston and Sophie watched him walk out the door. They were surprised he showed any emotion. They had never seen him anything but stoic. Not a doctor, you would say, had a good bedside manner.

Houston looked at Sophie, "twins?"

"Yeah, what a surprise. Are you happy about it?"

"I'm thrilled. And we know for sure one of them is a girl. Just like in your dream."

Sophie sat up and pulled her top down. "Can we manage twins?" Houston helped her off the table.

"Together, we can manage anything," he smiled and kissed her.

Sophie wanted a snack, so they went to the cafeteria. Houston spotted Lawson eating, so they headed to his table. "Tell me what you want, and I'll grab it, Sophie," Houston said.

"I'd like orange juice, pancakes, blueberry syrup, strawberries…and whipped cream," she rattled off.

Lawson looked up and saw them headed his way. He stood and pulled out a chair for Sophie.

"Hi, what are you doing here today?"

"I had an ultrasound."

"That's exciting. Did you ask about the sex of the baby?"

"Yes."

"Ok, don't keep me in suspense," Lawson said.

"I should wait for Houston so we can tell you together. I'm sorry you had to leave the festivities early yesterday." Sophie said.

"Me too. The entire family doesn't get together like that but a few times a year. And Chantel will be having her baby in December. So, I doubt she can come at Christmas this year. And we never know when Blaze can come. He is so popular with the people. His team calls him out to every PR event they have," Lawson recited.

"Yeah, I wish we all lived closer. And now Houston's family is so far away. I don't know how we will be able to see them as often as we'd like," Sophie said.

Houston came with a tray full of food. He placed her orange juice, pancakes, syrup, strawberries, and whipped cream in front of her. Then he put his BLT, fries, and banana pudding on the table. Sophie looked up at him.

"What's with all that."

"I'm eating for three," he laughed as he set the tray on the stand meant for returns.

"Three?" Lawson asked, puzzled.

"Sophie didn't tell you?"

"Tell me what?" Lawson looked back and forth at them.

Sophie smiled, "We are having twins; one we know for sure is a girl."

Lawson stood up and lifted her out of her seat to hug her, and then he went over to Houston and hugged him. "Congratulations. Oh, the family will go nuts when they hear this."

They all sat again. "I know. I had no idea twins were in either of our families," Sophie said.

"Me either."

"They could be fraternal twins," Lawson said. "Which means it wouldn't necessarily be genetic."

"It would be cool to have a boy and a girl," Sophie said. "But sisters would be cool too."

"I'll be happy with either. I am hoping the next ultrasound will give us a clear view," Houston said before he took a big bite of his sandwich.

"Will this deter your plans to open a detective agency, Houston?" Lawson asked. Houston looked over at Sophie.

"I don't think so. Fons is joining us as soon as we have office space. When Sophie feels she can't work any longer, Fons and I will make adjustments until she's back."

"True, I don't want this to slow down our plans," Sophie said.

I was still sitting in the cafeteria. I'd finished eating but was still mulling over what to do. I wanted to keep Rob out of it. I was gathering my garbage when I overheard the end of the conversation next to me.

The doctor asked the couple if they still planned to open a detective agency. The man said that he had another man who would be working with him when his wife was indisposed.

If they are a new agency, they might not charge too much. I can't just walk over there and insert myself into their conversation. But I've seen that doctor around. I can ask him the next time I see him.

I got up and tossed my garbage, taking another look at the couple.

CHAPTER FIVE

I didn't tell Rob what I learned in the cafeteria. His eyes were closed, but I knew he wasn't asleep. I sat in the recliner and let him rest.

A few hours later, an orderly rolled in another patient. The cute nurse followed, hooked him to a monitor, and transferred his IV to the stand attached to the bed. She pulled the curtain for his privacy and left him.

A woman walked in and hesitated like she thought she was in the wrong room. Then, cautiously moved beyond the pulled curtain.

I heard her trying to whisper so she wouldn't bother us. But in this room, the sound traveled.

"Oh, Milo, how did this vacation go so wrong. I thought I would lose both of you," Odett cried.

Milo took her hand, "we're alright, darling. I'll be out of here tomorrow. We have the best doctor in the country taking care of our little girl. Candy will be fine."

Odett sat on the edge of his bed, "Dr. Lawson said he would like to keep an eye on her for four weeks. He asked if staying in Austin for that long was too much of a financial burden. He said if we can't stay, he will find the best pediatric heart doctor in Colorado and give us a referral."

"No, we will stay. I'm not taking Candy anywhere until I know she is 100%."

"But your business, Milo?"

"It's just me and Simon. He can take walk-ins. I can work from here on my computer. We'll stay as long as we need."

"I could stay by myself, and you could go home."

"No way. We stay together. One lesson I learned is that we never know how long we have. I want us to spend that time together," Milo said. Odett bent over and laid her head on his shoulder and cried.

I had fallen asleep. Rob was watching TV when I woke up. I checked my watch. It was 4 pm.

"I'm sorry I fell asleep, Rob. Did you get lunch?"

"Yeah, the pretty nurse ordered it for me after she checked my vitals."

"I must have been in a deep sleep if I missed all that."

"You were man. You were snoring loudly," Rob laughed.

I moved closer to his bed and spoke softly. "Did the lady leave from over there," I nodded to the curtain.

"Yeah, she took her husband out in a wheelchair. He hasn't come back yet," Rob said. "You don't have to whisper."

"It sounded like they were on vacation here. And their little girl got really sick. Then something happened to him too."

"Yeah, I heard her tell him their little girl was on the second floor. That's where they went," Rob said.

I saw someone in my peripheral vision and turned my head. It was the doctor I saw talking to the couple that were detectives. He walked over to the other bed and saw it was empty.

"His wife took him to the second floor," I volunteered.

"Thanks. Will you let him know I'll come by again before I leave for the night?"

"Sure, no problem," I said. He started to leave. "You're Dr. Lawson, right?"

"Yes. Can I help you?"

"No, but I was sitting in the cafeteria at a table next to you earlier. I heard your friends say they were detectives."

"Yes. That's right," Lawson was getting a little leery about where this was going.

"I need a detective, but I don't know any. Do you think I could get their number?" I asked.

"I wouldn't feel comfortable giving out their number. But if you give me yours, I will pass it on," Lawson said.

"Thank you. My name is Felix, and this is my brother Robin. Can I text it to you, or do you rather I write it down?"

"Write it down for me."

"Please let them know the matter is urgent," I said.

"I'll pass that along."

The Doctor took the paper I gave him and headed out the door. I could hear him talking to someone in the hallway. Then, the doctor, the man in the wheelchair, and his wife returned to the room.

Odett helped her husband back into bed. "Doctor, Candy looks better," Milo said.

"She is improving, but she still has a way to go. I told your wife I would like to follow up with her once she leaves the hospital for four weeks. But if you can't stay, I will find the best pediatric heart specialist in Colorado for you."

Milo took Odett's hand, "We already decided to stay. I want my girl to have the best possible care."

"Good. Now, let's turn our attention to you. Your vitals and blood tests show you are responding well. If nothing changes, I will release you in the morning."

"What detective?" Rob asked me.

"When I was eating in the cafeteria, I heard the doctor talking to a couple. They said they were opening a detective agency. I figured they wouldn't cost as much if they were new at this."

"Felix, getting a detective is a crazy idea. What are you going to tell them?"

"I don't know yet."

"The doctor came by while you were asleep. He said he is going to release me in the morning."

"Good."

Houston unlocked the cottage door to let Sophie in. Then he walked across the patio to knock on Emmett's door to get Bully. There was no answer, so he headed back to the cottage. Sophie looked for Bully when he walked in.

"Where's Bully?"

"Emmett wasn't home. He said he was going to stake out our lot for the foundation. I wonder if he is still there. Do you want to go look?" Houston asked.

"Yes. Let me change my shoes first. Did Emmett say when they would be starting construction?"

"They have to excavate first. We'll be able to watch it progress."

As they walked to the property, Sophie asked, "Do we want to let everyone know about the twins?"

"Are you thinking you want to keep it a secret?" Houston asked.

"No, we have to tell your family, and I want to tell Lizzy and Sienna right away...and Fons and Carol. You see the problem. If we tell some and not others...I don't want to offend any of our family."

"How about we tell people as it comes up."

"That works," Sophie said.

As they walked through the gate they saw Emmett, Jared, and the construction manager on their property. Bully came running to greet them. Sophie leaned down and rubbed Bully's face and neck.

Jared came up. "I'm glad you are here. I want to make sure this is where you want your house situated. There are setback regulations, so you can't put it closer to the street, but you can put it further back," Jared informed them.

"I think it would look strange if our home is set back further than the others," Houston said.

"I've always encouraged the client to keep it uniform. But it's up to you."

"What do you think, Sophie?" Houston asked.

"I would rather have more room in the backyard. I prefer the front to be set back like the others."

"Good. We put up stakes. I understand the outside design is set in stone now," Jared said.

"Yes, we won't change the structure of the outside. We are still making changes inside," Houston said.

"That's fine until the interior walls start going up. After that, making interior changes will be costly," Jared told them.

"I understand, Uncle Jared. We'll finish the blueprints with CJ this week," Sophie promised.

They watched the men put in the stakes and string them together. Sophie and Houston walked inside the perimeter, imagining the interior design.

"Houston, on the plans, is the kitchen and sitting area over here?" Houston walked to her.

"Yes. Do you want it moved?"

"No, it's perfect," she wrapped her arm around him and laid her head on his chest. "Twins," she whispered.

He kissed her forehead, "twins."

Before they walked home, the gate opened, and Wes and his family drove in. They all hopped out of the car to see the outline of where her foundation would be.

"This is going to be a beautiful home," Lady Bee said.

"Thank you, Lady Be. We are excited."

"We were getting ready to 'ave denner. You moehst eat with oehs. Blaze 'as to leave tomorrow," Scarlett insisted. Her accent tended to be more prevalent when she relaxed.

Wes invited Jared and Emmett too. But they said they had work to do.

"Are Piper and Xander home?" Cade asked.

"They didn't come out. They may be at Aunt Carmen's," Sophie said. She thought for a moment. "Do you mind if CJ and Lizzy come?"

"Not at all, dear. We hired a chef for this week. There will be plenty of food," Lady Be said.

Blaze came up behind Sophie. "You got an ultrasound today, didn't you? Are you going to tell me the sex of your baby?" Sophie smiled at him and whispered.

"No one knows yet, but we are having twins, and we know one is a girl."

Blaze wrapped his arms around her. "Congratulations, sis. I get two nieces or nephews for the price of one," he laughed.

Xander and Piper pulled into the gated community before the others sat down for dinner. China saw their car drive by.

"Ma, Xander and Piper just got home. Do you want me to run over and invite them to dinner?" China asked.

"Yes, of course dear."

Wes said the blessing as soon as Xander and Piper said their hellos. The food platters and bowls of food were passed around the table. It seemed everyone talked more than they ate.

"Chantel, I'm so happy we are having children so close together. I hope they will enjoy the closeness we all do," Sophie said.

"Me too, Sophie."

Blaze blurted out, "Sophie's having twins." Everyone looked at her.

"My dear brother, whom I love very much, has no concept of timing, but it's true we are having twins," Sophie laughed.

Everyone was thrilled with the news. Drew was sitting next to China.

"I'm going to call Mom and Dad. They will love this."

"You better wait until dinner is over. You know how Pa feels about cell phones at the table."

After an evening of playing games with the family, they walked home. It was dusk, still light enough to walk without a flashlight.

"I can't get over that Blaze Cornish is your brother. He is the coolest guy. Fons will be jealous we ate with him tonight."

"A beautiful movie star was there too, but *you* were star struck over a soccer player?" Sophie teased. "Well, our plan to let people know about the twins generically went out the window," Sophie laughed.

"Yeah, I'll call Mom and Dad in the morning and let them know."

"I'll call Izumi, Kim, and Ojisan," Sophie said. Bully stopped in his tracks and turned his head.

"Bully, no. You need to let your little friends rest," Houston said. His cell rang, he looked to see who was calling. "It's Lawson," he said as he answered. "Hello, Lawson."

"Hi, Houston. When we were in the cafeteria, a young man was sitting next to us. Apparently, he overheard you were detectives. Later, I saw him again, and he said what he heard and asked if he could have your number.

"I didn't feel comfortable doing that, so I took his. I told him I would get it to you. He said it was urgent."

"It's a little strange he wouldn't go to someone established in town," Houston said. "Do you mind texting it to me?"

"Not at all. I'll do it now. We're playing basketball on Saturday morning. Are you coming?" Lawson asked.

"I'm not sure yet. I'm hoping Emmett will take me around to look at office space. If I don't find anything tomorrow, we'll head out again Saturday."

"Ok then, see you Sunday."

"Yes, you will," Houston responded and hung up.

"What was that about?" Sophie asked.

"Lawson said a young man heard us say we were detectives and asked if he would have us contact him. He said it was urgent." Houston heard his phone ping.

He looked at the text. Felix Wynne. He turned the phone so Sophie could see.

Bully stood by his bowl, waiting for his evening meal. Houston looked at him.

"Bully, after all the panhandling you did at dinner, I should make you wait until morning."

Bully whined and laid down. Houston caved and got a package of Carol's homemade dog food out of the refrigerator. He only gave him half the package.

Sophie came out of the bathroom in her pajamas and headed to the couch to see what was on TV. Houston got changed for the evening too.

Sophie was scrolling through the guide when Houston sat down next to her. Bully went to his bed and laid down.

"What do you think? Should we call this guy?" Sophie asked.

"Where would we meet him. I don't want any of our clients to come to our home."

"I agree. I could ask Uncle Manny if we could use his conference room," Sophie said while stopping on 'Blue Bloods' and clicking it.

"Are we ready to go right into another case?"

"Might as well, while I'm still able to help. If the case gets problematic, we could pay for Fons' airline ticket and have him come. Carol could come too and look around for a home."

"Fons texted me the other day saying they had been called in on a mission. He thought it would take a week or so. But we don't even know what this case is yet."

"So, what do you think?" Sophie asked.

"I sent in our applications for our Texas private investigators license, along with our qualifications, references, and background check forms. I checked the site and saw they had accepted our qualifications and cleared our background checks.

"I've been taking the class online after you go to sleep. I took the final test the other night. I haven't seen the results yet. But if I passed, I could call and see if they would expedite my license," Houston told her.

"Wow, I'm only halfway through."

"So, we call him?" Houston asked.

"I'll call Uncle Manny to see if we can use his conference room. I heard you tell Lawson you would look at office spaces tomorrow. Did you ask Grandpa to take you around?"

"I mentioned it when we were out on the yacht. Emmett said that would be fine. And I heard you making arrangements with Lizzy and Sienna to meet at the bakery tomorrow for lunch."

"What about Bully?"

"He'll be fine in the backyard," Houston said. Bully wagged his tail when he heard his name.

FRIDAY

Houston called his family and told them about the twins. Sophie called Izumi, Kim, and Katsumi. The conversations were happy.

Houston tried to call Felix Wynne, but no one answered. He decided to try again on Monday. He needed to spend the time looking for office space. He and Emmett were heading out in an hour.

Sophie, Piper, and Lizzy went to lunch at the bakery so Sienna could join them.

Sophie stopped by the law firm on her way home. She wanted to ask Uncle Manny if they could meet with clients in his conference room until they had an office. He had no problem with it.

When Houston got home, they went over to say goodbye to Scarlett and Bridget, who were leaving in the morning. Blaze had already left.

When they got home, he told her about the office space they had seen so far. Neither of them was impressed.

SATURDAY

In the morning, Houston got up early and quietly got dressed. He was heading over to Emmett's to start looking for offices again.

Before he left, he shook Sophie, "Darling, I'm leaving."

Sophie mumbled something incoherent. He shook her again.

"Did you hear me, sweetheart?" Houston asked. She mumbled again. He kissed her forehead and headed out. Bully followed him. He let him out to do his business and then put his breakfast in a bowl. Before he left, he gave Bully instructions to take care of Sophie.

Emmett was waiting for him. "Good morning, Houston. How is my granddaughter this morning?"

"Still sleeping."

"Good. I checked around and found some more buildings near the law firm, but they are downtown. It's more expensive down there."

"You know this city, Emmett. What do you think?"

"You have leeway. People looking for a private investigator are not usually drop-ins. So, you don't have to worry about foot traffic. But being closer to the town center has its benefits."

"Sounds good to me."

Sophie woke up to Bully sitting next to the bed with his nose on the bed almost touching hers. She was startled and laughed. "What's the matter, Bully, you bored?"

She got up and headed to the bathroom. When she got out, she called for Houston. No answer. "Houston," she called out again. Sophie walked into the kitchen. She didn't see him. "Bully, where did Houston go?" Bully looked at her. Sophie dialed his number.

"Hello, sweetheart. Did you just wake up?"

"Yes, where are you?"

"I'm with Emmett. He's showing me more office spaces. Don't you remember me telling you last night?"

"Oh, yeah. Why didn't you tell me you were leaving?"

"I did. I woke you twice."

"Oh."

"Are you and Lizzy going to the bakery again today?"

"Yes, Lizzy's picking me up at 1 pm. We are working on Sienna's wedding."

"Alright, darling, have a good day."

"You too, love," Sophie said.

Lizzy picked Sophie up at 12:45 pm after she had dropped Jett off with Grandma Ruby.

"Sienna's wedding is just a few weeks away. I hope she can sit with us today. Yesterday, all we did was talk about the fourth and Liam's date," Sophie chuckled.

"All the baking should be done by now," Lizzy said.

As they walked in, the bell rang, and Teresa looked up. She came around the counter and hugged Sophie.

"Twins," she said with a big smile.

"Yes."

Teresa turned and hugged Lizzy. "Guess what?"

"What," they both asked as they found a table by the window.

"You remember my friend, Aubrey?" Teresa asked.

"Yes, you two spent a lot of time together," Lizzy said.

"Well, she called me a few days ago and is going to the same culinary school in Dallas as I am. We are going to find an apartment together. I'm so excited."

"Oh, Teresa, that is awesome news. Have you found an apartment yet?" Sophie asked.

"Sorta. The school has an arrangement with an apartment complex close by. Aunt Sienna and Jean-Paul are taking us, Kato is coming too. We will look at the apartment next Saturday and the school."

"Who's going to watch the store," Sophie asked.

"Jean-Paul hired an assistant part-time. And, of course, the bread maker..."

"And I'm going to watch the front," Lizzy interrupted.

"We aren't leaving until 10:30. Most of the baking will already be done. Jean-Paul's assistant will make the lunches."

Sienna came around the corner, hearing what was said. "I am going to miss my sweet Teresa when she is gone," Sienna said.

Teresa hugged her, "and I will miss you too, Auntie."

After Sienna set lunch on the table, she hugged Sophie. Twins? How wonderful."

"Neither of us had any idea. We do know one is a girl."

"We will help you find baby names," Lizzy said.

"Oh, I have no doubt there will be plenty of input. China, Emily, Drew, need I go on." They all laughed.

Teresa heard as she brought them out drinks. "I'll help with names too."

"Thank you, Teresa," Sophie said.

"She is so excited about school. It will be hard to not have her around. And Aunt Anna and Uncle David asked if Kato could live with them while Teresa is in school."

"What do you think about that?" Sophie asked.

"It's hard for me to imagine my apartment without them in it. I know it's only been three years, but they made my apartment a home. But Kato doesn't do well without Teresa around. Drew will take the edge off."

"With finishing your wedding plans and going on your honeymoon. You'll be busy, at least for a time," Lizzy said.

"True, we are training people to work while we're gone. And when we return, we want a second day off during the week. We are doing well enough now to hire help."

"CJ said Houston didn't play basketball with the guys today," Lizzy said.

"No, Emmett is taking him around and showing him office spaces. He wants us to get up and running. Fons and Carol are coming down to work with us as soon as we are ready for them."

They finished their sandwiches, and Teresa brought them over the dessert Sienna had made for them.

"Crème Brulée? I love it, Sienna." Sophie said. "Now that I'm eating for three, I will indulge. Just a little," she laughed.

"You are still coming over Sunday to help me wrap the guests' gifts, aren't you. Mom plans on being home. She wants us to go over there after church."

"Of course, we'll be there. I'm hoping I don't get too much bigger by the end of August, or I might have to have my dress altered," Sophie patted her belly.

They finally got down to the wedding business when Sophie heard the bell. She looked over to see Houston walking in. He went over to the table and kissed his wife on the cheek.

"Good afternoon, Sienna, Lizzy." He saw Teresa come out from the back. "Hello, Teresa. I hear you are leaving for school soon."

Teresa gave him a hug. "I have to be there by September first. I can't wait."

"Houston, would you like a sandwich?" Sienna asked.

"No, thank you. Emmett and I went to the BBQ place down the street from the law firm. He's at the firm now, talking to David. He had to work on a case that goes to court on Monday. I told him I'd get a ride home with you. I want to show you a couple of office spaces."

"Oh. I rode with Lizzy."

"Maybe Lizzy and Sienna would like to look at the spaces too?" Houston asked.

"I would," Lizzy said.

"Me too," Sienna said.

A DESPERATE CHOICE

CHAPTER SIX

Lizzy drove as Houston showed them the office spaces available in town that Emmett took him to. The last one was two blocks south of Sienna's bakery.

"Well, this one has some points for being close to the bakery," Sophie laughed.

"Emmett knows the guy who owns this one. He gave Emmett the key. We can go in and look if you want."

"He gave you the key?" Sienna asked.

"Yes."

Lizzy parked in front of the building, and they all stepped out. Sophie looked in the window while Houston unlocked the door.

"I don't remember ever paying attention to this building. Does anyone remember what it used to be?" Sienna asked. They stepped in.

"I don't, but I like the entry. It goes up above the mezzanine. Could it have been a small bank?" Sophie asked.

"Maybe, it's one of the only buildings on the street with a small parking lot. The other stores have only street parking," Lizzy commented.

"Look, Lizzy, there is a metal gate in this room," Sophie said. "Like it could have been for bank deposit boxes."

"Yeah, but where was the safe?" Sienna asked.

"Here. The safe door is gone, but it looks like it was taken out here. And by the markings on the floor, it was thick," Lizzy said.

"Come look upstairs," Houston said. They took the stairs to the mezzanine.

69

"This is great," Sophie said. "Houston, what's on the floor above us. Can you get to it from here?"

"No, it has a separate entrance. But it might be an apartment. Emmett didn't have the key for that."

"I like that idea. This place is much nicer than the others you showed us. It has more potential and a parking lot, so our clients won't have to fight for street parking. What do you think, Houston?"

"That was my thought, too. I think it might be for sale."

"Oh, I like that idea," Sophie said.

"Lizzy, can you drop us off at the law firm. I'll have Emmett see if he can get ahold of the owner."

"Sure, do you want me to wait for you?"

"No. We'll get a ride." Houston said.

They dropped Sienna off first, then headed to the law firm.

THE WYNNE HOME.

I had poured sand on the bloodstains on the garage floor when I came home to change on Wednesday. Rob was lying on the couch resting, watching 'Animal Planet'. We used to watch it with my dad. But I had too much on my mind. I came out to try to sweep up the sand and scrub the stain out of the concrete.

I was kneeling on the concrete, scrubbing cleaner into the stain when Rob came out holding his ribs.

"What are you doing?" he asked.

"If I wait too long to scrub the stains out, they may be permanent."

"Did those detective people call?"

"A call came in from an anonymous number. I didn't answer. It could have been them. I'll answer it next time. It's the weekend. If they don't call Monday, we'll have to do something else," I said.

"Like what?" Rob asked.

I stopped scrubbing and looked up at him. "Like rob a bank."

"What? No way we are robbing a bank, Felix."

"Look, Rob, you don't have to do anything. I got us into this mess. I'll get us out." I started scrubbing again.

"Felix, we are not robbing anyone. That's just trading one problem for another."

"Maybe, but jail is better than being hacked to pieces by DeLeon when we can't pay him."

"No, we would be better off going to the cops and turning ourselves in."

"We aren't doing that, Rob. Let me handle this."

"What about poker?" He asked.

"Poker?"

"Yeah. You know I'm an excellent player. If we can get a stake in a game, I can build up our money a little at a time," Rob said.

I looked up at him, "that's not a bad idea. The guy across the street offered to buy the Jeep. If I can get him to give us five thousand for it, we could start with a smaller game and build up."

"I could see if the underground card game I used to play in is still around."

"Do that. After I clean up these stains, I'll go across the street and try to sell the Jeep."

Emmett was in David's office having a cup of coffee. Sophie stepped in, and the men stood to greet her and Houston. Sophie hugged her grandpa and uncle. Houston shook hands.

"Did you like any of the properties, Sophie?" Emmett asked.

"Yes, the one down the street from Sienna's bakery."

"That used to be a bank. It's been closed for years. I think there may be an apartment upstairs." David said.

"Emmett, would you mind calling the man and seeing if he would talk to me," Houston asked.

"Sure," Emmett left the room to make the call.

"Hello?"

"Hello, Akito, how are you?" Emmett asked.

"I'm as good as I was this morning when you came to get my key," he laughed.

"Good. I know it's Saturday. But if you aren't too busy, could you meet Houston at the property? He would like to talk to you about it. Can you meet them in an hour?"

"Yes. I can be there at five."

"Thank you, Akito. I won't be with him. But he has the key. He will return it to you."

"That's fine, Emmett." They said goodbye and hung up.

David suggested Houston call CJ to see if he would meet them there.

"He can tell you if structural damage can be easily repaired or if you should just walk away. Some repairs are worth making if you can get the right price. Jonathan, Luke, and I tore this place down to its studs. It was worth it."

Houston called CJ. He agreed to meet him in twenty minutes at 703 W. 12th Street.

Emmett returned to the room and said Akito would meet them there at 5 pm.

"Houston asked CJ to come look at it," David said.

"That gives you an hour and a half to go through it with him."

"Thanks, Emmett. We'll get a taxi and head over there."

"No, take my car. David said he's almost done. I'll ride home with him."

"Are you sure?"

"Yes," Emmett took the keys from his pocket and handed them to him.

"Thanks, Grandpa," Sophie said and kissed his cheek.

Before CJ arrived, Houston took a video of the entire property, inside and out. He wanted to send it to Fons in case they got serious about it. Fons had a right to have a say in it if he was going to be a partner."

CJ walked in. Houston thanked him for coming.

"This used to be a bank. It should be structurally sound."

"How come you remember what it was. None of us remember this building at all."

"I have researched many of the old buildings in the downtown area. It's my job to know," he laughed.

"I want to tell you upfront, CJ. I am paying you for your time and expertise. And if we buy this building, we want you to draw up its remodel."

"Houston, I don't charge family for my services."

"CJ, I accepted your generosity for the blueprints to our home because of your relationship with Sophie. But this is business. You have to make a living, and if you don't let me pay you, I'll go somewhere else," Houston said.

"Houston!" Sophie said, surprised.

"No, Sophie. I want to work with CJ for many years, and if he won't let me pay him, it isn't right. I don't have anything to exchange for barter."

CJ smiled. "Your friendship is a fair exchange."

"I'm serious, CJ. I want to pay you."

"Alright. I'll give you a friends and family discount. How about that?"

"I can live with that." They bumped fists and laughed.

CJ spent an hour going through all the rooms. He asked to get upstairs, but Houston didn't have the key. Sophie waited downstairs while Houston and CJ used the access ladder on the back of the building to climb up on the roof.

"From what I can tell, the owner has kept up repairs. The roof is in good condition. There is no indication of mold or asbestos inside. The bank would have had to remove it if there was. It was still open when those laws were passed.

"I can't see any problem with the plumbing or electrical. But you need to get a professional out here to check on that.

"Another advantage is the parking lot. Very few properties on this road have private parking. They use the alley for the employees' parking.

"It's a nice building, Houston, but is it more than you need?" CJ finished his assessment of the building, except for the upstairs.

"Maybe, but if there is a decent apartment above the business, it will help to pay for it. And someday we might grow into the downstairs," Houston said.

They heard a vehicle pull into the parking lot below them.

"That must be Mr. Lam. Do you mind waiting? I'd like you to look at the upstairs."

"No. I'm in no hurry." They climbed down the access ladder and greeted the owner.

"Mr. Lam, thank you for working on a Saturday. I'm Houston Townsend, and this is CJ..."

"Hello, Mr. Townsend. I know CJ. What did you think of my building, CJ."

"I should have known it was yours, Akito. I just told Houston; it looked like the owner had kept it up."

"I had to replace the roof and do some repairs on the outside. The plumbing and electrical downstairs are still good. I did upgrade them upstairs, though."

"Mr. Lam, we couldn't get upstairs. Do you mind letting us see it?"

"Not at all," he moved to the side door.

"I'll be right up. I need to get my wife. She's inside."

CJ was checking the water pressure and fittings when Houston and Sophie walked in. Mr. Lam was in the living room.

Houston stepped up to him, "Mr. Lam, this is my wife, Sophie."

"Please call me Akito," he said. "Sophie, are you Emmett's granddaughter?"

"Yes," she reached out to shake his hand.

"I didn't know you had come home. Emmett spent many nights worrying about you."

"I know, I caused heartache for my family," Sophie lowered her eyes.

"No. He understood why you left."

"Do you mind if we look around?" Houston wanted to change the conversation.

"No, take your time."

Houston went to the kitchen where CJ was, and Sophie walked around the apartment. It was bigger than she expected. There were three bedrooms, and the master bedroom had an ensuite bath. Unusual for a building this age. *Someone must have upgraded this not too long ago, she thought.*

After looking at the rest of the apartment, she walked back to the owner, "Mr. Lam..."

"Akito, please."

"Akito, how long have you owned this building?"

"Four years. I remodeled the apartment and rented it out for three of those years. The couple bought a house and moved out. I decided to sell the building, so I didn't try to rent it out again."

"I was wondering because it looks so much newer than the downstairs. You put in the ensuite bath?"

"Yes, and I did redo some of the plumbing and electrical up here, as I mentioned to your husband."

"I like the design. The kitchen is set up almost like a chef's kitchen."

"My wife insisted. She said the wife picks the family home, so we catered to that. She insisted on the TV room off the kitchen too."

"Your wife is very smart."

"Indeed, she is," he laughed.

"Akito, what are you asking for the building?" Houston asked as he and CJ returned to the living room.

"Four hundred fifty thousand. The parking lot adjacent adds value to the property."

"Yes, I can see that. Tomorrow is Sunday, but can I sit down with you Monday and discuss it."

"Yes, I would be happy to. Call me when you are free. We can meet at David's offices. He'll let us use the conference room."

"Perfect. It might be later in the afternoon. Is that all right?"

"Yes."

"Good. See you on Monday." Houston said as he handed the downstairs key back.

"No, keep it. You may want to come back again before Monday," he took the apartment key out of his pocket and handed that to him too.

"Thank you, Akito."

Houston thanked CJ for coming and said he would let him know what happened.

On the way home, Sophie asked, "I really like it. The downstairs has potential, and we can rent the apartment upstairs to help pay for it."

"True, but is it more building than we need, Sophie?"

"Maybe now. But we may grow into it like Dad's firm did," Sophie said.

"We could rent some of the empty office spaces downstairs, if you want," Houston commented.

"I don't know about that. When our babies come along, I plan to take them to the office with us. That could be disturbing to tenants."

"It's four hundred fifty thousand. That's a big loan, Sophie."

"We've never gotten loans before, except from our savings," Sophie said.

"Sweetheart, we are trying to pay for our new home, and that's just the beginning of the expense involved in new construction."

"I don't check our accounts often. I leave that to you. But the last time I checked, there was more than enough money. And I always charge a small percent of interest for the loan."

"True, and we will get a big return on our home in DC when we decide to sell."

"Ok, then, when we have done our due diligence. We'll pay cash," Sophie decided.

Houston nodded and kept driving. "We need to call Fons and Carol and see what they think about the building. Fons is our partner, he needs a say."

"What are you thinking each equity partner should pay?" Sophie asked.

"We need to ask Fons if he is ok with us owning the building and the agency paying rent to us. If he is, then the partner equity should equal the cost of remodeling the building and the cost of furniture, maybe a little operating money. It could be three hundred thousand or more," Houston said.

"Yes, maybe more. That would make it a hundred thousand each. Can Fons afford that?"

"You're thinking of a three-way partnership."

"Aren't you? I'm a partner," Sophie asked.

"Yes, of course. If Fons can't afford it, we will let him pay in payments as he can."

"I'm good with that. Do you think he expected it to be that much?"

"I don't know, but we'll figure it out. I want Fons to be our partner," Houston said.

"Me too."

As soon as they pulled into the driveway, they heard Bully at the gate, barking.

"Oh, Houston, he's been outside all day by himself. He had no one to play with."

Houston laughed, "He's a dog. I'm sure he found a way to entertain himself." Sophie gave him that look. When she unlocked the gate, Bully's whole body was shaking with the excitement of seeing them.

David's SUV pulled up behind them, and Emmett stepped out. Sophie waved at her uncle and headed with Bully into the cottage.

"Houston, what did you think of Akito's property?" Emmett asked.

"I like it. I'm wondering if it might be more than we need," Houston paused. "He is asking four hundred fifty thousand. I have no idea if that is a fair price. Do you know why he is selling?"

"He had it assessed before he bought it four years ago. He bought it for half the assessed value because the previous owner was in a forced sale. He told me it was assessed at four hundred thousand, then."

"Why is he selling?"

"Akito and his wife have worked hard all their lives. He came here as an immigrant at eighteen. He had nothing but saved every cent he made doing odd jobs. He applied to my construction company and got a job. I was lucky to have him. He bought his first property and lived in a small trailer, renting out the home. He worked his way up to owning over thirty properties. When he met his wife, she insisted they move into one of the properties.

"Akito's wife recently found out she has breast cancer. It scared him, even though she should be fine after surgery. He told me he wasted so many of their years together working. He wants to retire and enjoy the rest of their lives."

"I'm sorry to hear that. It helps to know how willing someone is to negotiate. Thanks for taking me around the last two days."

"My pleasure," Emmett said as they headed in.

Sophie was feeding Bully when Houston walked in. Bully was bouncing with excitement like he hadn't eaten in a week.

"What a ham," Houston said under his breath and laughed. "Sweetheart, what do you want for dinner?"

"Something light. I'm still full of my late lunch with the girls."

"We have salad fixing. Will that work?"

"Do we have shrimp or chicken to toss in with it?" She asked.

"If we do that, it's not light," he laughed. "I can bake the chicken breasts we bought yesterday."

"That sounds good, and some mashed potatoes and corn on the cob," she added.

"Sophie, in what world is that a light meal?" Houston asked, teasing her. Sophie stopped what she was doing and gave him a look.

"I am carrying two of your babies. The least you can do is feed them," Sophie said seriously. Houston couldn't help it. He burst out laughing. Then he hugged tight.

"I'll feed you whatever you want, sweetheart," he finally said when he was done laughing.

"That's better."

After dinner, Sophie asked, "Houston, don't you think we should call that young man. He told Lawson it was urgent."

"Did Manny say we could use his conference room?"

"Yes."

"I called once, but he didn't answer. I'll call again on Monday. It's too late today, and I don't want to start doing business on Sunday unless it is unavoidable."

"I agree with that policy."

"Then I'd like to call Fons before it gets too late."

CHAPTER SEVEN

WYNNES

"Rob, are you sure this is the address? This area is deserted."
"It's the right address. These card games are literally underground. See that abandoned warehouse. It has a basement."

"How do we get in?" I asked.

"Follow me."

They walked up to the door, where I spotted a keypad for the first time. Rob entered a number, and the door opened. It was dark inside, with only small night lights allowing them to maneuver. Rob headed straight for the downstairs. When he opened the door at the bottom of the stairs, the place was lit up, and ambient noise could be heard.

There was a bar at the far end, and waitresses moved around the ten tables of card players. Each table held six players. What looked like a bank teller was behind a teller window in an enclosed cage.

Security stood next to the inside door, and the owner walked around, watching the activity. He noticed Rob and came over.

"I haven't seen you for a while, Rob. I was surprised to get the call you wanted to play," he said.

"Thanks for letting me," he nodded to Felix. "This is my brother Felix. He doesn't play. He just wanted to come."

"No problem. You play poker, right?"

"Yes."

The owner looked around. "There is an empty seat at table two. You have your buy-in money, right?"

"Yes. It's still $500?"

"Yes."

"What's the rake?" Rob asked.

"Three percent. Good luck," the owner said, nodding to me, and walked away.

"What did you mean, rake?"

"Every table pays 3% to the house from every pot."

"Oh," I said as we headed to the cash cage.

"Felix, you have to sit at the bar. You can't sit by me while I play. These guys are paranoid about someone cheating."

I handed Rob the envelope with the five thousand in it that I got from selling the Jeep. Rob exchanged two thousand cash for chips.

"Can we call Fons and Carol to let them know about the building?" Sophie asked.

"Yes." Houston grabbed his cell.

"Hello, Houston. Do you have news for us? You're on speaker. Carol is here."

"Hi, Carol," Sophie said.

"Hello, how are you feeling?" Carol asked.

"I'm feeling great…"

"As long as I keep feeding her," Houston teased. Sophie jabbed him in the ribs. "Oww."

"Have you found an office?" Fons asked.

"I'm sending you a video of a place we're looking at. I'll send it to Carol's phone so you can watch it while we talk."

They heard the ping on her phone acknowledging the receipt of a text.

"We have options. And you must be very honest with us, so we know what you're thinking."

"We're watching the video now. Wow, that place is huge," Fons said.

"It's not quite as big as it looks on the video. It was a small community bank. It has a parking lot with it. Be it a small one. The only one on the block. The other stores have to use street parking."

"I can see the potential," Carol said.

"Are you thinking of buying or renting?" Fons asked.

"I'm thinking of buying. The owner wants four hundred fifty thousand, but he would negotiate. There is an apartment upstairs that will help pay for it."

"Wow, Houston, do you think we should go into debt like that?" Fons asked.

"Here are our options. Sophie and I are considering buying the building ourselves. If we do that, we will rent the downstairs to the business at a discounted rate. Or, if you want to, we can partner up with you on the building. The other option is to walk away if you think the space downstairs is more than we need.

"Emmett took me around this morning, and I looked at the office space available. I wasn't crazy about what I saw. Although, we don't necessarily have to be downtown for our type of business."

"How much was the rent at the offices you saw?"

"The largest one was $2000. The smallest $1250."

"What was the square footage?"

"The large one was 1500 sq. feet. The smallest 800 sq. feet."

"What's the square footage in the building?" Fons asked.

"The main floor is five thousand, and the mezzanine is less than half that," Houston said.

"The apartment upstairs is large, so it will carry most of the cost. I'm thinking $2000 a month," Houston said.

"Houston, no way can we get that much square footage for that price."

"We can if we own it..." Houston said. Sophie broke in.

"Fons, you know I don't invest in the stock market. I put my money in real estate or gold. I will keep the interest on the property low and still make more than having it sit in a savings account."

"Sophie, it is not right that you guys bear the brunt of the cost of our partnership," Fons insisted.

"Fons, it's how I invest. We don't have to buy the building. We can go another route, but I will invest in real estate here in Austin. Why not get something that can benefit us now?"

"I see your point. The building does have huge potential. What about the remodel?"

"That's where our partnership equity funds will come in. If we agree on this building, the money would be used to remodel. It would also cover office equipment and cover our start-up operating expenses. The remodel would be cheaper at one of the other offices, but in the end, this will be a nice place to work. And in time, we will need a place for Matt and Sissy if they are still interested."

"I hadn't thought about that," Fons said.

"Fons, we never talked about how much equity we all would put in. Now remember yours would only be one-third of the cost."

"One-third?"

"Yes, there are three of us in this partnership. You, Sophie, and me."

"But you and Sophie should only pay one portion."

"That's not how partnerships work. I need to know what you can comfortably afford. And Sophie and I have no problem if you want to pay it in installments."

"No, I don't want to be a liability to this partnership. We have gone over our savings, and we have an offer on our house. With the cost of the move and the estimated time it will take for us to be profitable. We could put in $100,000 and still be able to put a decent size downpayment on a home."

"That's perfect. That's what we were thinking too. If we do a majority of the work, the remodel cost should be manageable, and we don't have to fill the place with equipment right now. But we will need our spy craft tools."

"Yes, I agree."

"Carol, until you decide where to buy or rent a place, you and Fons are welcome to use the apartment upstairs. It's very nice and has a large kitchen. No charge, of course," Sophie said.

"No, if we use it, we'll pay for it," Carol insisted.

"Let's compromise. No charge until the business is remodeled and up and running," Sophie said. Carol thought about it.

"Ok, I can agree to that. Thank you."

"Houston," Fons said. "I'm excited to get this done. How long before you will need us?"

"Aren't you on a mission with the task force right now?"

"Yes, but we will have that wrapped up in a week."

"Good. If we get this building, closing will take a while, even with a cash sale. But there is something else."

"What is it?" Fons asked.

"We received a message from a young man who needs a private investigator. The message said it was urgent. I tried to call, but no one answered. I will call him back on Monday. I have no idea if we can help the young man or what it's about. I'm sure we can manage it, but if not, I'll call you."

"You don't know what it's about?" Fons asked.

"No. And I'm not having anyone come to where we live to find out. Manny said we could use his conference room on Monday."

"If you need me, I'll come down."

"Thanks. I'll be glad to have my partner back," Houston said.

"Me too. We miss you guys," Fons said.

"It's lonely here without you," Carol added.

"I'll call you about the building and the job this week," Houston said. Then they said goodbye.

WYNNES

We'd been at the gambling joint for a couple of hours. I couldn't see Rob well from where I sat at the bar, but his stack of chips looked bigger.

I sat wondering if the private investigators would actually call. We won't need the detectives if Rob can win what we need.

I sat there for another four hours. Rob had moved to another table that allowed for bigger pots. He was right across from me. I'd never seen this side of my brother. He was calm, with a deadpan expression on his face. Nothing that happened fazed him in any way. Even when he lost.

It scared me a little. I don't want my brother to have to do this. This is all my fault. Yes, he played before all the trouble, but it was entertainment. Now, our whole future lies on his shoulders.

Rob had accumulated stacks of chips. I had no idea how much, but he hadn't returned to the cash cage to buy more, so it must be winnings.

Then I saw Rob lay his cards on the table. I heard grumbles while others threw down their cards in disgust. Rob stood.

"Well, gentlemen, I need to call it a night."

"Aren't you going to give us a chance to win our money back?" A man in a suit shirt with rolled-up sleeves asked.

"Another night," Rob smiled.

I watched as the dealer collected the chips. He took out the house's cut, placed the rest in a black plastic bowl, and handed it to Rob.

Rob looked over at me and nodded. I met him at the cash cage, he exchanged his winnings, and we left.

"Rob, how do you do that?"

"What?"

"You are like a different person in there, and I had no idea you were so good," I said.

"It's a game. I'm playing a part. Although, it is much harder when your life depends on it. And less fun."

"How much did you win?"

"We'll talk at home. It's too dangerous to stick around. And make sure we're not followed home this time."

We reached the car, and I drove home, constantly looking in the rearview mirror. I closed the garage door, and we went inside.

Rob pulled out his winnings and the envelope with the three thousand dollars left from the Jeep sale. He placed it on the kitchen table.

I counted out two thousand, put it back in the envelope, and then counted what was left.

"Thirty-three thousand," I smiled.

"Wow, this could work. How long do you think it would take to win the whole $125,000."

Rob looked at me, "I don't know. I can't go to the same place every night. And I won't win every time. The trick is to win more than you lose, but it's a 60/40 proposition, with the sixty being losing."

"Why can't we go back every night?" I asked, being ignorant of this lifestyle.

"Because these gamblers are serious and dangerous. If they even think I could be hustling them, DeLeon won't be the only one we will be running from."

"Ok, so what's the plan?"

"I know of one other den that knows me and will let me play. If I go once a week to each and win about the same, we could have the money by the end of the month."

"That's great, Rob," I patted him on the back.

"Felix, the chances of me winning every time are slim to none. It could work, but we still need to sell everything we have. And we need to see what Dad had in the safety deposit box."

"Ok. At least we have a plan," I said, not quite as excited that we had solved our problems.

SUNDAY

After church, the families went to the BBQ at Whiteings. Sophie, Piper, and Lizzy went to Ailene Pierce's house. They met with Sienna, Teresa, and her cousin, Veronica, to work on the wedding.

Aileen greeted them with a beautifully laid-out lunch in the backyard on the covered patio. She hugged all the girls, and they enjoyed the meal.

"Sienna, did Jean-Paul tell you where you are going on your honeymoon?" Veronica asked.

"He's taking me back to Paris. We both love it there. He has made us a reservation in a luxury hotel a few blocks from the river Seine."

"I'm so excited for you," Lizzy said.

"Me too," Sophie added.

Aileen stood, "All right, ladies, we are here to get work done. I have things ready to put together in the family room." As everyone headed in that direction, Aileen stepped over to Sophie. "The First Lady and I were so happy for you when we heard you were having twins. Congratulations."

"Thank you, Aileen, and please tell the First Lady thank you for her well wishes."

When Sophie got home, Houston was on the couch watching 'Swat'. Bully was lying on his bed, his legs moving like he was dreaming of catching critters.

Houston put his show on pause and got up to greet her.

"Were you able to get everything done?"

"Not even close, but we still have time. I'm concerned that by the end of August, I won't fit into my bridesmaid dress."

"When it gets closer, can you have a seamstress adjust it?"

"The problem is the bodice doesn't flair out. I don't know how much material the seamstress will have to work with," Sophie said.

"Don't worry about it, babe, it will work out," Houston said.

"Easy for you to say. You don't have to fit into it. How was lunch with the family?"

"Good, I got to talk to them about the building. Most remembered it, and Emmett, Jared, and Henry had accounts there until it closed six years ago.

"They think it's a sound investment and a good location for a business."

"That's encouraging," Sophie stood. "I'm going to get changed and go to bed. I'm tired."

Houston looked at her, "Are you alright?"

"Yes, it's been a long day. Finish your movie and let Bully out before you come to bed."

Sophie heard Houston mumble, "like I'm not the one who does that every night." She laughed and heard him unpause his show.

MONDAY

After breakfast, Sophie mopped the floor and turned on the dishwasher, while Houston took Bully out. When he came back, he pulled out his cell and found Lawson's text. He found the young man's name and number. Sophie was sitting at the table with him. He dialed the number and put it on speaker.

"Hello?" a young man answered. His sounded like the phone woke him up.

"Hello, is this Felix Wynne?"

"Yes."

"I was given your number by Doctor Lawson Cornett."

"Are you the private investigator?"

"Yes. I am Houston Townsend, and my wife, Sophie Townsend, is also on the line. You asked us to call, that it was urgent."

"Mr. Townsend, I'm not sure you can help. I'm desperate and grabbing at straws."

"Let's not talk about this on the phone. We don't have an office set up yet. However, the firm of Scott, Young, Star, and Diaz on 10th downtown is letting us use their conference room. Do you know where that is?"

"Yes, I know the area."

"Can you meet us there at 1 pm?"

"Yes. How much will it cost to find out if you can help me?"

"We won't charge anything until we know that we can help. Is that fair?"

"Yes. I'll be there…. Thank you," Felix said and hung up.

Sophie looked over at Houston, "That was strange."

"I agree. I don't know what we can do for this young man, but he is obviously in a dire situation. That brings up the question. What will we charge, and are we charging by the hour or the case?" Houston asked.

"It has to be by the hour, plus expenses. I don't see any other way to do it."

"Ok, so how much?"

"For now, let's play it by ear. I doubt this young man has money to burn, and we don't have any overhead yet, so let's see what he can afford."

Houston and Sophie told the receptionist they were expecting a young man to be looking for them. Sophie asked her to direct him upstairs to Manny's conference room. Then they went upstairs and said hello to Manny.

"Thank you, Uncle Manny, for letting us use your conference room."

"Anything you need, honey," he turned to Houston. "Did you talk to the licensing division?"

"Yes, before we came. I picked up my private investigator's license on the way here."

"Good for you. When will you have yours, Sophie?"

"I should be taking the test in a week...I hope," she said.

WYNNE

I was eating cereal when Rob woke up and walked into the kitchen. He grabbed a bowl and poured the last cereal from the box and the last milk into it.

"We need milk and cereal, Felix."

"Yeah, I can see that," I said, looking at him sideways. "The private detectives called." Rob dropped his spoon in his bowl.

"No, Felix, we don't need them. We have a plan."

"A plan, you said is very iffy. I'm just going to talk to them. They said they wouldn't charge me for that."

"Ok, but I'm going with you."

"No, Rob. This is all my doing. I don't want you getting in any deeper," I told him.

"That's a stupid thing to say. I'm gambling, trying to pay off our debt. How much more can I get involved."

"Yeah, I guess. But you don't have to come," I told him.

"Hey, brother, good or bad, we are in this together," Rob reached over and put his hand on my shoulder.

CHAPTER EIGHT

Houston headed to the conference room while Sophie stopped by the restroom. Felix and Robin were coming up the stairs. Houston spotted them and closed the gap.

"Are you Felix Wynne?"

"Yes, and this is my brother Robin. Are you Mr. Townsend?"

"Yes, let's step into the conference room." Houston directed them to chairs and sat across from them. He wanted to read their faces as they told their story.

Felix leaned over and mumbled to his brother. "This guy looks like he stepped off an FBI recruitment poster." Rob nodded.

Sophie walked in. Houston stood to pull the chair out next to him and introduced her. "This is my wife and partner, Sophie." Houston took the remote to darken the glass room and then took a seat.

"Wow, she's beautiful," Rob didn't realize he said it out loud. Felix jabbed him in the ribs. Houston and Sophie acted like they didn't hear it.

"Mr. Wynne, what can we do for you?" Houston asked.

"Well, you see, we got this thing from a man and hadn't paid for it yet. Then, when we got home, some big dudes beat us up and took it. We need it back."

"Mr. Wynne…"

"Please call me Felix," he nodded to his brother. "And you can call him Rob.

"Ok, Felix. That explanation tells us absolutely nothing. You are going to have to be more specific than that. Like, what was the item stolen? Do you know the men who stole it? Things like that," Houston said.

"Do private investigators have the same thing like lawyers? I mean, you can't tell anyone what we tell you, like the police, right?" Felix asked.

"If we are hired by an attorney on your behalf, then it's true. But if you don't tell us your issue, we can't help you. If we think you need an attorney, we will bring one in," Houston said.

"I take it, Felix, that you have done something illegal," Sophie said.

"Yeah. We did something really stupid because we were desperate. Now, we are even more desperate. Can you help us?" Rob asked.

"We won't know until you tell us what *it* is," Sophie said.

Felix and Rob whispered between themselves, then Rob nodded, and Felix spoke up.

"Do you want me to start from the beginning?" Felix asked.

"That would be best," Houston said.

Felix went through everything from the time his mother died. At first, he was talking so fast that it was hard to keep up with his story. He finally slowed down and got to where he was in the cafeteria and heard them talking to the doctor.

No one said anything for a moment. Then Houston said, "You don't have any names for these guys other than Dante and Gideon?"

"No. My cousin Willy and I went to the bar where he met them, but no one knew them or has seen them since."

"Ok. Can Willy give a description? I know they wore masks when you saw them, but surely your cousin told you what they look like," Sophie questioned.

"Willy said they were white; one had longer dark hair, was over six feet, and was muscular. The other was maybe 5'11", dirty blond hair, cut short, with a medium build."

"They said they were from Dallas?" Houston asked.

"Yes."

"I can already see problems with finding them. But that's not the real problem. There is no way we will steal your drugs back so you can sell them on the streets," Houston said.

"I agree. And gambling to try to win the money to pay DeLeon back is in itself a gamble," Sophie commented.

"We have to do something. DeLeon will chop us up into pieces," Rob said.

"I'm not saying there isn't a way out, but you aren't going to like it. It's risky and could be dangerous," Sophie said.

"We need your help, we're desperate," Felix said.

"If we agree to help you, you will have to do things our way," Houston said.

"How much will it cost?" Felix asked.

"How much can you pay?" Sophie asked.

"Rob won $33,000 at poker last night. We could give you that."

"We will charge you by the hour. We won't need to take all your money, but I have one stipulation. No more gambling. You don't need to get in any deeper than you already are," Sophie said.

"But what if in the end, you can't help us? We still need to pay DeLeon," Felix said.

"We'll figure it out if it comes to that. Sophie and I need to speak for a moment. Wait here," Houston opened the French doors to the balcony, and they stepped out.

"Sophie, I don't know about this. We'd be moving headlong into conflict with a drug cartel from Mexico," Houston said.

"Houston, I recognize the name Luis DeLeon. My dad and uncles had a run-in with him over a loan he made to a friend of my grandpa's. These are two dumb kids who made a mistake. I don't think they are criminals. They will never get out of this on their own."

"I understand that, but a cartel kingpin?"

"Remember our first task force. Nikko Morano was the head of a drug empire. We took him down."

"With a large multiagency task force, Sophie."

"Ok, so do you want to send them on their way to fend for themselves?" Sophie asked him.

Houston turned and looked over the railing. He never said a word.

"What is it, Houston? I know you are not afraid."

"That's where you are wrong. I am afraid. I'm afraid of something happening to you and to our babies."

"We can't walk in fear, love."

"No, but the Lord expects us to use wisdom."

"Ok, it's up to you. If you don't want to take this case, so be it," Sophie said.

Houston turned to look at the two young men, who were watching them discuss this. "Alright. But we need to bring in an attorney for them. Because I know what you are thinking."

"And what's that."

"You will want them to work with the local DEA to take Luis DeLeon down. But in doing that, we are exposing their involvement in purchasing drugs to sell. We have to make sure they are protected."

"Exactly," Sophie said and took his hand. "Let me see if Rex is available. He runs the criminal division at the firm."

"David, Manny, and Jonathan need to be brought in, so they know what's going on. They may not want to have the firm involved at all," Houston said.

"Ok, let's present the idea to our clients first. Then we'll go from there."

Houston and Sophie walked back into the room; he held the chair for her as she sat.

"Felix, it's possible we could find these guys, but then what. You want us to pull a gun on them and tell them to hand over the drugs they stole?

"I am certain by now they have been sold. Then what? You want us to call the police to arrest them for assaulting you? If we do that, the police will find out about the drugs," Houston said.

"Sophie and I have a plan. I think it will be the best way for you two to get back on the right track," Houston turned to Rob. "You want to go to mechanic's school, right?" Rob nodded. "And you want to have your own tire shop, right?"
Felix nodded.

"First, we have to get you out of this. Rob, let's say you win enough money gambling to pay Luis DeLeon back. What makes you think he will let you quit? He will have you under his thumb for the rest of your lives. Which, based on your lack of criminal prowess, may not be long.

"We can help you. We will set you up with a criminal attorney who will make sure you are given immunity. Then we will deal with the DEA to help them take down Luis DeLeon," Houston finished.

Felix abruptly stood up; his chair scooted back a couple of inches. "You want me to set up one of Mexico's most dangerous cartel kingpins? Are you crazy? Come on, Rob, we're getting out of here."

"No, Felix. They're right. DeLeon will have his thumb on us for the rest of our lives. He'll figure we could make him money if we can sell that many drugs in a month."

"Rob, we would have to leave Texas. Even if Luis goes down, his men will come after us."

Rob looked at Houston, "That's true, isn't it?"

"Yes, Rob. More than likely, the US Marshals will move you to another state. But think about it. Your parents are gone. I'm sure you want nothing to do with your cousins anymore. What do you have to lose?" Houston asked.

"You can sell your house. When Rob finishes school, you can take that money to open an auto repair and tire shop," Sophie added.

Felix sat back down, "Where would we go?"

"Montana's nice," Rob said. "I watch the fishing channel, and they always fish up there."

"Is it dangerous? Yes. Do we know what we are doing? Yes. Of course, it's possible that something could go wrong in an operation like this. But I can guarantee things will go wrong if you continue on this path," Sophie said.

"Can my brother and I go out on the balcony and talk about it?" Felix asked.

"Yes, of course," Sophie said.

I closed the French doors behind us. "Rob, you're crazy if you think this is a good idea."

"I don't know, Felix. I trust them. You said yourself he looks like he stepped out of an FBI recruitment poster. Maybe he really was FBI."

I turned to look at the couple. "Yeah, they sound like they know what they are doing. But do you really want to leave Austin? We grew up here."

"Life here has always been tough. Even with both Mom and Dad working, we just scraped by. Maybe our luck will change if we move somewhere else."

"It's dangerous, Rob. I don't want you to get hurt. If we decide to do this, I do it without you."

"I know you want to protect me, Felix, but I kinda like the idea of doing something good for Austin. Taking down a kingpin like Luis DeLeon could save lives. I watch TV. I see how the police have been trying to rid the State of drugs coming from Mexico."

"You're fooling yourself if you think getting rid of Luis will stop the drug trade in Texas."

"I know that. I'm not stupid. But if the police felt like that, criminals would run everything," Rob said. "I want to do it, Felix."

I stood there looking at my little brother, who was a better man than me, and decided that if he was brave enough to do it, I was.

"Ok. We'll do it. But I don't know if our money will pay for them and an attorney."

"I guess we'll have to find out."

"I'm going to call Uncle David, you are right, we can't get Rex involved without the firm's partners agreeing. The fall out could land on them too, if things go wrong."

"Find out if they are all here. If the brothers agree, we will ask the partners to meet with us," Houston said. Sophie made the call.

"Hello, Sophie. Are you still in the building?"

"Yes, we are in the conference room upstairs. This case we're taking on is…well, it's complicated. If these young men hire us and we agree to take the case. I would like the firm's partners and Rex to hear the case."

"I'll be here until five. Jonathan should be back soon, and I heard Rex's voice. I don't know about his schedule. Is Manny upstairs?"

"Yes, he is here. I'll call you in a few." As Sophie hung up, the brothers opened the French doors and walked in.

After they sat down, Felix said, "My brother and I have decided it would be in our best interest to listen to you. I'm already worried about paying you. How much is an attorney going to cost?"

"Felix, we can work all that out. What's important is that you get out of this mess," Sophie said with a smile.

"Ok, then, what do we do next?"

"Next, we speak with an attorney for you and the firm's partners and get their input," Houston said.

"Oh, you work here?" Rob asked. "I thought you were independent."

"We are, but I know these people very well and trust their opinion. The most important thing in all of this is keeping you safe and out of jail," Sophie said. "We are going to talk with them first and then bring in your attorney if he agrees to take your case," Sophie stood. "Excuse me while I make a call." Sophie stepped out of the room.

"Sophie?"

"Yes, Uncle David, can you all talk to us in Uncle Manny's office?"

"We'll be right there."

Sophie stepped back into the conference room. She explained that she and Houston would leave the room for about ten minutes. "You are welcome to turn on the TV if you like. The remote is next to the coffee pot on the credenza."

"Thank you," Felix said.

"Houston, we need to fill Uncle Manny in. He has no idea I called for the partners and Rex."

Houston knocked on the door frame. Manny waved them in.

Sophie was filling him in when the other men walked in.

"Let's sit at the table," Manny directed. They all found a seat and waited for Sophie to explain the case.

"We are taking the two young men in the conference room on as clients. They have gotten themselves in a mess with Luis DeLeon." Sophie saw name recognition on her uncles' faces. She went on to give them an abbreviated version of what had happened.

"Sophie, you were a kid, but you must remember our run-in with Luis DeLeon. He is an incredibly dangerous man. And now you are telling us he has moved from Mexico to Austin?" David asked.

"Yes. And these two young men had no idea who he was when they got involved with him. They were desperate and made a desperate choice.

"I'm telling you all this because we want to work with the DEA and try to get evidence against DeLeon. But they will need a criminal attorney to ensure they have complete immunity. And we need to ensure the US Marshals will move them once it's over."

"We know this is not the kind of law you generally practice. Recruiting one of your attorneys could potentially bring danger to your doorstep. We want to know if you would rather, we go somewhere else?" Houston asked.

No one spoke for a minute. "I will help you in any way I can," Manny said.

"David and I will too," Jonathan said. "But we only have one criminal attorney in our firm. It has to be up to him."

Sophie looked at him. "Rex, this could be dangerous. I want you to do it for the right reasons. You don't owe us anything."

"Are you kidding me? I remember when Luke and Manny helped to track down a serial killer. It seemed cases like this regularly found him. I always wanted to be like your dad. I'm in," Rex smiled.

"Alright, let's introduce the young men to their new attorney," Houston said.

They stepped back into the conference room. Felix and Rob were watching a fishing channel. Felix turned it off.

"Felix, Robin, this is attorney Rex Ford. He has agreed to be your lawyer for the criminal case," Sophie said as they sat down. Felix and Rob stared at him, not sure what to say.

"To keep everything you tell me, privileged, I will need a retainer. If you wish to hire me, that is," Rex said.

Felix rummaged in his pocket and took out twenty dollars. "Will this work, for now, Mr. Ford?" Rex nodded. "But as I explained to Mr. and Mrs. Townsend, we only have thirty-three thousand dollars. Will that be enough to pay you both?"

"Let's not worry about that right now. Everything Houston and Sophie do will also be privileged because I will retain them on your behalf." Rex handed Houston the twenty dollars as a retainer. "What I need is for you to tell me in your own words exactly what happened. Especially your part in any illegal activity."

Felix told the whole story again, giving a little more detail.

"We have 25 days left to bring Luis DeLeon his cash, or he will chop us up a piece at a time," Rob added at the end.

"First off. No more illegal gambling. If the DEA catches you doing anything illegal after we make our agreement, those crimes will not be under the immunity agreement. Understood?" Rex asked, then continued.

"Houston and Sophie will contact the DEA and the DOJ. They will see if they are interested in what you know about Luis DeLeon. That's where I come in. I will make sure there are no loopholes or back doors that can allow them to get out of your immunity agreement. But you will have to cooperate with them."

"We understand."

"Alright, for now, when the Townsends are finished talking with you," he nodded to Houston and Sophie. "Go home and stay there until we can get an agreement in writing and signed on the dotted lines." Rex stood and shook the young men's hands. He turned to Houston and Sophie, "Let me know as soon as you have contact with the DEA and DOJ."

"We will. Thank you, Rex," Sophie said.

"So, you just go to the Drug Enforcement Agency and tell them you want a deal?" Felix asked.

"Something like that. We have contacts," Houston said.

Felix spoke under his breath to his brother, "I told you."

"Right now, no one, including Luis DeLeon, knows you are about to turn State's evidence. I don't feel you are in any danger. But if that changes, we will get you protection. Ok?" Houston asked. They nodded.

"It is vitally important that you do not speak of this to anyone. You can't even allude to it. Do you understand?" Sophie asked.

"Yes, ma'am," they both echoed.

"This could take a few days. Call me if you get nervous or have any questions," Houston handed Felix his cell phone number. "Don't put it in your contacts. Memorize it and get rid of the paper."

"Like a spy movie," Rob smiled.

Sophie laughed, "Yes, exactly like a spy movie." They all stood and shook hands.

CHAPTER NINE

"Sophie, I need to get ahold of Akito Lam. I told him we would meet with him this afternoon."

"We can meet him here now if he's available," Sophie said.

"Ok, we agree on the purchase of the old bank building?" Houston asked.

"Yes. Do you want to make contingencies for inspections?" Sophie asked.

"I don't think so. CJ and I went through the building pretty thoroughly. I know the plumbing upstairs was refurbished a few years ago. There isn't much in the way of plumbing downstairs. We will likely add our own," he thought for a moment. "Maybe we should call for an electrical inspection. Other than that, I'm ok. What do you think?"

"What about asbestos?" Sophie asked. "I remember there was asbestos in this building, and the men had to take the walls down to the boards and have it removed."

"CJ said if the building had asbestos, the previous owners would have had to remove it. But I'll put that in there, too, if you like."

"How much are you going to offer him?"

"He wants four fifty. I was thinking four."

"That seems fair since we will have to do a lot of work downstairs."

Houston called Akito. He said he could be there in half an hour.

WYNNES

"Felix, we need food. Stop at a grocery store." We picked up groceries and headed home.

"Why are you doing that," Rob asked, watching me lock the doors and pull the curtains. "Sophie said we are safe for now. We are not supposed to act differently."

I stopped, "You're right, but I'm still not sure this is a good idea."

"It's not like we have a choice, Felix."

Before I could answer, I heard a car pull up and I looked out the window.

"What is he doing here?" I asked myself out loud.

"Who?"

"Derreck. He's never been to our house before." I went to the door and let him in. Willy was with him.

"Hey, Felix...Rob. How are you doing, cuz?" Derreck asked.

"How do you think, Derreck. We're scrambling to come up with the money we owe DeLeon."

"I feel bad about turning my back on you," Derreck said. "I brought over some of my cocaine stash. If you can sell it, you can keep the money. It's worth fifty thousand."

"We don't need it," I said. "Rob is playing poker; he's winning enough that we should be able to pay DeLeon back by the end of the month."

"That's a gamble," Derreck laughed at his own joke.

"Not when Rob plays."

"Ok, good. But just in case you need it; I'll leave it with you," Derreck said. "And Willy thinks he found out the last name of one of the dudes that beat you up."

"Yeah, I've been asking around, the Dante guy, his last name is Vita. And he lives right here in Austin. I have the address."

"We'll go with you and give him a beat down. And if he has any money left from selling your drugs, we'll take it from him," Derreck said.

"No. We are done with all that. We should never have gotten involved. He could come after us again with more of his thugs. It could end up in a feud that will get us all killed," Rob said. Derreck got a strange look on his face.

"What's going on, Felix? You came to me desperate for money, and now you just... What? Something else is going on."

"Nothing is going on. But that beatdown we took shook us up, Derreck. Rob is still recovering. It was supposed to be a one-time thing anyway. We don't want to be drug dealers. We want to open our own business."

"Yeah, well, Felix, just where are you going to get the money to open this pipe dream of yours. You always thought you were better than me and Willy. But you're the one who's desperate for money."

I got into Derreck's space. "We never thought we were better than you until you backed out of our deal when the cocaine was stolen. You left us hanging. Now we are done. Get out of here," I yelled at him.

Derreck turned to leave, then stopped and turned to me again. "That's why I brought you this," he lifted a bank bag. "It's all packaged and ready to sell. I feel bad about leaving you hanging." Derreck tossed the bag onto the couch. As he left, he said, "When you're over yourself, come by, and we'll play cards."

Willy lifted the paper with the address, so I'd see it and placed it on the coffee table.

I watched them get in the car and leave, then locked the door behind them.

"I don't want that product in our house, Felix. Our attorney said we can't get caught doing anything illegal."

"I know. I'm calling Mr. Townsend," I took out the paper with his number on it and dialed.

"We were supposed to get rid of that," Rob said. I gave the note to him. "Throw it away. It's in my phone now." I let it ring until it went to voicemail. "It's me. Please call. It's important."

"We need to hide that," Rob pointed to the cocaine, "until Mr. Townsend calls us back."

Sophie told Houston she would meet him downstairs. She had to use the restroom again. David was walking out of Manny's office.

"Hey, sweetie, we are all so excited about your twins. Anna, Carmen, Ruby, and Zoey have been looking at baby paraphernalia for days."

"Thank you, Uncle David," she hugged him. Then she lowered her head. "Uncle David, I never had the chance to apologize for deserting you in your grief after Duke was killed." Sophie lowered her head as her eyes filled with tears and ran down her cheeks.

David put his finger under her chin and lifted her head. He used his thumb to wipe away some tears. "Sophie, we knew the pain you were in. You just lost your dad and were heading to the church to marry Duke when he died in your arms. That was more than anyone could handle.

"It was a tough time for all of us. But we never thought less of you for leaving. We loved you then, and we love you now, we never stopped loving you. We are just glad you came back to us," David said, wrapping her in his arms.

"Thank you, Uncle David," he let her go and kissed her forehead.

"Look at me," he said. Sophie lifted her eyes. "If you need any help with this investigation, you tell us. We will be there for you."

"Thank you. I love you, Uncle David," she paused. "Akito Lam is on his way. We decided to buy his property."

"Is he meeting you here?"

"Yes. If we come to an agreement, we'll need papers written up."

"Jonathan handles Akito's business dealings, but if he is gone, I can do that for you."

"Thanks."

Downstairs, Sophie saw Houston and Mr. Lam in the small conference room. Houston and Mr. Lam both stood to greet her when she walked in. Sophie walked over to Mr. Lam and stretched out her hand.

"Mr. Lam, thank you for meeting us today. I'm sure you had better things to do."

"Akito, please. My pleasure, Sophie. My wife and I were working in the garden. It's more her thing. I appreciated having a reason to leave her to it," he smiled before everyone sat.

"Akito, we are interested in buying your old bank building. The apartment upstairs and the small parking lot are an extra bonus.

"But as you know, there will be a great deal of remodeling downstairs to make it work for anything other than a bank. With that in mind, we would like to offer you four hundred thousand dollars for it, cash. With two minor contingencies."

"Which are?"

"I'd like electrical and asbestos inspections done."

"Cash? That makes it an appealing offer. As to the asbestos, I had an inspection done when I bought it. I can give you the final report if you want it, or you can get your own. As to the electrical, I had an electrician do work upstairs, but I have no problem with you bringing in an inspector."

"Your asbestos report will satisfy us. We're not afraid of doing some electrical work if we need to. We just want to know what we are getting into," Houston said.

"I understand. You are savvy purchasers. I would expect no less," he paused for a moment. "Four hundred thousand is less than I had intended to take for that building. Cash makes it much more appealing. I can make a reasonable profit if we can agree on four hundred twenty-five thousand. If you agree, we can write it up while we are here? Jonathan takes care of all my legal affairs."

Houston looked over to Sophie, who nodded. "Yes, we are ready. You can bring a copy of the report on the asbestos at your convenience, and we will leave it out of the sale agreement. Hopefully, we can have this closed in a week or so. Emmett has an electrician he uses on the homes he builds. I'm sure he can get him to come out right away for us," Houston said.

"Yes, I know him," Akito said. Houston left to see if Jonathan was available. Sophie and Akito waited in the room.

"Your grandfather and I are good friends. I met him when I was young and looking for work. I was living in a little trailer, doing odd jobs. I owned next to nothing. He gave me a job and spent time training me to put in foundations, a skill that has benefited me ever since. He befriended me. I was very young and shy. I didn't know how to make friends. He would invite me to go places with him on Saturdays or Sundays. He never worked us on the weekend unless we were on a deadline. He led me to the Lord.

"I was raised Buddhist. Not that I was practicing. But I knew nothing about the Christian God. It was two years before I went to church with him, but my life has never been the same. I owe him everything. I was ambitious enough to make money. But I would never have had the happiness in my soul without him leading me to Jesus.

"I went with him once when he thought he had a lead on where you were. He didn't want the others to know because he feared it was just another dead end.

"I see the spark has returned in his eyes now that you are back. I can see why, Sophie. There is something special about you. Your grandfather has not confided in me about your life while you were gone, but I know your work saved lives."

"Akito, you are kind to say that. But if you see anything good in me. It is only Jesus. When I walked away from here, I also walked away from my faith. I fell into a dire situation, but Jesus never abandoned me and helped me to find my way back to Him. Any good thing I do is only because of the mercy he showed me."

Houston and Jonathan walked in.

"Hello, Akito," Jonathan shook his hand, and he and Houston sat down. "Alright, I need the address of the property, the sales price, and any contingencies," Jonathan said, ready to take notes.

"I have to say that was the easiest property purchase we have ever done," Houston commented.

"It did seem to fall into place. I'm hungry, can we get something to eat? Bully is with Jett. He won't miss us."

"Where do you want to go?"

"The BBQ pulled pork place Grandpa took you to, down the street. Dad loved that place. Can we go there?"

"Sounds good to me," Houston drove the few blocks and pulled into the parking lot. Before he got out, he looked at his phone. He remembered he put his cell on mute. "It looks like I have a voicemail from Felix." Houston put the phone on speaker to listen to the message.

"It's me. Please call. It's important."

"We better call him back," Sophie said.

Houston dialed. Felix picked it up right away. "Mr. Townsend, thank you for calling back. We have a problem."

"Sophie is on the line too. What is it?"

"Is it safe to talk on the phone?"

"Is there any reason to believe someone is listening to your conversations?"

"No... I don't know..."

"You should probably tell us what's going on."

"As soon as we got home, Derreck and Willy showed up. Derreck said he felt terrible leaving me hanging when the...product was stolen. He brought us some of his, thinking we could use it to make up part of the loss we need to come up with. And Willy said he found out the last name of one of the guys who stole our...product. He lives here in town.

"I told him I didn't want his help, but he started getting suspicious. He offered to go with us to tune up the guy who stole from us and get back whatever money he may still have from its sale.

"I told him again I wasn't interested, that I should never have gotten involved in the first place. He was surprised at our reluctance. When he left, he tossed the bag with the product on the couch. I don't know what to do?"

"It's in your house?" Sophie asked.

"Yes."

"This could be a setup. But why? That's what illudes me at the moment." Houston said.

"Is there a reason your cousin would set you up?" Sophie asked.

"Not that I can think of. We aren't exactly close, but we have a decent relationship."

"Houston, he could have gotten picked up by the police. He may have been offered a deal if he leads them to someone higher up," Sophie said.

"We are not higher up," Rob said.

"I know, but he wouldn't dare give him Deleon's man, so he promised them his supplier."

"But he is the one that supplies to his street dealers," Felix said.

"The DEA may have just stumbled upon him. And if Derreck didn't have but a small amount on him. He could have lied and said he was a small-time dealer," Sophie said.

"So, why didn't the DEA break down our door?"

"Because Derreck knew you had nothing on you. He had to set you up. He probably gave them a reason, like you were out of town or something, or he didn't know where you lived," Houston said.

"We can't know exactly what transpired, but I have little doubt we are right about this," Sophie said. "And if that's the case, you must get rid of it immediately. We can't go to your house, but we can meet you somewhere. Go out the back door. Take the bag with you and make sure you are not followed. Where is the closest bar to your house?"

"Barley's, it's three blocks south of here."

"Sophie, do you know where that is?" Houston asked.

"No, what else is around it?" Sophie asked.

"There is a strip mall with a Wienerschnitzel fast food joint in the parking lot."

"I know where that is. There are only two in town," Sophie said.

"You want us to take it with us? What if we get caught?"

"You can't leave it at the house. Strap it to your back with your belt and put a shirt over it. Then put a light jacket on," Houston said.

"But it's hot out. Won't that look suspicious?" Rob asked.

"I have my short-sleeved work shirt that the tire company I worked for made me wear. I could put it on and leave it open with a T-shirt underneath," Felix said.

"Perfect. Now hurry. Go into the bar and walk out the back. We will head there now. If we aren't there, check for security cameras. If you don't see any, find somewhere to hide outside. If there are, go out of their range and wait," Houston said.

"Ok."

"Don't turn your phones off until we pick you up. We might need to call you," Sophie said.

Sophie gave Houston directions. Getting to that side of town took fifteen minutes.

"There, Houston."

Houston drove into the bar's parking lot and pulled around back. He looked for cameras. He didn't see any, so he pulled to the far side of the lot and looked for any sign of his clients.

Sophie spotted dumpsters. Then saw movement. "Drive over there," she pointed. Houston pulled in front of the commercial garbage containers. Two young men stepped out and got in the car. Houston drove away.

"Do either of you know where some construction is going on in town?" Sophie asked.

"Uh, construction?" Rob asked.

"Yes, they usually have Honey Bucket Latrines for the workers. We are going to dump the drugs in there."

"Oh, yes. Home Depot is building on this side of the river, just outside of the downtown area," Felix said.

Houston asked for directions.

As they drove, Sophie directed them to take the battery out of their phones.

Houston spotted a line of latrines behind the building site. He didn't see security. Hopefully, they could get in and out before they got spotted.

Sophie turned to the back seat. "I want you to go in there and dump the drugs into the hole. Not the bag, just the drugs. Make sure every one of those packets gets into the latrine," she handed him a pin light. "Check the seat and the floor; make sure it's all down there."

"Got it," Felix said as he exited the car.

Houston kept his eye out for security. Felix was back in less than five minutes with the empty bank bag.

Sophie pulled Purex Wipes from the glove box and reached for the bag. She wiped the bag down inside and out.

"Houston, find me a place to dump this," Sophie said. Houston pulled behind a hair salon that was already closed and found the dumpster. He took the bank bag from Sophie, using the wipe for protection. He grabbed another wipe to open the garbage can. Then he got back in and drove off.

"How do you know to do all that?" Rob asked.

"We had a similar situation not long ago. You can't go home until we have secured a deal with the DEA. We will drop you off close to a motel. You need one that will let you pay with cash and no ID. Do you know any place like that?"

"Yeah, when I graduated high school, a group of us wanted to play poker and drink all night. We went to a motel on the other side of the river," Rob smiled.

"Direct me to it, and I will take you a mile from the motel. You can walk the rest of the way. Don't give the motel your real name and pay with cash. Do you have any cash?"

"Yes, we grabbed the poker winnings before we left the house," Rob said.

"Ok, if you reach behind the seat, you will find a duffel with a ball cap, a pair of sweatpants, and a couple of T-shirts. They're clean. Dump everything else out and take the duffle. There should be deodorant and a razor too," Houston added.

"You can use the hotel phone for now. Call us and give us the number. Do not call anyone else. I know you'll have to go out for food. Don't sit in a restaurant. One of you buy food to-go and make sure the ball cap is pulled down low. Don't use a credit card, and don't use an ATM. Do the same routine if you have to go to a store," Sophie said.

"How long?" Felix asked.

"We will try to call my contact in the DEA tonight, but it will at least be a day or two before it is safe for you to come in. If our contact says there is no file on Derreck, this was all for not. But we still had to get rid of the drugs," Houston said.

"Ok, Mr. Townsend, the motel is about a mile from here. We can walk," Felix said. Rob opened the back door and grabbed the duffle. Felix scooted over to get out. "We don't deserve your help, but I don't know how we would get out of this without you."

"You're welcome, Felix. If we all got only what we deserved, we would all be in a bad way," Sophie smiled and patted him on the arm.

CHAPTER TEN

"Were you thinking we should contact Director Cosby to give us a contact in the DEA," Sophie asked.

"No, he's FBI. We need DEA; SAC Hampton is my first choice. I heard he moved up to a supervisory position, he is now assistant administrator of the New York State offices. But I'm sure he can help us."

"I had his cell number at one time. When you traded in my phone for a newer one, did you transfer all my contacts?" Sophie asked.

"Yes, dear," Houston teased. Sophie poked him in the ribs.

"Oww. How do you always manage to get the same rib."

Sophie scrolled through her contacts. She asked, "What do you think of this whole Derreck scenario I came up with. Is it a little farfetched? Do you think Derreck would do that to his cousins?"

"I don't know the guy, but he sells drugs, so I don't put much past him."

"It does seem a little out there, even for me... I found it. How late is it in New York?"

Houston looked at the dashboard clock. "It's a little after ten in New York. But he used to stay up late."

"Houston, I'm starving. Can we go back to the Wienerschnitzel?"

"Sophie, we are at least 20 minutes away from there. You said there were two. Where is the other one?"

"Way on the other side of town. Please, I'm starving."

"We passed a Kentucky Fried less than a mile back."

"No, I need a hot dog," Sophie insisted.

"Kentucky Fried has hot dogs," Houston said. Sophie turned and stared at him. He didn't look. He could feel it.

"No problem, sweetheart, I'm happy to take you to Wienerschnitzel."

"Thanks, love. I'll call Hampton on the way. He may not answer since my number comes up as a private caller," Sophie said.

"He's DEA, his curiosity will kick in," Houston said. Sophie dialed.

"Hello?"

"Assistant Administrator Hampton, Sophie Star Townsend here. Sorry to call so late." She emphasized his title.

"Sophie?"

"Yes. Houston is here with me. I'm going to put you on speaker."

"Hello, Houston. Are you in trouble?"

"No. Again, sorry for the late call. We need a favor."

They could hear someone on his end speaking.

"I'm heading to bed, honey. Don't stay up too late." Hampton responded, "I'll be up soon, dear."

"Sorry, that was my wife. I thought I heard through the grapevine that you both retired from the President's Task Force."

"We have, sir…"

"Call me James. You don't work for me anymore."

"Sophie was injured in the last mission," Houston said. "We both felt it was time to quit. We are starting a family."

"You're pregnant, Sophie?" James sounded pleased.

"Twins," Sophie said.

"No kidding? Congratulations," James responded with a chuckle. "I get my news from Deputy Chief Cartwright. We stay in touch and still see each other on occasion."

"Don, is Deputy Chief now? He didn't tell us that, the last time we saw him," Sophie said.

"It just came through. He was going to turn it down, but now that Melina said yes to his proposal, he decided he wanted to take the raise."

"Amazing. I'm so happy for them," Sophie said.

"You said you called me for a favor. How can I help you?"

Houston ran him through the condensed version of what had happened so far.

"What we need, James, is to see if we imagined Derreck's motives or if he was picked up by DEA or the police. If he was picked up in Austin, would you be able to see a file on him?" Sophie questioned.

"I have my DEA secure laptop with me. Give me his name again."

"D-e-r-r-e-c-k W-y-n-n-e," she spelled out his name.

They could hear James typing on the laptop. No one spoke.

"Ok, I found a file on him dated yesterday. He was pulled over for a broken taillight. The police officer saw a gun, then pulled his and told him to get out of the car. He handcuffed him and put him in his cruiser. Then called for backup. He searched his car and found ten one-gram packages of cocaine. He arrested him."

"How did he end up in the DEA's custody," Houston asked.

"The DEA and the police all across Texas are working together to stop the influx of drugs coming over the border. A task force of sorts. In the last 10 years, drugs have increased exponentially in Texas. A cartel kingpin has moved from Mexico over the border into Austin. He has a brother there. Obviously, he didn't come across legally."

"Luis Deleon," Sophie said.

"Yes, how did you know?" James asked.

"He is the man our clients bought the drugs from," Houston said.

"Oh, you left that part out."

"My father and uncles had a run-in with him years ago. He wasn't living here then," Sophie said.

"What is your plan, Sophie?"

"We wanted to get ahold of the DEA and make an immunity deal for our clients. In exchange, they would cooperate by giving the State evidence against DeLeon. We also want our clients relocated to a place they choose when it's over."

"James, can you give us an *in* to work with the DEA? We have no connections here. Otherwise, they will just dismiss us," Houston said.

"I wouldn't be so sure about that. Our task force takedown of the Morano drug empire is taught to all our new recruits. It is the same with the release of the trafficked women from the Chinese gangs.

"They will recognize your names, but I will make a few calls for you in the morning and clear the way."

"Thank you, James. Do you think Derreck was trying to trade our clients for his release?"

"I'm sure that's exactly what he did."

"How does the file say he got released the same day?" Houston asked. James typed on his laptop.

"It says they are using him as a registered CI. However, I don't see names of anyone he has given up yet."

"It was so nice to speak with you again. Please tell your wife we apologize for the late call," Sophie said.

"Me too," Houston chimed in. James paused.

"It was nice to talk with you again. I'll always remember the work we did together. It was the best I've ever done. Keep in touch."

"We will. Goodnight. I'll text you my number," Sophie said.

"Well, I guess it wasn't so farfetched after all," Sophie said. When she looked up, she saw the Wienerschnitzel ahead.

Houston pulled up to the takeout menu board. Someone welcomed them over a speaker and asked what they wanted to order.

"We'll need a minute, please," Houston said.

"No," Sophie leaned over him to get closer to the window so the girl could hear her. "I want a plain dog for Bully…"

Houston interrupted, "Sophie, I don't like feeding him people food."

Sophie ignored him. "Two chili cheese dogs, one with the toppings in a separate container so the bun doesn't get soggy. Two BBQ pulled pork dogs, one with the topping on the side. A mini corn dog, Ranch chili cheese fries, and a chocolate shake."

Houston stared at her. "Sophie, have you lost your mind."

"Anything else, ma'am?"

"Houston, put in your order."

"I'll have a double cheeseburger and a root beer, please."

"I'll give you your total at the window. Please pull forward."

"Sophie, what possessed you to order so much food?"

"It's not all for me. I got the plain dog for Bully, the other chili cheese dog for Lizzy, and the second BBQ pulled pork dog for CJ."

"Sophie, that still leaves a ton of food."

"Just a chili cheese dog, a mini corn dog, a BBQ pulled pork dog, and the chili cheese fries. Oh, and the chocolate shake. And you know very well you will eat half of it. And I will have leftovers for the morning."

"Alright, sweetheart, whatever you say."

Houston pulled into the restaurant's parking lot to eat his hamburger and share the chili cheese fries.

By the time they got to Lizzy's house to pick up Bully, Sophie had eaten the mini corn dog, part of her chili cheese fries, half her milkshake, and was working on her chili cheese dog.

Sophie could see Bully move the curtain to see who pulled up outside. She grabbed the bags with CJ and Lizzy's hot dogs and stepped out. Houston came around, and they headed for the front door. Lizzy opened it, and Bully ran out. She handed the bags to Houston and bent down to pet Bully, who was wagging his body in excitement.

"Once Jett went to bed, Coco went to bed too. Bully's been laying by the door waiting for you," Lizzy said. CJ came out to greet them. Sophie stood and took the bags back from Houston.

"Look what I brought you, Lizzy?"

"Oh, awesome, Wienerschnitzel. Is it a chili cheese dog?" Lizzy asked in anticipation.

"Yes, and a BBQ pulled pork dog for CJ. I had them put the toppings on the side so the bun didn't get soggy."

"I haven't had one of these in…forever. Why were you out by the Wienerschnitzel?"

"We had to pick up some clients in that area," Sophie said.

"Did you get yourself something?" Lizzy asked.

"The whole store," Houston snickered. Sophie gave him the *death star* stare.

"Eat with us," CJ said.

"We're just now headed home. I'll catch up with you tomorrow," Sophie said.

"Everything alright, Houston?" CJ asked as Sophie walked Lizzy to the table to set the bags down.

"We took on clients today. It seems their situation is much more precarious than we thought. We had to find a place to hide them," Houston said.

"That sounds bad."

"It is, CJ. But we may have a way out for them."

"If there is anything I can do to help, let me know," CJ offered.

"Thanks, CJ. Ready to go, Sophie?"

"Yes," she hugged Lizzy. "We'll talk tomorrow."

"Thanks for the treats," Lizzy said, and she and CJ watched their friends get into the car before closing the door.

"That was a nice gesture, sweetheart," he looked over at her. "Bringing them the food," Houston said.

"Wienerschnitzel has always been one of those places for us. If any of us were close to one, we always brought something back for the others."

"I like that. Small gestures sometimes make a big impact."

Bully was sniffing the food. "Hold on, Bully, I brought you something too," Sophie said.

"Houston, does it bother you if I mention Duke? Lizzy and CJ are hesitant to bring up any history that includes him," Sophie said, turning to him.

"No, sweetheart, it sounds to me Duke was a good guy and kept you out of trouble. I appreciate he was there for you," Houston reached for her hand. "I am secure in your love for me. You've never given me any reason to think I was a second choice."

"Oh, love, you are not a second choice. You are the love of my life and the father to our twins," Sophie said. Houston lifted her hand to his mouth and kissed it.

As Houston pulled into Emmett's driveway, Sophie gathered all her goodies. She handed them to Houston to carry. She got out and opened the door for Bully.

"Are you done with these, Soph? I'll dump them in the garbage out here, so we don't smell up the house."

Sophie stopped in her tracks. "Don't you dare throw away my hot dogs. Put them in the refrigerator, and I'll eat them tomorrow."

"Ok, ok, don't get upset. Refrigerator it is."

TUESDAY

When Sophie woke up, Houston was in the bathroom. She used the guest bathroom, let Bully out, and headed for the refrigerator. She pulled her BBQ-pulled pork dog out and put it in the microwave to heat up. Bully started barking at the front door.

Sophie let him in and asked him if he wanted breakfast. He ran to his bowl, half sat, and half stood waiting for his food. Sophie grabbed one of the packages of dog food Carol made for him out of the fridge and scraped it into his bowl. She patted him on the head and said, "Sorry, no more hot dogs for you. You ate yours last night. Bon Appetit."

The microwave dinged. Sophie grabbed a plate, a fork, and a knife and set them on the table after taking her treasure out of the microwave and placing it next to her plate. She reached into the refrigerator, grabbed the milk, and filled a glass to the top.

Sophie slid the pulled pork dog off the to-go container onto her plate, taking a sip of milk to give it time to cool. After saying her blessing, Sophie dug in. "Mmm…" she closed her eyes. She didn't hear Houston come in and jumped when he spoke.

"Sophie, you can't be eating that for breakfast!"

"You startled me. Why not? It's wonderful. And your kids love it."

At that, burst out laughing. "If you say so," he kissed her on the forehead. "I'm making eggs and bacon."

"Make some for me too," Sophie smiled. Houston knew better than to respond. "You know the doctor said I needed to gain some weight."

"Yes, sweetheart, but I don't think he meant to gain it all in one day."

Sophie finished her hot dog and headed for the bathroom to shower and dress. "Let me know when the bacon is done."

Sophie stepped out of her room, dressed and ready to go to the DEA headquarters. James had texted earlier and said he had paved the way for them to meet with SAC Emil Ramos.

Sophie wore a flowing A-line poplin skirt in an amber peach color with a white sleeveless silk top. She accessorized with light peach color, three-inch heels.

Houston wore khaki pants, loafers, and a light blue button-up, short-sleeved shirt.

They didn't want to be seen as federal agents, and Hampton had arranged for them to enter through the back door.

"You look beautiful, sweetheart," Houston said as he handed her a piece of bacon."

"Thank you, love, but I just brushed my teeth," Sophie gave it to Bully, sitting beside her.

"So, is this how it's going to be. I say no to the kids, and you say yes," Houston teased.

Sophie walked over to him and placed her hand on his chest. "You don't fool anyone. This thin layer of tough agent guy covers layers and layers of a softie. I see you sneak food to Bully. And I have no doubt you will be the one who spoils our children so badly that no one will ever let us come over."

Houston laughed, "Is that what you think of me?"

"It is," she said, then kissed him. "And you look very handsome too.

Houston grabbed Bully's service vest and secured it on him. Bully heeled to Houston's every move and watched for any command. He was on duty, and he knew it. Houston grabbed the older duffle by the door he restocked for the SUV. He grabbed Bully's leash on the way out.

Houston opened the back of the SUV, grabbed the loose stuff Felix dumped in the back, and slipped it into the old duffle.

Sophie opened the back door, and Bully jumped in.

"Houston, are you sure you want us to be dressed this casually? The SAC may not take us seriously."

"Yes, if we are going to live here and work as private investigators, we don't want people to think we are agents."

Houston pulled up to the security gate and gave the officer his name. The man looked at a clipboard and opened the gate. Houston pulled into the back parking lot. He got out and came around to open Sophie's door, extending his hand to help her. Then he opened the back door, hooked the leash onto Bully's collar, and Bully jumped out.

Sophie left her purse in the car and put her phone in her skirt pocket. There was no handle outside the door, only a keypad and an intercom. Houston pushed the intercom and waited.

"Yes"

"Houston Townsend, we are expected." The door buzzed and opened on its own. Someone was waiting for them on the other side.

The man said, "I am Assistant Special Agent in Charge Griff Berry. I will escort you to SAC Ramos' office on the fourth floor." He extended his hand. Houston and Sophie both reciprocated as Houston introduced himself.

"Thank you. I'm Houston Townsend, and this is my wife, Sophie Star Townsend..."

"I know who you are. And this is Bully," the man looked down at him. Then directed them to the elevators in the entry. Sophie looked over at Houston, questioning how the agent knew them. Houston shrugged.

On the fourth floor, the elevator opened to a bullpen. Men and women were working at their desks or talking on the phone. Some desks were empty, though it was evident agents worked from them.

One agent was standing in the aisle. Bully stopped and bared his teeth at him but did not growl, something Bully seldom did. Houston took note of the man and moved on.

As they continued walking down the aisle, the agents looked up to watch them pass.

The door to the office was open, and the man sitting at the desk stood when he saw them coming, greeting them at the door.

"Mr. Townsend and Mrs. Star Townsend, come in. I was expecting you," he extended his hand to one, then the other, and they shook.

It was a large office with a small conference table and a sitting area. The SAC directed them to the two chairs before his desk as he returned to his seat. Bully lay down next to Houston. ASAC Berry stood leaning on the door frame.

"The head of the New York state DEA offices called and vouched for you. He said you worked for him."

"Yes, I worked for him when he was SAC in New York," Houston said.

"He mentioned that. Of course, I am aware of who you are, Ms. Star. The success of the Morano task force and the Chinese gang trafficking case are almost legendary. But what is it you need from me?" Ramos asked.

"Sir, my wife and I have retired from the agency. We are now private investigators. We have clients that have gotten themselves into a situation that crosses over into your jurisdiction."

"I see. Do we have an open case file on them?"

"No."

"Then I think you better explain."

Houston gave the SAC a capsulated version of what happened. Leaving out names and critical elements. He needed to read the man.

"I'm a little confused. If we don't have an open case on them and they don't have the drugs anymore, why come here? They are in no jeopardy of getting arrested."

"When the drugs were stolen, they knew they couldn't pay the supplier. Now they owe a dangerous man a lot of money."

"I'm sorry, but that's not our problem. That is on them."

"We understand that, but they will cooperate and help you make a case against the man who gave them the drugs. The man told them if they did not pay on time, he would chop them up a piece at a time."

"That's just how they keep their dealers in line," Ramos laughed.

"Not this man, sir. He will do it," Houston said.

"If the man is that dangerous, we must have a case open on him."

"Do you? His name is Luis DeLeon." Houston spotted the split second of surprise on the SAC's face.

"Your clients are lying to you. There is no way some low-level, first-time dealer got a face-to-face with Luis DeLeon. No one gets that close to him. We can't get a want or a warrant on him because he is insulated so well."

"They are not lying. I can't explain how they stumbled into a face-to-face with him, but they did. And you just registered a CI planning to give you false information."

"How could you possibly know that?"

"Because he will try to feed you our clients as his supplier. Which is a lie. He gets his product from one of DeLeon's men. He tried to plant drugs on our clients."

SAC Ramos sat in his desk chair, rocking it, and staring past his guests into the bullpen. Then he picked up the phone and made a call. Houston and Sophie only heard one side of the conversation.

"Captain Sung, can you come over to my office?" Ramos listened.

"Yes, DeLeon." He listened again.

"As soon as you can," Ramos responded.

"That would be fine, thank you." Ramos hung up the phone.

"Captain Sung's division of the Austin police has been working with us trying to bring a case against DeLeon. He has taken over the biggest portion of the drug trade in Austin."

"Are you saying you will work with us?" Sophie asked.

"That depends on what you mean by work with," Ramos said.

"Generally, we like to devise a plan and coordinate it with whatever agencies that make up the task force. Our main concern is the protection of our clients. We will want an immunity agreement in place. And a guarantee they will be relocated to a state and city of their choice," Sophie said.

"I know how you work, Ms. Star, but we don't do things that way here," SAC Ramos said.

"I can appreciate that, sir," Houston said. "But we won't work with you if we can't actively protect our clients."

"We can talk about that, and I don't mind having your input. But I want to assure you, I will be in charge. I would like to speak with your clients."

"SAC Ramos, we will not bring our clients in until our stipulations are met. And our clients have an attorney who will want to be the one to make the agreement with the DOJ."

"I see."

"And this needs to stay compartmentalized. A small task force would be optimal. We don't want DeLeon finding out," Houston said.

"Are you saying there is a leak in our department?" Ramos was insulted.

"No, sir. There doesn't need to be a leak. An overheard conversation could get back to DeLeon," Houston said.

Ramos was about to reply when he saw Captain Sung coming.

CHAPTER ELEVEN

SAC Ramos stood to greet her. "Captain, this is Mr. Houston Townsend and Mrs. Sophie Star Townsend."

Houston stood. The Captain extended her hand, and Houston reciprocated. Sophie greeted her with a smile and a nod.

"Why don't we go into the small conference room," Ramos ask ASAC Berry to join them as he directed them into the room.

As they were seated, SAC Ramos gave a condensed version of what had transpired as he saw it.

"Are you telling me that your clients met with Luis DeLeon face to face, and he was the one who gave him the drugs?"

"Yes," Houston said.

"Well, that puts a new spin on things," Sung said.

"What we are trying to do, Captain, is to free our clients from DeLeon. They will never be free until they pay him back, and since the drugs were stolen, they can't do that," Sophie said.

"So, they will cooperate with us to get evidence on DeLeon?" Sung asked.

"Yes, with stipulations," Sophie said.

"Which are?"

"Immunity, of course, and a guarantee of relocation. But Houston and I also need a say in the operation. We need to be certain our clients aren't taking undo risks," Sophie said.

"I understand, but you don't mean you want to run the operation, do you?" Sung asked.

"To some respects. In the other task forces we have been involved with, Houston and I ran them."

"Other task forces?"

"They worked with the FBI and DEA in DC and New York. Ms. Star ran the operation that took down the Morano empire."

"I'm afraid that won't be possible here, but I have no problem with your input," Captain Sung said.

"We will need your clients to come in," Ramos emphasized again.

"Not until there is a plan in place and DOJ has signed off on our stipulations," Houston said.

"Alright, give us the afternoon to come up with a plan, and we will contact you," Ramos said.

Houston and Sophie stood. "Thank you," Houston said and wrote down his number on a yellow pad on the conference table.

"SAC Berry will see you out," Ramos said.

"Thank you," Houston said. Bully stood and heeled next to Houston's right side.

Once they entered the elevator ASAC Berry said, "SAC Ramos is out to make a name for himself. He will never let you get credit for an operation."

"ASAC Berry, we aren't looking for credit. We are trying to save our clients from a dangerous man," Sophie said.

"I hate to say it, but SAC Ramos will not care if your clients' lives are at risk."

"ASAC Berry, if that is how you feel about him, why haven't you transferred?" Houston asked. "This sounds a little bit like sour grapes."

"No, sir. I'm staying to try to keep someone else from dying."

"Someone else?" Sophie turned to him as the elevator doors opened on the main floor. ASAC Berry moved them out of the entry toward the back door.

"We had another dealer who agreed to cooperate to get out of doing time. Ramos pushed him too fast to get info on DeLeon. He started asking too many questions. He was found dead in his bed a week later," Berry said.

"Oh, that's awful. But we can't do this without backup. What about Captain Sung?" Sophie asked.

"She keeps him in line as much as she can. I trust her, but you would be better off if you could go over Ramos' head to get someone else to run the operation. Your clients will have a better chance of making it out of this alive." ASAC Berry opened the back door and let them out. Nothing more was said.

Houston opened the car door for his wife, then let Bully in the back seat. When he got behind the wheel, he didn't start the car.

Sophie looked at him, "Well, I wasn't expecting that."

"I'm not sure how to take what Berry said. But if it is true, there is no way we will put our clients in Ramos' hands."

"What can we do about it. Now, whether we bring in our clients or not, he will try to locate them."

"And they have Derreck, who is more than willing to give them up. They just haven't put it together yet," Houston said.

"We have to keep them hidden until we know the DEA's plan. If they plan to send them in to pay off their debt and try to buy more cocaine. I think Ramos will be very disappointed. These boys fell into that meeting by a quirk of fate. No way will they ever meet up with him again." Houston said.

"Maybe not fate. It could be the Lord is giving us a way to get rid of DeLeon," Sophie said. "I'm hungry."

"Please, no more chili dogs. The car still smells of them," Houston said.

"No, I'm thinking pizza. I can see if Lizzy wants to meet us at CJ's office, and we can eat lunch together," Sophie said.

"Sounds good to me."

Houston brought in two pizzas. Jett ran headlong into Houston's leg and wouldn't let go. Sophie grabbed the pizzas. Houston dragged Jett along, while the boy stood on his shoe, giggling.

Bully's service vest was off, and he ran circles around Houston and Jett. Coco followed suit.

"It is so much fun to watch how the dogs love Jett. It's like he's their toy," Lizzy laughed.

"What kind of pizza did you bring us," CJ asked.

"A pepperoni and olive, of course, and a Canadian bacon and pineapple. Houston thinks pineapple on pizza is an arrestable offense. But I ignore him," Sophie chuckled. "Lizzy said you had soda in the mini fridge."

"Yes, take out what you want. You can grab me a root beer if you will," CJ said.

CJ pulled the highchair out of the little storage room in his office and set Jett in it. Lizzy held Jett over the sink, washing his hands and face, drying them with a paper towel. She sat him in the highchair and gave him a pizza slice without the toppings. She placed the extra toppings on her piece. Bully and Coco sat strategically, knowing who would give them scraps. Jett was always their first choice.

After saying blessing and taking a couple of bites, CJ asked. "How did it go at the DEA?"

"Not like we hoped. They made it perfectly clear we were not in charge but would listen to our input," Houston said.

"The problem is, his second in command, ASAC Berry, warned us that SAC Ramos is out to make a name for himself. He said one CI had already lost his life because Ramos pushed him too hard, too fast."

"Oh, that's not good," Lizzy said, wiping off Jett's face and telling him not to give the dogs his pizza.

"What are you going to do?" CJ asked.

"One thing is for sure: we are not turning our clients over to them unless their plan is safe. I think we could do better on our own," Sophie said.

"We can't do an operation like this without proper backup," Houston said.

Jett kept throwing pieces of his pizza to Bully and Coco. Lizzy took the food off his tray and fed it to him, so he'd get some of it into his mouth.

"Houston, do you think Assistant Administrator Hampton would find some reason to call SAC Ramos to a training session in New York or DC? We could work with Ramos's ASAC, Berry, and maybe even Captain Sung." Sophie asked.

"We can ask him. All he can do is say no. Director Cosby would have more clout with something like that, but he is FBI, not DEA."

Houston's phone rang, but he didn't recognize the number, "Hello?

"Mr. Townsend, I thought I'd give you a heads up. SAC Ramos is sending out a team to search the house that I think might be your clients. A CI told us it is where his supplier lives and there are drugs in there. I didn't know if these were the brothers you were talking about. I wanted to warn you." ASAC Berry said.

"Are there arrest warrants?"

"We have them available, but we won't arrest them if there are no drugs. Or if we can't find them," Berry said.

"ASAC Berry, there should be no drugs in that house. If there is, someone planted them. Please keep an eye out. I have a bad feeling about this," Houston thanked him and hung up.

"I need to make sure Felix and Rob are nowhere near their house. SAC Ramos is raiding it." Houston dialed the number they texted to him last night.

"Hello, Mr. Townsend," Felix answered.

"Tell me you are nowhere near your house."

"No, we are at the motel, like you told us."

"What's going on, Houston?" Sophie wanted more details. He told her and Felix at the same time.

"Derreck gave up Felix and Rob like we thought. ASAC Berry told me Ramos is sending out a team to search their house and arrest them if they find any drugs."

"Mr. Townsend, I promise you we don't have any drugs except what Derreck left, and we got rid of that."

"I believe you, but I would not put it past Derreck to go back and plant more to ensure you get caught with it."

"Didn't you tell the DEA what happened?"

"Yes, it didn't go so well. I never gave your names or address, so the DEA only has it if Derreck gave it to them."

"I can't believe he would do that to us," Felix said, telling Rob what was happening.

"I'm putting you on speaker. Sophie wants to talk to you."

"Felix, I think we will need to send you out of state. You won't be able to go back and get your things. Let us call you back," Sophie told him. Houston hung up and gave Sophie his attention.

"What are you thinking?"

"I'm thinking one of our families in Trenton could take him in until we have this taken care of. If the DEA gets their hands on them, it will be too late for a good deal."

"Mom and Dad would take them in."

"I'm thinking Katsumi, it would be a great experience for the brothers to hear how God can change a life."

"Ok, let's head home and make some arrangements," Houston said. He and Sophie picked up the paper plates and empty pizza boxes.

"Leave it," Lizzy said. "I can take care of this. You take care of those young men."

"SAC Ramos is cutting us out of the equation. Berry was right," Houston said. "We can't trust him."

"If they don't find drugs and still want to bring them in for questioning, we'll know they plan on intimidating them into meeting with DeLeon on Ramos' terms," Sophie said. "I'm going to call Katsumi and give him a heads-up." Sophie dialed.

"Musume, I am so happy to hear from you."

"Ojisan, I miss you. I hope you are well."

"Very well, now that I hear your voice," Katsumi said. Whenever Sophie called Katsumi, she knew better than to try to get to the point until the pleasantries were out of the way.

"Ojisan, I have a big favor to ask you."

"You know I will do anything for you."

"Houston and I took on as clients two young men who are brothers. They had gotten into a desperate situation and made terrible decisions. We thought we might help them out of it, but the agency we were trying to work with is cutting us out. I am afraid these young men could be in danger.

"If it is necessary to get them out of town, would they be welcome to stay with you? These young men could be served by hearing the testimony of your life."

"I am honored to be asked to help. They can stay as long as you need."

"They won't be able to take anything with them. But they do have some money to get clothes. I will send you some money for their keep," Sophie said.

"If you do that, musume, you will insult me clear to my heart. With all that God has done for me, it is a little thing to share my worldly goods," he said.

"Of course, Ojisan. I didn't mean to offend you. We will know by this evening. I'll call you back," Sophie said and hung up after the goodbyes.

As soon as Sophie hung up, Houston's cell rang.

"Hello?"

"Mr. Townsend, ASAC Berry here. The search did not produce drugs, but SAC Ramos wants us to bring the boys in for questioning. He has put a BOLO out on them."

"What's his motivation for doing that if the search produced nothing?" Houston asked and put him on speaker so Sophie could hear.

"When the CI came in and gave us a tip with the address of his supplier. It didn't take much of a leap for the SAC to connect the CI's tip to your clients. He knows they were willing to cooperate, so Ramos figured the brothers are scared enough he could bully them out of calling you and just do what he wants.," Berry paused. "I've seen him do that before. He's relentless and will threaten them with harsh sentences if they don't."

"Thank you ASAC Berry, I won't forget this. But why are you telling us this? I know you said you don't want another CI to die. But there has to be more than that. If Ramos ever finds out you warned us, you put your whole career on the line."

Berry was still for a moment. "Mr. Townsend. I didn't just listen when they taught us about your operations in the Training Academy at Quantico. I read every transcript, after-action report, summary, and teammates' personal statements.

"To a man, everyone said the mission's success was directly related to the leadership of Ms. Star, you, and Agent Rodriguez. And you used the same team for other operations, which produced the same results and comments.

"That's the kind of team I want to be on. I don't care if I'm at the top. I just want to be a part of something like that."

"Maybe you will not find the kind of leader you are looking for here. But when it is your turn to lead, you can become that kind of leader," Houston said. "Thank you, ASAC Berry," Houston said and hung up.

"I would have liked to have him on one of our teams," Sophie said.

Houston pulled his vehicle into a parking lot. "We need to get Felix and Rob on a flight to Trenton as soon as possible. But I'm afraid to meet them at the motel. SAC Ramos could have us followed, although I haven't noticed a tail."

"I'll call the airlines to see when the next flight out is."

While Sophie was doing that. Houston was thinking about the logistics of getting them from the motel to the airport. A problem being if the DEA sent the BOLO out to the bus stations, trains, and airlines, they would be picked up trying to board the plane.

"Sophie, hang up. They can't fly commercial."

"Why?" Then she thought about it. "SAC Ramos could have sent the BOLO to all transit locations. Do you think he would go that far?"

"Yes. A man with the ego of SAC Ramos will do anything if he thinks he can catch a big fish like DeLeon. Ok, here are our two problems. We can't pick up our clients at the motel if we are being followed, and we can't get them on a commercial flight out of town."

"If Uncle Jared is available, we can pay for the fuel and see if he will fly them to Trenton. And we can ask Uncle Manny to pick them up at the motel," Sophie said.

Houston headed downtown to the law firm to talk to Manny.

Manny was upstairs with a client, so Houston and Sophie waited in the conference room and made some calls.

"Uncle Jared, I have a big favor to ask," Sophie explained the situation with the young men. "Is it possible for you to fly him to Trenton tonight? Since this is business, we will pay for all the fuel and your time."

"Sophie, no need to pay me. My guess is these young men don't have the money to pay your fee as it is, and you are footing the costs yourself. I can take them in the morning, but they can stay here tonight so you know they are safe."

"Thank you, Uncle Jared. We are waiting at the law firm to ask Uncle Manny to pick them up. We're afraid we may be being followed."

"Take your time. I'll be home the rest of the evening."

Sophie thanked him and hung up. Houston had just hung up the phone too.

"Uncle Jared said the young men could stay with him tonight, and he would fly them out in the morning."

"Good, I talked to Felix. I told them not to leave the motel for any reason, and we would send someone to pick them up."

Sophie saw Uncle Manny walk his clients to the stairs. She stepped out into the hall to greet him, Bully followed her. "Hi, Uncle Manny."

"Hi, Sophie," he gave her a quick hug, then patted Bully on his head.

"Do you have time to talk to us?"

"Sure, come into my office."

Houston shut the door behind them. "Manny, you already know the story with our clients. We went to the DEA today, and things did not go as well as we hoped. The SAC is locking us out and is using the information the CI told him, even though he knows it's a lie. He asked us to bring Felix and Rob in. We refused to do it. He plans on threatening them with arrest and imprisonment if they don't do what he wants."

"But Rex is their attorney. He can protect them."

"They young men will not be able to handle SAC Ramos. He'll keep putting off their call. We are sending them to Trenton until we can get this under control," Houston said.

"What is it you need my help with, Houston?"

"We have Felix and Rob stashed at a motel. We can't pick them up ourselves for fear we are being followed. We know SAC Ramos has put a BOLO out on them," Houston said.

"Uncle Jared said they can stay with him tonight, and he will fly them to Trenton in the morning," Sophie added.

"Alright, I can do that. Give me the address," Manny said.

Houston texted it to him. "It will take me twenty minutes to get there. Call them and tell them to look out for my Black Jeep in twenty minutes."

"Thank you, Uncle Manny. This work is so much harder without a backup team."

"Sophie, we will always be there for you," Manny said.

A DESPERATE CHOICE

CHAPTER TWELVE

After Houston called Felix to let him know Manny was coming for them, he and Sophie stopped by Rex's office. He was typing on the computer but noticed them in his peripheral vision.

"Hello, come on in."

"Hello, Rex, we have had some complications with our client's case," Houston said.

"Fill me in."

"Sophie and I went to the DEA to make a deal like we said. It did not go well. SAC Ramos won't work with us. We never divulged names, but the cousin using them as a scapegoat did. And even though I told the SAC he was lying; he raided the Wynne's house. Now he has a BOLO out on the brothers to bring them in for questioning."

"Did they find drugs when they searched the house?"

"No, we had gotten rid of the drugs his cousin brought over to frame them with."

"Did the police take the brothers in?" Rex asked.

"No, we had stashed them in a motel. I was afraid the police would get to them before we made a deal."

"Rex, I want to send the brothers to Trenton, New Jersey. They are not safe here, not from DeLeon or the DEA."

"You are sure there is no arrest warrant pending?" Rex asked.

"Not that I'm aware of. We were told they were wanted for questioning, but no drugs were found. What could they arrest them for?" Sophie asked.

"As long as you aren't helping them illude justice, it should be fine. If we find out later that there is an arrest warrant, we'll need to bring them back," Rex said.

"Rex, do you think we should call and find out if there are arrest warrants before we move them out of state?" Sophie asked.

"No. In this case it is better to ask forgiveness then ask permission, as the old saying goes. To our knowledge right now there are no arrest warrants. True?"

"Yes," Houston said.

"Rex, if SAC Ramos tries to get ahold of us to see where the brothers are, can we refer them to you?" Sophie asked.

"Yes, absolutely. I can require him to show me his evidence for an arrest warrant or, for that matter, to show cause to question them."

"Thank you, Rex," Sophie said.

On the way home, Manny called and said he delivered the brothers to Jared.

"After eating and feeding Bully, we can walk to Jared's. We can go out the back gate in case we brought a tail home with us," Houston said.

"Do you really think we have a tail," Sophie asked.

"If I were the SAC, it's what I'd do."

Sophie called Jared to tell him they would come over through the back door. It was open when they made it to his house.

Jared, Felix, and Robin were waiting for them, sitting at the kitchen table. Houston and Sophie took a seat as Bully laid down in the corner to take a nap.

"Hello, Uncle Jared. Thank you for doing this."

"I'm happy to help, Sophie. We'll leave at eight in the morning."

"Do we really have to go?" Rob asked.

"Sorry. Rob's never been out of state. He's nervous. And the fact we can't go back for any of our things is hard," Felix said.

"I understand, and if you give us your house keys and a list of what you want. We'll go over there when it's safe and send you what you need," Sophie said.

"Ok. But where are we going?"

"Houston and I have family and friends in Trenton, New Jersey. No one will look for you there. Mr. Katsumi has agreed to take you in. He is very kind and will ensure you have everything you need."

"Will he take us somewhere so we can buy some clothes and toiletries?" Rob asked.

"Yes. And we will stay in contact with you. Only use Mr. Katsumi's landline. No cell phones. And don't call anyone else. Your cousin traded you guys in to save his own skin."

"What about the money we owe DeLeon? If we don't pay him, he will never stop looking for us," Felix asked.

"We'll get all that cleared up. We still have three weeks, right?" Houston asked.

"Yes, August 4th is the due date. Mr. Townsand, how will we be able to pay for all this? A private flight to New Jersey alone will take all our money," Felix asked.

"We'll keep an accounting of the costs. When you open your auto and tire shop, you can pay us monthly," Houston said.

"It could take years."

"That's fine, Felix, we trust you," Sophie said.

"I'll land at Trenton's private executive airport. Do we have someone meeting us?" Jared asked.

"Yes, I called my dad before we came over. He said he would pick up Katsumi and take him to the airport. He just needed me to text him the estimated arrival time," Houston said.

"We should be there at about 12:15 pm their time. It's just over a three-hour flight," Jared said. Houston texted that information to his dad, asking him to pass it on to Katsumi.

Sophie reached out and touched her uncle's arm. "Thank you. It seems I'm always thanking you for something."

Jared put his hand over hers, "Sophie, there is no limit to what I would do for you. Remember that."

"I know Uncle Jared."

"It's no inconvenience. I was heading to New York anyway. Liam and Ricky want me to check out a man who wants to do business with them. Neither David nor Jonathan was available."

"We insist you use our SUV; it's stored at my dad's. Don't rent a car," Houston said.

"And Jack has the keys to our penthouse. I want you, Ricky, and Liam to stay there for as long as you want," Sophie added.

"I'm sure they have a hotel room," Jared said.

"Absolutely not. I'll call and have some food delivered to the condo."

"Thank you, both."

Felix handed over his keys to the house and the Mustang. He gave them a list of what they would like sent to them from the house. He thanked them again and promised to pay them back for everything. Then he asked.

"Why are you doing all this for us?"

Houston looked at Felix, "Felix, you and Rob have made bad decisions. Decisions that you cannot recover from without help. The help we give you is temporary. You can go right back out and make the same mistakes over and over again. Something needs to change inside of you. Jesus can help you in a way that will change your life forever. While you are gone, you need to think about what you want the rest of your life to look like."

"Houston and I will do our best to help you," Sophie said. "We promise you that."

Houston opened the cottage door. Sophie went to get her pajamas on while Houston locked the door and filled Bully's water bowl.

Houston raised his voice so Sophie could hear him through the bathroom door. "I'm going to call Fons. We need his help on this," he heard a muffled reply from the bathroom.

"Ok, love. I'll be out in a minute."

Houston went into the living room, turned on the TV to the news channel, and muted it. Then he pulled out his cell and dialed Fons.

"Hello, partner."

"Hey, Fons. Do you have a minute?"

"Of course. What's going on?"

"I told you we were meeting with clients yesterday. Felix and Robin Wynne. We are going to need backup. This is way more complex than we expected." Houston went on to tell him every detail of what they knew and the events that had transpired.

Sophie walked in with a big bowl of popcorn, one glass of ice for herself, and two sodas. She sat beside him and motioned for him to put it on speaker.

"I'm putting you on speaker, Fons. Sophie's with me."

"Hi, Soph."

"Hello, Fons. Is Carol with you?"

"She went to bed; she has an early catering job in the morning," Fons paused. "So, the SAC wouldn't work with you?"

"No. Even though we told Ramos the CI was lying, he used his information as an excuse to search the Wynne home. They found no drugs, but he still put a BOLO on them. He wants to question them. If he picks them up, the advantage of us approaching the DEA first for a good deal will go out the window."

"So, you are sending them up here."

"Yeah. Manny and Jared are helping us out, but we need backup. I know you have to finish the operation you are on for Director Cosby. Do you know how much longer it will be?"

"We arrested the targets of the operation today. Tomorrow, we will wrap everything up and do our after-action reports. Cosby hasn't said anything about a new operation yet. But I can put in my two week notice and tell him I'll be in Austin until he needs me back to finish my time."

"Fons, I know this isn't giving you time to prepare things. How is Carol going to feel about this?" Sophie asked.

"Sophie, Carol and I have already packed up our entire apartment. We were just waiting for your call. We'll have to return to arrange for our things to be shipped once we find a place to live, but we are ready."

"Having you here will make Sophie and I feel better. Sophie's dad had a run-in with Luis DeLeon years ago. He knew then how dangerous DeLeon was."

"Keep things stable until I can get there. I may go down to Trenton to speak with the brothers before we leave," Fons said.

"That would be a good idea. They may remember something more that can help us. Find out everything you can about their meeting with DeLeon."

"I feel better already, knowing backup is on the way," Sophie said."

"Keep me informed of any changes in the circumstances," Fons said.

"We will."

Houston disconnected his cell and let out a breath. "That's a relief."

"I'm glad they are coming. Would they want to stay in the apartment above the office until they decide where to live? It's a great apartment, and the kitchen is perfect for Carol."

"We'll offer it to them. I forgot to ask Emmett for the electrician's number," Houston stood and looked out the window. "His light is still on; I'll run over and talk to him."

Bully saw him go to the door and scrambled off his bed to go with him.

WEDNESDAY

Sophie was still sleeping, but Houston woke early and couldn't go back to sleep. He got up, went into the kitchen, and made himself a cup of coffee. He let Bully out and the front door open, so Bully could come in when he was ready for breakfast.

It had been hot outside since their return from Henderson. The only moisture was the dew in the morning. But today, a sprinkling of rain left a fresh smell outside that Houston welcomed.

Bully lopped in, shook his coat, sprayed water mist on the door, and headed to the kitchen. Houston grabbed a towel from the linen closet and told Bully to come. He dried Bully off, rubbing him down.

"Are you happy here, buddy?" He asked as Bully's tail wagged, and he licked Houston's hand. "You have all the critters to chase you could ever ask for. Your mom likes it here too. That's all we care about, isn't it, boy."

Houston got up and put Bully's breakfast in his bowl. He washed his hands and took breakfast ingredients out of the refrigerator when his cell pinged. A text from Jared.

'**On the tarmac now, should be in Trenton at 12:15 as planned.**'

Houston forwarded the text to his father. A reply came immediately.

'**Will be there. Miss you, son.**'

Houston replied with. '**Miss you too.**'

Houston missed his family. It wasn't that he didn't love Sophie's family. And he enjoyed his relationship with CJ, Jean-Paul, Xander, Dex, Cade, Blaze, and Lawson. *I would never have thought of myself as one who would be homesick. I've been so spoiled, always living so close to my family. I took that for granted. Leaving my comfort zone is a little harder than I thought. But this is what Sophie needs and she is so happy. I am, too, for the most part.* His cell ringing brought him out of his musings.

"Hello, ASAC Berry."

"Mr. Townsend, a heads up. SAC Ramos wants you brought in. The police can't find the Wynne brothers, and he thinks you know where they are."

"He hasn't called."

"No, he is sending one of our Agents to pick you up."

"How does he know where I live?" Houston asked. It was quiet on the other end for a moment.

"He's been having you tailed."

"He is crossing some lines here."

"Yes, he is. I told you he wants to make a name for himself. Taking down Luis DeLeon will do that."

"Thank you, ASAC Berry." Houston hung up and called Rex immediately.

"Hello?"

"Rex, I know you're not at the office yet, but I got a heads up. SAC Ramos is sending someone to take us in. You'll represent us, won't you?"

"Yes, of course. When the agent comes, tell him you will meet them at the DEA offices in an hour. Then call me. Don't ride with him. You are not under arrest; he can't make you go with him."

"Thank you, Rex."

Bully was lying next to Houston when he raised his head and growled. It startled Houston, and he looked up as Bully ran out the door. He ran after him and saw a man coming through Emmett's gate.

"Bully, leave it, heel," Houston ordered. Bully continued to growl but stopped in his tracts.

"Heel," he ordered again. Bully didn't turn away from the man but backed up until he was next to Houston. He recognized the man as the same one Bully bared his teeth at, while walking through the DEA bullpen.

"You should know better than to just walk into someone's backyard," Houston said. He noticed Emmett had come out the back door when he heard Bully growling. Emmet didn't make his presence known to the intruder but waited and watched.

"You better keep that mutt under control, or I'll have to put him down," the agent said.

"I'd rethink that if I were you," Houston said.

"Mr. Townsend, my name is Special Agent Vogt. SAC Ramos sent me to bring you and your wife in for questioning."

"Questioning about what?"

"I'll let him explain that to you, sir."

"Tell SAC Ramos my wife and I will be there in an hour."

"No, sir. He wants you to come with me now."

"Am I under arrest?"

"No."

"Then I'll be there in an hour," Houston saw a flash of anger cross the man's face, then it was gone.

"I'll pass that along," Agent Vogt said as he left.

Emmett stepped out, "What's that all about, Houston?"

"We went to the DEA to get a deal for our clients, but SAC Ramos wouldn't work with us. Now he is trying to get his hands on our clients to force them to cooperate with him on his terms."

"Why would he do that?"

"The man we would give state's evidence on is Luis DeLeon. He is more worried about making a name than protecting our clients."

"Luis DeLeon? We had a run-in with him years ago. We had to hire Security First to watch our homes for a week after we dealt with him."

"Sophie mentioned your run-in with him."

"You were afraid for your clients. That's why you had Jared fly them to Trenton this morning."

"Yes. And we are afraid of what Ramos would do too. He wants to bully them into doing something that could get them killed."

"Are you taking David with you?"

"Rex is going to meet us there."

"Good. Let me know how it turns out."

Houston's back was turned, closing the door when Sophie spoke from the kitchen.

"What's going on? I heard Bully growling."

Houston turned to see his wife. Her hair was tousled, her pajamas were tight around the middle, and she had no makeup. A huge smile crossed his face as his heart melted like it did every time, he saw her. At that moment, he knew he would go anywhere, live anywhere, do anything to make her happy. *Wherever she is, is home.* It was settled in his heart.

When he reached her, he said, "You are so beautiful, sweetheart," and kissed her. She looked at him quizzically. "Sophie, when I was in middle school, I saw how much my dad loved my mom and how much she loved him. I prayed that one day, I would love someone like that and be loved back. All my prayers were answered in you."

"Houston, why so sentimental today?" She asked. Houston shrugged. "You have it all backward. I didn't know to pray for you because I didn't know a man like you existed. I'm the one that was blessed beyond measure."

Houston held her tight for a few minutes. Then, told her what was going on. "SAC Ramos sent one of his men over. He wants us in his office for questioning. I already called Rex. We need to be there in an hour."

"He wants us to tell him where the Wynne brothers are," Sophie said.

"No doubt. You get dressed first. I'll make you eggs and bacon."

"I won't have time to eat it."

"SAC Ramos can wait. My children need to eat," Houston said.

As the bacon was cooking, Houston called Rex and told him he agreed to be at the DEA offices in an hour and would meet him in the back parking lot. He warned Rex they may be a little late.

Houston drove into the Federal Building complex fifteen minutes late. Rex met them at the back door, and Houston hit the intercom. ASAC Berry buzzed them in and led them upstairs. Berry didn't say much, which made Houston wonder if his boss found out he gave them a heads up.

The elevator opened on the fourth floor. Bully heeled to Houston's left as they walked to a conference room. SAC Ramos was standing at the door.

"Mr. and Mrs. Townsend, thank you for coming," he turned to Rex to explain his presence.

"Good morning, SAC Ramos. I am Rex Ford, their attorney," Rex extended his hand. It took a moment for Ramos to reciprocate.

"You brought your attorney? You are not under arrest. This is just a friendly conversation," he said as he directed them and ASAC Berry to sit at the conference table.

"The fact that you sent your agent over to bring us in instead of just calling us made me think otherwise. And then there is the fact you are having us followed," Houston said.

"What makes you think I'm having you tailed?" Ramos asked.

"How else would you know where we live?" Houston asked. Ramos did not reply.

"Mr. Townsend, I need to know where your clients are."

"Why. You don't even know their names. I never divulged that information. Or their address, for that matter. My wife and I came hoping to help you with one of your biggest cases, and you didn't want our help. As far as I'm concerned, that ended our collaboration."

"We have our own sources, Mr. Townsend. We know your clients are Felix and Robin Wynne."

"How would you know that?"

"We have a CI who gave us a tip."

"A tip that didn't produce anything," Houston retorted.

"Based on that tip, we searched your client's home. Now, we need to question them."

Rex stepped in, "Did you recover any drugs, based on your CI's tip."

"No, but we know he had some, based on what Mr. Townsend told us himself."

"Mr. Townsend will neither confirm nor deny who his clients are," Rex said. Ramos turned to Houston.

"Listen, Mr. Townsend, you don't want to be on the left foot of the DEA if you plan to work in this town. Your clients made an illegal drug purchase, and if they don't agree to cooperate with me, I will arrest them."

"Based on what evidence, SAC Ramos. You told us yourself there were no drugs in the Wynne home when you searched it. You have nothing but the word of a CI who fed you bad information. Let me guess, you told him you would drop the charges on him if he gave you someone else," Rex said with authority.

"Mr. Townsend admitted it," Ramos blurted out.

"He did no such thing. He never gave any names," Rex insisted. "Mr. Townsend, it's time for us to leave," Rex stood.

"I'm warning you, Mr. Townsend, if you are harboring a fugitive, I will prosecute you and your wife. She could end up having that baby in prison."

Houston jumped up, knocking over his chair, and pointed a finger in Ramos' face. Bully stood to his feet, his hackles raised, and growled at Ramos. "You do anything to jeopardize my wife and babies. I will make sure you never work for another federal agency again." Sophie laid her hand on his arm to calm him.

"SAC Ramos, contact me if you have any further questions about Felix and Robin Wynne. Do not contact my clients again," Rex said, getting Houston's attention away from Ramos. Houston turned, picked up the chair, and set it back on its feet. Then walked out with Rex and Sophie.

ASAC Berry walked them to the back door, "I'm sorry, Mr. Townsend. SAC Ramos has a fire in his belly to get Luis DeLeon."

"I can see that. Thank you for giving us the heads up," Houston said, then walked Rex to his car.

"Houston, what got into you? We've been threatened before. You've never got heated over it," Sophie said.

"I can't explain it, but something is wrong. I don't think Ramos is dirty, but something isn't right in his command. I can feel it."

"Things like that tend to come out. It won't stay hidden for long," Rex said.

"Thank you for being here, Rex. I let him get to me in there. Thanks for stepping in."

Rex extended his hand, "Anytime, Houston. And you are right about one thing for sure. That man's ego will eventually cause him to cross the line."

"Do you think we need to worry that we sent the brothers away?" Sophie asked.

"No, they admitted they have no evidence against them." With that, Rex got in his car.

CHAPTER THIRTEEN

"What are we going to do next?" Sophie asked.

"We're going to see if Assistant Administrator Hampton will find a way to lure him out of town. But first, I need to call Jared and see if Fons and Carol can hitch a ride back with them.

"I'll call him. They should be landed by now." There was no answer. "I'll have to try again later," Sophie said.

"Emmett gave me the name of his electrician. Let's see how soon he can come to look over the bank property. I'd like to have the sale closed as soon as possible." Houston dialed his number.

"Hello?"

"Hello, Mr. Peretz, Emmett Scott gave me your number. I hope that was all right."

"Yes. Emmett sends me business all the time. Sorry, that was presumptuous. Maybe you are calling for another reason."

"No, Mr. Peretz, it's business. I am purchasing the old bank building downtown at 703 W. 12th. Mr. Lam is the owner."

"Yes, I know Mr. Lam and the building. He hired me to upgrade the wiring upstairs. He refinished that apartment and upgraded the fixtures."

"Yes, that's the one. I was hoping to have you look at the downstairs. We want an idea of what it will cost to bring the wiring up to date and add new wiring. I assume you do not think the upstairs will need any work."

"No, I stand by my work. If you have any issues, all you have to do is call. Akito had me do a quick review of the downstairs, so I can tell you right off it will need a new electrical panel."

"Can you meet us there when you have time?"

"I'm finishing a job right now. Should be done in two hours. My men will have a few days off. Our next job doesn't start until Monday," he paused. "If you want, I could stop by on my way home about 2 o'clock."

"Perfect. We will be there."

"See you then."

"Well, the timing on that couldn't have been better," Houston said.

Houston wanted to talk to CJ about the remodel. But Sophie wanted to meet with Lizzy and Sienna at the bakery to get caught up on the wedding plans. Houston dropped her off there and headed to CJ's office.

He drove into the parking lot at CJ's office. Before he got out, he called Hampton.

"Assistant Administrator Hampton's office, may I help you?" A man's voice said.

"Yes. This is Houston Townsend. Would you see if he has a moment to speak with me?"

"One moment, please." Houston waited, listening to the elevator music. "I can connect you now."

"Thank you."

"Hello, Houston. How did things go with SAC Ramos?"

"Not well, I'm afraid. Ramos locked us out and tried to get his hands on my clients. They raided their home and then put a BOLO out on them."

"Did they find drugs in the house?"

"No. Ramos said he was bringing them in for questioning. But I know he plans to threaten them with jail time if they don't let him use them for bait to get DeLeon."

"How do you know that?"

"Because he threatened to put Sophie in jail if we didn't tell him where the brothers were," Houston said, his voice angry.

"What?"

"Yes. He's been having us tailed, and then he sent one of his agents over to bring us in for questioning this morning. My attorney told me not to go with him but to say we would voluntarily meet them there an hour later. Which we did."

"And the interview didn't go well."

"No."

"Houston, do you know where the brothers are?" Hampton asked. Houston didn't answer right away.

"I don't think I'm going to answer that. There is no evidence against them, and there is no arrest warrant. They have the right to go and come as they please."

"True. Ok, what is it you need my help with?"

"SAC Ramos' obsession to make a name for himself will get someone killed. I don't intend that to be our clients or my wife. But ASAC Berry is the opposite. He just wants to do his job.

"Is there some way to call Ramos to New York for training or something that would stroke his ego? If he were gone, I would contact ASAC Berry and work with him."

There was silence on the line. "Quantico is having a two-week training session for all federal agencies. The training sessions are to update cyber techs on innovative technologies. The criminals use the most up-to-date techniques while we still use outdated ones."

"That would be perfect, but that wouldn't include him."

"No, but I can make a special invitation for him to come along to hobnob with the higher-ups," Hampton said.

"That would do it. When is that happening?"

"The training session starts next Monday. Let me see if he has signed up his computer forensic tech," Hampton said. Houston could hear him tapping on his keyboard. "No. That will give me an excuse to call him."

"Thank you, James. I know you don't have to help us."

"It's alright. I want to evaluate Ramos for myself. We don't need an SAC that is only out to make a name for themself. I'd like you to keep me updated with the operation."

"No problem. Talk to you soon." After hanging up, Houston let out a breath.

Bully pranced in the back seat when he saw they were going to CJ's office. Houston let him out, and it took all the control Bully could muster to walk with him. When they got to the door, Bully barked.

Houston opened the door, and Bully ran the office perimeter looking for Jett. When he realized he wasn't there, he walked to the corner where Jett's toy box was and laid his head on a fallen toy.

TRENTON, NEW JERSEY

The tower directed Jared to a hangar where he could stow his plane. After doing his shutdown checklist, he grabbed his duffle and opened the door.

"Come on, I'm sure Jack and Katsumi are waiting for you at the terminal. Felix grabbed the duffle with the few things Houston had given them, including the new packages of T-shirts, underwear, and socks Jared gave them.

"Mrs. Townsend spoke of the man we are staying with a little cryptically. Is he strange?" Rob asked Jared.

Some might call him that. This man had unlimited control and power over thousands of people. He gave it up for something better. You'll get to understand him in time."

"How much time? We aren't going to be here very long," Felix said.

Jared smiled and locked the plane's door behind them. There was a cool breeze that swept by them as they walked to the terminal. As soon as he opened the door, he spotted Jack and Katsumi.

"They are over there," Jared said to the brothers and pointed, then headed in that direction.

Jack spotted them, and he and Katsumi bridged the gap. Jack gave Jared a hug and shook the young man's hands. Katsumi bowed slightly in greeting. Felix and Rob didn't know how to respond, so they mimicked his gesture. The men started walking through the terminal.

"Jack, Houston insisted I use his SUV while I was here. Is that all right with you?"

"Of course."

"I'll be driving to New York in the morning."

"I have the key to Sophie's condo. I'm sure she also insisted you stay there."

"She did. Thanks." Jared realized he had turned his cell off and pulled it out of his pocket to see if he missed any calls. They made it to Jack's car.

"I missed a call from Sophie. Do you mind if I call her before we go?"

"No, we are in no rush," Katsumi said.

Jared dialed Sophie. No answer, so he tried Houston's number.

"Hello, Jared. I take it you made it to Trenton safe and sound."

"We did. I missed a call from Sophie."

"She's with the girls. They were probably laughing so hard she couldn't hear the phone. I have no idea what they talk about that makes them laugh so much."

"Houston, it's been that way since they were little. You'll just have to get used to it," Jared laughed. "Do you know why she called?"

"Yes. I asked Fons to come down and help me with this case. There is an element of danger that could be involved. Without the DEA's support... anyway, he just finished an operation in DC and said he could come down on Friday. I wondered if you wouldn't mind company on the way home."

"No problem. Like I told Sophie, I'm meeting with Ricky and Liam in New York. Something about this guy that wants to do business with them concerned them. But it's a big contract, and they don't want to dismiss it out of hand. When we're done, we are going to see a live performance. They will be flying home with me too. Will Carol be coming?

"Yes, they will drive as far as Trenton. I can't thank you enough for this, Jared. I still want to pay you."

"There is no need. As I said, I was coming anyway. It worked out perfectly."

"How are Felix and Rob doing. This is hard for them, leaving everything they have and everyone they know," Houston said. Jared looked over at the young men. Jack and Katsumi were speaking with them.

"They will have to grow up fast. It will be good for them."

"Let me know when you will be arriving home. I'll pick you up," Houston offered.

"No need. I left my car in the airport parking lot."

They said goodbye, and Jared headed over to Jack's car so they could head out.

As he walked to the car a text came from Sophie.

'I'm having groceries delivered to the condo. When you leave, please take what's left to Lily in Trenton. Thanks. Enjoy your stay.'

Jared smiled as he texts back and smiley emoji.

When Houston got off the line, CJ asked. "I have an idea for the bank remodel. I'll draw out a rough draft, and you can have it before you meet with Mr. Peretz."

"Thank you," Houston called Fons while CJ was busy with the draft. There was no answer. A text pinged almost immediately.

'In a wrap-up meeting. It will be done shortly. Will call.'

Houston texted him back. **'Don't buy airline tickets. Jared is in town. He will fly you here.'**

For the next hour, CJ drew a remodel for the bank and, with Houston's input, ended up with a rough draft that he could show Fons and Sophie.

"CJ, if I show this to Mr. Peretz, will he be able to tell me an estimate of the cost to upgrade the bank's electricity?"

"Usually, I give him a blueprint that spells everything out. But this will give him enough information to give you a vague idea of what it will take."

"Perfect. Thanks, CJ. Do you take debit cards, or do I need to write a check?"

"I haven't billed you yet," CJ said.

"I know. I want to give you a five-thousand-dollar retainer. Then you can tell me when you have used that up."

"You don't need to do that, Houston. I'm not worried about you running out on the bill," he laughed.

"I know, but it's how I like to do business."

"Let me call the firm's bookkeeper. She does my books too. If she's here, she can run a debit card." CJ pressed the landline button that connected to the bookkeeper.

"Ms. Todd. A friend wants to put down a retainer for services with his debit card. Do you have time to do that now?"

"Yes, that will be fine."

CJ disconnected and stood. Come on, Houston, I'll walk you back there. He put the rough draft in a manilla envelope and handed it to him. "Don't be afraid to change it but do it in pencil so I can see the original lines."

"Thanks, CJ."

Bully woke up when he heard the door open and ran to meet up with them.

Houston walked into the bakery. He heard the ladies laughing and followed the sound.

"Hello, ladies."

They all looked up at him. "Hello," they echoed.

Teresa came over to see if he wanted anything. He thanked her but said he had an appointment.

"Are you ready to go, sweetheart?" Houston asked. Sophie stood, and Lizzy and Sienna stood with her. They hugged.

"Ok, we are set to work on centerpieces on Sunday."

"Yes, come right after church. Mom plans to have lunch for us," Sienna said.

"Is she making her lasagna?" Lizzy asked.

"Yes, please," Sophie added.

"I'll ask her to make it," Sienna said with a smile.

When Houston pulled into the bank's parking lot, he noticed a parked truck. Peretz Electric was written on the side. A man was sitting in the car. Houston stepped out and went around to open the door for Sophie. The man stepped out of the truck and walked over to them.

"Mr. Townsend, Shaul Peretz," he extended his hand, and Houston shook it. He nodded to Sophie, "Hello, Mrs. Townsend."

"Hello, Mr. Peretz. Thank you for coming at such short notice. Please call me Sophie." They headed for the side door.

"Mr. Peretz, CJ drew a rough draft of what a remodel might look like. I don't know if it will help you to see what changes might be needed."

"Call me Shaul, please. All right, let me look around first and see what shape the existing wiring is in."

"Thank you, and please call me Houston." They stepped in, and Peretz went straight to the electrical panel. Bully ran through the building, checking things out.

"I didn't know CJ drew a remodel. Let me see," Sophie said. Houston handed her the manila envelope. They moved over to where a counter was still standing.

"I like that he kept the entry with the high ceiling. Oh, and I see he made a space for the twins. I like that," Sophie said.

"Yes, and we have at least seven offices, two conference rooms, a potential room for a forensic specialist, and a small command center."

"You thought of everything. I like it."

"Fons and Carol should be here in a few days, and we'll see what they think. It will take time to get the remodel done. But I think Fons and I can do much of the work," Houston said as his cell rang. "It's Fons," he said, answering the cell. "Hi, Fons, are you done with the debriefs?"

"Yes, and I told Cosby I was resigning my commission but would be available if he needed me in the next two weeks. He said he was expecting it. He didn't exactly exude happy thoughts toward our new adventure," Fons laughed.

"Does he know you will be in Austin for those two weeks you offered him?"

"Yes. You texted that Jared will be in Trenton, and we can fly to Austin with him. That's great."

"He plans to leave Trenton on Friday. Will that work?"

"Yes, Carol has everything ready for us to leave when I get home. We should be there tonight. Can we stay in your apartment in Trenton until Friday?"

"I expected you to. Dad has the key. You'll talk to the brothers tomorrow, then?"

"Yes. What's happening with the old bank building?"

"Sophie and I are here now. We have an electrician looking through the place to make an assessment. CJ drew us a rough draft of a remodel. I'll take a picture to see what you think. We'll discuss it when you get here."

"You said there was an apartment upstairs?"

"Yes, Carol would like it. It's in great shape if you want to stay there until you get a place. Emmett said you are welcome to stay with him as long as you like."

"I think we'll take him up on that until we decide what to do," Fons said.

"I'm glad you're coming, partner."

"Me too. See you soon."

Shaul met them at the counter, and Houston showed him the rough draft.

"I see, this changes things. The existing electrical panel will handle what's here. I'll have to add to it for the small kitchen and break room. But the command center and the computer forensic room will have to have their own panel," Shaul paused. "Mr. Townsend, I would estimate that the cost to rewire and upgrade could cost up to ten thousand. And that is if you take down the sheetrock for the new wiring."

"Thank you, Shaul. How far out are you scheduled?"

"Three weeks. And I can give you the name of the company that did the plumbing upstairs. He could put in the small kitchen and the shower in the upstairs bathroom." He wrote the number down on his invoice pad and ripped it off.

"I'll call him, thank you."

Houston and Sophie walked Shaul out to his truck and locked up.

In the car, Houston asked, "Did you make any plans for tonight?"

"No. Did you want to do something?"

"No. I thought cooking at home and having a quiet evening would be nice."

Sophie grabbed his hand. "I'd like that."

CHAPTER FOURTEEN

THURSDAY. LUIS DELEON COMPOUND.

"Luis, come to our TCL Grauman's Chinese Theater opening. There is a big after-party at the Chinese 6 Theater. The studios require other celebrities to support openings. It will be fun," Diego said. Celina walked up to him and placed a hand on his arm.

"Please come, Luis. We could never have made it this far without your support."

Luis put his hand over hers. "All right if you insist. It will be fun to star-watch," he laughed. "I never saw myself as one of those fans who like to meet their favorite celebrities. But it would be interesting. When are you leaving?"

"We leave on Monday. The opening is on Wednesday night," Diego said.

"I'll meet you there on Tuesday. Where are you staying?"

"The studio puts us up at the Loews Hotel because it's nearby. I already had them reserve a room for you. Who knows, brother, you may find the love of your life while there," Diego chuckled.

"Who knows," Luis smiled. He had loved a woman once when he was young, before he got into 'the business' he is in now. But when he couldn't find a job and started doing errands for the cartel, she told him she didn't want to see him anymore. He could have quit the cartel then, but the money was good, and he liked the job. She left the next day, and he never saw her again. He'd had women around him since then, but never one he wanted to marry.

Luis' right-hand man, Tacito Ibarra, a man he knew from childhood, came to the doorway. Everyone called him Taco. Luis acknowledges him. "Taco?" He spoke in his native language.

"Una momento, Jefe."

"Si," Luis moved to the doorway, where Taco was waiting.

"Uno de nuestros distribuidores ha sido recogido por la DEA."

"Quien?"

"Derreck Wynne," Taco paused. "Fue recogido y dejado ir en un par de horas."

"¿Crees que lo convirtieron?"

"No sé."

"Ve a verlo. Descúbrelo con seguridad," Luis looked over at his brother. Taco nodded and was leaving when Luis stopped him. He spoke in English, "Don't do anything that can be led back to us." Taco left.

"Everything alright, Luis?" Diego asked. Luis slapped his brother on his back.

"Nothing for you to worry about, Diego."

Xander and Piper arrived home from Dallas. Piper was helping her father light a set of a reality show he contracted with. He had moved his company up here from Hollywood when Piper married Xander. She was their only child, and they didn't want to be that far away.

"Come in, Houston, Sophie. Thank you for coming over. And you too, Bully."

"Thank you for inviting us for lunch. We missed you," Sophie said, giving Xander and Piper hugs. Houston and Xander bumped fists.

"I can't wait until your house is built. It will be so nice to have neighbors right next door. I love it when Wes and his family are here," Piper said.

"Isn't China still here?" Sophie asked.

"Yes, but she stays with Drew when her family is gone," Xander said. He directed them to the back porch, where a hot brick pizza oven was ready for homemade pizza.

"Oh, I hadn't noticed that before. A brick pizza oven. What a great idea," Sophie said. Xander placed two pizzas in the oven as the others sat around a beautiful glass outdoor table on cushioned rod iron chairs.

"How did the filming go in Dallas?" Houston asked.

Xander laughed. Piper answered, "I can't imagine working with those reality stars. They are such divas and treat the crew like their personal servants. I had one lady ask me to get her coffee.

"Dad, put a stop to that real quick," Piper snickered.

"I can't believe Arlo is putting up with it. He has too much clout in the industry to tolerate that behavior," Xander said.

"Xander, Daddy has a year contract. They pay well, and there aren't as many sets to work on in Dallas."

"Piper, your father has enough money to retire and live more than comfortably for the rest of his life."

"Can you imagine my father with nothing to do?"

"Point taken," Xander said. "Sorry, guys, I didn't mean to leave you out of the conversation."

"No, I love hearing about it. Tell me more about the cast," Sophie leaned forward and smiled. Houston's cell rang, and he excused himself and stepped into the kitchen.

"Hello, Fons."

"Hey, Houston. I'm at Katsumi's. He invited the entire family for dinner since we are leaving tomorrow."

"I'm jealous."

"You should be. Anyway, I spoke with the brothers, and they told me the same things they told you. When I prodded them to think harder, Felix said he saw a portrait of a couple in the living room. Luis told him it was his brother and his wife, and that his brother was a director, and his wife was a famous actress."

"That's interesting. I'll let Sophie know. Thanks Fons. Have fun tonight. We'll be waiting for you tomorrow."

"Don't worry, we'll have a blast with this group. See you tomorrow."

Tacito was Luis' frontman for the drug cartel and the only one a buyer had contact with. Derreck had met with him many times, usually at a warehouse out of town. Today, Taco went to his house to catch him off guard. Tacito knocked at the door. Derreck answered in his skivvies, still half asleep. He woke up really fast.

"Taco?"

Tacito pushed his way inside. "You mind if I come in."

"No, of course not," Derreck looked outside to see if anyone came with him.

"You alone?"

"Yes. What's going on?"

"Let's sit and have a talk," Tacito said. Derreck led him to the kitchen table.

"What are you doing here?"

"I have ears everywhere, derdedor. You tell me."

"I don't know what you're talking about?"

"Don't do that, Derreck. You have seen what I do to unos mentirosos."

"I'm not lying. It's nothing. The police stopped me, and they found cocaine on me. They turned me over to the DEA. But they didn't have enough to hold me."

"Cuánto?" Tacito asked. Derreck was tempted to lie but was afraid he already knew the answer. He had moles everywhere.

"Ten grams."

"No way, they caught you with that much and let you go, estúpido," Tacito said, knowing he had to have made a deal. "You snitched...."

"No, never, Taco. I'd never do that."

"I don't believe you."

"They thought I was a street dealer. They wanted my supplier, so I gave them my cousin Felix. The one that I sent you. There was no way I was going to turn on you. I'd never do that."

"I don't know this, Felix."

"Whoever answered the phone told me to send him to this address." Derreck wrote it down on a napkin.

"Felix met Jefe. Now he can finger him. Eres un hombre muerto."

"I just did what I was told. How was I supposed to know he would meet the boss? You told me no one ever met him."

"It was a random occurrence. Where is Felix now?"

"I don't know, the police raided their house after I planted some cocaine there. But Felix and Rob were gone, and so was the cocaine. I think they left town."

"Why would they do that?"

"I don't know. I gave them enough cocaine to sell to pay for half the stolen product. At least, that was what I told them. I had to make sure there was cocaine there when the DEA came looking."

"What stolen product?"

"After they picked up the cocaine. Someone followed them home. When they pulled into their garage, two men attacked them and stole it. They are terrified they won't be able to pay their debt, so Rob is gambling to try to win the money. They might have sold the drugs I gave them and taken the money to Las Vegas to win the rest back."

"You think they are in Las Vegas?"

"I don't know for sure."

"That means the DEA is going to come back to you for more information," Tacito shook his head. "You have made trouble for me, Derreck. I can't have that," Tacito slid his gun out of his waistband under the table. He took the silencer out of his pocket and screwed it on the end.

"Honest, Taco. I would never snitch on you. I swear."

"I don't believe you." Taco took out his gun and shot Derreck. His chair tipped back, and he rolled out of it dead before he hit the ground.

After eating two pizzas, the two couples enjoyed the banana cream pie Xander had bought from Sienna's bakery.

"I never bake anymore," Piper said. "Sienna's desserts are so good; we buy everything we want from her. Oh...." Piper got up and went into the kitchen. When she returned, she handed Sophie a box. "I picked these up for you. I know how much you like them."

"Macarons! I love them. Thank you, Piper," Sophie said.

"There is a dozen in those boxes, and she won't share one with me," Houston teased.

"You can buy your own," Sophie held the box to her chest. Houston laughed.

"Next time, I'll buy you your own box, Houston," Piper chuckled.

"Xander, do you know an actress and a director named DeLeon?"

"Yes. Celina DeLeon is fairly new to the Hollywood scene but was famous in Mexico. Her husband Diego is a director. She made 'B' movies for years. Then, several years back, they moved to Austin, and Diego got backing to make a big-budget movie starring his wife. It was successful, so the studios considered her for their 'A' list movies.

"As a matter of fact, we are attending one of her movie openings at TCL Grauman's Chinese theater next week."

"You know them well enough to be invited?" Houston asked.

"No. The studio requires celebrities to appear at different openings so that the event draws more press and fans. Mom and Dad were supposed to go, but Mom is working on Sienna's wedding with Aunt Aileen, so she asked us to take her place."

"Why are you asking, Houston?" Sophie questioned. Houston explained the phone call from Fons.

"Who are the brothers he was talking to," Xander asked.

"They are our clients. They've gotten in a bad spot with Luis DeLeon, Diego's brother. He's a cartel kingpin, and they owe him money. We tried to work with the DEA to get evidence against DeLeon, but they didn't want to work with us. So, we are on our own for now."

"Wow, I had no idea," Xander said.

"Grandpa had a friend who had gotten tangled up with the DeLeon's when he was desperate for money. He got a loan from Diago. He didn't know the money came from his drug kingpin brother Luis. Dad and the firm had to meet with Luis to pay him off. When the guy couldn't pay him back, Luis wanted to legitimize himself by becoming a partner in the man's construction business. Dad said they couldn't let that happen. Emmett lent him the money to pay Luis off," Sophie said.

"I don't remember that," Xander said.

"I think they tried to keep it quiet, but Dad said Luis was dangerous," Sophie paused. "But this gives me an idea. Would you guys want to be a part of an undercover operation?"

"Really?" Piper sat up straight.

"What are you thinking, Sophie?" Houston asked.

"I'm thinking if I can get my name floating around Luis' ears. Then, when I try to get a meeting with him, he will be intrigued enough to meet with me himself," she paused. "I will have to think this all the way through."

"Well, you are welcome to come with us if you like," Xander said.

"Thank you. We'll have to have a clear plan in place before we go," Sophie said. "You are coming to Aunt Aileen's Sunday to help with the centerpieces, right?"

"Yes, Sienna sent me a text. I'll be there," Piper said. Sophie hugged her goodbye, and Houston called for Bully, who was trying to reach a squirrel who rejected his offer to play by running up a tree.

DELEON COMPOUND.

Luis was in the kitchen having a glass of iced tea. He sat in the kitchen nook, looking out the large bay window at his beautiful garden. Diego had asked when he would find a woman and get married. It was a natural question for a brother to ask. But a woman who would be ok with his business was one he wouldn't want to raise his children.

Tacito watched his boss for a moment. He knew he was lonely. But that wasn't something he could help him with.

"Luis, un momento?"

"Sí, por favor, tome asineto."

Tacito switched to English as he sat, "I met with Derreck. He was stopped by the police, and they found ten grams of coke on him. They turned him over to DEA."

"He turned?" Luis shook his head.

"Not on us, but on his cousins. They thought he was a low-level street dealer, so he told them his cousins were the suppliers. They went to pick up his cousins, but they have disappeared."

"Are they running with our product?"

"No, I don't think that's it. Apparently, two men jumped them when they got home that night and stole it. The younger cousin is a talented card player. Derreck gave them some product to sell. He meant it to back up his story to the DEA when they raided his home. But he thinks they sold it in Las Vegas so Rob could get into a high-stakes card game."

Luis thought about it. Ok, let's give them the three weeks they have left. If they don't come with our money, then you know what to do."

"Sí."

"What about Derreck? The DEA will return to him for more information and interrogate him until he gives them someone else."

"Sí. He is no longer a problem," Tacito said, looking at Luis. Luis nodded.

"Tacito, we have to be careful here. They will search for the killer, no matter that the victim is a dealer. We don't own the police in Austin," Luis picked up his tea and took a drink.

"Entiendo, Jefe."

"I will be leaving Tuesday for Las Angeles; I'm going to Diego and Celina's opening at that famous Chinese Theater."

"You must be proud of them."

"I am. When I got into this business, Diego wanted to follow in my footsteps. He followed me around for a while. When my boss told me one of the shop owners needed a lesson, Diego came with me. What he saw put him in a catatonic state. It took a week for him to come out of it. From then on, I refused to get him involved. He doesn't have the seared conscience for this kind of work," he turned to Tacito. "Not like you and me. We belong here. I'll leave you in charge."

"I will take care of everything, like always, Jefe."

"I know you will. Don't call unless it's something you can't handle."

Tacito thought for a moment before he spoke next. "Diego hopes you will find a good woman there," he smiled.

Luis chuckled, "he has always been a romantic."

When Houston and Sophie got home, Bully went straight for his food bowl. Houston fed him and filled his water bowl. Bully scarfed his food down and went to bed in the living room.

Sophie sat down at the kitchen table. "What is this plan you're thinking about, Sophie?" Houston grabbed the orange juice from the fridge and poured some for Sophie. He grabbed a Pepsi for himself.

She thanked him. "If Xander takes us to the opening. He might notice me. Then, at the after-party, I'll head to the bathroom. Xander and Piper can pay their respects to the DeLeon's, and she can ask Celina to go to the lady's room with her."

"Isn't that a little weird?" Houston said. Sophie looked at him like he didn't have a clue.

"Houston, have you ever seen me go to the lady's room without someone else?" He thought for a moment.

"No. Why is that?"

"It's a time for us to gossip about people's clothes, and we just like to."

"Ok, go on. So, you are in the bathroom, and Celina and Piper head in there..."

"So, I time coming out of the stall as they walk in. I wash my hands, say hello, and then return to the table. That gives Piper a chance to feed Celina the gossip.

"She complains that the studio made them invite me. That I have connections. Celina will ask why Piper doesn't like me. Then she'll say that I was arrested in New York for being the head of a drug empire.

"Celina will ask why I'm not in jail. Piper will tell her there was some sort of misconduct by the DA's office, and they had to let me go. Then she'll say she thinks I paid someone off."

"Ok, but how does that get us to Luis DeLeon? We don't even know if he'll be there."

"It won't matter. After Xander and Piper quickly excuse themselves. Celina will pass on all the juicy gossip to her husband and Luis if he is there. At that point, we will leave. The last thing we want, if Luis is there, is for him to want to meet me. I need to stay mysterious. And if Luis isn't there, his brother and Celina will tell him about the after-party. Including me."

"Ok, but you never mentioned me in this scenario."

"You will be monitoring our earpieces and mics."

"I don't want you in there by yourself, Sophie."

"I agree. I would have a bodyguard if I'm supposed to have a drug empire. Fon's can do that. The plan gets more complicated after that."

"Keep going. I'm not liking being left on the shelf so far."

"I'll make sure Diego and, hopefully, Luis gets a glimpse of me as I leave. I'm hoping he remembers me..."

"That's not a problem," Houston mumbled, annoyed.

"What?"

"Nothing, go on."

"So, when we get back here. I show up on Luis' doorstep. Felix said the place is walled, with men and dogs protecting the place. He said there was a monitor and intercom. Fons will drive me and let them know I want to speak with Luis DeLeon."

179

"What makes you think he will let you in?"

"Curiosity. I'm sure he will go straight home and look me up."

"All the police records with your name were destroyed. Yes, but the articles are still out there somewhere. I'll have Sissy make sure there is no trace of our detective agency and bring up all the articles of my arrest. I'll have her store a hard copy, then delete them from the internet when this is over."

"Ok, he is too intrigued to not let you in."

"Hopefully. Then, I will say two men contacted me saying they had cocaine and wanted to know if I was interested, not knowing I'm out of the business. I'll say they also didn't know the ones they stole it from had asked for my help to recover it.

"From there, I'll play it by ear. But eventually, I will let Luis know I have a partner and husband, which is when you come into the picture."

"Finally."

"Were you feeling a little left out, honey?" She laughed and kissed him.

"Then you are thinking we find some way to make a deal with him. A deal where he will have to show up at the exchange like Nikko."

"That's what I'm thinking. Or Luis may show us his operation. Something that will connect him to his cartel."

"That's all good, but you are ignoring the danger."

"I'll find a way to step out of the picture, somehow. And I'm still hoping ASAC Berry will be working with us."

"You better give Sissy a call. If she is working on another job. She might not be able to get right to it."

"You're right. I'll call her now," Sophie dialed Sissy and explained the plan.

CHAPTER FIFTEEN

FRIDAY

Houston was up and dressed. He let Bully out and filled his food bowl. Sophie was in the bathroom drying her hair. He went to open the door so Bully could come back in. When he did, he saw his best friend standing there with his wife. Bully was getting his favorite type of greeting from his friends. Carol scratched behind his ears and kissed his forehead. Fons did the same. Houston grabbed Fons and gave him a hug.

"I'm so glad you're here," he let go and hugged Carol.

"Where is Sophie," Carol asked.

"Drying her hair," Houston directed them inside.

"I'll go surprise her," Carol smiled.

"Let me help you get your suitcases and get you settled in Emmett's."

"Already done. Jared helped me. He and Emmett want us all to come over for breakfast."

"I'll tell Sophie we'll be at Emmett's and meet them over there."

When Carol stepped into view through the mirror behind her in the open bathroom door, Sophie was drying her hair. She turned around, gave a little squeal, and hugged her.

"I'm so happy to see you," Sophie said.

"Me too. It was so lonely in DC without you."

Houston stuck his head in and told them he and Fons were headed to Emmett's for breakfast.

"We'll be right there," Sophie said.

Carol put the lid down on the toilet and told her to sit. She would finish drying her hair for her.

Emmett handed Houston some mail when he walked in.

"Thanks, Emmett," he put it on a small table by the back door. "Sophie and Carol should be here in a bit."

"Good, sit. Do you want coffee or juice?"

"Coffee," Fons and Houston echoed.

"Jared, how was your trip to New York?" Houston asked.

"I'm glad I went. Ricky and Liam were meeting with a man who wanted to do a licensing deal with them. But they had a bad feeling about the guy and wanted someone else's opinion.

"We met with the man, and he gave us a really good speel. But something wasn't right. We told the guy we would consider it over lunch and return in two hours. We took the contract with us and sent it to Jonathan immediately.

"Twenty minutes later, Jonathan called back. He said the man had deftly added that he would have the right to see the proprietary code. Jonathan told us to rip up the contract and walk away. So, we did.

"Then we grabbed their things from the hotel they were staying at and went to your condo. Thank you. By the way, that is a great place."

"You are welcome to it anytime you go to New York," Houston said.

"Thanks, Houston. Anyway, we went to see 'The Lion King' on Broadway. It was spectacular, and then we went to a late dinner. When we returned to the condo, Ricky and Liam found the snacks Sophie had sent up. They fought over the Dorito Cool

Ranch. Which left the bear claws for me. In the morning, we took our time getting up and made omelets, hashbrowns, and bacon. We boxed up the rest of the food, took it to Trenton, and gave it to Lily. Katsumi invited everyone to dinner at his house that evening. Needless to say, the food was delicious, and the company entertaining. You have a great family, Houston."

"How were Felix and Rob," Houston asked.

"I think they were overwhelmed. Everyone treated them like long-lost family. But you could tell they were homesick. They didn't interact much but seem to have connected with Katsumi."

"Homesick or not, they can't return right now, maybe never. This is a problem of their own making," Houston said. Sophie and Carol walked in. Sophie went to give Fons a hug, then gave one to Jared and Emmett.

"Are you making me waffles, Grandpa?" Sophie asked.

"What else? Do you want blueberries in it?"

"Not me. How about you, Carol?"

"Yes, I love blueberries. Thank you, Emmett."

They visited and ate at Emmett's for two hours. Houston grabbed the mail as they went back to the cottage with Fons and Carol. Bully had been playing outside. He saw them going home and followed.

Houston went over Sophie's plan. "It's still in the preliminary stages. But with tweaking, it could work," Houston said.

"Houston, if we don't have some agency backing us up on this, I can see us in legal jeopardy.

"I also have a problem with part of your plan. I have no doubt you will be able to get in to see Luis DeLeon, but we don't know if he will trust you. My other issue is it's not our responsibility to take his cartel down. We are no longer agents.

We should aim to pay off the boys' debt and hopefully satisfy DeLeon. If we stick to that, we won't need the DEA," Fons said.

"That's a good point, Fons. I'm still acting like we have an obligation to put the DeLeon cartel out of commission. Our goal is to get our clients out of trouble. If DeLeon initiates a desire to work with us, we will bring in the DEA and maybe even Director Cosby," Houston responded.

"If that happens, we will need an attorney to get an immunity deal signed by the DEA and maybe the DOJ. We aren't covered by the task force's immunity anymore," Fons said.

"I agree. If we can't get that, we might have to go about this another way," Houston said.

"Now that that is settled. Let's go show you the apartment. If you like it, you can stay there until you are ready to buy or build," Sophie said.

"Do you mind if we look at the lots in the gated community first? Fons' sale on his house was closed before we left, and we have the money to buy a lot if we want to," Carol said.

"That would be wonderful. We can walk there from here," Sophie said.

Houston used his remote to open the gate, and they walked over to the property Houston and Sophie bought. Houston had to call Bully to quit chasing lizards in the desert and come.

"Fons, this is the most beautiful setting I've ever seen. I would love to live here. Who lives in those houses?" Carol asked.

"The one there," she pointed to Xander's mansion. "Belongs to Xander and Piper Whiteing."

"Are you talking about Xander, the movie star and director?" Carol asked.

"Yes. And over there," she pointed. "Is where Blaze Cornish built a home for his family."

"Blaze Cornish," Fons looked at Houston. "The famous soccer player?"

"Yes, you remember him from the hospital."

"Yes, I do, but I had no idea he would be our neighbor. He is the coolest guy ever."

"I know, I keep telling Sophie that," Houston said.

"Sophie, we could never afford houses like this," Carol said, disappointed.

"Carol, there are no size requirements here. And construction is less expensive in Texas than it is in New York. Houston and I don't plan to build a mansion. We'll show you the blueprints. They should be ready soon."

"How much are the lots?" Fons asked.

"We paid one hundred fifty thousand, but all the utilities are up to the lot. We'll also pay a minimal amount for mobile security and security around the perimeter."

Fons looked over to his wife. "What do you think?"

"We figured the lot would be at least that," she turned to Sophie. "Which lots are available?"

"Grandpa was asked to save the cul-de-sac for family, but the lot right next to ours and down to the gates are not spoken for. As far as I know," Sophie said.

"This one here, right next to you?" She asked.

"Yes. Oh, Fons, this one would be perfect. Look at it."

"Honey, maybe they don't want us that close to them," Fons said.

"No, we'd love it," Sophie said.

"Fons, you lived above us for years. Was that a problem for you? Cause it wasn't for us. But you are the ones who have to make that decision," Houston said, placing his arm on his shoulder.

"Ok, we'll talk to Emmett tonight when we go home," Fons said. Carol wrapped her arms around him and kissed him.

Piper caught a glimpse of people outside through her front window and went to see who it was. "Oh, Sophie, hi," she said when she opened the door.

Sophie turned, "Piper, come out here. I want you to meet your potential new neighbors," Piper hurried over.

"I remember, from the hospital, Agent Alfonso and Carol Rodriguez, right."

"Yes, it's a pleasure to see you again." Fons said.

"Are you thinking of buying a lot?" Piper asked.

"Yes. But we won't build a mansion like yours," Carol said.

"Oh, this place is too big. I don't know what Xander was thinking. It was what he was used to. He did tone it down some," she laughed.

"Where is Xander?" Sophie asked.

"He went to help his dad. Some outside lights went out, and he wanted to replace them with new ones."

"I plan on calling Lizzy and Sienna. I thought we would go shopping and eat at the food court. I was hoping you would come with us." Sophie offered.

"I'd love to. Are you looking for baby things?"

"Some, but my clothes are getting a little tight."

"Ok, you want me to pick you and Carol up at three. We can pick up Lizzy too."

"No, we won't be here, but we'll meet up with you guys at the bakery and follow you from there."

Houston opened the door to the apartment above the bank, and they headed in.

"Oh, this *is* nice, and it's so much bigger than our apartment in DC." They walked through the rooms. "Fons, look at this. It's a chef's kitchen."

"That means you're sold without looking at the rest of the apartment," he laughed and put his arms around her.

"No, of course not...well maybe," she smiled. They went through the rest of the rooms.

"I can put my office in here," Fons said.

"Look at this master bath," Carol hollered out to him. He met her there.

"Will you be happy here until we build?"

"Yes, very. I only wish the apartment was closer to Sophie."

"We'll be spending a lot of time preparing the office downstairs," Fons said. Carol nodded.

"Houston, we won't live here for free. I need a number."

Houston turned to Sophie; she nodded. "We don't want you to pay us. But if you insist, can you afford to pay what you paid in DC without causing hardship? But we don't want you to pay anything until we have the office up and running."

"Houston, this place is twice the size. It is worth more."

"No, like we said, rents are cheaper here in Austin."

"Ok but are you sure you can wait for rent until we open."

"Yes, absolutely."

"Okay, deal," Fons stretched his hand out, and they shook on it.

"Houston thinks the property will close by the end of next week. We'll come to help you disinfect the apartment and have the rugs shampooed when it closes," Sophie said.

"I'll have to go back to DC after this case and make arrangements for our things to be sent."

"I'll go back and help you. I'll need to meet with a real estate agent too."

With that settled, they headed downstairs. They walked through the building and then looked over the rough sketch CJ had made for them.

"I like it, Houston. It might be a little big, but I can see how we can grow into this. I suggest we combine the command center and computer room and make it a SCIF. We may not be dealing with top-secret materials, but the criminals are tech-savvy. We don't want them hacking into our case information.

"It would be worth paying Timms and Smith to come here and set it up with the right cable and accessories. Sissy and Matt too."

"I agree with you, Fons. If we are going to find missing persons, we need to have the best equipment to do it."

Sophie looked at her watch, "Houston, Carol, and I need to go. If we take the vehicle, how will you get home?"

"Don't worry, we'll walk over to the law firm. It's pretty close. I want to talk to Jonathan anyway. I'm sure David will let us use his SUV.

"Good," Sophie kissed him as he handed her the keys. Carol kissed Fons goodbye on the way out.

Before Houston and Fons headed to the law firm, Fons asked, "Do you have our corporation and partner papers drawn up?"

"Yes, Jonathon is waiting for your signature. Sophie and I already signed."

"I have my equity money. I'm ready to sign on the dotted line and get this rolling."

"I have mine and Sophie's equity money too. We can settle this today if Jonathan can spare us a minute."

"Houston, I don't think I have ever been more excited about anything except marrying Carol."

"Me too, Fons. Let's head over there."

"Can you take me to rent a car? We should have one while we're here," Fons asked.

"Sure."

Houston and Fons walked into the law firm and nodded at the receptionist. They headed to Jonathan's office but saw David and decided to ask him about borrowing his vehicle.

Houston knocked on the door frame. David looked up and waved them in. "David, you remember my partner, Fons."

"Yes, of course," David extended his hand to Fons. They shook, and David said, "I know how happy Houston and Sophie are that you accepted their invitation to be partners."

"It's a dream for all of us."

"David, I hate to ask, but the ladies went shopping with Lizzy, Sienna, and Piper, and they took my vehicle. Can I use yours to take Fons to get a rental? Then we'll bring yours back."

"Since you bought your own SUV, Dad isn't using his. He much prefers to drive his F150. Let me call him and see if he doesn't mind lending it to Fons until he gets a vehicle."

"David, I don't want to put your dad on the spot like that. He is already letting us stay in his home," Fons said.

"There is no sense in leaving a car to sit in a garage," David called his dad and got an immediate yes. He said he planned to offer it when you came home that evening.

"Take my car home. I'll have Jonathan take me to Emmett's to pick it up."

"No, David, we will drop it off at your house and walk to Emmett's," Houston insisted.

As they stood, David said, "Houston, I need Sophie to come in and settle her dad's estate. She didn't want to deal with it when she left and asked me to manage it. I need to close it out."

"I'll tell her," Houston said.

Jonathan was on the phone but waved them in, putting his finger up to signify he'd only be a minute.

When he hung up, he said, "Hello, Fons, it's nice to see you again."

"Carol and I are happy to be here."

"How can I help you, Houston?"

"If you have a few minutes, we would like to finalize the partnership agreement you drafted for us. We have our equity funds ready to deposit."

"Ok," Jonathan pulled open his bottom drawer and removed a file from hanging dividers. He opened it and gave Fons a copy to read one last time.

"A three-way corporation partnership with a stipulation upon the death of an equity partner. The equity amount will be returned to the partner's surviving spouse or children. Also, the business will pay key man insurance on all partners," Jonathan explained.

After Fons finished reading the agreement, he nodded and reached for a pen. He signed both copies next to Houston and Sophie's signatures. Houston reached for his wallet to get out his debit card, and Fons pulled a cashier's check from his wallet.

"I'll have you take those to the accountant. Fons, you need to sign the signature card for the business checking account Houston and Sophie have already signed. Then, I can transfer the funds to your business from our trust account. I set you up at Austin Telco Credit Union. You can change it at any time."

"Thank you, Jonathan. I am still waiting to receive a bill from your office. I'd like to pay for it now. I know where your accounting office is."

"Houston, you, and Sophie will never receive a bill for legal fees from the partners. Her father is still a named partner and always will be."

"Thank you, Jonathan, but that's not how I like to do business."

"It's not up to you. It's up to us."

"Thank you. And we have had an electrician look over the property. So that contingency is met. We are ready to have the property close as soon as possible."

"Ok, Akito is coming in on other business tomorrow. I will let him know and call the title company." They all stood and shook hands.

After taking their money to the accountant, Houston and Fons headed to David's SUV. They both stopped in the middle of the parking lot and did a little whoop and high-fived.

"I'm so stoked about this," Fons said.

"Me too," Houston laughed.

The ladies had been shopping at the mall for a couple of hours. They headed to Nordstrom. Piper and Lizzy headed to the men's department to pick up blue jeans for Xander. Sophie and Sienna went to the maternity section.

"Look at this, Sophie," Sienna held up a pink blush maxi dress with semi-sheer sleeves and an overlay of lace.

"Oh, that's pretty. What do you think of this?" Sophie took a white cropped top with a scalloped edge to the waist and a flowing white skirt with a chiffon layer.

When Piper and Lizzy returned, Sophie had four outfits in the dressing room. She modeled them all. The light blue top with three-quarter-length sleeves went well with her maternity jeans, and the dresses fit her well. The girls insisted she buy them all.

It was time for food, and they headed to the food court. They found a place to sit with their trays, said grace, and dug in.

Sophie saw someone come up in her peripheral vision. She looked over and saw Cash Ruiz.

"Sophie, is that you?" Cash asked.

"Cash, how are you? And who is this?" She asked about the boy with him, who looked about eight years old. "Pull up a seat."

"I can't. My son is going to his first birthday party sleepover. We had to get a present for him to take," Cash acknowledged his other friends at the table. He recognized Piper from all the photos of her and Xander in the paper attending charity events. Sophie introduced Cash to Piper and Carol.

"How is your father? Is he still working hard in his restaurant?" Sophie asked.

"No, he retired. He passed it on to me. I didn't think I wanted to own a restaurant. I saw how hard my father worked. But I love it. And since Dad did all the demanding work to make it successful, I can still have a life with my wife and family. She runs the front of the house, and I cook. My sous chef is covering for me now so I can take my son to the party."

"Cash, I can't be happier for you. But you never told us your son's name," Sophie reached out and touched the boy's arm.

"My name is Duke," the boy piped up proudly. Sophie's eyes got big, and she looked up at Cash. His eyes watered.

"Duke was such a good man. Someone to look up to. My boy's name is Angel Duke Ruiz, but we call him Duke."

Sophie took his hand. "I know he would have been honored."

"I hope so. We better go," I hope you are here for a while."

"Yes, I am. We'll eat at your place soon. It is good to see you."

"You too. Lizzy, Sienna, nice to see you. It was a pleasure to meet you, Piper, Carol." He nodded to them.

"You too," the others echoed.

Lizzy looked over at Sophie to see if she was all right. She saw her brush a tear from her eye.

CHAPTER SIXTEEN

Sophie walked into the cottage burdened with packages. Houston and Fons were at the table working on something. Houston got up, grabbed some packages, and put them in the bedroom.

"Hello, sweetheart, it looks like your trip was successful," Houston chuckled.

"It was."

"Where is Carol," Fons asked.

"She said she wanted to research caterers in the area and look at popular menus. She knows she will have to adjust to the local tastes. I think the thought of all the work of moving her life from DC to here is becoming overwhelming."

"I'll check on her in a bit," Fons said.

"We're trying to figure out how we will charge our clients," Houston said. Sophie put the rest of the packages in the bedroom, gave Bully a proper greeting, and then sat down.

"What are you thinking?"

"We agreed the rent for the downstairs should be two thousand dollars. I'm guessing utilities and insurance will be another five hundred. So, we are trying to figure out how to have a steady income to cover the basic expenses. And if we will charge clients by the hour or the case." Fons said.

"Uncle Manny told us that he had the same concern. He took on big corporations that ran through employees needing background checks. He has one man who does only that and surveillance for insurance companies."

"I can see how that would pay the bills. But are we interested in doing surveillance for insurance companies?" Fons looked at Houston.

"Yeah, not really. But background checks we can do. That is if Manny doesn't have all the big corporations locked up already."

"Uncle Manny also said he could send us his overflow of investigations and background checks." Sophie said.

"What do you mean?"

"He gets requests from other law firms that don't have in-house investigators. Sometimes, he doesn't have enough men to take them on. He said he would outsource them to us. He would get the business, but we would get the pay for the job minus ten percent."

"That would be great. It could help us get started. We want to specialize in missing persons. But we all know that will not be enough to keep us in the black. It's too limiting a specialty."

"We figured that too. We'll talk to Manny about it when we open," Houston said.

"That still leaves the question whether we charge by the hour or case." Fons said.

"I don't see how we can charge by the case. Do you?" Sophie asked.

"Not really. By the hour, it is. But the bookkeeping to prove hours spent will be taxing," Houston agreed.

They talked about it for another fifteen minutes, then Fons headed to Emmett's.

Houston noticed the mail he hadn't opened. "Look, it's from Burly," Houston opened it and found a letter and a check for five hundred dollars.

"Read it out loud," Sophie said.

"Dear Houston and Sophie, I am returning your retainer. I hope you are both well. Luna, Bently, Axel, and I are becoming good friends. Bently sometimes goes fishing with Axel and me on his days off, and we go to dinner at Luna's house once a week. We have breakfast at the diner several times a week. I think Bently and Luna are becoming more than friends.

"Axel is still writing articles on the takedown of years of corruption by a small group of police officers in the Hendersons Police Department. His grandson will be here soon. He will live with Axel while attending school in Las Vegas to be a journalist. Axel's excited to see him again and for the companionship.

"Luna is working hard to get well. Bently convinced her to ride on his Harley. As long as she wears the helmet, she can do it. He also helped her to step off the property and walk down the alley a half block.

"Luna facetimes with Teresa and Kato at least once a week. Teresa told her she will visit her culinary school this weekend and get an apartment nearby in Dallas. It's hard for Luna to miss these milestones in Teresa and Kato's lives.

"We all miss you. You made a mark on our lives, and I hope we stay in touch. Please let us know when your baby comes. Sincerely, Burly."

"I am so glad Burly and Axel have become friends. I hope Luna can overcome her anxiety," Sophie commented.

"Me too. Do you want a late dinner?"

"No, we ate at the food court."

"When did that ever stop you," he laughed. Sophie smiled.

"I guess I could go for a waffle...or two."

"There she is. Coming up right now," Houston said and kissed his wife on the top of her head.

SATURDAY

Houston and Sophie drove Fons and Carol around the city and the outlying areas. They wanted to get an idea of what the city was like. They spent time at the aquarium and then dinner at

Cash's restaurant. The food was excellent, and Cash sat and visited with them for a while. He introduced his wife, who was very welcoming and attractive.

They were driving home when Houston got a call.

"Hello, ASAC Berry," Houston pulled over and put the cell on speaker.

"I don't know how you managed it, but SAC Ramos is gone for two weeks. Are you still interested in helping us get evidence on Luis DeLeon? If you are, I would be willing to work with you.

"ASAC Berry, my partner Alfonso Rodriquez, and I discussed it. We decided to help our clients in another way. If it goes any further than that, we will contact you."

"I'm sorry to hear that. If you change your mind, let me know. One more thing, Mr. Townsend. Derreck Wynne is dead."

"What? When?"

"He was found dead by his cousin, Willy, Thursday evening. The ME said he'd been dead since the morning. SAC Ramos told me to get ahold of you and tell you he wants Felix and Rob Wynne here now to answer questions." Berry heard Sophie gasp.

"My wife is with me. You are on speaker. He can't believe our clients had anything to do with this."

"Of course, he does. I can't blame him."

"You said this happened Thursday. My clients were out of town. They had no wants or warrants, so I told them they could leave for their own protection."

"I see. I'll take your word for it. But SAC Ramos won't. When he gets back, this could be a problem."

"Thank you, ASAC Berry. If we come across any information that will assist you in your investigation, we will pass it on." With that, they hung up.

"Houston, it has to be over drugs," Sophie said.

"Yes, but not necessarily anything to do with Felix and Rob."

"It's a good thing you sent them out of town," Fons said.

"Houston, it had to be DeLeon. He must have heard Derreck got picked up by the police," Sophie said.

"He may not stop with Derreck. Even if we do settle the debt for them with DeLeon. They can never come back here."

SUNDAY

After church, everyone headed to Carmens for a BBQ. Sienna's friends went to Aileen's to work on wedding stuff. Carol went with them.

"This is a beautiful place, Carmen," Fons said.

"Thank you. We use it as much as we can to entertain our friends. We also have charity events here. Jean-Paul and Sienna will have a small reception party here after their wedding at the church."

"Carol and I liked the Pastor's message this morning. We will want to join when we finally get settled in."

"I know how hard it is to move so far away from what you are used to. But I hope you allow Austin to make it feel like home," Carmen sympathized.

"We will. Being with Houston and Sophie is enough to start with."

MONDAY

Xander and Piper came by to make final arrangements for the opening in Hollywood.

"Are you still wanting to do this?" Xander asked.

"Yes. If we subtly get Sophie's 'history' within Luis DeLeon's hearing, he will likely let her into his compound. That will allow her to make a deal to get our clients off his radar," Houston responded.

"Piper, you were with me when I bought the dresses. Will any of them be stylish enough for the red carpet?"

"I don't think so. But you can rent something at an event clothing store not far from here. Let's go see if we can find something for you."

While Sophie, Piper, and Carol went to find a dress for Sophie. Xander went to visit with Emmett while Houston and Fons headed to Manny's office to see if they could borrow surveillance equipment.

After the group had dinner at the cottage, they repeated the scenario, trying to see what flaws might emerge in their thinking.

"What if Celina won't go to the restroom with you," Carol asked.

"That's a valid point."

"In that case, I can point out Sophie as she heads to the lady's room and whisper the gossip to her, as Sophie passes," Piper said.

"That could work," Fons said.

"Ok, Fons, you will go in as Sophie's bodyguard. Xander and Piper will be her escort, and Carol and I will watch out for any trouble from the hotel room."

"Thanks to Manny for letting us use earpieces, mics, and a monitor for the operation," Fons said.

"We have to leave in the morning. My dad wants me to pitch an idea to the studio while we are there," Xander said.

"Do you know what hotel the DeLeon's will stay at?" Sophie asked.

"Yes, Loews, that's where the studio puts up all the stars involved with the opening. It's only a block away."

"Are there any rooms available for us?" Sophie asked.

"Piper and I have a room there. Let me call and see if there are any rooms left," Xander stepped into the living room to make the call.

"What are you thinking, Soph," Houston asked.

"If we stay in the same hotel, I'm thinking we should go tomorrow too and try to let them get a glimpse of me, so I seem like I belong."

Xander came into the room with his cell to his ear, "Hold on," he said into the phone. "They only have the penthouse suite available. The studio won't pay for that for its stars. It's one thousand seven hundred fifty a night."

"Take it. I'm sure it has two bedrooms, and it will send the message we want," Sophie said.

"Yes, we'll take it," Xander said into the phone. Put the room under the name..." he waved at Sophie to tell him what name.

"Sophie Star," she said.

"Sophie Star. Yes, put it on my card," Xander said and hung up.

"I'll give you the cash for the room, Xander," Houston said.

"We can settle up later." Xander waved him off.

"Houston, there is no way those two young men can pay for this," Fons said.

"I told them I would front them the money, and when they open their tire and auto shop, they can pay us in installments," Houston responded.

"We know we can't do this regularly. But the brothers were upfront with us about their financial situation, and they will end up dead if we didn't help," Sophie said.

"Ok, then, let's go over the plan again."

TUESDAY, HOLLYWOOD.

Xander and Piper left on an early flight. Houston, Sophie, Fons, and Carol took the afternoon flight after dropping Bully off with Lizzy. Drew was going to take Bully to his house after Jett went to sleep. They didn't want Bully lying at Lizzy's door and whining.

They had a medium-sized durable plastic case with their surveillance equipment along with their luggage. Houston chose it as his carry-on since they needed it to do the job, and it didn't belong to them.

It was only a three-hour flight, and once they picked up the rental car, they headed for the hotel. Before they went in, they agreed Fons and Sophie should go in with their luggage first and sign in. Houston and Carol would bring up the rest of their things and meet them at the penthouse a few minutes later.

As Carol and Houston waited in the car, Carol noticed a handsome man, "Houston, that looks like the man in the picture. The one you are targeting."

Houston pulled up Luis DeLeon's picture on his cell. "Good eye, Carol. I'll text Sophie to linger at the desk."

The registration desk was busy, and Sophie was next in line. She showed Fons the text. He took a sweep of the large foyer and saw him walk in.

"He is walking in now."

"Next, please," the woman behind the counter called out.

"Welcome to Loews. May I have your name?"

"Sophie Star," she said a little louder than necessary.

"Oh, I see you are in the penthouse suite," the woman said. She waved over a bell boy with a gold luggage cart.

"Please take Ms. Stars' luggage to the penthouse suite." The front desk clerk turned back to Sophie while the bellhop loaded her luggage. "We have a fruit basket waiting for you, and of course, all the beverages in the refrigerator are on the house."

"Thank you. And I was told my suite had a second bedroom for my bodyguard. He doesn't like staying in another room without a connecting door." Sophie again raised her voice a little louder than necessary.

"Yes, ma'am. There are two bedrooms. If you need anything, call the concierge. He will see to what you need immediately."

"That's very kind," Sophie turned and headed toward the elevator where the bellhop waited for them. She made sure she turned enough so Luis DeLeon could get a good look at her face without making it obvious.

Sophie texted Houston, **'At least we know he is here.' We are on the way to the penthouse. See if there is another entrance so you don't have to come through the foyer.'**

Once they settled into the penthouse, Houston and Fons set up the monitor for tomorrow. Xander called and said they were at the hotel. Sophie invited them up.

Their room must have been close to theirs because it was less than two minutes until a knock came on the door. Carol opened it.

"Hi, how did your meeting with the studio go?" Carol asked.

"They liked the movie pitch. They said they'd look it over and let us know."

"Do you think they will pick up the option?" Sophie asked.

"If they don't, we'll back it ourselves. It's a good script. And I prefer to do it that way. Dad and Mom like the perks the studios give the actors. Things that they can't do when they back their own films."

"Will you guys be gone for a long time when you start shooting?" Sophie asked.

"No, a lot of it will be shot in Texas. We'll do the editing in LA," Xander and Piper sat at the table with the others. "What's next on our case."

"Our case?" Sophie chuckled.

"I think I would make a good detective. I played one in a movie once," Xander laughed.

"I think Xander, Piper, and I should be seen having dinner together," Sophie said. "We know Luis is here. Have you seen Celina and Diego?"

"No. You saw Luis?" Piper asked.

"We did. He is a handsome man. I didn't expect that," Carol said.

"He is, huh," Fons teased.

"Not as handsome as you, dear," Carol patted his face. The others laughed.

"I know what you mean. If Luis were being cast in a show, he would have pockmarks and a scar or two," Xander said.

"Have you eaten here, Xander?" Sophie asked.

"The H2 Kitchen is less high-end than you would think, and the menu is not large. But the food is good, and many of the guests eat there."

"Is there any way to know if the DeLeon's have made a reservation?" Sophie asked.

Piper smiled at Xander. "Well...I made a point to make *friends* with the concierge when we started in the business. I felt he would be a good man to know."

"Excellent. Can you call and see if the concierge will let you know if the DeLeons are eating there this evening?" Sophie asked.

Xander put his cell on speaker so the others could hear and dialed the concierge number in his contact list. Sophie raised her eyebrow at that. Xander shrugged.

"Asher?"

"Yes, sir."

"Hi, it's Xander, I'm here for the DeLeon opening."

"I didn't see you arrive. I apologize. How are you and Piper, sir?"

"We are well, thanks for asking. Could you do me a solid and tell me if Diego and Celina have a reservation at H2 this evening?"

"Let me check for you," Asher tapped on his computer. "Yes. They have a reservation for eight o'clock."

"Would it be possible to get seating for three at the same time?" Xander read Sophie's hurriedly scribbled note, saying not close to them. "Not close to their table, just at the same time."

"Done, sir. And I want to say I saw your last movie. It was very inspirational."

"Thank you, Asher. That's high praise coming from you," Xander thanked him again and hung up.

"I'll sit at the bar. That way, I can watch Luis and see if he notices her," Fons said.

"Yeah, and you can wear an earpiece, a mic, and this button camera," Houston said.

"I think I'm going to pick your brains and write a detective story," Xander laughed.

"Piper, how dressy is this place?" Sophie asked.

"The white crop top and the flowing skirt should fit in nicely."

At eight, Xander and Piper left their room and headed to the mezzanine H2 restaurant. Sophie came out of the bedroom, ready to go ten minutes later. Houston walked over and kissed her.

"You look beautiful, sweetheart."

"Thank you, love. Let's hope he notices me." Sophie and Fons took the elevator to the mezzanine.

The Maître D' asked her name and led her to Xander's table. Fons followed, looking for the DeLeons sitting three tables closer to the door. Fons watched as Luis noticed Sophie and watched her until she sat down at Xander's table. Xander and Piper had seen where the DeLeons were sitting when they arrived. They left the seat open, that allowed Luis to see Sophie. The Maître D' pulled out her chair.

Once she was seated, Fons found an empty stool at the bar and discreetly kept an eye on Luis. Fons whispered into the mic.

"Can you see Luis and his brother?"

"Yeah, you have them square in your camera's view."

"Did he notice her on the way in?" Houston asked.

"What do you think?" Fons responded.

The DeLeon's finished their meal first and left. Luis took one last look over at Sophie and followed his brother and wife out of the restaurant.

Houston saw them leave. "Now that they are gone, how about you order food for me and Carol?" Fons put their order in to go and one for himself. The to-go order was ready by the time the others were finished with their meal.

Back in the suite, Houston and Fons ate their 'smoked pork belly,' and Carol ate the 'charbroiled salmon'. Piper and Sophie ate the dessert they brought and an extra for Carol, 'key lime cheesecake'.

"I love all this spy stuff. Do you think we accomplished anything tonight?" Piper asked.

"I watched Luis checking Sophie out. So far, we have his attention," Fons said.

"Does that bother you, Houston?" Xander asked.

"No, it doesn't matter where we go. Sophie always turns heads. I have no doubt about my wife's commitment to me. And I know she doesn't seek anyone else's attention."

"We must leave for the TCL Grauman's Chinese Theater at 6 pm. The red carpet will be out, and the film stars should arrive at 7 pm. Piper and I will have to go through the step and repeat for publicity pictures," Xander said.

"I don't want to do that. That's too much exposure if we want to stay undercover on another case," Sophie said. "I'll go find seats."

"No problem. Just go past us on the red carpet, and head inside. We'll look for you inside."

"Ok. Thanks for all your help with this. We couldn't do it without you," Houston said.

"See you tomorrow," Piper said, hugging Sophie and Carol before leaving for their room.

"I'm tired too, Houston. I'm going to bed," Sophie said as she tossed the empty to-go containers in the trash.

"Me too," Carol said as she grabbed what was left on the table and took it to the small kitchen in the suite.

"Fons and I are going to go over tomorrow's strategy again," Houston said.

CHAPTER SEVENTEEN

WEDNESDAY

The couples ate their breakfast in the room. Sophie wanted to avoid getting overexposed and possibly have Luis approach her before they got back to Austin.

Xander and Piper had commitments all day and said they would meet us in the penthouse at 5:30 pm.

Sophie spent the afternoon helping Carol come up with ideas for her catering business. She wanted to get it up and running.

"Carol, aren't you going to continue doing your vlog? It's been really successful for you. And you know Houston and I will continue to order our meals from you. We will understand if you need to up your prices."

"No, that's not necessary. And I do plan to continue my vlog. But if I get some good catering gigs, I can put away money to help us build our house. We have a good down payment, from the sale of Fons' home, but I don't want a big mortgage. Fons doesn't want to use any more money in my savings from selling my condo. I didn't have a lot of equity in it when I sold it. But it did give us a nice savings. I used some of it on our wedding. I used more of it for equipment to get my catering business up and running. The vlog was next to nothing to start up. I was supposed to put the money back into the savings from my catering gigs. But we ended up using it for other things. If I use what's left in the savings, it will help us build our house sooner. Fons is against it. I know in Texas; each county fixes its property tax rate. That and insurance will add to our monthly mortgage payment. Getting a house and starting a business simultaneously is a lot."

"Are you sure this move is what you want? I can see it's harder than you thought," Sophie asked.

"No, Sophie. I couldn't be happier to be with you all again, and Fons was miserable without his partner. It's just a huge change. And I want to live close to you in that beautiful, gated community. I'm just worried we are reaching too high too fast."

"Carol, CJ can make blueprints for your home that can be designed to be built in sections. It will look complete from the outside, but when you are ready to add on, the infrastructure will be in place."

"Really?"

"Yes. Houston and I considered that too."

"Oh, that makes me feel better. I don't want to have the dumpy house that brings the property value down," Carol said. "I mean, really. I'll be living next to the rich and famous."

"So will Lizzy and CJ and Houston and me. None of us want to build a mansion like theirs. This gated community was made to have a safe place for our family and friends. Not so we could impress the neighbors.

"I'll tell you something in confidence. Grandpa, Uncle David, Uncle Jared, Liam, and Ricky are all multi-millionaires. Liam and Ricky are the richest of all. But they don't live to impress anyone.

"Drew is even richer than Liam and Ricky. Uncle David and Aunt Anna adopted him when he was a baby. He had no idea until they felt he needed to know."

"Who were his parents, and what happened to them?"

"His mother was the heir to the Windsor fortune. Her estate is worth over a billion and belongs to Drew. His father married his mother for her money. She had no idea the man had run through his own family's fortune. He was having an affair, and the woman he had the affair with, killed him and then Drew's mother. Uncle David was her attorney. He was there that night right after it happened. He took Drew home, and they adopted him. I'm sure they never told Drew the details of his parent's death."

"Oh, Sophie, what a horrible story."

"I'm only telling you, so you understand. Money isn't what drives our friends and family. It just isn't."

"Thanks for telling me all that. Fons works hard to make a good life for us. I want to help as much as I can. And I want a beautiful home with the perfect kitchen, next to you guys." she smiled.

"I want that for you too," Sophie said.

After a light lunch, Sophie took a short nap. By four o'clock, Sophie got up, showered, and was working on putting her hair in a chignon. The formal dress she rented was a sleeveless, light peach floor length, with a wide ribbon, just above her waist, with a thin chiffon overlay on the bottom. It was almost impossible to tell she was pregnant.

Carol came in to help her finish her stylish, messy chignon with loose hanging tendrils around her face. She wore more makeup than usual since it was an evening event and three-inch heels.

When she stepped out of the room, Houston went to her, "You are stunning as always, sweetheart. How are our babies doing?"

"They are cranky. They don't like me wearing heels," Sophie complained.

"Well, let's get you back here and in your fuzzy slippers as soon as possible." He kissed her and took her hand to have her do a 360° turn for him.

Fons came out in his tux, Sophie whistled. "Don't you look dapper," she laughed. Carol stepped up to him and whispered something in his ear that made him smile.

"You are no slouch either," Fons commented.

A knock came at the door, and Carol opened it to Xander and Piper, who looked stunning individually and as a couple.

"You look wonderful, Sophie," Xander said. Piper went to her.

"You look great. No way, Luis isn't going to notice you."

"The limo is waiting," Xander said.

Houston walked his wife to the elevator and kissed her. "I'll be watching," he said with a wink.

The limo pulled up to the red carpet. Sophie had watched these opening nights on TV, but she wasn't prepared for the noise of the fans. The fans lined up on either side of the carpet, held back by gold stanchions and red velvet ropes.

A doorman opened the limo door and helped Piper out, who looked gorgeous in her fitted sparkly black gown. Xander was in his tux, which Sophie knew wasn't a rental. When the couple were out of the limo, the crowd started hollering at them. They turned to the fans so they could get pictures.

The doorman reached for Sophie's hand. She didn't know how to get past the fans without being noticed. She took his hand and stepped out. She kept her head down, and Fons followed her out. He walked next to her, trying to shield her from the cameras that were closest to her. The crowd started to yell for her attention, then realized she wasn't a celebrity, and Sophie was able to walk past them quickly. Xander, with Piper at his side, accommodated his fans.

When they were all inside, Xander said, "The DeLeons should be in the center box upstairs. So, let's sit in easy view of that box. Xander led them down the sloping aisle to the center of the theater and seated them about a third down the row. Fons stood by the entrance of the seating area with the other bodyguards. There were seats in the back wall to accommodate them if they wished to sit.

Forty minutes later, they knew the film stars had arrived because of the volume of the crowd outside. The seats around them were full now, and many of the stars Xander worked with stopped by to say hello.

"Ok, it won't be long now. The film will start, it will be approximately one hour forty-five minutes. Then we will head to the after-party. Piper and I will have to walk the 'Step and Repeat', but you can bypass that and go inside and find a table for us. The DeLeons will have to stay and take pictures with the film's other stars. That will delay their arrival at the party by about thirty minutes.

"Thanks for talking me through this, Xander. It's a little nerve-racking."

"Anything for you, sis," Xander said. Sophie squeezed his arm.

Luis was all right with the cameras and the crowd. He wasn't one to seek it out, but it didn't bother him either. His brother and Celina loved the attention and spent time working the red carpet. They patiently spoke with talking heads shoving television cameras and microphones in their face. He moved along and stepped into the theater.

Luis thought the theater a little gauche for his taste, but this was Hollywood. Everything had to be over the top.

Luis' mind went back to the woman he noticed at the restaurant the night before. She looked like a movie star and was with Xander Whiteing, a big celebrity, but he couldn't figure out who she was. He knew the Whiteings would be at the after-party. Maybe she would be with them.

Diego and Celina finally made it inside and headed up to their box. Before the lights dimmed, Luis noticed Xander and his wife sitting in the audience. Next to them was the woman.

Maybe I will find out who she is after all, he thought. It wasn't only that she was beautiful. It was the way she carried herself with a mysterious air that impressed him. *I might still meet an interesting woman after all.*

While Xander and Piper walked the 'Step and Repeat', Sophie entered the after-party room. Piper had told her the lady's room was down the hall left of the entry. Xander explained the larger table in the center of the room was reserved for the stars of the opening.

Fons followed Sophie inside. They picked a table two rows up from the celebrity table and two rows over. She took the seat, allowing her to glance around the room without being conspicuous. Fons moved to the wall on the left and stood. He could see the entire room from that position, but more importantly, he could watch Luis.

Xander and Piper came in ten minutes later. The trio decided to go through the buffet line and grab something to eat.

"I'm a little disappointed in their food. Carol would have put together a much nicer buffet," Sophie commented.

"I agree, they never have good food at these things," Piper said.

"The movie was directed and edited well. And I think Celina did justice to her role," Xander commented as they returned to the table with their plates. Waiters came around to take beverage orders.

They all chose iced tea.

"It was a little strange that they left you hanging at the end of the movie. They didn't reveal if Celina was the one who killed her husband," Sophie said.

"I think it's a play off the old Hitchcock movies. I think it was her husband's business partner. He loved Celina and didn't like how he treated her," Piper said.

"I didn't consider that, but I think she did it."

"I liked that they left us hanging. That way, I can decide for myself how it ends," Xander said.

Houston and Carol were watching from the hotel. Houston noticed Luis DeLeon come into the room first. Someone must have instructed him where to sit because he headed for the large middle table.

"Hey, Fons, have you finished all the requirements for your private investigator license in Texas?" Houston asked through his earpiece.

"Yes, I just needed a local address. Now that we have one for us and one for the business, I should be set," Fons responded.

"I can take you to the Division of Professional Licensing downtown when we get back. If your requirements are posted in the system, they will give you your license while we wait. I need to ask Sophie if she's finished her test."

"Sounds like a plan.... Ok, I see Diego and Celina coming in."

"Did Sophie notice?"

"Yes, she glanced their way. She just made it back from the buffet line."

"I hope there was something healthy for her to choose from. She eats too much junk food."

"Are you going to be the one to tell her that?" Fons chuckled.

"Not if I want to stay married to her," he laughed. Carol poked his arm.

"Hey, how would you like to carry around two little people in your tummy?"

"Point taken," Houston laughed.

Xander knew that the guests at the party would flood around the stars when they first came in. The plan was to let the crowd die down, and then Xander and Piper would go and speak with them.

It took about thirty-five minutes for the crowd around DeLeon's table to whittle down. Xander stood and reached his hand out for Piper.

"Ok, Sophie, give us a few minutes to schmooze with them," Xander said.

Xander and Piper approached the table. Diego stood to greet him. "Xander, I saw you were on the list. Let me introduce you and Piper to my brother first, then tell me what you thought?

"Luis, this is Xander Whiteing and his wife Piper. Xander is the son of Henry and Carmen Whiteing. Xander, Piper, this is my brother Luis, and you already know Celina."

Xander extended his hand, "A pleasure to meet you, Luis."

"The pleasure is mine," he turned to Piper. "And you, as well, Piper."

Piper smiled and nodded, then sat in an empty chair next to Celina. While Xander told Diego how much he enjoyed his film, Piper spoke to Celina.

"Celina, you were a perfect fit for that role. And the ending was such a surprise. I told the woman who came with us I thought it rivaled a Hitchcock movie."

"The woman?" Celina looked over to the table where they had been seated.

"Yes. The studio insisted Xander, and I accommodated her. She has connection to someone high up on the food chain."

"Oh, I thought she might be a star in one of Henry's movies."

"No, she is not an actress." Piper saw Sophie stand and head to the bathroom. She wanted to give Sophie a few minutes, so she made more small talk.

"Celina, would you walk with me to the ladies' room? There is a woman I want to walk you by. I don't know who she is, but she seems very friendly with the casting director. I'm wondering where his wife is."

"Oh, let's check her out," Celina said as they got up from the table.

They headed to the ladies' room and Piper nodded to the woman in question. "I recognize her now. She is a reality star on one of those Real Housewives Shows. I am trying to remember her name, but she was married to a big television star until about six years ago.... Why can't I remember her name?" Celina giggled.

In the bathroom, Sophie stayed in the stall until she heard Piper's voice. Then she stepped out and went to the sink and washed her hands.

"Piper, I would have waited for you if I knew you were heading this way," Sophie said.

"No need to worry. This is my friend, Celina," Piper said.

"Yes, of course, Celina Charron, you are married to Diego DeLeon. I loved how you portrayed your character. It was very convincing. I enjoyed it. But I'd really like to know if you were the one who killed your husband?"

Celina laughed. "Thank you, Ms..."

"Star. I'm Sophie Star."

"Well, Ms. Star. That is a secret I will have to take to my grave," Celina smiled at her.

Sophie pulled the lipstick out of her purse and reapplied it. Celina and Piper brought out lipstick and mascara for themselves. Sophie paused, then said.

"I guess I'll see you back at the table, Piper."

"Yes, in a minute," Piper said turning away from Sophie, snubbing her.

"I'm so happy we had a chance to meet, Mrs. DeLeon," Sophie said.

"Please call me, Celina. A pleasure to meet you too."

When Sophie left the room, Celina commented, "You don't seem to like her very much."

"Well, if you knew the whole story, you would understand."

"What story?" Celina asked. Piper checked to see if anyone else was in the bathroom.

"Ms. Star was arrested in New York a few years ago for running a huge drug syndicate. She was joining up with another drug empire run by Nikko Morano. They were caught red-handed with millions of dollars worth of drugs by an FBI and DEA task force. It was a huge deal, all over the news."

"How is she still out on the street?" Celina asked. A woman came in, and the two waited for her to leave before they spoke again.

"The DA in New York had either mishandled or planted some evidence. I can't remember which. But anyway, Morano got caught, but the judge had to let her go. Nikko Morano jumped bail and ended up dead."

"No kidding. That sounds like a plot to a blockbuster," Celina said.

Piper laughed, "Yes, it does. I'll have to tell that to Xander."

"But I don't understand how you got stuck with her."

"Who knows how these criminals manage to ingratiate themselves into the hierarchy of our business. From what I heard; she has a lot of money."

"I have to tell Diego and Luis about this. I noticed Luis looking at her earlier. She is a beautiful woman."

"Yes, but I would certainly steer him away from her."

"It's not likely they would meet again."

"She just moved to Austin. You never know," Piper said.

The ladies headed back to the table. Piper stood next to Xander and reminded him they had another commitment."

"Congratulations again, Diego, on the excellent directing job. And Celina, you played the lead beautifully. Luis, a pleasure to meet you."

Xander and Piper stopped at their table and said something to Sophie. They gathered their things and headed out. Fons came up behind them.

Luis had noticed Sophie sitting at the table earlier. He had considered going over to introduce himself. But Xander and Piper came up, and he didn't want to be rude to his brother's peers.

Luis watched her until she was out the door. Celina came up next to him and placed her hand on his arm.

"That woman you were watching...you won't believe who she is..." Celina went on to tell the whole story with embellishments of her own.

Luis knew she was telling him this to make him think less of her, but all it did was add to his interest.

When the trio got into the limo, Piper laughed. "That was so much fun," she turned to Xander. "I could be an actress in one of your movies."

"Sweetheart, you are already a star in my eyes," Xander kissed her hand. Sophie laughed.

"It's time for us to get out of town, Fons. I want to avoid running into them tomorrow. I'll go to registration and tell them we will be gone by noon tomorrow. You can sign for the bill."

"Piper and I have to stay. I received a text from my dad. He said the studio already contacted him and wanted to get more details. So, we will be here a few more days, but we'll move to the Hyatt. It's more comfortable."

The limo pulled under the portico, and the doorman helped the ladies out. The foyer was almost deserted. Most of the guests were still at the after-party.

Fons and Sophie stopped at the front desk. Xander and Piper headed for the elevators to wait.

"Yes, Ms. Star," the woman behind the desk said.

"We are leaving tomorrow. If anyone asks for me or if any calls come for me, please tell them I have left."

Yes, ma'am."

"Mr. Rodriguez will settle the bill."

"Yes, ma'am. We at Loews hope you enjoyed your stay and will come back again."

Sophie met up with Xander and took the elevator to the penthouse suite.

When Sophie walked in, Houston met her and headed for the couch. As soon as Sophie was seated, Houston removed her heels and rubbed her feet.

"Oh, that feels good," Sophie leaned back on the cushion and started removing her jewelry.

Xander and Piper seated themselves on the couch across from Houston and Sophie, a coffee table between them. The door opened again, and Fons stepped in. He removed his tux jacket and tie, putting them over a chair at the table, and went to sit with his wife on the loveseat.

"Piper, tell us about your Emmy winning performance," Sophie smiled.

"I really played up your cover story. Celina was eating it up. But if she tells Luis, won't he try to look it up online?"

"That's what we are hoping for. Our computer expert has gathered all the archived articles written about it and brought them up for easy access," Sophie said.

"What are you talking about? This is all made up, isn't it?" Piper asked, surprised.

Fons looked over at Houston, then answered. "That case was the first undercover we worked together. Sophie worked it with us, and we brought down one of the largest drug families in New York."

"Oh! That's amazing. I had no idea," Piper said. Xander looked at Sophie, knowing there was much more to that story. Xander hoped she would share it with him someday. The family had lost all contact with her when she left after her father and Duke died. No one knew what happened to her.

"Alright, sweetheart, we need to go. Do you guys want to eat breakfast together before you leave," Xander asked as he stood and put his hand out to help his wife up.

"If we order in. We can't take the chance of running into the DeLeons."

"Is nine o'clock good for you?"

"Perfect, but I'll still be in my jammies," Sophie smiled, then stood and hugged the couple before they left.

CHAPTER EIGHTEEN

THURSDAY. HOLLYWOOD.

Everyone was at the kitchen table having coffee. Sophie finally got out of the shower and walked out of the bedroom at 9 am.

"I ordered for you, sweetheart."

"Waffles?"

"Yes, with strawberries and whipped cream on the side," Houston smiled. "Just the way you like it."

"Now I remember why I married you." Sophie wrapped her arms around his neck from behind where he was sitting and kissed his cheek.

Fons heard a knock on the door and looked through the peephole, opening it to let Xander and Piper in. They were dressed casually and found a seat around the table.

"How is my cohort in espionage," Piper chuckled.

"Good. Which one are you? Cagney or Lacey?" Sophie asked.

"Which was the smart one," Piper quipped.

"I don't know. Lacey, maybe." Sophie teased. "Does that make me the not-so-smart one?" There was another knock on the door, and Fons let the room service cart in with their breakfast.

The friends visited over breakfast and continued the conversation in the living room.

Luis had stayed up late the night before. When he returned from the after-party, he used the hotel's computer to look up

Sophie Star. He found a dozen articles about the arrest and subsequent release of Ms. Star. Some more in-depth articles came out after the initial sensationalized reporting.

It seemed the Morano family had a criminal empire for decades. The father started it when he brought his family to the States from Italy. They were hugely successful because of the way they organized their syndicate. No one knew who was at the cartel's top except for the family, Nikko Morano's number two man, and their strategist/accountant. The strategist was a woman who increased their profit and kept them insulated from the police. She set up the purchase of cocoa farms in Mexico and initiated stringent protocols.

Luis had a feeling that the strategist/accountant was Ms. Star. Maybe she left the Moranos, went out on her own, and came back to merge with them when the DEA caught onto them.

He spent hours trying to discover what happened to her after she was released. The only mention of her again was a year later when an Italian hitman tried to kill her but was gunned down instead.

This woman has nine lives, he thought.

When Luis woke up, the articles were still on his mind. *I wonder if she is still here at the hotel.* Luis picked up the phone by his bed and called the operator.

"Hello, Mr. DeLeon, how can I help you?"

"Can you connect me to Ms. Star's room please?" There was a pause on the line while the operator tapped on the keys.

"I'm sorry, Mr. DeLeon, Ms. Star has checked out."

Even though he had yet to meet her, he felt let down.

Houston and Carol left first. Houston carried the black hard case with the surveillance equipment and his suitcase. Carol rolled her suitcase behind her. They went down two flights of stairs and found the freight elevator. They pushed the button that led to the covered parking.

"I'll let Fons know about this elevator. I think it's the safest way to get them out without being seen." Houston called Fons as he loaded up the rental car.

Sophie wore a pair of jeans and a cotton top. She added a baseball cap, pulling her ponytail through the hole in the back. Fons opened the door, looked both ways and placed both suitcases in the hallway.

"Ok, Soph, let's roll." They took the stairs down. Fons heard the stairway door open as they passed the floor below them. Fons was carrying both suitcases.

Luis was heading downstairs to meet with his brother for breakfast. He habitually took the stairs in most hotels for exercise and heard someone else going down ahead of him. Luis looked over the banister out of curiosity and saw a woman. He couldn't tell who she was, but he recognized the man with her. It was Sophie Star's bodyguard.

"Ms. Star," he called out.

"Keep moving," Fons whispered to Sophie. They were already at the door to the next level. As soon as they passed through the door, they ran to the freight elevator around the corner.

Luis stepped through the door a few moments behind them. He looked both ways but didn't see where they had gone.

She might have thought I was a reporter trying to get a story.

Fons and Sophie got on the elevator and pushed the button for the parking garage.

Sophie let out a breath, "that was close."

Houston was there waiting for them and took Sophie's suitcase.

When they finally got into the car, Sophie laughed. "That little episode really did feel like a spy movie. Piper would have loved it."

"What?" Houston asked. Sophie explained.

Houston dropped Fons and Carol off at Emmett's from the airport, and he and Sophie went to pick up Bully.

When they pulled up outside Lizzy's and got to the gate, they could hear Lizzy in the backyard playing with Jett and the dogs. She had the hose with a sprayer on it, and every time Jett got close, she would spray a little water on him. He would laugh so hard he would fall down. Coco and Bully would nudge him to get up again.

Sophie stopped Houston and watched. "Isn't that the most precious site in the world?" Sophie looked at Houston.

"Yes, and we are going to have those for ourselves soon," he wrapped his arm around her from behind and patted her tummy."

FRIDAY

Houston and Sophie were headed to the hospital for their appointment with Dr. Banerjee. She had called earlier and asked if they could do another ultrasound. They wanted to see if the other baby moved enough to know the sex.

Houston handed Fons the keys to the apartment and office. They wanted to see it again and Fons said he would get keys made.

Fons and Carol decided to stop at a national brand furniture shop and get a couple of chairs. There needed to be somewhere to sit in their new apartment. The store had a sale on sectionals. Since this apartment was twice the size of the one in DC, they decided to buy the two end pieces. It came in white and a pretty mint color.

"Don't you want the white one, Carol," Fons asked.

"Fons, Sophie is having twins. No way white can survive babies. And we will have our own children too," Carol said. Fons stopped in his tracks.

"Are you saying we are...."

"No, not yet. But we want kids, don't we?"

"Of course," Fons went off to find a salesperson.

"Oh and tell him we want it sprayed with spot protection. See if they can deliver it today," she said loud enough for him to hear.

The next stop was the hardware store to make keys. Then they went to the apartment.

"I would have loved to have this kitchen in DC. It will make a beautiful set for my vlogs."

"It's going to take a while to fill this place up, but it feels like home to me already," Fons said. He saw a look come over Carol. He went over to her. "Honey, I can tell something is bothering you. If this move is not what you want, I can call Director Cosby and get my job back in DC or work with the US Marshals in New York. I would never be happy if you weren't. I don't want you making this kind of a sacrifice for me. I mean it."

Carol walked into the living room and looked out the window. "No, Fons. Sophie asked me the same thing, but that's not it. I have made more friends here in a week than in all the years I lived in New York," she turned to look at Fons.

"What then?"

"I never cared about having a house. It wasn't a big deal to me. But when I saw that gated community, I fell in love with it. It made me want it all. The house, the yard, and the best friend next door."

"Ok...."

"Fons, we can't afford it. Moving, starting a new business, putting equity money into the partnership. It will take everything we have, even what's left of the profit from selling my condo in New York. I won't put the burden of a large mortgage on us like that.

"I'm not looking for a mansion like Xander's. Even a nice comfortable house will be too much right now," she turned back to the window. "I've been trying to figure out how to get enough catering jobs to help pay for the construction. It will take years," a tear fell from her eyes. Fons wiped it away and hugged her.

"Honey, sit here with me," they sat on the carpet. "Look, we have three hundred thousand left from selling my house after I paid my equity share. We'll need some of that to have our belongings shipped here...."

"Not if you rent a U-Haul truck and bring it yourself," Carol broke in."

"True. Houston and I agreed to work double time to get our bread-and-butter clients like Manny did. That and your vlog income will allow us to live without touching the house balance.

"Now, there are two ways we can do this. We can pay cash for the lot, so we don't add any extra expenses on us right now. Keep the other hundred seventy-five thousand dollars aside and add to it until we have enough for a comfortable down payment."

"Or?"

"*Or* we can use the one hundred seventy-five thousand as a down payment and get a bank loan and just build the house. Houston said that building a house here is not like in New York."

"Finding out what it will cost to build is the first step. We can pay CJ to do our blueprints and have Jared price it out for us," Carol turned her face to Fons. "We want Jared to build it, right?"

"Yes, I trust him. And from what Houston said, he and Emmett are only building homes for the gated community right now."

"I promise, darling, if the cost is more than we want to borrow, I won't overextend us. I'll wait until we have a better down payment," Carol said.

"Don't you worry about it. One way or the other, you will have your dream home...soon."

Houston and Sophie headed to the doctor's office. "I think Fons and I should contact Luis tomorrow," she said.

"Ok, we'll work on the plan tonight. Right now, let's see if we can get our little one to cooperate with us and let us get a peek at him or her."

As they walked into the doctor's office, she asked, "You are hoping for a boy, aren't you?"

"Boy or girl, whichever one will make me happy."

The doctor checked out Sophie's vitals and her weight. "Sophie, you are still a little underweight for carrying twins."

"Doctor, how is that possible? She eats all the time," Houston blurted out.

"Hey!" Sophie slugged his arm.

"I can see she has gained some weight. Let's ensure what you eat is good for you, Sophie." Dr. Banerjee commented. "Ok, let's see if your baby moved enough to get a good look." The Doctor rubbed the gel on her abdomen and started running the probe over it.

"Look, Soph, there is our little girl," Houston said. Sophie looked over at the screen and smiled.

"Ok, now let's see if we can get around her a little so we can see her twin." He moved the probe around and finally saw the baby's body, but the doctor couldn't get a good look. He moved the probe around more and finally saw what he was looking for. "A boy!" He said.

"Can you point him out, Doctor," Houston said. The Doctor pointed to the monitor and used his finger to circle the proof.

"I see," Houston laughed. "We are having a boy and a girl," he leaned down and kissed his wife's forehead. She laughed.

"Thank you, Doctor Banerjee. Is there any way to tell if they are fraternal?" Houston asked.

"Well, there are two placentas and amniotic sacs. But that happens with fraternal twins, too, sometimes. So, I would say no."

"Do they both look healthy?" Sophie asked.

"I'll get your blood work results tomorrow. But so far, everything looks good. I think your little boy is a bit bigger than his sister."

"Thank you, Doctor," Sophie took the paper towel he offered her and wiped the gel off.

Once she sat up, he said, "Sophie, it wasn't that long ago you had a traumatic injury from the fall into the ocean. Although I don't see any signs of it now, your body is still not fully recovered. As the twins get bigger, it will be more taxing on your body. You need to take care of yourself and exercise. Nothing overtaxing. Just keep yourself strong. You'll have to stay off your feet more at the end of your pregnancy."

"Don't worry, Doctor. I will keep an eye on her," Houston said.

"I know you will," the doctor smiled and left the room.

"Sophie, isn't it great? We are having a boy and a girl," Houston hugged her.

"I knew you wanted a boy," she laughed. He winked at her.

Fons and Carol walked into Emmett's with bags of groceries. Emmett was outside throwing a ball for Bully to chase after. He was watching Bully while Sophie was at the doctors. He heard them come in.

"Hey, what's all this?"

"I wanted to make lasagna for everyone. I hope that's all right?"

"You bet. I'll never turn down tasty food. I need to meet with my partners in our downtown commercial building. I'll be back later. Bully is outside. He's fine if you have somewhere else to go."

"No. We are here for the night. Thanks, Emmett."

"Please don't wait on me to eat. I don't know how long I'll be gone."

"I'll make sure to set a plate aside for you," Carol said.

Houston pulled into the law firm's parking lot. "Do you want to come in while I return the surveillance equipment?"

"No, I'll wait here. I want to make a grocery list. We need to pick up groceries on the way home."

"Alright, I'll be right back."

At the grocery store, Houston kept putting in fruits, vegetables, meat, and fish. Sophie went for the goodies.

"Sophie, does it bother you that I tease you about how much you eat? Honestly, I wouldn't care if you gained a hundred pounds. I just can't believe how much you eat and don't gain weight."

"It bothers me sometimes. I never was a healthy eater. I like sugar. But I do want to be more careful, for the babies' sake. A little teasing is all right."

"Shall I BBQ chicken tonight? We have enough for all of us."

"Sure."

Fons heard Bully barking at the gate when Houston and Sophie opened it. Houston's arms were full of grocery bags. Sophie bent down to say hello and rub Bully's face and ruff.

"Hey, let me help you with some of those," Fons said.

"Better not try to transfer them. But if you could open the door, that would help."

Fons grabbed the keys from Houston's finger and unlocked the cottage door.

"Houston is grilling chicken tonight," Sophie said.

"Oh, Carol is putting together her lasagna for us," Fons said.

"Ooh. I love her lasagna. We can have chicken another time, Houston."

"Fine by me." Houston put the groceries away and visited with Fons while Sophie changed into her jeans and a cotton top. She put her hair in a French braid and slipped on her fuzzy slippers.

"I think we need to go see Luis tomorrow," Sophie said as she took the glass of orange juice Houston handed her and sat down at the kitchen table.

"Ok, I'm in. How do we want to do this?"

"Let's keep it simple. You can drive me to Luis' compound and see if he will let us in. If not, that trip to Hollywood was a waste of time."

"I want you carrying, Fons," Houston said.

"My thought exactly. Never leave home without it, right?" Fons smiled.

"I'll try to keep to the script. As we agreed, our only goal is to get our clients out of trouble. I'll ask for time, saying we were contacted to find the men who stole their product and get the money from them.

"I think we should tell him we are fixers using a detective agency as a front. We live here, and unless we change our minds about putting him behind bars, he could see us around town," Sophie said.

"I agree, Fons is right. We aren't the police anymore. That's their job. But if we run across any information that will help the DEA or Austin Police, we will pass it on. Fons, I'd like you to record it on your cell," Houston said.

"That shouldn't be a problem. Other than carrying my gun, I don't think we need to take any other precautions," Fons said.

"I don't think we will be in any danger. My concern is if Luis rejects our request," Sophie said.

"Felix said Willy gave him the name of one of the guys who stole his cocaine. If we can find where they stash their goods. We could do a civilian 'sneak and peek'..."

"Houston, there is no such thing. That's a law enforcement tool, used with a delayed notification search warrant," Fons interrupted.

"I just invented it. We have to make sure there is something there. Then we can get the DEA involved. And if they find a big enough stash of cocaine or money, we could get an informant's fee on what they confiscate. We aren't law enforcement, so we are eligible for the reward. If it's enough, we could pay Luis what is owed, and our clients would be off the hook. It may even pay for part of our expenses, so we don't start out in the hole," Houston said.

"I'm still FBI," Fons said.

"We'll leave your name out of it," Houston said.

"Is it ethical to pay off Luis with the DEA's money?" Fons asked.

"We aren't the ones giving it to him. We are representing our clients to save their lives. I don't have a problem with it," Houston said.

"When I approached the DEA with my offer to take Nikko down, I insisted on a percentage of what we confiscated from Nikko. I was afraid I would have to hide for the rest of my life and needed money to do that. The take was big enough that my portion was substantial."

"Is a percentage larger than a CI's fee?" Fons asked.

"Yes. We'll negotiate for that," Sophie said.

"Ok, so we are set to meet with Luis tomorrow, and based on how that goes, we will initiate our plan B," Houston said.

"If plan B doesn't work, the Wynne brothers will have to sell their house to pay off Luis. That is if I can get enough of an extension from him. They can never come back here anyway. I'm sure his parents paid off their home. Felix said they lived there since he was born. So even after paying off Luis, they should have enough to pay for Rob's trade school and start the tire and auto shop they want."

"One more line of defense. I want Bully to go with you, Sophie," Houston said.

Carol stepped out the back door of Emmett's and hollered, "Dinner is ready."

CHAPTER NINETEEN

SATURDAY

Fons came over at 12:30 pm to pick Sophie up. He wore dress pants, a button-up shirt, and a lightweight sports jacket to cover his Glock 22.

Sophie had on a pair of cream-colored slacks that still fit her. She tucked in a dusty blue sleeveless silk top, then bloused it to help hide her tummy. Sophie added a light cream sweater with three-quarter lengths sleeves to the ensemble and two-inch heels. She placed white gold hoops on her ears and an inverted pear ruby necklace on a white gold chain around her neck, keeping her wedding ring on her finger.

The plan was for Houston to follow them to Luis' property line. He would stay out of sight unless things went wrong.

Carol stayed at Emmett's. Fons said she was searching for recipes for her business.

Fons pulled up to the monitor/intercom at the gate and pushed the button.

"Yes," a man's face came on the little monitor.

"Ms. Star wishes to speak with Mr. DeLeon."

From the back seat, Sophie watched guards with dogs walking the perimeter of the gated compound.

Luis had been on the phone all morning dealing with an attack on his warehouse just over the border in Mexico.

He had been spending a lot more time at his home in Texas. The other cartels saw that as an invitation to take over his territory. Luis had a big enough army to keep them at bay for now, but it cost him men and product. He needed to go back to Coahuila. His home there was also beautiful, but he liked living close to his brother, and he liked Austin.

Luis hung up the phone and headed to the kitchen to get coffee. He noticed Tacito speaking into the monitor with someone at the gate.

"I'm sorry, but Mr. DeLeon does not take meetings without an appointment," Tacito said.

"Will you please leave Mr. DeLeon a message? Tell him that Ms. Star stopped by and will try again when it is more convenient for him."

"Si...." Tacito started to say. When Luis came up behind him.

"Did he say Ms. Star is at our gate?"

"Yes, Jefe. But I don't know who she is, and she has no appointment."

"I know her. Let them in."

"Jefe...."

"Let them in!"

"Mr. DeLeon will meet with you. Please pull into the compound and park by the front door. I will meet you there."

"Jefe, no sabemos quiénes son estas personas. Podrían ser un problema."

"No, Tacito. I know who she is. She won't be a problem. I'll meet her outside."

Fons pulled the SUV into the compound and parked as directed. He got out and opened the door for Sophie, extending his hand to help her. He whispered.

"Adjust your earring if you get uncomfortable or want out of here. I'll get you out."

"I'll be fine, Fons, but thank you." Bully jumped out of the back seat after her. Fons took hold of his leash.

Before Sophie and Fons reached the door, Luis DeLeon opened it and stepped out. Carol and Piper were right. She had only seen him from afar. Close up, he was even more handsome and well-dressed, likely in his mid-forties.

Luis stepped up to her, "Ms. Star," he said, kissing her hand when she extended it instead of shaking it.

"I apologize, Mr. DeLeon. Have we met?"

"No, but I know who you are. I saw you at my brother and his wife's opening in Hollywood, Wednesday."

"Oh, I see. I'm sorry I didn't get to formally meet you there."

"Please come in and call me Luis. May I call you Sophie?"

"Yes, I would prefer it."

Luis walked Sophie into his living room. It had a glass wall, looking out on a lake.

"This is beautiful, Luis." Sophie turned when she heard Bully growling. Fons refused to give up his weapon to Tacito.

"Luis, I'm afraid my bodyguard will cause a stir if you require him to give up his weapon. I assure you we mean you no harm."

"Of course. Tacito, leave it be," Luis saw Tacito was not happy.

"I know it was rude of me to stop by unannounced, but I had no way of contacting you by phone," Sophie said.

"It is no bother, Sophie. Can I get you something to drink in the kitchen? Iced tea or something stronger?"

"Would you happen to have lemonade? I love lemonade in the afternoon on a hot day," Sophie said.

"Tacito, please ask Dulce if she would make lemonade for me and my guest."

"Oh, no, please. I shouldn't have asked. I don't want to inconvenience anyone," Sophie was testing his resolve to give in to her whims. She needed him to get used to saying yes to her.

"Not at all. Lemonade sounds perfect for a day like today." Luis directed her to a white half-circle kitchen nook with light mint seats and back cushions. The large bay window also overlooked the lake.

"Your home is exquisite, Luis."

"I like it here. I also have a home in Coahuila. The grounds there are beautiful."

"I'm sure."

Tacito returned with an older woman who could have been Luis' mother. She busied herself making lemonade. Fons and Tacito stood just inside the kitchen doorway. Bully sat at alert next to Fons.

"Luis, I'm afraid I have come to ask a favor of you. I know it is presumptuous of me. You have no idea who I am and owe me no deference. But I humbly ask that you hear me out."

"I am intrigued, and if possible, I will happily accommodate you," Luis said. Dulce brought over two glasses full of ice and lemonade. Sophie took a sip and smiled.

"I am a fixer and have been engaged by clients in your debt. It happened that my clients had purchased products from you. Two men attacked them as they drove into their home and stole it.

"They came to me, asking me to locate and retrieve their stolen items. There is a time limit on the payment that is due you. I am here to ask for an extension until I can locate the men who did this to my clients."

"I am aware of this incident and planned on giving the young men the full 30 days to find a way to pay. What I don't understand is, if they can afford to hire someone like you, why wouldn't they just pay me."

"Very astute, Luis. These young men do not have the money. The only asset they have is their home. Which was left to them by their father. They don't have enough time to sell it and pay you off. However, if I can locate the thieves and retrieve the stolen property or the money. I can pay you. And for this service, they will have to sign their home over to me," Sophie paused and looked up at him. "So, for what I hope is little effort, it is possible I will make three hundred thousand dollars or more.

"Now, if I can't retrieve the money from the culprits, I will pay you off when I sell the house. My profit will be cut, but I will have made a friend...you. I hope."

"When I saw you at the opening, I will admit I looked you up. You ran a drug empire in New York. This seems a little out of your wheelhouse."

"Then you know I was arrested. I learned a lot through that experience. One thing is for sure. I never want to put myself in that position again. They could not file against me, but I knew I did not want to go to jail. So, now I can make significant amounts of money without taking that risk. As a licensed private investigator in the state of Texas, I can do things for an elite clientele they can't do for themselves. Mostly legal, some, not so much. But nothing worthy of the DEA or FBI catching wind of me and hunting me down again.

"I am a woman of modest dreams, Luis. Having multiple millions of dollars without the threat of jail is much more appealing to me than having a billion and fear being hunted." Sophie drank more of her lemonade.

Luis looked at Sophie while he followed suit. He did not believe for a moment she was a woman of modest dreams. "I still don't understand why you would take such a small case."

"I may seem like a hardened criminal to most. But those who know me well know I have a soft spot for fair play and justice, albeit my own kind of justice. My clients are not drug dealers but desperate young men who were losing their home. They reached out in the only way they knew to make quick money. I understand this business is a 'do it at your own peril' type of enterprise. But these young men were robbed.

"They heard about my detective agency and asked if I would help them... And I can take on a charity case now and then. I am just as charitable as those fancy celebrities in Hollywood who like to snub me," Sophie laughed.

Luis laughed with her, "Yes, they can be snobs, can't they."

"I didn't intend to come here and take up so much of your valuable time, Luis. And there are no hard feelings if you insist on keeping my client to the original time limit."

"How much time are you asking for, Sophie?"

"As I understand it, their deadline is the end of this month. If I have an additional 30 days, I will have the money for you, one way or the other. And I assure you if I can't sell the house by then or find the thieves. I will pay you out of my own pocket."

Luis sat there, not saying a word. He never extended the due date. But if he didn't work with her, he would likely never see her again. She was beautiful and interesting, and he may need her services someday.

"Alright, I will give you the extension. But I would like to hear more about your operation in New York. Would you have dinner here with me next week? I have to go to Mexico for a short business trip."

"Luis, I would love to have dinner with you. But I don't want to lead you on. I am married, but if that invitation extends to both of us, we would be happy to come."

Luis was disappointed, but he had noticed her wedding ring. He still felt knowing her could be beneficial. "I would be honored to have you both."

They stood, and Luis walked Sophie to the front door. As Luis passed, Bully bared his teeth but did not growl.

"How will I contact you?" Sophie asked.

"Let me give you my private cell number," Luis said. Sophie handed him the burner phone they bought for this purpose, and he put his number in it.

"Thank you for your hospitality," Sophie said outside as he opened the car door for her. "And please apologize to Miss Dolce for me for interrupting her afternoon."

The smell of Mexican food filled the room as the group walked into the cottage.

"Oh, Carol, that smells delicious," Sophie said.

"I'm trying new southwestern recipes to add to my catering menu. I have several things I want you all to taste."

On the table was laid out seasoned shredded beef, seasoned chicken, and homemade corn and flour tortillas. Individual bowls were filled with Pico de Gallo, shredded lettuce, grilled onions for fajitas, jalapeños, and shredded cheese.

"This looks amazing. Let's talk shop after we eat," Sophie said.

"Carol, how did you do this in a few hours?" Houston asked.

"It took longer than that. I did most of it at Emmett's this morning. I packed it all up and finished it here for when you came home." Carol watched as everyone packed their plates and sat down. "I want your opinion on the seasonings of the chicken and beef. I found several old seasoning recipes online. I decided to try my hand at making my own. The first few I tried didn't go well. But these two are my favorite. Since Mexican food is so popular here, it will be hard for me to compete if I don't have something that sets me apart."

"Mmm...the seasoning on the chicken is scrumptious," Sophie said with a mouthful. Are you going to come up with a salsa?"

"I hadn't thought of coming up with salsa. I'll look into it. I knew you would give me an honest critique of the seasonings, Sophie. I figured the guys would just scarf it down," Carol chuckled.

"Not true, Carol, I can tell you the shredded beef is fantastic. It tastes like it came from over the border," Houston said.

"What do you think, darling," Carol asked Fons.

"I'm too busy scarfing it down to give a critique right now," he said. Carol chuckled.

"I'm thinking of showing how to cook this on my vlog. But I'm wondering if I should package the seasoning and sell it rather than give the recipe away."

"Oh, you should definitely package it. I'll help," Sophie said.

"Yeah, honey, it will give you another revenue stream. No sense in giving it away," Fons said.

After all the food was devoured, Sophie helped clean up. She was a little disappointed there were no leftovers for a late-night snack. The group went outside and sat on Emmett's patio. He had gone over to Jared to work on a business deal.

I could eat that food every night, Carol," Sophie laughed. "I think it's the twins' favorite too."

"By the way, how did the doctor's appointment go yesterday?" Carol asked.

"Dr. Banerjee did another ultrasound, and we saw the other twin..." Sophie paused.

"Don't leave us hanging, Soph," Fons said, looking at her. Houston blurted it out.

"It's a boy."

Fons and Carol whooped and hollered with excitement.

Houston looked at the time. "Let's listen to the recording of your meeting with Luis."

After hearing the conversation, Houston agreed their time in Hollywood was well spent. She had him at 'Hello'.

"Did Felix ever give us the name of the man that beat him up? The name Willy gave him," Houston asked.

"No, but we need to have it. Let's call Felix. I'd like to go check him out," Fons said.

"Sophie, can you call Katsumi's house and talk to Felix."

Sophie hesitated, "We need to tell him about Derreck."

Fons and Houston were silent for a moment.

"You're right. He needs to know," Fons finally said. Sophie dialed.

"Hello?"

"Hello, Ojisan. It's me, Sophie."

"My missing musume. I thought you had forgotten about me," he teased.

"Never. I hope the guests we sent you are not too much trouble," Sophie said.

"Not at all. They were homesick at first, but I asked them to help me work the grounds here and at the church. They are quick learners and enjoy the work.

"I was able to talk to them about my life and how Jesus took my wasted life and forgave my sins."

Sophie could hear Katsumi getting choked up. He always did when he talked about what Jesus had done for him.

"They kept asking questions. They see there can be more to life, but only time will tell if it makes a difference."

"I knew they could relate to you, Ojisan. You are a testimony to the greatness of God."

"I hope that could be true. I will do my best to do for them what you and Houston did for me," Katsumi said. "How are my grandbabies?"

"I have news. Yesterday at the doctor, the twin moved enough to give us a glimpse of her brother."

"Ah, such a miracle. A boy and a girl. How will I have time to spoil all of my grandchildren?"

"I'm sure you will find a way, Ojisan," Sophie laughed.

"I will do my best," he chuckled.

"Is Felix there, Ojisan. I need to speak with him."

"Yes, he is over at Izumi's. I can get him. He has been spending time at my son's factory learning how to work the machines. He seems to be intrigued with the whole process."

"I can speak to Rob if he is closer," Sophie said.

"Yes, he is helping Mr. Jo fix the sink in the kitchen. I will get him." Sophie could hear Katsumi walk into the kitchen and tell Rob I was on the phone and wished to speak with him.

"Hello, Mrs. Townsend. Has something happened?"

Sophie hesitated, "Yes, Rob. Derreck was murdered Thursday." Sophie listened for a response, but all she heard was a gasp.

"It was DeLeon, wasn't it. He found out Derreck got picked up by the DEA."

"We think so."

"Felix and I would be dead too, if you hadn't sent us away," Rob said, choked up.

"It's possible. One thing is for sure. You can never come back here. I have met with Luis DeLeon, and he is giving me more time to come up with the money. What I need from you is the name and address of the man Willy gave you. The one that took the cocaine and beat you up."

"Yeah, he had it on a piece of paper. When Felix told him we were done with the whole thing, he put it on the coffee table. I never looked at it. I'm sure it's still there. If you need it, you can go into the house."

"Ok, we will. We are trying to find a way to get the money to pay back Luis. But if we can't, you will need to sell your house. Even if you don't ever come back here. A man like Luis DeLeon could want to make an example of you if he isn't paid and hunt you down."

"Yeah, I figured. How can we do it from here?"

"I'll have Rex contact you. You can give him the power of attorney to sell the house for you and hire a realtor. Houston and I can hire someone to pack up the house and store your things. We can get them to you when you decide where you want to live."

"DeLeon really killed Derreck?"

"I'm sorry, Rob. But a lifestyle of drug dealing is a risky business. Though no one deserved to be murdered, Derreck got into this with his eyes open."

"I know. Mr. Katsumi told us how you and your husband introduced him to Jesus. It's hard to believe that this gentle, humble man was once the head of the world's most brutal Akuza crime families."

"It's amazing what God can do with one life. If you let him," Sophie said.

"I'll let Felix know what you've told me. He's been working with Mr. Izumi. Felix really likes him."

"Remember, don't contact anyone but us."

"I understand."

"May I speak with Mr. Katsumi again, please."

"Mr. Katsumi, Mrs. Townsend wants to speak with you again." Sophie heard him hand over the phone.

"Ojisan, Rob seems to have settled in. Thank you."

"How could I call myself a Christian if I did not help a lost lamb find his shepherd."

"I hope to see you soon, Ojisan. Aishi te iya masu."

"Watashi mo musume aishi te iya masu."

CHAPTER TWENTY

"Fons, what do you say we go pick up that address at the Wynne's house and check on this guy tonight?"

"I'm in."

"What kind of tools did you bring with you?"

"I have my lock picks and alligator clips," Fons said.

"I do too, and I have binoculars and flashlights," Houston said.

"Do you have the key to their house?"

"Yeah, he handed it over before they left."

Houston drove. As they got closer to the Wynne home, they were concerned that the police might be watching the house. There was still a BOLO out on the brothers. And now that Derreck was murdered, the DEA made it their priority to get their hands on Felix and Rob.

"I'll drive down the street, Fons. Check out the parked cars." As Houston drove, Fons looked for unmarked car plates with someone sitting in it.

"There," Fons said.

"Ok, I'll park around the corner, and we can walk down the alley and go in from the back."

Houston turned at the end of the block and parked. It took a few minutes to walk to the Wynne home. There was an unlocked gate that opened into their backyard.

"The key opens the door to the kitchen from the garage. They went in the unlocked garage's side door and used the key to get inside.

There was enough light still coming through to see. Flashlights would have drawn attention from the police surveillance outside.

"They tossed this place pretty good. Let's hope that piece of paper survived," Houston said.

"It looks like they used a snap gun on the front door to get in, then secured the door when they left."

Houston looked all over the coffee table, "I don't see it."

Fons stepped over and helped him search around the floor. With the dimming light, it was harder to see now. Houston moved the coffee table. A small square piece of paper was stuck under the corner.

"I got it," he looked at the name and address. "Dante Vita. Let's get out of here."

"The address is Lakehurst Dr.," Fons said.

"I'm not that familiar with Austin. Punch it into the GPS."

Fons watched the directions come up. "It's off E. William Cannon Dr.," Fons said.

"That is a one-way main artery. I can get us there."

Fifteen minutes later, they drove down Lakehurst, looking for the correct house. They drove by and spotted it. Houston parked around the corner, and they walked back to it in the alley. It was dark now, but the ambient light allowed them to see where they were going.

There was a light inside, but when they drove past the house, they saw no cars or signs that someone lived there. But that didn't mean a car wasn't in the garage. There was a six-foot rock wall around the backyard. The house to the left looked occupied. The place to the right had a for sale sign and looked empty. They jumped the fence next door and walked closer to the target house. Houston saw a camera over the back door. He recognized the brand.

"That uses a cone shape to show the biggest part of the property. If we jump the wall here and flatten ourselves against the house, we should be out of range," Houston said. They double-checked to be sure there were no other cameras and hopped the fence.

Houston went one way and Fons the other. They looked in windows to see or hear any sign that someone was home, choosing not to check the front.

"I don't think anyone lives here, Houston. Look, no chairs on the patio. The garbage can is brand new and empty. The yard is mowed, but there are no bushes or flowers. I think this is a stash house."

"Smart, putting it in a middle-income neighborhood."

Houston and Fons put on gloves, and then Fons picked the lock. When they stepped in, they heard the chirping of an alarm. Fons quickly removed the keypad's cover and hooked alligator clips to bypass the system.

The one light that was on allowed Houston to scan the entry and the hallway. He didn't see any cameras until he looked into the first room on the left, an office. There was a desk with a computer. Across from that was the kitchen. He didn't see any cameras in there. They stepped in there to figure out how to search the place without being picked up by the cameras.

"I'm going to call Sissy," Houston said, taking out his cell.

"Good evening, Houston. You realize we are two hours ahead of you. Don't you?" Sissy teased.

"Oops. Sorry, but we are in a precarious situation."

"What's up?"

"We are in what we think is a stash house. Fons has bypassed the alarm system. But there are cameras. We can't search the place without getting caught." Houston could hear her get up and walk to her computer. He heard Matt comment in the background that he thought we retired.

"Most security cameras are hooked into the computer. Do you see one?"

"Yes, but there is a camera in there."

"Use your flashlight to blind the camera and turn on the computer."

Fons shined his flashlight directly into the camera while Houston turned on the computer.

"Hit the start menu. Then type '**cmd**' in the search bar."

"Ok, done."

"Type in '**ipconfig**' and hit enter."

"Ok. Done."

"Read the IP address to me."

Houston read the IP address, and Sissy had control of the computer in seconds.

"What are you going to do?" Houston asked.

"I'm going to record a loop. You need to stand somewhere where a camera cannot see you for fifteen minutes. Then, I will erase the flashlight from the recording and plug in the loop. I'll keep replaying it until you tell me you have completed your search. Then I'll restore it back to normal function."

"That's why you get paid the big bucks, Sissy," Houston laughed.

"Right. Remember that when I send you the bill."

Houston and Fons waited in the kitchen, keeping Sissy on the line until she told them it was safe to move around.

"It's on a continuous loop. Call me when you are done searching."

"Thanks, Sissy. And tell Matt, this is me retired," he chuckled.

"I'll take the computer room," Houston said.

"I'll start in the living room."

"They looked for any kind of trap in the floor or anything on the walls or paneling that was loose and could be removed.

Houston felt along the panel wall, pushing, and knocking along the way. It didn't take long before he heard a hollow spot. He searched for a way to open it. He pushed on all the corners; nothing happened. Then he kicked the baseboard. The paneling opened, and inside were narrow shelves with stacks of cash.

"Fons look at this," Houston hollered. Fons stepped in.

"Let's get this documented. There has to be more," Fons said, taking pictures with his cell.

When they were done searching, they found four more wall traps and five-floor traps. Three of them were empty. Four of them were filled with money. The others were filled with fentanyl or cocaine.

They were getting ready to call Sissy back when the landline rang. They stopped in their tracks. The answering machine picked up.

"We need to hear the messages on that phone," Fons said.

"Messages usually go straight to the carrier," Houston commented.

"Can we retrieve them from here?"

"Most carriers use the standard, *99, to retrieve your messages from home. Let's try," Houston put it on speaker. He hit *99, and the voice said, "You have two new and six saved messages. To hear your messages, hit 1." Fons used his phone to record what they heard.

"A tip just came in that one of the Mexican cartels is bringing in some fentanyl for his dealers. The product is supposed to be at the closed diner on Hiline Road at Emerald Point on Monday at 6 pm. You need to get there with your partner before the supplier shows up and catch him off guard. You want to avoid being there when the dealers come for their product. I will pass on the tip but adjust the time."

"To erase this message, press 7; to save it, press 9." They listened and recorded all the messages, then hung up.

"That sounded like Special Agent Vogt."

"Who?" Fons asked.

"A man we met at the DEA. I knew there was something about him that wasn't right."

"You can't know that for sure, Houston. We'll need to get a recording of his voice and analyze it."

"We can do that, but I know it's him."

"Ok, so what exactly is going on here?" Fons asked.

"Vogt is getting inside information then passes it on to his accomplishes. They steal it by any means necessary and bring it here. Then he sells the drugs and stores the money, giving his men a cut."

"I have to say, that's not a bad plan. Who knows how long this has been going on? He could have a fortune in a Cayman Island account," Fons said.

"It's time for us to get out of here. I'll call Sissy. You check to make sure everything is back in its place."

Houston and Fons walked into the cottage.

"Did Carol go to Emmett's?"

"Yes, she is mapping out a route with MapQuest for you to drive a U-Haul back from DC with your belongings."

"Yeah, we talked about that."

"Sophie, you need to hear what we recorded," Houston said. "First, we need to fill you in. We went to the Wynne house. An unmarked car was watching the place. We entered through the alley. We found the paper with the name of one of the guys that beat up Felix and Rob.

"Since we had the address, Fons and I decided to check it out. The place was empty, with cameras and a security system. Fons picked the lock and disabled the alarm. I noticed cameras inside, so I called Sissy to work her magic." Houston paused while Fons opened the pictures he had taken.

Fons handed his phone to her. "We found ten traps in the stash house."

"What are you thinking?" Sophie asked.

"I know exactly what is going on. Now I want you to listen to the recording," Houston asked Fons to play it. Sophie handed him back his cell.

They all listened to the messages. It didn't take long for Sophie to figure it out. "There is an agent in the DEA using tips to steal drugs and money. He is paying a percentage to these guys for stealing it."

"Exactly. And I know who it is," Houston said.

"How?"

"He is the one who came her that day to take us into the DEA. Special Agent Vogt," Houston said.

"Are you sure?"

"I am, but I'm going to get Berry to take a recording of his voice so I can send it to Sissy so she can analyze it."

"It won't be good enough for court, Houston."

"I know. But once we make a deal and have the police raid the place, we can get the original recordings, which will be enough."

Sophie leaned back on the couch where she was sitting and took a deep breath. Bully sat next to her on the sofa until Houston came in. Then he laid down on the floor by her feet.

"Unbelievable," she asked to look at the pictures on Fons' cell again. "It's possible three-quarters of a million dollars are in that house."

"And another million in drugs," Fons added.

"Yeah, but I'm not so sure we can trust the local DEA to give us a percentage," Sophie said.

"And how do we work with them when it's one of their own agents who is corrupt," Fons asked.

"I trust ASAC Berry," Houston said. "If we can get the DOJ to sanction our raid. Then I wouldn't have a problem with getting him involved with a few of his men that can be trusted."

"We don't know the local AUSAs," Houston said.

"No, but all these federal agencies are under the auspices of the Attorney General. The local DEA will have to honor a deal made by AUSA Trindi Martin."

"Let's make a deal with her first. Then we'll contact Berry and feel him out," Fons said.

"Ok. Good. We can't call Trindi until Monday. We'll have to pray they don't move the stuff out of the house before then," Houston said. Fons got up from the overstuffed chair he plopped in when they walked in the door. Houston was sitting next to his wife.

"Since we can't do anything else until Monday, I'm going to bed. I'll see you in the morning."

"Goodnight, Fons," Houston and Sophie echoed.

"Wow, if this works, it would be good all around. The DEA needs to know they have a crooked agent. DeLeon will get paid, getting the boys off the hook, and we may even make a dollar or two."

"It may not be that simple, Sophie. If the DEA raids the place and all the contraband is gone, we will have shown Vogt our hand. It could make him very dangerous."

SUNDAY

Houston was up first and let Bully out, leaving the door open so he could come in when he was done. He hadn't realized it rained last night. There was a fresh smell in the air. Houston put food and water down for Bully. Sophie came out of the bedroom in her pajamas.

"Do you want me to make breakfast?" Sophie asked.

Houston chuckled and kissed her forehead as she sat at the kitchen table. "Is that a real question?"

Sophie looked up at him and shrugged, "Maybe." Bully came in from his morning jaunt and headed for his breakfast.

"No, you get ready for Church."

Sophie's timing was perfect. Just as she came out fully dressed and sat at the table, Houston put a waffle in front of her. She slathered it in butter, jelly, and syrup and took the first bite. "Mmm," she moaned, closing her eyes as she savored it.

Houston sat with his own plate of eggs and bacon. He couldn't help but smile, watching her enjoy her waffles.

After church, all the ladies went to Aileen's to work on the decorations with Sienna. Her wedding was only a few weeks away. Anna, Ruby, and Zoey headed to Carmen's house with Aileen to work on the reception. Carmen offered to have it at her house. They were over there figuring out how they wanted it set up.

Lizzy, Sophie, and Carol made the big white bows for the end of the pews in the aisle. Flowers would be added to them on the day of the wedding.

"You've worked a lot this week, Lizzy. I missed you," Sophie said.

"CJ and I want to push the date up for the construction on our house. We have had our blueprints for years. Now that you are building, it has brought back the excitement of moving forward."

"I can't wait. Carol and Fons are thinking about buying property there too," Sophie said.

"Oh, that would be awesome," Lizzy commented.

"The setting there is so inviting. I fell in love with it. It will take a while for us to build, but we want to buy the property right away."

"We won't be building a mansion like Xander and Blaze's, that's for sure. But our design is two stories, bigger than we need, but I'm sure we'll fill it up. We are going with wood and brick construction to help blend in with the other homes," Lizzy said. "CJ said Houston opted for that exterior too."

"Yes, for the same reasons," Sophie said.

"When I saw those mansions, I was initially concerned about buying there. I figured no way," Carol said. "But Sophie said she wasn't building a mansion either."

The men had the BBQ at Jared's all to themselves today for once.

Bully and Coco kept Jett occupied, and Drew and Kato were swimming in Jared's pool. China and Teresa were with Sienna, helping wrap bows around the wedding guest's gifts.

The men had brought out a big-screen TV. They watched the Texas Rangers play against the New York Mets and worked the grill.

"I could enjoy doing this more often," David said.

"Don't let Anna hear you say that," Jonathan laughed.

MONDAY

Sophie was the first to wake up. Unusual for her. *Houston must have worn himself out watching sports,* she thought. She decided to make breakfast for him. He ate the same thing every morning. Today, she would shake things up and make him pancakes with his eggs and bacon.

Bully stretched and followed her. Sophie bent down and gave him a good rub down his face and over his back. He loved that. Then she let him out and filled his bowls with food and water.

Sophie was mixing the pancake batter when she heard the shower. Houston came out fully dressed as usual, and she put a plate of pancakes, eggs, and bacon in front of him.

"Thank you, sweetheart, this looks good."

"Why do you say that like you're surprised. I can make a decent breakfast," Sophie chided him.

"Yes, you can." He grabbed her hand and kissed it.

"I'm going to take a shower and get dressed. Will you make your children waffles?" Sophie asked, going behind his chair and putting her arms around his neck.

"And there's the rub," Houston laughed and patted her arm.

Sophie came out dressed just as Houston laid her breakfast on the table. Bully had already eaten and was stretched out in the sun's rays through the front window.

When she finished her meal, she asked, "Do you want me to do the dishes?"

"No, you call Trindi."

"If you insist, honey," Sophie looked at him and fluttered her eyelashes.

Houston chuckled and filled the dishwasher, then wiped and put away the syrup, jelly, and butter, Sophie always slathered on her waffle.

Sophie's cell was charging next to her bed. She grabbed it and returned to the kitchen table, putting it on speaker. She dialed the DOJ attorney Trindi Martin.

"AUSA Trindi Martin."

"AUSA Martin, Sophie Star Townsend here."

"Ms. Star?"

"Yes, how are you?"

"I'm well. Why on earth would you be calling me? Aren't you and your husband retired?"

"Yes. But we have a case that falls under your authority."

"Aren't you in Texas?"

"Yes. But we don't know the AUSAs here. We trust you."

"I'm sure you can trust them, Ms. Star."

"Please, hear me out." Sophie explained the situation with the corrupt DEA agent and that they can't trust that making a deal with them will be honored. "We have proof that will stand up in court. But we want the DOJ to pay us a percentage of what is confiscated. Ten percent, like when I worked on the Nikko Morano case."

"Agents aren't eligible for that," Trindi said.

"We aren't agents anymore. Remember?" Sophie responded. Trindi was silent for what felt like a long time.

"Ms. Star, when you were working for the President's Task Force, it was nearly impossible for me to say no to you. I would have never approved of some of the demands you made, except for that.

"Now, you don't have that same clout. But I have a feeling if I ran this by the Attorney General, he would still insist I accommodate you. So, give me the particulars, and I will write this up...but you must bring in a federal agency to raid and arrest."

"Understood." Sophie gave her the name of the corrupt agent, his accomplices, and the address of the stash house.

"I'll have this signed and send it to you by email."

"Thank you, Trindi," Sophie said.

"I admit, things are a little less interesting without you."

"That's the nicest thing you have ever said to me," Sophie chuckled.

"Don't let it go to your head. And find someone down there you can bother next time."

Sophie said goodbye and looked at Houston. "Well, that was the first step."

"We have a problem, Soph. We know of a crime being committed tonight but haven't reported it."

"I know. But we need a plan before contacting ASAC Berry." Sophie saw Bully's ears perked, and he got up to greet someone coming to the open door.

Fons walked in. After rubbing behind Bully's ears, he said, "We have an issue."

"Yeah, we know," Houston said. "Want some coffee?"

"Sure."

"What's Carol doing?" Sophie asked.

"She's researching recipes for Taco Soup to develop her own version."

"I hope that means we get Taco Soup for dinner today," Sophie rubbed her hands together.

"I'm sure," Fons said and sat down where Houston put a steaming cup of coffee.

"Ok, first, AUSA Martin is writing up a 10% informant's fee agreement on all contraband confiscated in this operation," Houston said.

"Perfect. Now, what do we do about the crime happening tonight?" Fons asked.

"Hear me out," Sophie said. "We contact ASAC Berry. We tell him we know of a drug supplier bringing in fentanyl and give him the correct time and location. Forty-five minutes before the raid, he tells his men to put their phones in a box he provides. Then, he informs them about the operation and makes Vogt his second in command. He keeps Vogt by his side until the raid happens. That way, Vogt won't have time to warn Dante.

"After the raid, Vogt will worry Dante will spill his guts. He will have to go to the stash house to clear it out. We make sure there is another team waiting there for him. We can ask Sissy hack into the stash house camera so we have a copy of every move he makes inside. The DEA takes him down, and we collect our money."

"I like it," Fons said.

"We'll have to meet Berry somewhere we can be certain no one will see us together," Houston said.

"He could go into Sienna's bakery. She could lead him to the stairs to her apartment. We can talk up there."

"Ok, we need to get this done right away."

CHAPTER TWENTY-ONE

An hour later, ASAC Berry knocked on Sienna's apartment door. Houston opened it, and they all sat at the table.

"What's with all this secrecy?" Berry asked.

"ASAC Berry, we have some information you need to know," Sophie said, then turned to Houston to fill him in.

Houston told him everything they knew. Then Fons pulled out his cell, showed him the proof of the stash, and let him hear the messages.

"That does sound like Vogt, but that's not enough proof for me to arrest him," Berry objected.

"No. We don't want you to arrest him. We want to catch him in the act. You heard him say a drug deal is going down at a closed diner at Emerald Point. Vogt plans to give you that information but at the wrong time. He will only tell you after 6 pm for fear you will want to have someone sitting on the property. Forty-five minutes before six, you get your team together and tell them you received a tip about a drug deal. You can make Vogt your second and keep him in your line of sight until the takedown. Everyone will need to turn in their cells so nothing can leak. We can't let Vogt get ahold of Dante.

"After you arrest the suppliers and Dante and Gideon, Vogt will have to run, for fear Dante will sell him out. He will be forced to get to the stash house and grab the money and drugs and run," Houston explained.

"ASAC Berry, the men you pick to be at the stash house waiting, have to be men you would trust your life to. If Vogt gets wind, this is a trap, he will run. Chances are we will never find him. He likely has money stashed out of the country," Fons said.

"It's a solid plan, but we have never taken the cells from our agents before a raid. That may tip him off."

"You can say you heard from Ramos, and that was one of the new policies he learned in DC," Sophie said.

"That could work. What I can't believe is Vogt is dirty. I've worked with him for five years. Our office had some bad information from informants, but that happens. You're saying he sent his accomplices there first to steal the drugs and money." Berry looked at each one of them. Fons nodded.

"That's what we are telling you."

ASAC Berry looked at his watch, "It's 1 pm. That doesn't give me much time. We'll need a warrant to enter the stash house if we want the arrest to stick."

"Can you call and say you had a tip about a stash house and get a warrant?" Sophie asked.

"If Vogt's attorney is good, he will want a discloser on who the tip came from," Berry said.

"One of the guys who beat up our clients is Dante Vita. Derreck's cousin, Willy, found this address where he thought Dante lived. That's the tip." Houston said.

"We can't give you these pictures or audio. But when the raid happens at Emerald Point, your men at the stash house can go in and take their own pictures and listen to the messages," Fons said.

"Can you do it? Or do we need to call in the APD to help?" Houston asked.

"No, we can manage it."

"Fons and I will wait at the stash house with your men."

ASAC Berry stood, paused, then said, "I hope you are wrong about Vogt. I know you could have bypassed me and gone to the APD. But I appreciate you letting us clean up our mess." Berry shook hands and left through the bakery the way he came.

When they walked into the cottage, they could smell the Taco Soup.

"We didn't expect this until dinner, Carol," Sophie said.

"It was easier than I thought. Come sit down. I need your honest opinions."

They sat at the table Carol had already set. Bully watching Carol's every move. Hoping it was something he could get a taste of.

Carol served the soup. "I want you to take the different condiments on the table and add them a little at a time. Then tell me what works and what doesn't."

They looked over the bowls of onions, chopped tomatoes, chopped jalapenos, shredded Mexican cheese mix, corn, green onions, and sour cream. There was a big bowl of tortilla chips in the middle.

The men dumped spoons full of everything in their soup, but Sophie took a spoonful of one thing at a time and tasted it in the soup. Carol did the same. When Bully realized he wouldn't be getting scraps. He went to bed in the living room and took a nap.

"Carol, really, this is amazing. I like all of it," Houston said as he scooped up the meat and beans with a tortilla chip and put it in his mouth.

"Me too, honey. Perfect." Fons was using the tortilla chips as his spoon.

"Carol, I like that you give the people a choice. If you include corn in the soup, it will give it a crunch. But the jalapenos are hot and could cause a problem for some people. I'm unsure about the sour cream, but some people will like it."

"Thanks, Sophie. I knew the guys would not follow my instructions. I needed you to give me an honest critique."

"We need to help you pay for groceries. You are feeding us on your dime," Sophie said.

"No, I'm using it as a business expense. I do have a question, though."

"I need to start my vlog up again. I only had two weeks prerecorded. Do we have any idea when the property will close?"

"I'll call Jonathan this afternoon. He is in contact with the Title Company," Houston said.

"Thanks, Houston."

"Emmett said I could do it from his kitchen for as long as I need, but I like the look of the chef's kitchen at the apartment."

ASAC Berry pulled aside five men he trusted completely. He spoke with them one floor below the DEA level of the federal building in a small conference room. Berry explained everything he knew. After a stunned reaction from the men, he told them about the operation that was going to play out in a few hours.

"You will meet behind the fire station two blocks from the stash house. Mr. Townsend and Mr. Rodriguez will be part of the team.

"Special Agent Barber, you will have to get the code for the alarm once you're inside. Agent Vogt can't know anyone has breached his stash house."

"I have the equipment to do that, sir."

"Agent Singh, you, and the rest of the team will go in and confirm that it is a stash house and take pictures and record the messages. You and Agent Barber will hide inside the house with Townsend and Rodriguez. The rest of the team will hide behind the rock wall next door.

"Griff, how sure are you about this?" Agent Percy asked.

"You now know what I know. What do you think?"

"I think we need more."

"And if this wasn't all going down tonight, we could get more. But even if it is not Vogt, that stash house belongs to someone. And we will be there to take whomever into custody," Berry said. The others nodded their agreement.

"I've gotten approval from SWAT to use one of their frequencies to communicate using your comms. The team at the diner will be on the DEA assigned frequency.

"I will be with the other team raiding the closed diner where the drug deal should go down. Mr. Rodriguez is an active SAC with the FBI. He will be the highest-ranking member of the team, even though he is not doing this in his capacity as an agent.

"Don't return to the squad room, and do not call anyone. This operation is black ops. I do have a warrant to enter the stash house from an AUSA,"

"Does SAC Ramos know about this?" Barber asked.

"No," was the only answer he gave.

ASAC Berry was getting ready to call the rest of the squad into the conference room. It was almost 5 pm. When the squad was assembled, ASAC Berry told them he had gotten a tip, and they would head out in five minutes. He explained the operation.

ASAC Berry put a box on the table and said, "I need everyone to put their cell phones into this box. We will only be using our comms."

"Since when," Vogt asked, "do we give up our cells?"

"It's a new protocol SAC Ramos has learned up in DC. No phone calls or cell phone use until the operation is over. You can discuss it with him when he gets back, Vogt, if you have a problem with it."

"No...no problem."

"I want you as my second, Vogt. You're next in line."

"I'm with you."

"Special Agent Lund if we have to split up you will lead the other team."

"Yes, sir," Special Agent Lund said.

"Where is the rest of the squad?" One of the team asked.

"I lent them to SWAT, to help on a training exercise." That seemed to satisfy everyone. "Ok, we have an unmarked van waiting for us downstairs. Grab your vests on the way out, and let's move. This is happening now."

Agent Vogt had no way to warn Dante. But there was no way he could let him, or his partner be arrested. *How did Berry get this tip? My informant knows not to talk to anyone but me. He must have a guy of his own. This is not good.*

I can't get paranoid; this raid is not connected to my stash house. But if Berry gets his hands on Dante or Gideon, they could talk. I'll have to make sure they can't.

Agent Vogt grabbed his Kevlar vest and followed the team downstairs.

Houston and Fons had gotten a text and headed to meet the DEA team assigned to the stash house in Emmett's SUV. Both were armed. Carol was working on her script for her next vlog, so Sophie and Bully walked to Lizzy's to visit.

Bully chased a rabbit for a while, but then the rabbit stopped, turned, and looked at him. Bully got down to a crawl position and slowly came up on the rabbit. Bully sniffed him, and the rabbit bolted. Bully lost interest and went to meet up with Sophie.

When they reached the houses. Bully did his best to stick by her side, but he got too excited when he figured out, he was going to see Jett. He ran ahead to Lizzy's porch to look in the picture window.

Jett didn't take long to hear Bully barking and came to the window excited to see his friend. Coco ignored Bully as usual.

Lizzy opened the door before Sophie made it up the stairs. "Hello, Sophie, come in." They hugged. Jett came to her, and she lifted him up in the air like Houston always did. CJ came out of the kitchen to say hello.

"Where is Houston?"

"He and Fons are working the case, and Carol is working on her new vlog she will be putting online this week."

"I've been watching her vlogs. She is an amazing cook and makes it fun to watch," Lizzy said. "What do you want to drink, Sophie. I have Dr. Pepper."

"That sounds good. Do you have a copy of the blueprints to our house here, CJ?"

"Sure, you want to look at them?"

"Yes, I want to go through it with you and Lizzy. I didn't know we were having twins when we first designed it."

"Good point. You may want a connecting bedroom or a larger nursery," CJ agreed.

Houston and Fons pulled in behind the fire station and saw a white van with a cable company logo behind the fire station. Five men in Kevlar vests and DEA Jackets were standing around.

Agent Singh went up to them and introduced himself, shaking their hands. Agent Barber came up behind and did the same.

"ASAC Berry said you were the lead on this, Special Agent Rodriguez," Agent Barber said.

"I'm here to work with you, not to run the show. How did ASAC Berry say he wanted this handled?"

"ASAC Berry said, I need to disarm the alarm system by pulling the code from the control panel's memory. The team goes in next and verifies with pictures the tip is good. Then you, Mr. Townsend, me, and Agent Singh remain inside. The rest of the team will wait next door. I understand you have someone controlling the cameras inside?" Barber asked.

"Yes."

"As soon as we get the text from ASAC Berry that they have moved to Emeral Point, we will move to the location," Agent Singh explained.

ASAC Berry had his men out of site at the diner. The property was surrounded. At 5:30 pm, they saw two men pick the lock on the door and go inside. A half-hour later, a black van appeared, and two large men got out. One had an AK-47; the other a sidearm. Their tats indicated they belonged to a Mexican cartel.

"This is it, men," Berry said through the comms.

One man stood watch as the other opened the back of the van and grabbed two plastic storage bins. ASAC Berry could see there were three more bins in the van.

The man with the AK-47 had a key and unlocked the door. The other man dropped the containers inside the door and returned for the rest.

"Ok, Lund, you and your team will take down the guard. Wait for the other man to finish loading the drugs into the diner. Vogt and I will go through the front. We will wait to hear you take down the guard before we enter. The suspect inside will be looking toward the back door when he hears you taking down the guard. That should give us an opportunity to get behind him and cut off his other escape route. Wait for my command before you come in."

"What about the other two men inside?" Lund asked.

"Vogt and I will deal with them."

"Understood," Lund said.

ASAC Berry and SA Vogt made their way to the front door without being seen. Vogt picked the front door lock and waited for Lund's team to take down the guard.

"When we get inside, I'll look for the other two men. You get into a position to stop the suspect from fleeing out the front. I'll meet you after I've located the other two," Berry whispered. "When I locate them, I'll have Lund send one of his men around to help me take them down. You keep your eye on the dealer."

Vogt didn't know how he was going to reverse the situation so that he was the one to look for Dante and Gideon. But there was no way he could let them be taken into custody. He was going to have to wait for an opportunity.

The team watched the guy with the AK-47. It was obvious the cartel had used this location before without incident, because after looking around for threats he stood by the door and pulled out his cigarettes. After lighting one he put one foot on the wall and leaned back; relaxed. His AK- 47 was pointed down to the ground.

Special Agent Lund used hand signals to direct the men to either side of the building toward the guard. They waited at the end of the building. When Lund was certain the guard had not heard them, he tapped his comm, which was the signal for them to come out and take him into custody.

The team was only a few feet from the guard when they started yelling commands. The suspect was taken off guard.

"DROP THE WEAPON AND PUT YOUR HANDS UP!"

They kept repeating the command. They could see the man was deciding if he wanted to live or go down in a blaze of gunfire. He decided to live. He put his weapon down and two agents turned him to the wall, patted him down and cuffed him.

Special Agent Lund ordered the same two agents to take him to the van and guard him. The others waited for a signal from Berry to enter the diner.

Berry and Vogt slipped into the diner. The inside man had his gun pulled, aiming it at the back door. They were maneuvering around tables and chairs trying to get a good angle on the man before making their presence known.

Vogt saw the only place for his accomplices to hide was on the left. Berry had gone in first and was on that side. Vogt moved in around him forcing Berry right. He needed Berry to be the one cutting off the dealers escape route so he could look for Dante and Gideon.

Vogt knocked into a table giving away their position. The man at the door turned and shot. Berry gave the command for the other team to enter while he took cover. The suspect ran into the storage room by the back door, shutting himself in and barricading the door.

"I'll check the rest of the diner for the other two men," Vogt told Berry.

Berry hadn't planned on Vogt being the one to look for his accomplices, but now they had an active shooter, and his plans went out the window. Someone had to make sure Dante and Gideon didn't ambush them. He nodded to Vogt and went after the dealer.

Berry made it to the back door as three of Lund's team entered.

"YOU ARE SURROUNDED. COME OUT WITH YOUR HAND UP."

The suspect's response was to shoot through the door.

Vogt bumped into the table on purpose. He knew this was his one opportunity to switch things around. Having an active shooter forced Berry to deal with it. Berry had no choice but to have him look for the other two men.

Vogt cleared several rooms before entering the kitchen. Dante and Gideon were standing there with their guns pointed in his direction. When they saw it was him, they lowered their guns.

"Boy, am I glad to see you. You have to help us get out of here," Dante said.

"Can we get out the front without being seen?" Gideon asked.

Vogt raised his Sig Sauer P2260 and aimed it at them. "Drop your weapons."

Vogt knew his time was limited; he could hear Berry ordering the suspect out with his hands up.

Lund and another agent were on one side of the storage room door. Berry and another agent on the other side.

"OPEN THE DOOR. DROP YOUR GUN AND COME OUT WITH YOUR HANDS UP," Berry ordered.

After another minute Berry continued. This time lowering his voice to try to calm the man down.

"Look, there is no way out of this for you. You have a choice to make. Either you leave in a black bag, or you walk escorted to a police cruiser."

The suspect responded by shooting through the door again.

Dante spoke again, drawing Vogt's attention back to him.

"This is perfect. They are all focused on the dealer. We can get out now."

Vogt kept his gun aimed at Dante.

"What are you doing? We can still get out. You can say you didn't see us," Gideon said.

Vogt whispered, "I don't think so. This is a perfect setup to tie up loose ends. I think it's time for me to leave the country."

"Don't do this, Vogt," Dante repeated, pleading with him.

"I'm sorry, Dante, but I think your usefulness has ended."

When Dante realized Vogt was going to shoot him, he raised his weapon in self-defense, but Vogt shot first. Gideon dropped his gun and raised his hands. Vogt shot him in cold blood.

ASAC Berry and the agent with him, came running to back-up Vogt when they heard the shots. As soon as he stepped in the kitchen, he saw the two men on the ground; Vogt's gun still aimed at them. ASAC Berry told him to holster his weapon and then went to see if either of the men was still alive. They weren't. Their guns were on the ground close to their bodies. He looked over at Vogt.

"They drew their guns on me," Vogt said. Berry knew he was lying. "I managed to shoot first."

ASAC Berry felt horrible. He should have foreseen that Vogt would kill them to keep them quiet. He told Vogt to hand over his gun to his teammate, standard procedure, and go wait outside.

ASAC Berry worked to coax the man out of the room for another fifteen minutes. Finally, the man opened the door, slid out his gun, put his hands up, and walked out.

Special Agent Lund called in the ME to manage the dead bodies. After searching the building again, ASAC Berry called in the evidence techs and turned the scene over. They called out a transport van to haul the prisoners to the federal building for interrogation.

SAC Berry spoke to Agent Vogt as they got in their van to return to headquarters. "Can you explain how those two men ended up dead."

"I already told you..." Vogt was angry he was being questioned about the shoot. "I cleared the other rooms when you were dealing with the active shooter. When I entered the kitchen, the two men had their guns pointed at me. I tried to talk them down, but they wouldn't listen. When I saw the bigger one was going to pull the trigger, I shot first. The other man was still in an aggressive posture, so for my own safety I shot him too."

"You were certain he was going to shoot?" Berry asked.

"Are you questioning whether it was a good shoot?" Vogt asked. ASAC Berry weighed up what he said next. They still had another live operation happening.

"No, I just wondered why it was necessary to kill them both. I would have liked to interrogate them," Berry said.

"I would have liked that too, but it didn't work out that way. I startled them when I came into the kitchen. They had their guns aimed at me. When they didn't obey my commands, I had no choice but to defend myself."

"Ok, when we get back to headquarters, let's get these after-action reports done before news gets out about this operation."

When they returned to the squad room, Vogt asked ASAC Berry if he could have personal time. He said he had arranged to meet up with a roofer.

ASAC Berry knew it was time to let him go. Berry texted Agent Barber to inform him Vogt should arrive in ten minutes.

Agent Singh had already picked the lock, and Barber opened the face of the alarm control panel. He used a handheld monitor attached to a ribbon cable holding parallel wires that was fastened to a black plastic end the width of the ribbon. The plastic end held sharp connectors that were inserted into different types of systems. Barber hooked it into the port on the control panel and in seconds, the alarm code showed up on the monitor. He punched in the code before the alarm went off.

While they were waiting to go in, Houston contacted Sissy to aske her to start the loop and let it run until he tells her Vogt was on his way. Then he wanted her to have the cameras recording everything that happened and to save a backup.

The team took pictures of all the traps Houston and Fons showed them and recorded the messages. They were looking for more traps when Barber got the text from ASAC Berry that Vogt was on his way. The team assigned to wait outside left and Barber reset the alarm.

Houston hid in the bathroom and sent Sissy a message. Fons hid in the closet of the computer room. Singh hid in the pantry, and Barber hid behind a louver door in the hallway closet.

Ten minutes later, they heard the back door open, and Vogt turned off the alarm. He had several duffle bags in his hands and went directly into the computer room. He opened the wall panel and shoved the money into one of the duffels, then headed for the living room and moved the couch. He opened a trap door on the floor. He was taking bricks of cocaine from the floor trap and putting them in another duffle.

Vogt's hands were occupied. Agent Barber and Agent Singh were the closest to him and decided to make their move. They made it as far as the entry to the living room before Vogt heard them and looked up.

"**PUT YOUR HANDS IN THE AIR AND MOVE TOWARD ME, VOGT**," Barber growled. "How could you betray your team like this?"

"It's not what it looks like. I got a tip..." Vogt stopped talking when he saw Houston and Fons come into the room. "You...you did this?" Three more of his team came up behind them. All of them were aiming their guns at him.

"I said to come around the couch toward me, Vogt."

"You have it all wrong. I got a tip about this stash house. I wanted to check it out before calling it in to ensure it was a good tip."

"Is that what the phone messages are going to tell us? And what about the security video on your computer?"

"I can explain everything..."

"Shut up, Vogt," Singh said as he directed Agent Percy to cuff him and pat him down. Agent Percy took Vogt's weapons and handed them to another agent.

"Take him out to the van and cuff him to the inside panel. Then stay out there with him until we are finished in here," Singh ordered.

As Vogt was marched outside in cuffs, Special Agent Barber turned to Houston, "You were right about Vogt. I never saw it coming."

"I know it hurts, Agent Barber. I'm sorry it turned out this way," Houston said. The men were all standing around, stunned that a man they worked with could have fooled them for so long. Singh spoke up to bring them out of their slump.

"Ok, Barber, call in the evidence collection team. They can search for more traps, record everything, confiscate the phone and the computer, and take the evidence to headquarters."

Houston and Fons headed outside to wait for the techs. When they stepped out, they saw Agent Percy on the ground, not moving. They ran over to him and noticed his gun was missing, and a set of cuffs were lying beside him.

"Agent Barber," Houston hollered as he checked Percy's vitals. Agent Barber and Agent Singh came running out. "Percy's alive, but Vogt is gone."

Agent Barber went to Agent Percy who was still not moving and looked for his injuries while dialing 911 for an ambulance. Agent Singh checked the back of the van for himself. He pulled out his cell to call Berry. "Sir, Vogt escaped custody. We need more men."

Houston stepped up next to Fons. "Go after him. I'm going to call Sophie to bring Bully over. We can start the search while they wait for the rest of their team." Houston dialed Sophie and gave her the address of where to bring Bully. "Bring his leash and his vest. We're going to start searching. I'll keep the line open, so I can direct you to where we are."

Houston asked Singh if he had anything with Vogt's scent on it.

"I saw his DEA jacket on the couch. I'll grab it," Singh said. Houston waited for the coat while Fons was tracking.

CHAPTER TWENTY-TWO

Fons looked up and down the alley to try to find any sign of where Vogt went. He saw disturbed gravel like someone had stumbled. Fons started running in that direction. Houston saw which direction he had gone and headed that way. He saw Fons running down the middle of the street a block ahead and ran to catch up. Fons slowed for him, while keeping an eye out for Vogt.

When they got to the corner, they saw a glimpse of someone turning a corner two blocks ahead. They sped up.

Sophie was there in less than fifteen minutes and followed Houston's directions. She found them standing on a corner waiting for her. Houston opened the car door and let Bully out of the back. Sophie rolled down her window.

"I'll follow you in case you need a car."

"Alright," Houston put Vogt's jacket to Bully's nose, then tossed it into the car.

Bully sniffed the air, then headed down the street. Houston had the leash, and he and Fons ran, trying not to slow Bully down. Sophie was trailing them in the car.

Houston and Fons heard sirens coming in their direction. Bully followed the trail from the middle of the street to the sidewalk. Then he ran along the side of a house with no fence. He kept going and ran across several lawns and crossed the street again. Bully kept pulling them forward. This went on for blocks, going from street to yard to alley.

They heard a scream, and Bully took off. Houston dropped the leash and let him go. They saw Vogt pulling a woman out of a car and throwing her to the ground. Bully got there as Vogt closed the door and took off. Bully tore out after the vehicle. Houston whistled the command for him to return. Fons read the plate number aloud and called Agent Barber.

"We had Vogt in sight. He just hijacked a woman's car and took off. We are going to go after him. The plate on the car is GLM-6721. It's a red Lexus."

"Roger that, we will get a chopper in the air. What is your location?"

Houston went to the street sign and read it off to Barber, while Fons checked on the woman.

The woman had gotten up. Fons asked her if she was all right. She said other than skinned-up legs, she was fine. Fons told her to wait. Police were on the way. They would get an EMT to check her over.

Houston got in the front passenger seat. Fons opened the back door so Bully could jump in, then got in after him.

Sophie saw the red Lexus turn left at the corner. She floored the accelerator, screeching the tires as she rounded the corner.

"There, Sophie, he turned again," Houston said as he pointed out the red Lexus. Fons was still on the cell phone with Barber, calling out the streets so they could catch up.

Houston noticed this wasn't their SUV. "Who's car is this?"

"We had walked to CJ's when you called. He heard what was happening and told me to take his SUV."

Bully was standing in the center of the backseat, his front paws on the center console. He was looking out the front windshield. Bully knew they were in hot pursuit. He had an uncanny ability to stabilize himself in a moving vehicle.

"He's two blocks ahead of us," Fons told Barber.

"Tell Barber we'll never catch up to him at this rate. We need air support to spot him so we can find a way to cut him off." Fons passed it on.

"Barber says they have a chopper in the air. They are trying to locate us," Fons relayed, then put Barber on speaker.

"He's heading for the interstate. It's a mile ahead," Sophie said.

"You know this area?" Houston asked.

"Well enough, in high school, a serial killer chased Lizzy and me not far from here. He ended up ramming us."

"You'll have to tell me the rest of that story when we get home," Houston said.

They couldn't gain ground on Vogt but didn't lose him either. They heard a chopper overhead and asked Barber to connect them to the pilot.

Barber hung up with Fons and had the helicopter pilot call him.

"Flight officer, Yeager here."

"Special Agent Alfonso Rodrigues, here. I'm with Houston and Sophie Townsend in the car following our suspect. What we need from you is directions on how to cut him off."

"Can do. You are in the black SUV?"

"Yes. Agent Vogt is in the red Lexus a few blocks ahead of us."

"Got it. He is heading for the interstate. You won't be able to catch up to him before he gets on it. You could parallel him on the access road, but you will run into traffic and lights."

"How is traffic on the freeway?"

"No problems going east. West is slower. But if he knows the area, he won't go west."

"Ok. He will get off the interstate if you call for a roadblock ahead of him. We'll take our chances on the access road," Houston suggested.

"Ok, I'll call for a roadblock as soon as I know he is going east."

"Please stay connected to us," Fons requested.

"Whoa, he almost hit that car by running that red light," the flight officer said.

"Sophie, you can slow down a bit now that we have eyes on him."

Sophie didn't slow down except at lights and stop signs to make sure she didn't cause an accident.

"I have a problem up here. A news chopper is interfering in the chase," Flight officer Yeager said, reporting to someone on his headset. Yeager got instructions to order the news chopper out of the area. They could hear Yeager speak directly to the news helicopter over Fons' cell.

"Police Air One to Channel Six news helicopter. You must leave the area. You are interfering with a police chase. Repeat, you must leave the area."

"Understood, Police Air One, we will stay out of your way."

"He's on the freeway, going east," Yeager said as his attention returned to the car chase. Sophie turned east on the access road.

"This would be much easier if we had sirens," she complained.

"He has sped up now on the freeway. I'm told the police have gotten on the freeway a mile ahead. They are slowing traffic down slowly, so they don't cause an accident."

"Good, are we closing in on him?" Sophie asked.

"You are going to pass him. Pull over until we know what he is going to do."

Vogt knew why the cars were slowing down. They were setting up a roadblock. He needed to get off. The meridian was a wide grassy separation between the East and westbound lanes.

There was a slight slope to the center and a slight rise to the other side. He drove onto the meridian and started to drive across it to the west going lanes.

The chopper relayed the information, and Sophie turned under the overpass and drove on the access road West.

"His tire is stuck on the west side of the meridian. He's reversing and going back to the center. Now he is driving down the center and slowly inching up the grassy incline to the freeway."

Sophie rushed to catch him; she knew he would get off at the next exit. She got there as the Flight Officer gave them an update.

"He is getting off at the exit you are approaching."

"We see him. We should be right behind him once he crosses the intersection," Fons said.

Vogt tried to fly through the intersection without slowing down.

"Sophie gasped as she saw a truck try to screech to a stop. It was too late. The GMC box truck hit the red Lexus broadside on the passenger side. The car spun 360°.

Vogt was stunned, and it took him a moment to realize what had happened. He got out of the car and ran across both lanes and onto the freeway on ramp.

Fons opened the door; Bully jumped over him and ran after Vogt. Houston and Fons followed. All the cars at the intersection were at a complete stop, so Sophie maneuvered between vehicles to cross the intersection and followed the men.

Bully was gaining on Vogt, who was limping. Vogt had Agent Percy's gun in his right hand. Bully caught up to him and jumped to grab Vogt's arm with the weapon, causing Vogt to stumble. Vogt turned onto his back, but the dog refused to let go of his forearm and crossed over as he turned.

Vogt saw a broken piece of concrete curb and stretched to grab it. He swung it and hit the dog. He heard a yelp, but the dog wouldn't let go of his forearm and was now shaking his arm, causing the skin to rip. The gun was already out of his hand. Vogt swung and hit the dog again. He was ready to hit him a third time, aiming for his head, when Houston grabbed his arm and wrenched it until he let go of the piece of concrete.

Fons came right behind him and aimed his gun at Vogt's face. "Stop fighting, Vogt."

"Get that dog off of me," Vogt yelled in pain.

Police cars pulled up from all directions, and Houston let go of Vogt when a police officer took his arm. Houston gave the release command to Bully so the police officer could cuff Vogt.

Bully let go and limped to the side of the road. Sophie got out of the car and ran to him. She got down and held him, running her hands down his body to see where he was hurt. He yelped when she touched his ribs and again when she felt his hip. She held him close and kept telling him he was a good boy. He licked her hand and her cheek and wagged his tail.

Houston hurried over, "Where is he hurt?"

"I think his ribs and his hip. We need to get Bully help," Sophie had tears in her eyes. Houston checked him out for himself.

Fons ran over to them. "Flight Officer Yeager said he can land on the freeway. The police had put up a roadblock in both directions, so the freeway is clear for him to land. He can airlift Bully to the veterinarian the police use for their dogs."

Houston looked up and gave a thumbs up to Yeager. Then he lifted Bully and carried him. Sophie followed them up the exit ramp to where the chopper was getting ready to land.

"I'll get the address and meet you there," Fons hollered after them.

The Vet was waiting for them when the helicopter landed. He had a rolling gurney, and Houston laid Bully on it. Houston and Sophie followed the gurney inside.

The doctor rolled Bully into an X-ray room. Bully lifted his head when he didn't see Sophie anymore. She moved closer so he could see her.

"Stay, Bully, they are going to take care of you," she kissed his forehead.

Twenty minutes later, the Vet came out and told them that Bully had a cracked rib and a hairline fracture on his hip. The hip would heal in time, same as the rib.

"Is he in pain?" Sophie asked.

"Yes. I'll give Bully a prescription for something similar to Tylenol and an anti-inflammatory for the hip. That should help. I know it will be difficult to keep him still, but he needs six weeks to recover. He will be willing to stay down for at least one or two of those weeks, but after that, he will want to start getting up more. Do your best to keep him from running or staying on his feet too long."

"Can we take him home?" Sophie asked. The Vet looked at her. He could tell she was distressed, and there was no real need to keep him at the clinic, so he said yes.

"I'll give you some painkillers for tonight. Then I want you to take the prescription I will give you to your regular pharmacy. They should carry it."

"Thank you, Doctor," Houston said. "I'll give you my address so you can send the bill."

"No bill for police dogs," he said.

"Bully isn't a police dog," Sophie corrected.

"He was today."

Fons drove to the Vet's in CJ's SUV. He walked in while Houston and Sophie were speaking to the Vet. He stepped over and heard the last bit of information.

"Let me give him a shot of painkiller that should last several hours. I'll bring Bully out in a few minutes," the Vet said.

"How bad is it, Houston?" Fons asked.

"A cracked rib and a hairline fracture on his hip. He's coming home with us."

"Good. ASAC Berry wants us to go in and fill out an after-action report when we can."

"We don't work for him," Houston said.

"He knows that. He wants to talk about Vogt and the operation."

"I get it. There were a lot of moving pieces to this operation."

"Berry told me Vogt shot Dante and his partner in cold blood," Fons said.

"How was he alone with them?"

"Vogt gave away their position to the dealer. The dealer turned and started shooting. Berry had to address it. That's when Vogt went off on his own to find his accomplices."

"Can Berry prove it was murder?" Houston asked.

"No. Not unless Berry gets Vogt to confess," Fons said.

The doctor rolled Bully out to the SUV and Houston lifted him into the back seat. Sophie slid into the backseat from the other door and lifted Bully's head onto her lap.

Houston drove Fons to the Fire Station to pick up Emmett's SUV and headed home.

When they pulled into the driveway at Emmett's, Sophie noticed Lizzy's car parked on the curb. Fons pulled into the driveway beside them.

Lizzy opened the gate pulling a wagon behind her. She had put padding and one of Bully's beds inside. Sophie opened the door and slid out from under Bully's head.

"Lizzy, that's a wonderful idea. Thank you. But how did you know?"

"Channel 6 had part of the chase live on TV. When I saw Bully was hurt, I thought this would help to get him around."

Sophie hugged her friend. "Thank you, Lizzy."

"Are you alright?" Lizzy asked.

"I am, now that we are home," Sophie said.

Carol came out the front door of Emmett's and hugged Sophie.

"Sophie, how bad is Bully hurt?"

"He has a cracked rib and a hairline fracture on his hip. The Vet said it would take six weeks for him to be 100%."

Fons walked up to his wife. She turned and hugged him. "I'm so happy to see you."

"Me too."

Houston slid Bully out of the car and placed him in the wagon. "Thank you for this, Lizzy. It's brilliant."

As the group moved into the cottage. CJ came up carrying Jett and followed them into the cottage. CJ put Jett down and he walked over to Bully in the wagon and patted his head. Bully tried to get up to play, but Sophie came and told him to stay down.

"Kiss owie," Jett said and kissed Bully's forehead. Bully's tail wagged as Jett continued to stroke Bully's head and back. "Gooood boy."

Jett knelt down beside Bully, and half talked, half babbled to him.

Houston pulled CJ over, "CJ, I will take your car to get detailed and fill it up. I'm sorry it got caught up in the chase. We ran it pretty hard."

CJ smiled, "Houston, this isn't my first rodeo with Sophie or Lizzy getting caught up in something like this. Don't worry about it. I'll take it home and take care of it."

"No, that isn't right. I want to give it back to you clean."

CJ put his hand on Houston's shoulder.

"Houston, let me help. You have your hands full here."

Houston looked around, "Alright, CJ, thank you."

Emmett came in with grilled chicken and corn on the cob. "You all have to be hungry. I cooked some without spices for Bully. Is it all right if I feed it to him, Houston?"

"Yes, thank you, Emmett. He deserves it."

As everyone found a place to sit with a plate of food, Carol asked to hear the whole story.

Houston and Fons filled them in.

As the night progressed, the phone continually rang with friends asking how Bully was. Xander and Piper came over, as did Drew, Kato, and China. Lawson came by to examine Bully himself. Sienna and Teresa called and said they would come by the next day to check on him.

TUESDAY

Sophie had insisted Bully be allowed to sleep at the foot of their bed. Houston normally would have objected, but he knew it would make them both feel better. Houston changed Bully's doggie diaper in the morning. He moved him to the wagon to pull him into the kitchen while Sophie showered and dressed.

Houston was hand-feeding Bully when Sophie came out of the bedroom.

"Is he feeling better today, Houston?"

"I gave him one of the painkillers the Vet gave us in his food. He can lift his head, but he yelps when he moves more than that."

"Oh, Houston. He controlled Vogt so he couldn't shoot at you and Fons."

"I know, honey. This isn't the first time he's protected one of us and paid the price for it. He is a good partner."

Sophie knelt down next to Bully and kissed his forehead. He lifted his head to lick her. Houston lifted his bowl of water, so Bully could drink. It was awkward and messy, but he could get some water down.

"Sophie, we need to go to the DEA office. Would Drew, China, and Kato come to babysit Bully?"

"I'll call and ask. We also need to stop at the pharmacy to pick up more painkillers and the anti-inflammatory for Bully."

By the time the kids arrived, Houston had taken his shower and was dressed. He changed Bully's diaper one more time.

China was next to Bully, petting him. His tail was wagging. "Houston, is it ok for us to pull him around in his wagon outside so he can get some sun?"

"Yes. I'm sure he would like that. Thank you all for doing this for us."

"No problem, Houston," Drew said.

Sophie gave them each a hug. I don't know how long we will be gone. But if you have to leave, I think Carol will come to watch him. And there is plenty of food in the refrigerator. Eat whatever you want." Sophie bent down and kissed Bully and stroked his back. "You can pet him; just be careful of his rib and hip. And try to lift his water bowl so he can drink a little. It's messy, so you might do that in the kitchen or outside."

"We'll take good care of him, Sophie," China said.

"I know you will."

Agent Barber met Sophie, Houston, and Fons at the back door of the Federal building and let them in. They met with the squad in the conference room. ASAC Berry stood and spoke.

"I wanted to get everyone together to fill you all in on what was going on behind the scenes yesterday," Berry explained how Houston and Fons had come to him with proof of Agent Vogt's criminal activities. He explained the plan to catch him at the stash house.

"I believe he killed Dante Vita and Gideon Tellez in cold blood. Unfortunately, unless he confesses, he will never be convicted for it. Vogt was cleaning up loose ends, and I believe he was getting ready to run when we arrested him at the stash house."

"How is Agent Percy?" Houston asked.

"He is at home resting. Agent Percy told me he unlocked Vogt's cuff to attach one end to the railing in the van. That's when Vogt tried to grab his gun. They struggled outside the van for it. Vogt got control of the weapon and hit Percy with the butt hard enough to give him a concussion. The hospital kept him overnight for observation and released him this morning."

"How is Bully? He's become a hero to the public." Agent Singh asked.

"He has a cracked rib and a hairline fracture on his hip. The Vet said it will take six weeks to fully heal," Sophie replied.

"I'm getting requests for his name, and the news wants to write an article on him," Berry said.

"I'm sorry. If we want to use Bully when we do undercover work, he can't be on the news," Houston said.

"I'll send any letters from fans to you," Berry said. "You can imagine how hard this has been on this squad. I'm having Vogt brought up for questioning."

"ASAC Berry, I would like to be the one to interrogate him," Sophie said.

"Mrs. Townsend, Vogt has been working with us for years. I don't think he will spill his guts to you."

"ASAC Berry," Fons interrupted, "Sophie has been the lead on one of the most elite task forces in the country. She knows what she is doing."

ASAC Berry looked at her, not quite sure he believed it. "Alright, but I'm going in with you."

"I think he will let down his defenses better if I go in alone. He will underestimate me, like you did, and let his guard down."

ASAC Berry nodded. He told the squad he would send the interview to the screen in the conference room so they could see. "We all have an emotional attachment to this case."

"Does SAC Ramos know what's happened?" Fons asked.

"Yes, it made national news. He's on his way back here."

CHAPTER TWENTY-THREE

Marvin Vogt was brought up in a red jumpsuit with his hands cuffed to a chain around his waist. The color of his jumpsuit an indicator of his high-risk designation.

Sophie, Houston, Fons, and ASAC Berry watched him from the observation room. Sophie waited for twenty minutes before she headed to the interrogation room.

Houston walked her to the interrogation room door and said, "Are you sure you want to do this?"

"Yes," Sophie nodded. Houston kissed her cheek and went back to the observation room. Sophie waited until he was out of sight before she opened the door and walked in.

The guard had taken one cuff off the chain around Vogt's waist. He attached it to a metal bar that ran across the length of the table with stops so the cuff couldn't run the length of the bar. That arm had a thick layer of gauze covering the stitches he needed from the dog bites. Red spots had seeped through the gauze. Then the guard uncuffed his other hand.

Vogt smiled when he saw Sophie walk in. He leaned back in his chair, resting his uncuffed arm over the back of the chair. A move revealing, he thought she was no threat to him. "If it isn't the infamous Miss Star. I was never a fan. I take it Berry is. He's more of a sycophant than I thought if he sent you in here thinking you can get a confession out of me."

Sophie walked over to the chair across from him and sat at a slight angle, putting her hands in her lap. She didn't say a word. She knew he would fill in the dead air.

Or maybe Berry thinks I will spill my guts to a pretty face, is that it. He's an idiot."

"I asked to speak to you, Marvin. This isn't a formal interrogation. Someone else will do that," she looked directly at him. "Is it alright if I call you Marvin?"

"Sure, why not. And why is it you wanted to talk to me?"

"I wanted to know if you were simply A-moral or if you felt there were no real victims in your little enterprise," she paused. "I can understand that. You were stealing drugs and money from drug dealers. Who's the victim, right? And if the men you hired have a mean streak and like to beat up the guys they steal from. Well, that's on them." Vogt smiled but didn't answer. "You knew your squad might discover who you were if they arrested Dante and Gideon. You had to take things into your own hands and do something about it, so you shot them."

"You have the story wrong," Vogt smirked. "They pulled on me. I had no choice but to defend myself,"

"I know you want your team to believe that. But you were so afraid of them getting arrested and turning on you that you forgot to look for cameras."

"Mrs. Townsend…or may I call you Sophie?" Vogt smiled. Sophie shrugged. "Sophie, I'm not stupid. If there were cameras in the diner, they were not operating."

"ASAC Berry had your tech activate them. He wanted the capture of the cartel suppliers memorialized for court."

Berry looked at Houston, "The cameras weren't working."

Houston smiled, "They could have been if we had thought of it."

Marvin Vogt's face went pale, and he moved his arm from the back of the chair and placed it on the metal table. "I don't believe you."

"I saw it myself. Dante and Gideon looked relieved when you found them in the kitchen. They said something to you. You raised your gun, and then they pleaded with you. But you didn't care. Dante might have tried to defend himself; that wasn't clear, but Gideon, you shot in cold blood."

"They were criminals."

"So, you became judge, jury, and executioner. Convenient for you. Now they are dead; they can't tell anyone you were the mastermind."

"That's your version of what happened. Doesn't make it true," Marvin said. "Why are you involved anyway?"

"The two men you hired to steal cocaine from my clients savagely beat them. Putting one of them in the hospital. They weren't drug dealers, Marvin. They were desperate young men trying to keep the home they grew up in from getting repossessed. Yes, they made a desperate choice by buying cocaine from DeLeon, but they were just dumb kids."

"So, they hired you to what? To get the cocaine back?"

"They couldn't pay DeLeon. That's when we came to SAC Ramos to try to make a deal. He didn't want anything to do with us. So, we branched out on our own." Sophie paused and looked at him for a long time, trying to read him. "Did you leak the fact that Derreck Wynne was picked up?"

"I don't even know who he is," Vogt said. "And Dante and Gideon pulled that job on their own. I had nothing to do with it."

"Are you telling me another agent in your squad is betraying his oath?"

"No, I doubt it. My guess is someone in the police department talked too much."

"Marvin, don't you think it would be best to make a deal? If you have any information to trade for leniency, it would be best to play those cards now. Once an AUSA gets involved, they may want to make an example of you."

"I think I will take my chances with a jury," Vogt said.

"You will regret that, when the AUSA shows you shot Dante and Gideon in cold blood," Sophie argued.

"If you saw the video, then you saw Dante lift his gun."

"After he realized, you were going to shoot him. And what about Gideon," Sophie decided to take a chance on her gut feeling. "He dropped his gun."

"He dropped his gun, but how did I know he wasn't trying to trick me and pull out another one," Vogt said.

"That would be a hard sell since his hands were raised."

"Killing them was a public service," Vogt blurted out, then realized what he said.

Sophie leaned back in her chair and crossed her legs to give the illusion she was relaxed. She wanted more from him.

"Why be an agent, Marvin. I don't get it. You're smart. You've been getting away with this for years. Just be a good criminal."

"I worked at this gig for years before I became an agent. But getting the intel of who or where the small shipments or exchanges were happening was few and far between. I didn't want to mess with big cartels, like Luis DeLeon. I was careful to only steal from his rivals. But I was barely making a living from it."

"You stayed away from DeLeon's product until you stole from my clients," Sophie said.

"I told you, Dante and Gideon did that on their own. Dante told me about it. He didn't want me to find out some other way. He said they ran into someone at the bar, and the man had a big mouth and was talking about his cousin who was making big bucks. You know the type. They overheard a conversation on the phone when they were playing cards at that guy's house and jumped on it. They stole the cocaine and left me out of the transaction."

"So, you became a DEA agent to make more money stealing drugs and cash from drug dealers? That is out of character for a thief. The DEA application and training process is a twelve-month commitment."

"I had never been arrested, so my record was clean. I was thinking of the long game. I've been an agent for six years and amassed a fortune. I couldn't have done that, on my own. No promotion I could earn at the DEA could have given me a retirement like that. Plus, I put some bad guys behind bars."

"I hope someone read this guy his rights, ASAC Berry," Fons said.

"Yes, when he was arrested and again when he was processed. He doesn't realize she *is* the interrogator. It's like she said, he thinks her negligible, so he has let down his defenses. He wants her to know how much smarter he is than her, with all her laurels from Quantico. His ego is talking. He isn't processing that everything he says is being recorded to use against him."

"You can see why we wanted you to let Sophie talk to him," Fons said.

"Yes, indeed. I still don't think we can get him on the murder of Dante and Gideon."

"Let's see how this plays out," Houston said.

"You must be a patient man. I don't think I could look at it like that. Did you start out working with Dante and Gideon?" Sophie asked.

"No, I was a one-man show. It was safer that way. No one could turn on me. But it became more difficult when I finally got a spot in the squad."

"How did you recruit Dante and Gideon?"

"A call came in from a dealer. Can you believe it? It was a kid, maybe eighteen. He was a dealer and had been robbed of his product. He called the DEA," Vogt laughed. "How dumb can you be... He gave me a good description of the culprits, and I knew I had seen them around. So, I came back to the office and told the squad about the kid complaining about his drugs being stolen. I wrote it up without the descriptions, and the squad got a good laugh out of it.

"Then I found Dante and Gideon. We made a deal. We started making real money. I had to be careful how I used the information. Eventually, I had my own CIs and rarely used information from other agents. In time, I had to buy a stash house to hold the drugs, until I could get them sold."

"So, basically, you were always a criminal. Just a very smart one."

Vogt smiled. "Yes, I guess that's right."

"You made some big mistakes, Marvin."

"Why don't you enlighten me," Vogt smirked.

"You came across our path for one. The other was murdering your accomplices."

"It will be hard to prove, even if there is a video. Dante realized I was going to kill him, so he raised his gun. Self-defense. Gideon did drop his gun and raise his hands, but I can convince a jury he could have had another weapon."

Houston heard Berry gasp, "Does he know what he just said?"

"No, and it will take him a while to realize it too. You have everything you need for the AUSA to convince Vogt to take a deal. It would be better for the department if you don't take this to trial," Houston said.

"Yeah. I can't believe we were so blindsided. How could we have rooted him out earlier?" Berry asked.

"I don't know that you could have. Sometimes, things get past us. All you can do is be more diligent next time. My guess is Vogt didn't spend much off-time with his squad members. That can be something to watch for," Fons said.

"You're right. Vogt always had a reason not to mingle. I'll keep that in my mind from now on."

Houston went to the interrogation room door, nodded at the guard, and opened it. "Sophie, they have everything they need."

Sophie stood, "Marvin, I would advise you to make a deal with the AUSA. And no matter what happens, you have a God who loves you and will forgive you if you ask Him to.

"He paid the price for your sins on the cross. You may have to go to jail, but you can still be free, here," Sophie touched her heart and head. "I'll make sure a Bible is given to you."

The look on Vogt's face could be interpreted as surprise at Sophie's last statement. Or the realization he hadn't been speaking off the record to a civilian but had just given a full confession to the DEA.

Fons and ASAC Berry were in the hallway. Berry told the guard to take Vogt back to holding.

"I need to speak with you in my office," Berry said.

As they walked into the squad room, the men and women applauded. Sophie looked at Houston, questioning the reason.

"They saw the interrogation, sweetheart," he whispered.

In ASAC Berry's office, they all found a seat. He turned on his computer and waited for it to open. When it did, he went to his email and sent a page to the printer.

"I received this from the DOJ in DC, from AUSA Martin. It's an agreement for a Confidential Informant payment. She wants an itemized list of items confiscated on the operations you were involved with that concerned Agent Marvin Vogt." Berry turned, pulled the page off the printer, and handed it to Houston.

"Thank you. I'd appreciate it if you send in the final figures as soon as possible."

"At 10%, your portion of what has been calculated so far is over four hundred thousand dollars."

"There was that much at Vogt's stash house?" Fons asked.

"No, that was about two million, even though they found three more traps in the house. If the DEA can confiscate all his hidden accounts in and out of the country, it will be a lot more than that. The rest came from the diner operation. There were five bins of fentanyl with a street value estimated at nearly three million."

"Is there anything else you need from us," Houston asked.

ASAC Berry lowered his head. "It's my fault Dante and Gideon are dead. I hadn't planned on Vogt being the one to look for them. But when he gave away our position, I had to deal with the active shooter. I couldn't have two bad actors running loose who could ambush us, so I let him go in my stead."

"Griff, I'm not saying you can't learn something from this, but you can't be blamed for what Vogt did. That's all on him."

"Thanks for saying that. But it might take me some time to let it go."

"Is there anything we can do for you?" Sophie asked.

"No, but SAC Ramos might want to talk to you. We still have not solved Derreck Wynne's murder."

"All right, thanks for the heads up." Houston, Sophie, and Fons stood. ASAC Berry came around the desk and shook hands.

"Thank you. If you ever need help on another case..."

"We'll keep that in mind," Houston said.

Sophie stopped at the door, "Griff would you please see to it that a Bible is given to Vogt."

"Yes, I'll see to it myself."

Fons had brought his own ride. Houston had told him David wanted to speak with Sophie when we were done.

While they were standing by Emmett's SUV, Houston said, "This should close the case on our first client. And if it is all right with my partners, I would like to pay the cost of having the Wynne's home packed up. We can store it until they know where they want to live."

"I'm good with that, Houston. We are getting way more than expected, even after paying off DeLeon. We will consider the Wynne debt to us paid," Sophie said.

"I agree we should consider their debt paid, even though this money was for our work in taking down Vogt. It will help us to start out in the black. I'm happy with that," Fons agreed.

"Our first business meeting. Well done," Houston smiled.

"Do you know why Uncle David wants to talk to me?" Sophie asked.

"He mentioned he needed to close your father's estate. He said when you left, you asked him to manage it."

"I did, but it can't be much. Dad had an insurance policy that was split between Marci and me. The house was supposed to go to Marci because, at the time, he thought Duke and I would be getting married.

"Marci insisted the deed to the house be transferred to me. It was paid off from a mortgage insurance policy Dad bought. I didn't want to sell it. I asked CJ and Lizzy to move in rent free. All I asked was for them to pay the taxes and insurance. My mom left me money, but I used most of it during college.

"You don't know how much you have left?"

"I told Uncle David I didn't want to know how much was in there. I was afraid I would blow it. I used just what I needed to stay alive and eat until I got a job."

They pulled into the law firm parking lot, and Houston walked around and opened the door for her.

Sophie knocked on the door frame of David's office. He was typing on his keyboard.

"Come in. I'll only be a second. I need to finish my thought for this case."

"Take your time, Uncle David." They both sat in front of his desk.

David finished his thought and looked up. "Hello, Sophie, Houston, thanks for coming in. I saw the chase yesterday. Brought back some bad memories. I'm glad you are both all right. Drew said he, China, and Kato are watching Bully until you get home today. How badly was he hurt?"

"He has a cracked rib and a hairline fracture on his hip. The Vet said it would take him six weeks to completely heal. He wants Bully still for two weeks if he'll do it."

"I heard on the news Bully is being hailed a hero. The Channel Six News chopper caught the whole chase on their helicopter's action camera. Including Bully taking down the suspect and holding him.

"Drew, China, and Kato are at your disposal. They have been looking for things to do. They are getting bored."

Sophie laughed, "Thanks for volunteering them. I'll take you up on it."

David opened his bottom drawer and pulled out a file. "Sophie, when you left, you asked me to take care of your estate. It's time I close it out."

"Ok, Uncle David. I understand. There can't be much. Our house was probably Dad's most valuable asset."

"I'm afraid it's much more complicated than that. You took the debit card that accessed the money your mother left you. While in college, you used it to live on and pay for the dorm and classes. Six months after that, you stopped using it. There was still money in there. I left it in there in case you had an emergency and needed it. But you never did."

"I forgot about it, Uncle David. I thought I had used it all. I don't even know what happened to the debit card."

David pulled out a page from the file in front of him. It was a spreadsheet. I didn't want to tie it up, so I put it in a money market that allowed you access. So, the interest was low." He put the paper in front of her. She lifted it so Houston could see it too.

"This can't be right, Uncle David. I remember my dad telling me my inheritance was five hundred thousand dollars. We used it to pay for my years at Parkcrest and for college. No way there is still three hundred fifty thousand dollars in there."

"The interest paid back a little of what you used. But you were very frugal while you were in college."

"Wow, that's nice. It will help us pay for our house construction, Houston. Don't you think?"

"You know I don't like using your money for household expenses."

"Yes, but we agreed to use it for property."

"Thank you, Uncle David. This is a pleasant surprise."

"I'll have the money transferred from the trust to whatever account you give me," he paused and pulled out another spreadsheet. "Now, we need to go over your father's estate." He handed her the sheet of paper that said summary on the top. Sophie's eyes got wide.

"No, Uncle David, this is a mistake. Dad never had this kind of money."

"Let me explain. When we opened this firm and became partners, we added a clause to the agreement. It spoke to what would happen if one or more partners passed on. Our main concern was for the families. We wanted them taken care of. The agreement assigned that partner's profit distribution to the family. Marci said she knew Luke would want you to have it, so she signed off. All these years, your portion has been adding up. I felt obligated to be a good steward and invested much of it in gold, back when it was at a reasonable price. Now it is worth six times what I paid for it. The rest I invested in Liam and Ricky's business. I didn't do that lightly. I reviewed their perspectives and the games they were creating. It was a safe investment. All the families agreed and invested.

"That too has yielded a fat return. You will see what that investment is worth in the second section. Ricky and Liam are always willing to buy back the percentages of the business they sold to us. So anytime you want to do that, Jonathan handles that for them."

"Ok, but what is this," Sophie turned the paper to David and pointed at the third item on the page.

"CJ and Lizzy refused to live in the house without paying something. They knew you didn't want them to, so they settled on paying half of what it would be worth in the rental market. They paid one thousand dollars a month and the taxes and insurance. So that money is there in that third summary."

"It looks like it's not tied up in any investments," Sophie noticed.

"No, I felt I should leave something liquid if you ever needed money fast."

"Uncle David. Thank you for taking care of me like this. But as of the first of this year, I want you to stop putting in Daddy's portion of the profits. We don't need it, and it's been long enough."

"Sophie, we set it up to continue until we sell the business or retire."

"I understand that. But really, Uncle David, Houston, and I are doing well. It should go back to the partners."

"I'll talk to the others about it. You can see we never took your father's name off the sign. That is something we will never change. He was more than our partner. He was a brother to us."

"It is a memorial he would have been very proud of. He loved you all so much," Sophie covered her face and cried. Houston was going to hold her, but David came around the desk and knelt before her. He took her hands from her face and hugged her. She laid her head on his shoulder and cried.

Houston watched as David held her for what seemed like a long time. When she stopped crying, he handed her his handkerchief, got up, and leaned against the desk.

"As much as we loved your father, we love you too. You know that, right, Sophie?" She nodded but couldn't speak.

"You will always be a daughter to us," David said.

"Thank you, Uncle David," Sophie managed to say.

David moved back behind his desk. He let Sophie compose herself some more. Houston took her hand and kissed her palm. She looked at him with red eyes and gave a sad smile.

"Sophie, as you can see, we are dealing with over six million dollars. If you want to keep the investments, all I have to do is transfer the name on them. As for your mother's money and the money for the rental. Like I said, I will need your account to transfer the funds."

"Uncle David, could we have a reading of the Will, of sorts. I want to give Lizzy and CJ back their money, but they will never accept it. So, I would like it to look like it came to her as an inheritance from my mom. She would believe that. My mom treated her like my sister," she turned to Houston. "Is that alright with you, Houston?"

"Sophie, you don't have to ask me. It's your money. You can do with it as you please."

"No, Houston, what I own you own. I don't want it any other way."

"It would be a generous gift. Do it."

"Ok. Uncle David, how much did they pay over the years?"

"It looks like one hundred twenty thousand."

"Let's make it two hundred fifty thousand," Sophie said, excited about it. "How can we do this?"

"Bring her with you the next time you come here. I'll ask you to sign papers concerning your mother's estate in my office. I'll explain money was designated to be left to her. Two hundred fifty thousand dollars, and say the balance goes to you. I won't get into your dad's estate."

"That's perfect, Uncle David. Thank you."

"Can you let me know how you want me to distribute your money and investments? I really do want to close this trust account," David said. Sophie looked at Houston.

"David, can we have until Monday to get back to you? I'll need to look through our accounts and decide how to distribute it," Houston requested.

"Certainly. Monday will be fine."

Sophie got up and went around the desk to hug David again. He stood and held her tight.

"I'll bring back your handkerchief washed and ironed on Monday, Uncle David," Sophie said. David smiled.

Houston picked up the two sheets of paper with the summaries on it.

CHAPTER TWENTY-FOUR

As Houston drove home, he noticed Sophie was being quiet. He reached over and took her hand, kissing her palm. She looked over at him and smiled.

"What is it, sweetheart?" He asked.

"Daddy made sure I was taken care of if anything happened to him."

"Of course, he did. You were his life. It's obvious."

"I know, it's just...he was such a good man. He will never meet his grandbabies. Why did he have to die so young?" Sophie choked up.

"Sophie, we won't know the answer to that until we see our Savior in heaven. But your dad had a weak heart. Death comes early for some people. Even the best of us."

"Houston, you can't die. Our twins need you. Promise me you won't die," Sophie broke down.

Houston pulled into a parking lot and turned off the engine. He reached over and pulled her as close to him as the console would allow.

"Sophie, you made your dad promise, didn't you?"

She nodded and cried on his shoulder. "He broke his promise."

"Sophie. You know that's not true. He had no choice in the matter."

"Promise me."

"I can't make that promise any more than you can. All I can do is tell you I will fight to live to my last breath."

Houston held her until she calmed down.

Houston and Sophie walked into Emmett's backyard. China was walking Bully around the yard in his wagon. It made Sophie smile.

Drew, Kato, Carol, Fons, and Emmett were on the patio drinking iced tea. Emmett was grilling chicken. Houston and Sophie stepped over to the patio and found a seat.

"Hi, you guys look comfortable," Sophie smiled.

"Thought I'd grill for us tonight. Carol has been cooking for days," Emmett said.

That night, Sophie went to bed early. Houston lifted Bully onto the foot of the bed, then went into the kitchen. He spent time looking over the spreadsheets David had given them. Six million dollars was a total surprise for both of them. He felt David did an excellent job investing Sophie's inheritance. He decided to keep those investments intact for now.

The easily accessible portions of the inheritance would pay for part of their home construction. When the house in DC sold, they would have more than enough to finish the home. He had talked it over with her, but she generally liked him to manage it. As long as her money was making money, she was happy.

Houston liked the idea of her sharing her mom's inheritance with Lizzy. From all he could tell, Lizzy had been a sister to her, and sharing was a part of who Sophie was.

Houston was looking at their account on the computer when he heard Sophie crying. He went to the bedroom and cuddled beside her, wrapping his arms around her. He didn't need to ask why she was crying. He knew. Bringing up her father's estate brought his loss back and all the pain with it.

WEDNESDAY

In the morning, Houston felt his furry friend had scooted his way between him and Sophie. He got up, and Bully lifted his head.

"Come on, boy, let's get you changed and fed," Houston whispered. "And don't get used to this. As soon as you are well, you won't be sleeping on this bed anymore."

After Houston changed and fed him, he carried Bully to his bed in the living room by the window to lay in the sun.

Houston was in the shower when Sophie woke up. She went to look for Bully. Houston found her sitting next to him on the floor, stroking him.

"Good morning, sweetheart," Houston said, walking over to her and kissing her on the top of her head. "Are you feeling better this morning?"

"Yes. Houston, I'd like to close this case and pay off DeLeon."

"I know, we will do that as soon as the money comes in from the DOJ."

"No, I mean now. We can take it out of our account. We know it will be replaced. I want done with all of this."

"Alright, we can do that. And we can hire a company to pack up Wynne's house too."

"Yeah, we'll call them and let them know what happened."

"Ok, why don't you take your shower, and I'll make us breakfast."

"Ok. Did you ask Jonathan when the sale will close on the office?"

"Yes, he said it will close next Wednesday."

After breakfast, Houston called Katsumi's house to talk to Felix and Rob and let them know what happened. Katsumi took the phone to Felix, who was outside helping Mr. Jo in the garden. Rob was helping Kim clean the outdoor furniture.

"Mr. Katsumi, you have given those boys some good training," Houston laughed.

"They are good boys, Houston. They just needed direction."

"Here, I'll hand you off to Felix," Houston heard him explain to Felix that he was on the line. Then Felix hollered at Rob to come over.

"Hello, Mr. Townsend, Rob is coming," Houston heard Felix walking somewhere. Then he told Rob, who was on the line.

"Mr. Townsend, you are on speaker. Rob and I are both here."

"Sophie is here with me too. We want to tell you what's happened." Houston started with the conversation with DeLeon that gave them more time to pay. Then went through the two operations. "Because we had an agreement with the DOJ, we will receive an informant's fee. That fee will be enough to pay off DeLeon what you owe him. We will also pay to have your belongings packed and eventually shipped to you."

"Wow, I can't believe you managed all that so fast," Rob said.

"We can have the US Marshals relocate you as soon as a couple of weeks," Houston told them.

"Uh, I think we may want to live here. Izumi said he would train me to become a clothier. I could start by learning how to measure clients and then learn how the suits are made. Maybe I can even be a manager someday," Felix said.

"What about you, Rob?" Sophie asked.

"I'm not sure yet, but I no longer want to go to automotive school. There are so many more options out there. But I like Trenton. I wouldn't mind living here."

"We own an apartment building there. Katsumi can ask the manager if there are any open apartments when it's time for you to decide," Sophie said.

"We can't thank you enough for helping us. Looking back, it's hard to imagine that we made such bad choices. I don't know what would have happened if we hadn't found you guys. We'd likely be dead like Derreck," Felix said. Rob agreed.

"You are both welcome. And you can thank us by not making the same mistakes again," Houston said.

"We promise to pay you when the house sells," Felix said.

"No. The informant's fee will cover that too," Houston said.

"Do you mind putting Katsumi back on the line," Sophie asked.

They heard Felix holler for Mr. Katsumi. Sophie laughed, "Katsumi will correct that behavior."

"Houston, I'm here," Katsumi said, taking the phone.

"It's me, Ojisan. I wanted to say hello. I miss you."

"What's wrong, musume, you are sad."

"I am, a little. I spoke with the attorney who took care of my father's estate. It made me miss him."

"I'm sorry, musume. Such a loss never truly heals. It only lies beneath the surface. I am certain, by the fact that he raised such a wonderful daughter, that your father was an extraordinary man and that he is in heaven. I hope to visit him when I go home to be with my Lord. I will tell him of his most excellent daughter and how she has changed the lives and saved so many young women."

"Ojisan, you give me too much credit, like always."

"No, I saw with my own eyes how you worked to find one missing girl taken by traffickers. And by your sheer determination freed a thousand. That is indeed something to tell your father about."

"You helped me and protected me," Sophie said.

"I was not being altruistic; I was being selfish. I wanted to keep you alive, for my sake."

"No, I don't believe that. But thank you. I miss you, Ojisan. I know you will help those boys make good choices. And hopefully lead them to the One who can change their lives forever."

"That is my goal as well. Remember, musume, you will see your father again. And then, he can keep his promise to never leave you," Katsumi said.

"Thank you, Ojisan, you always make me feel better. Aishi te iya masu."

"Watashi mo anata wa aishi te iya masu, musume."

Fons and Carol came over in the afternoon to check on Bully. Carol sat by him for a while, petting him. "Is your case over now?"

"Mostly. We need to take the money owed to DeLeon over to him. Then we'll hire a company to pack up the brother's home and hire a realtor," Houston said.

"I'd like to get back to DC and haul our belongings back as soon as possible," Fons said. "Carol needs her cooking things."

"I need to hire a realtor to sell the DC house, too," Houston said.

"If I can speak with Luis DeLeon, we can make arrangements to give him the money," Sophie said.

"Did the money come from the informant's fee already?" Fons asked.

"No, we are going to pay it and reimburse ourselves when it comes," Houston said.

"Sounds good to me. I'd like DeLeon off our radar too," Fons said.

"We can call movers, but I don't think we should do anything until we get SAC Ramos off our backs. He wants us to bring in Felix and Rob to question them about the death of their cousin, Derreck," Houston said.

"So, what is the plan for today?" Fons asked.

"I think we need to talk to Ramos before we move forward," Houston said.

"I don't want to go back there," Sophie said.

"Fons and I can handle him."

"DeLeon had invited us to dinner on Friday. I'll see if that invitation is still open. We can pay him then." Sophie went to the end table to pick up her burner phone and dialed Luis' private number.

"Hello, Ms. Star," Luis answered.

"Mr. DeLeon, thank you for answering. I have good news. I have what is owed to you."

"Already?"

"The dominos fell in our direction."

"I saw on the news that two men were killed in a raid by the DEA. If I were a betting man, I'd bet they were the men that took your clients' property."

"You bet right."

"And the corrupt cop helping them. You orchestrated his capture, too?"

"He was in our crosshairs," Sophie said.

"You are more lethal than you look, Ms. Star."

"I was hoping my husband and I could come by and close the account with you on Friday at dinner. If the invitation is still open?" Sophie said.

"Something to look forward to," Luis said, pleased.

"And your interest in my clients will end with that?"

"I am a man of my word, Ms. Star."

"Thank you. Will six o'clock Friday evening work for you?"

"Yes, see you then," Luis said.

Houston's phone rang while Sophie was talking to Luis. He walked out of the cottage before he answered it.

"Hello?"

"Mr. Townsend, I would like you and your wife to be in my office this afternoon," SAC Ramos ordered.

"My partner Alfonso Rodriguez and I will be there. My wife will not."

"I would like to talk to her."

"Is she under arrest?"

"No."

"Then she won't be there."

"Fine, be here by four."

"We can do that," Houston hung up.

ASAC Berry met Houston and Fons at the back door. "Sorry about this. SAC Ramos was furious we took down a corrupt agent and made a huge drug bust when he wasn't around to get the credit."

"I figured," Fons said.

"He is determined to speak with your clients. He still wants them arrested for their part in all this."

"He'd have to prove it first. Maybe we should have Rex here with us," Houston said. "Can you give me a minute to call him?"

Berry stepped away. "I don't know who you're calling," he smiled.

Houston was able to talk to Rex and explain the situation.

"I can be there in ten minutes."

"Thanks, Rex. After what you all went through to expose a corrupt agent in his ranks, Ramos should give you a medal. Not come after our clients."

Ramos was waiting in the conference room for them. Houston introduced Fons. ASAC Berry went into the room with them. Once they were seated, Ramos spoke.

"I told you to stay out of this, Townsend."

"You told me you didn't want our help. So, we didn't help you. We did it ourselves."

"But you didn't do it by yourselves. You included my squad in your little operation. And you made a media sensation out of it. One we now have to clean up."

"What are you talking about?"

"Our squad is on the hot seat for having a crooked agent in our midst."

"How is that on us. It is true. You had a crooked agent in your squad. That's on you."

That did not resonate well with Ramos, who just got more upset. "And that ridiculous informant's fee. It is way out of bounds. I will make sure that agreement is quashed."

"Good luck with that. The AUSA who wrote it up works in the attorney general's office in DC. It was done with his approval. So have at it," Houston said. Ramos stared at Houston for a long time.

"We have a murder we need to solve, Mr. Townsend. And your clients still have to answer for their part in all this."

Rex stepped up to the door. Ramos was not happy to see him.

"What are you doing here?" Ramos asked Rex.

"I understand you have questions for my clients Felix and Rob Wynne."

"Who told you that?" Ramos looked over at his ASAC. Berry raised his hands, indicating he had nothing to do with it.

"Please go on. I'll listen in for now," Rex took the seat next to Houston.

"As I was saying. We still have an unsolved murder, and the Wynne brothers need to answer for buying drugs."

"Buying drugs?" Rex asked.

"They bought cocaine from Luis DeLeon," Ramos blurted out.

"I'm sorry, did I miss something. I was told that the tip you had that they had cocaine in their possession did not pan out. Didn't you execute a search on their home?"

"Yes."

"Did you find any cocaine?"

"No, but they weren't there. They could have taken it with them," Ramos said.

"And you have proof of that? Or is that speculation?"

"I know they bought cocaine. Mr. Townsend came here and told me himself."

"I never said the Wynne brothers were the ones who bought cocaine from Luis DeLeon. I came to you wanting to help you in your case against DeLeon."

"We know it was them," Ramos said.

"You don't know that. And unless you can show some evidence to the contrary, I want you to quit slandering my clients."

"What about Derreck's murder? Felix and Rob Wynne are persons of interest in that case. I need to speak with them."

"SAC Ramos, my clients were not even in town when that murder happened. How could they know anything about it?"

"I need to determine that for myself."

"No, that's what they hired me for. I can answer all your questions," Rex said. "If that doesn't satisfy you, you will need to get a court order to bring them back here. "

"Where are they, Mr. Ford?"

"Out of the state."

"I want them back here answering questions."

"SAC Ramos, I will say this for the last time. I have a pilot who will give testimony that he flew the Wynne brothers out of the state the day before Derreck Wynne was murdered. And I can tell you the brothers have no information about the case."

"I can have them extradited back to our jurisdiction."

Rex laughed aloud, "I'm sorry. I didn't mean to do that. No judge will entertain that with no solid evidence. The court will never put out the expense to have them expedited. You know as well as I do." Rex paused. "Let's settle this once and for all. I want you to stop this harassment of my clients, or I will have a judge order you to," Rex stood. "Now, if that's all, I have another meeting."

Ramos stared at him and finally nodded. "If I find out they knew anything about Dereck Wynne's death and didn't come forward. You will hear from me again."

"You know how to get ahold of me," Rex said, leaving the room.

Ramos turned his attention back to Houston and Fons. "I don't know how, but I have a feeling you had something to do with me being out of town when this went down."

"Really, SAC Ramos. That sounds a little paranoid," Fons said.

"If there is nothing else, we have other things to do today."

Ramos looked at them, "ASAC Berry will see you out."

When they reached the back door, Houston said. "I think you are in for some rough weeks with him."

"Yeah, but what we did was good for the department. I'll be fine."

"I'm glad we could work on this with you, Griff," Houston extended his hand. Griff shook it.

"I learned a lot seeing how you work. I hope I can use what I learned someday," Berry said, shaking Fons' hand.

THURSDAY

Sophie called and arranged to have a mover come over and pack up the Wynne home on Friday. The company had a storage facility that could hold the items until they called to have them shipped.

Carol, Lizzy, and Sophie headed to the house to take pictures of everything. Sophie had read it was the best way to ensure things didn't disappear. And if things were broken, they could send the photos to the insurance company.

"I'll have a picture of all the items in each room posted on the doors. Thanks for coming with me. The broker should be here soon. Emmett said when he needed a broker, he always used her."

"Happy to come. I was sick of looking up recipes. And I've already mapped out the route Houston and Fons will travel from DC, thanks to MapQuest," Carol said.

"That has to be at least 1500 miles. How many days will it take for them to get here?" Lizzy asked.

"It isn't just the travel time. They need to rent a U-Haul and load it. Then Houston has to meet with a broker."

"You figure a week?" Sophie asked.

"Regarding time on the road, they can get here in two to three days if they want to. The other stuff, I don't know," Carol said.

A knock came on the door. Sophie opened it and invited the broker in.

"Mrs. Townsend, I presume? My name is Tessa Kipling."

"Please come in. I need to explain up front I do not own this property. Attorney Rex Ford has the power of attorney, but I will be working with you. Once the owners approve your appraisal, the attorney will sign the broker's contract."

"I have worked with similar situations. I understand you will have the furniture out of here tomorrow?"

"Yes. I know some brokers prefer having furniture in a home to make it appealing to clients. But I don't think you will want it in this case," Sophie said.

"Very astute, Mrs. Townsend. No offense to the owners but it is evident they never updated the home."

"Please call me Sophie. And this is Carol Rodriguez and Lizzy Young."

"A pleasure to meet you. May I look around and take measurements."

"Yes, feel free. A car is in the garage, but we will have that removed too."

"If you don't mind me making an observation. It looks like the people who lived here literally dropped what they were doing and took off," Tessa said.

"It does appear that way, doesn't it," Sophie said, not giving any details."

CHAPTER TWENTY-FIVE

Sophie, Carol, and Lizzy cleaned out the refrigerator and dumped the garbage cans, and freezer. Then Carol took the garbage outside and put the can on the street for pickup.

"How much do you think this is worth, Lizzy?"

"If it were in town, it would be worth four hundred thousand or more. I'd say it's seventeen hundred square feet. That's a comfortable size. And with only a few modifications, the floor plan can be modernized."

"So, you think it will go for less outside the city limits?" Carol asked.

"Yes, maybe three hundred thousand if they're lucky."

"In DC, a house like this would cost double that outside the city limits and probability triple that in the city."

Tessa Kipling walked back into the kitchen. "When everything is out of the house. You will have the carpets shampooed and the place professionally cleaned?'

"Yes," Sophie said.

"I have all the measurements and checked the recent sales in the neighborhood before I came. It does have a good floor plan, and the rooms are all good-sized. There are only a few homes for sale in this area, and the neighbors keep up their homes."

"I know you have to do more homework, but can you estimate what it might sell for?" Sophie asked.

"Every seller asks me that," she chuckled. "You can't hold me to it. But I can see this going between three hundred and three hundred fifty thousand in this neighborhood. That is, after it's all cleaned up. It does appear the owners kept up the yard."

"That sounds good. Get back to me as soon as possible. You have my number?"

"Yes, from when you called," Tessa handed each lady a business card and left.

"You were right on, Lizzy."

"I live with an architect. He is constantly checking the values of homes in Austin."

They locked up and decided to go to Sienna's bakery for a snack before she closed.

Houston noticed Emmett's SUV was gone when they pulled in.

"I thought the ladies would be back by now," Houston said.

"Carol texted me saying they were headed to Sienna's to get a snack before the bakery closed."

"Of course," Houston chuckled. "Where else."

Houston paid Drew, China, and Kato for babysitting Bully.

"Houston, you don't need to pay us. We like taking care of Bully. He's a hero," Drew said.

"I know you don't expect to be paid. But I won't feel like I can call on you again if I don't do right by you."

China looked at the others, "Thank you, Houston."

"Would you be free Friday night?"

"Could we take him to my house?" Drew asked. "Ricky is bringing us another game to try out."

"Sure, if it's all right with your folks."

"Thanks, Uncle Houston," Kato said. Kato and Teresa felt they should call him uncle since they weren't related like China and Drew were to Sophie, who was more of a sister to them.

Houston pulled the wagon inside and changed Bully's diaper. He fed him and lifted his bowl of water so he could drink. Then he lifted Bully out of the wagon and onto his bed in the living room. He was asleep in minutes.

Fons and Houston sat at the table, looking over the map Carol had printed, showing the fastest way back to Austin.

"Houston, didn't you tell me Felix and Rob want to stay in Trenton?"

"Yes."

"One of the issues is getting them their belongings without a paper trail. Right?"

"Right."

"When Carol checked on the cost of a U-Haul, she found it cost more to rent a truck one way. What if the movers load Felix's belongings into a U-Haul, and we drive it up there instead of flying?"

"Not a bad idea. And Emmett has a flatbed. We can ask if we can use it. That way, we could haul his Mustang too. No way anyone would ever find out where their furnishings ended up."

"If we have a flatbed, I could haul my SUV here. That would be huge for Carol and me, Houston."

"We can call them and make sure that is what they want. They will have to find a large storage area to hold it all," Houston said.

When Sophie and Carol got home, they discussed taking the brothers' belongings to them.

"That would work out perfectly, and they did say they would like to stay there. We wouldn't have to involve the US Marshals," Sophie said.

"Yes, and the U-Haul is cheaper if you bring it back," Carol said.

"We need to call Trenton to make sure Felix and Rob want their stuff up there. If so, we need to call the movers to let them know there is a change of plan. Did you see the broker?" Houston asked.

"Yes. The company takes a 6% commission. I gave the broker Rex's number to get the contract signed. But Rex said he wants confirmation by email that the brothers want to accept her appraisal."

"Well, let's call them and finish this," Houston said. Sophie dialed Katsumi's landline.

"Hello?"

"It's me, Ojisan. I hope you and the family are well."

"Yes, musume. As well as we can be with you so far away."

"May we speak to Felix and Rob, please."

"I will get them for you. They are on the back porch barbequing. They wanted to try their hand at it. Mr. Jo, Yon Moon, and I are the king's food tasters," he chuckled.

Sophie laughed. "Ojisan, I do not think they intend to poison you."

"Maybe not on purpose," Katsumi teased. "Here they are. Felix, musume wishes to speak with you."

"Mrs. Townsend?"

"Yes, Felix, I need to speak with you and your brother. Can you ask Katsumi to watch the grill for you?"

"Sure," he handed Katsumi the tongs and told Rob to come inside. "We are both here now."

"You are on speaker phone with Houston, Fons, and Carol. We have information for you."

"Good news, I hope," Rob said.

"We are having your household items packed up tomorrow. Fons and Houston will be coming up that way and want to know if you want them to bring your things up with them. Do you know where you want to live?"

"Yes, Rob and I have talked about it. We love it here, and we have been going to church. We turned our lives over to Jesus and want to stay in this church."

"Felix, Rob, that is the best news we could have ever hoped for," Sophie said.

"I've never been around people who live what they say they believe. And they aren't boring," Rob chuckled.

"Life here is happy and moving forward all the time. We want that. So yes, we would appreciate it if you could bring our things up. What about my Mustang?" Felix asked.

"Fons and I are going to haul it on a flatbed behind the U-Haul," Houston said.

"That's awesome. I will have to find a shed to rent. Then we will have to find a place to live."

"Did you ask Katsumi to call our apartment manager? If there is an open apartment, you can rent it until your house sells."

"I will miss living here with Katsumi, but we can't impose on him forever. Did the broker lady say how much she thinks we can get for the property?"

"Yes, she called me back this afternoon. After more research, she appraised it for three hundred seventy-five thousand dollars." The line went silent, but Sophie could hear them breathing. "Felix?"

"We're here. We had no idea. We will have enough to take our time to decide what we want to do with our lives. Thank you."

"The broker takes 6%, and you will have to pay your attorney. Rex wants you to email him with your approval of the appraisal price. Then he will sign the contract with the broker as a power of attorney."

"Do you think it is a fair price, Mrs. Townsend?"

"I do."

"Ok, then I'll email him tonight. I have no idea where we would be right now without your help," Rob got choked up.

"Rob, the Lord had mercy on me when I was in the same state you were. He is no respecter of persons. Now, it is up to you to keep the fire inside burning."

"Fons and I will leave here on Saturday. We plan on being there on Monday. See you then," Houston said.

"You better go retrieve the tongs from Katsumi, or he won't relinquish them," Sophie chuckled.

They said goodbye, and Sophie asked Felix to say goodbye to Katsumi, Mr. Jo, and Yon Moon for them.

"Felix and Rob turning their lives over to Jesus makes this whole ordeal worthwhile," Sophie said.

"A life snatched out of the fires of hell. Nothing in the world is more important than that," Fons agreed.

FRIDAY

Sophie called the moving company to say there was a change of plans and the household items would be loaded into a U-Haul.

Houston and Fons hooked Emmett's flatbed to Houston's SUV by 7 am. Then Houston dropped Fons off at the U-Haul. Fons picked up the truck, and they met at the Wynne home. Houston unlocked the door minutes before the movers came to pack the house. They situated the truck to make it easy for the men to load. Fons stayed outside to help supervise the loading. Houston went inside to make sure no damage was done.

It took eight hours for the five-man crew to have the house packed and loaded into the U-Haul. Houston called the office and paid the bill with the business debit card.

When the truck was locked, Fons moved it so Houston could back up the flatbed. They unhooked the flatbed from Houston's SUV. Then, he moved his vehicle so that they could attach it to the back of the U-Haul. They found the car keys where Felix said they would be. Fons pulled out the two heavy duty equipment loading ramps on the flatbed to load the Mustang. They went back through the house, the shed in the back, and the garage to ensure nothing was left behind. Then, they secured the property.

"Fons, are you sure you want me to take the DeLeon money out of our business account?"

"Yes. I'm sure the money from the DOJ will come before we need it for the remodel," Fons said.

"If it doesn't, I'll replace it. If you take the truck home, I'll stop and get the cash and drop these house keys off at the law firm."

Houston arrived home in time to shower and change for dinner at Luis DeLeon's compound. Fons was waiting for him when he got out of the shower.

"Sophie's almost ready, Fons."

"Do you want me to take Bully to Emmett's? Carol will be happy to watch him," Fons asked.

"No, Drew, China, and Kato are coming. They are going to pull him in his wagon to David's house. Ricky is bringing over a new game for them to evaluate."

"Out of curiosity, I played one of their games on Emmett's unit. The way they made the action 3D without wearing goggles gives playing games a new meaning. No wonder they are making a fortune," Fons said.

"That's what I've been told. When things calm down, I'd like to try it myself."

Sophie came out. She wore the pink blush maxi dress she had purchased before they went to Hollywood. She wore the gold hoops she liked and a solitary diamond around her neck.

"You look beautiful, darling," Houston kissed her. He noticed she was wearing two-inch heels and not her usual three-inch ones.

The door was open. Drew, China, and Kato came in to pick up Bully. Houston lifted him to the wagon. Then, he brought over his water bowl so he could take a drink before they left.

"Will you make sure he drinks more water?"

"Sure, Houston. We'll take good care of him," Drew said.

"I know you will."

Sophie went over to Bully and loved on him. Bully's tail wagged, and he lifted his head and tried to lift his body but yelped from the pain. Sophie stroked him and told him to stay down.

Fons pulled up to the monitor and pushed the intercom button.

"Yes," came a face and a voice on the monitor.

"Ms. Star and Mr. Townsend here to see Mr. DeLeon."

The gate started to open. Sophie noticed there were double the number of guards on the compound. Fons drove up to the same parking spot as their last visit. Luis DeLeon opened the door and stepped out. Tacito wasn't with him. A guard Sophie didn't recognize stood by Luis.

Fons opened the door for Houston, then walked around and opened the door for Sophie. They stepped over to where Luis was waiting for them. Houston extended his hand and introduced himself. Luis reciprocated.

"Mr. Townsend, it is a pleasure to meet you," Luis said. Houston wasn't convinced he meant it.

"Thank you, Mr. DeLeon, for having us over and letting us settle this account. Please call me Houston."

"Ms. Star," Luis said, turning to her. Sophie extended her hand. Luis kissed it.

"I thought we were past the formalities, Mr. DeLeon."

"Yes, of course, Sophie, please come in." As they walked in, the guard asked to take Houston and Fons' weapons.

Sophie stopped. "Luis, my husband, and bodyguard will not give up their weapons. We mean you no harm, but as you have men here to protect you, they are here to protect me."

"Of course," Luis waved the guard away. "Please come into the dining room."

"Oh, I was hoping we could sit in that beautiful nook you have in the kitchen," Sophie said.

"It is a beautiful spot. I just wanted to impress you and your husband. However, if you prefer, we can eat there."

"Thank you," Sophie said as they walked into the large kitchen and sat at the table."

Dulce was busy doing the final preparations for the dinner. A man dressed as a waiter came over and asked what they would like to drink. He read off the options.

"I would like iced tea; if I'm not mistaken, my wife would like lemonade," Houston said. Sophie nodded.

Luis recognized that Houston was making sure he knew that Sophie was married. He smiled to himself. With such a beautiful wife, a man has to set boundaries around other men.

"Where is Tacito," Sophie asked. Fons was standing at the kitchen door with Luis' guard. Tacito had yet to make an appearance.

"I mentioned at your last visit that we had to return to Mexico to take care of some business. Tacito was injured on that trip. A doctor cared for his injuries, and now a nurse is tending to him."

"I'm sorry to hear that, Luis. What happened in Coahuila?" Sophie asked. Luis hesitated while the waiter brought the drinks.

"Ten years ago, three cartels in and around Coahuila were vying for dominance. There was a lot of violence between the cartels trying to take what the others had.

"The three jefes got together like your mafia bosses did years ago. We set boundaries. It worked. Everyone made money, and the death count dropped, keeping the Federales out of our state.

"Since I moved here, one of the jefes of the three cartels died. The son decided to try to make a move on my territory. I went over there to try to stop the attacks. That's when I found out his father made him head of the cartel before he died. He was not interested in keeping the peace."

"So now you are at war?" Houston asked.

"Yes, and Tacito was a casualty, along with two of our warehouses that were burned down. I brought him here so he could get the best care. But I will have to return to defend my business."

"I'm sorry to hear that. I'm glad I no longer have to worry about such things. It seemed someone was always trying to take what I worked for. Like there wasn't enough money to go around.

"It makes you wonder how much money one person can spend. When is it enough?" Sophie asked. Luis looked at her like he had a revelation.

"That is a good question. Is that what you asked yourself when you were arrested?" Luis asked.

"Yes. And Houston and I agreed. We had more than enough. But we still wanted to work. That is how we became fixers. It's much safer, and we enjoy it," she turned to Houston. "Don't we, love?"

"I didn't think it would be quite this...exciting. But not being hunted down gives us a chance to live our lives," Houston said.

The waiter brought a plate of homemade flour tortillas, a bowl of Pico De Gallo, and a jar of homemade hot sauce. He returned with a platter of Spanish rice, a sizzling plate of grilled onions, green peppers, and skirt steak that was cut into slices and seasoned. It smelled wonderful.

"Please serve yourselves," Luis offered.

Sophie took a homemade flour tortilla from the plate in the center of the table and set it on her plate. Houston lifted the platter of meat for her, and she used the spoon to take meat, onions, and peppers. Then Houston did the same for his plate and set the platter down.

Sophie spiced up her fajita with the Pico de Gallo and a dab of hot sauce. Before she took a bite, she scooped rice onto her plate. She and Houston lowered their heads for a moment and said grace silently. Luis noticed but said nothing.

"Luis, this food looks and smells amazing."

"I'm so glad to see a woman not afraid to eat."

They ate without speaking for a while, then Luis asked. "You said you already have the money Felix Wynne owes me. It seems you did not need the extension you asked for."

"We had a lead on one of the men that stole from our clients. We snooped around and found his stash house. We were able to recover what we needed. Unfortunately, the man's boss was not happy about it. We had to take measures to ensure no one would come after us," Houston said.

"The news showed the chase on TV. The police eventually showed up, but a dog apprehended the man with a gun. I could have sworn that was your guard dog, Sophie," Luis said.

"Yes, he is also recuperating from his injuries," Sophie said.

"And the men who stole from your client?"

"I'm afraid they didn't make it."

"I see."

"We had nothing in that part. The man they worked for shot them. He didn't want to leave loose ends," Houston said.

"This is a dangerous business," Luis agreed. "I have become a little tired of it myself. The constant warring among the cartels. The police are not a concern in Mexico as long as the Federales don't get involved. We pay a hefty fee to the local police, but they do have to occasionally make arrests to maintain some sort of posture. And the price seems to go up every year."

"The cost of doing business, I suppose," Houston said.

"I'm thinking of moving my stash from Coahuila to here. I'm returning next week to see if we can settle things down. I might have to live there for a while. I will miss this place."

"You think you will be gone for a long time then?" Sophie asked.

"Maybe. Unless, like you, I decide enough is enough. If that is the case, I may need your services."

"I'm not sure a fixer can solve your problems," Houston said. "But if you need us, we will do what we can."

"Thank you."

They finished eating and then went to the back patio. Dulce sent out Flan for dessert, and they watched the sunset.

Before they left, Houston paid Luis the $125K owed him. They shook on it, signifying the transaction was complete, and said goodbye.

CHAPTER TWENTY-SIX

As they pulled out of the compound, Houston said, "That's interesting. It sounded to me he might be looking to get out of the business."

"Time will only tell. But I don't know what we could do unless he wants to turn over evidence on the cartels to get a deal with the DEA. And I can't see that," Sophie said.

"He wouldn't really have to do anything. As far as we know, he has no wants or warrants in the US," Houston said.

Fons drove them home. Houston went to pick up Bully. The kids offered to walk him home, but Houston said it was dark outside, and he'd come pick him up.

SATURDAY

Sophie and Carol watched as the men drove off with the U-Haul towing the flatbed holding the Mustang at 6 am. Carol had loaded them up with food in ice chests and a bag of snacks.

Sophie went back to bed. Houston had changed Bully and lifted him into the wagon so Sophie could take care of him. Emmett said he would come over to lift Bully in and out of the wagon.

After feeding Bully, including a pain pill, in his late breakfast, Sophie made sure he had plenty to drink. Then, she went to take her shower and get dressed.

Sophie wore lightweight blue cropped pants and a sleeveless cotton top. Though it rained the night before, it was already in the 90s today. She planned on walking Bully over to Lizzy's, so he could spend time with Jett. Before she left, she noticed a missed call from SAC Ramos. Against her better judgment, she returned his call.

"Mrs. Townsend, thank you for returning my call. We have two bags of mail here from children for Bully. I would appreciate it if you would come to pick them up."

"Um. Mail for Bully?"

"Yes. Haven't you been watching the news? The video of Bully taking down Agent Vogt has been repeated daily since the takedown. And I heard it has gone viral online too."

"I had no idea. Yes, I'll come by today."

"Thank you. And the DEA has gotten good press for the operation. My ASAC says that most of the credit for its success goes to you, your husband, and your partner."

"I appreciate you recognizing that. I know you weren't happy about our involvement."

"Well, it turned out alright...this time."

They said goodbye and hung up. Sophie walked Bully over to Lizzy's after checking on Carol. She was preparing for her vlog, using Emmett's kitchen.

When Bully saw where they were headed, he started wagging his tail and trying to get up. Sophie patted him and told him to stay.

Sophie knocked on the door. Lizzy opened it and called for CJ to lift Bully from the wagon to bring him into the house.

Jett sat by Bully, patting him, and babbling on about something. Bully was thumping his tail, enjoying the conversation. Coco even lay next to him.

"I made lunch for us," Lizzy said.

"That sounds wonderful, but SAC Ramos from the DEA asked me to come by and pick up some mail that has come for Bully."

"Bully?"

"Yes. The video went viral on social media, and kids are sending Bully letters.

CJ offered to watch Bully so Lizzy could go with Sophie to pick up the mail.

Sophie dialed ASAC Berry at the federal building and asked him to let them in the back door.

"Wait there," Berry said. "I'll bring the bags to you and put them in your car."

"Thanks, Griff."

A few minutes later, the door opened, and Griff loaded the two bags of mail into the back of Lizzy's SUV.

"I'm sure there will be more coming. We are still getting calls from the local news channels wanting us to let Bully come on TV. They think he is a police dog."

"I'm sorry, but we can't put him out there. Like we said, if we go undercover, Bully being recognized as a police dog could get us killed."

"I understand."

"How is SAC Ramos treating you? I know he was pretty upset he missed the action," Sophie asked.

"He may have missed the action but has no problem taking credit for it. He's been interviewed several times. He never mentioned he wasn't in town during the operation," Griff laughed.

"Does that bother you?"

"Not really. If Ramos had been here, there is no way he would have taken your lead. The whole thing could have ended badly."

"Thanks for trusting us."

"When I learned of your other operations at Quantico, I always hoped I could be involved in one. Though this one was small potatoes compared to the others."

"I hope we can work together again," Sophie closed the back of the SUV. They said goodbye and headed back to Lizzy's.

"How many letters do you think are in there?" Sophie asked.

"I don't know. Maybe hundreds."

Sophie and Lizzy dropped the bags of mail in the living room. Lizzy cleared off the coffee table and Sophie opened one of the bags and dumped it on the coffee table. The letters filled the coffee table and spilled over onto the floor.

"We are going to need help," Sophie said.

"Let's call Drew, China, and Kato. Maybe they will help," Lizzy suggested.

Even with their help, they barely touched the pile from the first bag a half hour later. They heard a honk.

"Lizzy, that's Xander. We are meeting the guys at the YMCA to play basketball. I'll be back in a few hours, sweetheart."

"Ok, honey," Lizzy said as CJ came over and kissed her cheek.

"Drew, Kato, are you sure you don't want to come?"

"Thanks, CJ, but we want to help with these letters."

"Alright," CJ said as he headed out the door.

"Sophie, what are we going to do with all this. We can't just ignore the kids that wrote them," China said.

"We can't let Bully be a celebrity. It's too dangerous for us and him," Sophie said.

"I get it, but we have to respond," Drew said.

"How?"

"Letters would take too long. We could make a generic postcard, with..."

"It can't be his picture, China," Sophie said.

"How about his paw print. And he could have a cool saying on it, like... 'Be kind to someone today'. Something like that."

"Postcards do cost less to mail. Then, after we answer all of these letters, we can see if Liam will make Bully a website. That way, it would be much quicker and easier to respond," Lizzy suggested.

"That's brilliant," China said. "And Drew, Kato, and I could maintain it. We could give updates on how and what Bully is doing in generic terms. Like, he is working with his partners today. Or he is chasing lizards."

"I like it, but we can't give his real name."

"We can come up with a pseudonym," Lizzy said.

"Like what?" China asked.

"Hero dog," Kato suggested.

"Super dog," Drew laughed.

"What about gentle warrior?" China said.

"I like that," Sophie said, and the others agreed.

"Will you guys take the lead on the website? But you can't launch it until we get approval from Houston."

"Sure, that will be awesome. Do you want us to design a postcard to answer all these letters?" Drew asked.

"Yes, and we can put the website address on the postcard, so they won't write any more letters."

After a couple of hours of reading letters, Lizzy took a break to feed Jett and put him down for a nap. Then brought out the lunch she had made for her and Sophie. They had gotten caught up reading the letters, they forgot to eat. Lizzy brought out enough for everyone. The ate in the living rooms so they could continue to read letters. Sophie took a drink from her glass of Dr. Pepper. When China got her attention.

"Sophie, listen to this. 'Dear owner of the hero dog on TV. My son is in the Dell Children's Medical Center and talks about your dog constantly. He wrote you a letter, enclosed. I wanted to know if your dog could come to see my son. He is extremely ill, and it would mean a lot to him. Mrs. Tanni Herrmann." China paused while she put that page down and read the letter from the little boy. "Dear hero dog, I love you. I saw how brave you are. Even when that bad man hit you. I hope you are not hurt too bad. I wish I could see you. You are my hero. I am not brave like you. I'm sick, and I see my mom crying. I think she doesn't believe I will get better. I pray for you every day. Fabian."

"Oh, that is heartbreaking," Lizzy said. Sophie wiped away a tear.

"Bully isn't well enough to go to the hospital. But even if he was, people would take pictures, and someone would give it to the press."

"Maybe he is in a private room, Sophie. It's worth a try," China said.

"China, Bully can't even walk. How could we take him?" Sophie asked. No one answered.

"Why don't we call and find out how sick he is. You said Bully should be able to walk a short distance in a week," Lizzy said.

By the time they finished the first bag, there were three more similar letters. Not quite as heart-wrenching, but still.

They called it a night, and Sophie said she would call the mother tomorrow after church.

CJ packed Bully to his car and put the wagon in the back. It was dark, and he didn't want her walking home.

SUNDAY

Houston called late Saturday night. He said they should be in Trenton on Monday afternoon. Sophie told him about the letters and the little boy who was sick. He agreed that she should find out how urgent the matter was and then decide. If necessary, she could ask Emmett to help her get Bully inside with the wagon and make sure no one took pictures.

After church, Emmett said he would take care of Bully so Sophie could go to Aileen's to work on the wedding. Sophie called Mrs. Herrmann at the hospital before she went inside, asking Dell Children's Medical Center for the Fabian Herrmann room.

"Hello?"

"Mrs. Herrmann?"

"Yes,"

"My name is Sophie Townsend. You sent a letter to me. Or I should say to my dog. I wanted to know how your son is doing."

"Oh, yes, Mrs. Townsend. I didn't think anyone would respond. Let me leave the room. Hold on, please," she said. Sophie heard her tell her son she would be right back, then heard a door close.

"Fabian has heart disease. We brought him to Austin because of Doctor Cornett. The doctor has had great success with his device for children with a certain heart disease. But when he examined Fabian, he said he wasn't a candidate. The Doctor said he might be able to adjust the device to help my son. The hang-up is that the FDA must approve any changes made to the device. He also said he wasn't certain it would help."

"What about 'The Right to Try' legislation?"

"I've applied, but I haven't gotten a waiver yet. The application had to be sent to the FDA for their approval."

"Red tape."

"Yes."

"I'm calling because I would love to bring my dog to see your son, but he was injured in the incident that was played on the news. He can't walk right now. In a week, he may be well enough to try."

"Thank you. The doctors are giving him...," Tanni choked up. When she composed herself, she said, "They have tried everything they can and don't expect him to improve."

"The best I could do is bring my dog in a wagon. But that won't be much fun for Fabian. My dog is usually very affectionate with children, and I would like Fabian to see him as that."

"Mrs. Townsend, I understand."

"If I do bring him up, no one can take pictures. I can't have his face on the news or have the press pick it up. He works undercover with us. His celebrity could put us in danger."

"Can I tell Fabian you will bring him when he is better?"

"Yes, and I will make some calls and see if we can push your application to the front of the pile."

"You can do that?"

"I have no idea, but I can try."

"Thank you, Mrs. Townsend."

"I'll let you know what I find out."

Everyone was working on the tissue paper flowers to be attached to the back of the chairs at the reception. Sophie approached Aileen, who was talking with Carmen and Ruby about the reception.

"May I speak with you for a moment, Aunt Aileen?"

"Of course, dear, let's move away from the chatter. How is Bully?"

"He is still in pain, but I do see improvement. Aunt Aileen, I need your help with a dire situation. Your connection to the White House may make the difference."

"Oh, what is it, Sophie?"

Sophie explained the situation with the little boy at Dell Children's Medical Center. Aileen sat in the wicker chair on the patio. Sophie did the same.

"What is it you think I can do?"

"'The Right to Try' legislation should have allowed her to get the treatment. But if Lawson adjusts the device in any way, the FDA must sign off on it. It's being held up somewhere. It would be awful if the approval came too late."

"Oh, yes, that would be dreadful."

"Can you see if the First Lady will partner with you to push this through?"

"You know how highly Emma thinks of you. I'm sure she would help," Aileen said. "I'll be heading back to DC tomorrow. I'll talk to her then."

Sophie hugged Aileen. "Thank you, Aunt Aileen."

MONDAY

Sophie called Emmet. He came over and carried Bully off her bed and laid him on his dog bed in the living room. Sophie changed his diaper and hand fed Bully and gave him water. Then she called Lawson.

"Hello, Sophie."

"Hi, Lawson. Do you remember examining a boy named Fabian Herrmann at Dell Children's Hospital?"

"Yes, his parents brought him here from Denver, Colorado, hoping my device would work on him."

"Are you saying it won't?" Sophie was surprised.

"No, I'm not saying it won't, but the problem with his heart isn't what my device was built to correct. Liam designed a program that allows me to take a picture of a heart off a cardiac MRI and study it. I've been working on Fabian's heart issue. I believe I have figured out a way to adapt the device to fix what's wrong with it. But as you know, the FDA must approve any deviation from the original use or design."

"His mother applied for 'The Right to Try' legislation."

"I know, Sophie, but the FDA still has to look it over, and we haven't heard back yet."

"Mukhtar Hijazi only had to apply for 'The Right to Try' legislation to get his surgery."

"I know, but I had already adapted my original design to adults. And the new design was in the FDA's system. They had researched it. It just had yet to get to the approval stage. This is different. I'm redesigning it again to fit this one patient. The FDA hasn't seen it or been informed of the new use."

"I spoke with Aunt Aileen yesterday. I asked her to partner up with the First Lady and try to get 'The Right to Try' application off the pile and signed."

"Oh. That's great. If she can do that. I will take Fabian into surgery right away. But Sophie, you have to understand I cannot guarantee the results. My apparatus was not created for his specific problem."

"I know, Lawson, but better you try than let him waste away."

"True. Houston and Fons didn't play ball with us yesterday."

"Yeah, they are driving up to DC to pick up Fons and Carol's furnishings and driving them back."

"Oh, that's a long trip. How is Bully doing?"

"Improving a little at a time. I don't suppose there is any way to speed up his recovery?" Sophie asked.

"Afraid not. Only time."

"Thanks, Lawson. I'll see you soon."

Houston called at 1 pm and told her they were in Trenton. Izumi had a large shed behind his manufacturing plant that he wasn't using. He said Felix could use it until they decided what they wanted to sell and what they wanted to keep.

"Sophie, you should have seen Felix's eyes light up when he saw his Mustang. I get it. It's one of those cars where the older it is, the more you like it. It's not a classic, but it is close in its design."

"I'm glad you made it there in good time. How was the drive?"

"We were able to talk a lot about the company. What we want to do with it and our hopes it will be successful. Fons and I have always found a ton of things to talk about. It made the trip go faster. We only stayed in a hotel once. The traffic was bad, and we figured, why fight it."

"I miss you, Houston."

"Me too. I don't like being away from you for this long. We'll stay the night here with family and head to DC in the morning. Fons wants to take his SUV back with us. It will save them from selling it and buying a new one in Austin. I know he is worried about money. We plan to put our nose to the grindstone when we get back. We need to get those 'bread and butter' clients Manny talks about. We can start giving out paychecks once we cover the office expenses."

"Can we use some of the money from the confidential informants fee for payroll?"

"There won't be much left. We already paid DeLeon, and the movers. We will have to pay for the building's utilities, insurance, and rent. And we aren't sure yet what is coming in or how much we might need to do the remodel."

"When it comes in, if there is enough, I want Fons to get paid first. We can hold off on the rent, we don't owe a bank. I don't need the money. And when we do get cases, I want him, and you paid before me."

"I agree, sweetheart, but I don't think he will let us do that. He has his pride."

Sophie told him about the phone call to the sick boy's mother and about talking to Aileen. Then, they ended the call.

Uncle Manny knocked on the cottage door later that afternoon.

"Uncle Manny, how are you? Come in," she hugged him.

"Hello, Sophie. China called and asked if I would take a print of Bully's paw. They are all hyped up about answering the fan mail Bully has received."

"Yeah, the news replayed that scene where Bully took down Agent Vogt, over and over. They saw him injured and taken away in a helicopter. I guess it has stirred their imagination. It's gone viral online."

"They said they want to answer all the letters with a postcard and then set up a website for him," Manny smiled.

"I told them they can't put a picture of him out there or use his real name. He could be recognized if we went undercover."

"Yes, I figured as much." Manny went over to Bully, where he was lying in the sun on his bed. "How did your first case go? Other than taking out a crooked agent."

"Agent Vogt shot his accomplices, who were the men that beat up our clients. I should have seen that coming. They were criminals, but they didn't deserve to die."

Manny took Bully's paw print and stroked him for a while. Then, he got up and sat next to Sophie.

"Sophie, when you start a case, there is no way to know all the twists and turns of what could happen. If you can't live with that, then you need to let Houston and Fons manage the cases."

"I know you are right, Uncle Manny. It's just...."

"I know, you've always been that way. I did not like that the case involved Luis DeLeon. How did that turn out?"

"He accepted the money paid in full with no repercussions. He did say something. I don't know what to make of it. He said a cartel war is going on in Mexico, where he lives. I don't think he saw it coming; he wasn't prepared for it. He gave the impression he wanted out."

"I know the DEA wants to put him in jail. They may never get him if they don't find something on him before he's out of the business."

"Well, that's not our problem anymore. I'm thankful for that. I'm proud of the work we did on the task force, but I want to be able to choose our cases. And you know we want to specialize in missing persons. And yes, I know, we can't rely on just those cases, Uncle Manny."

"That reminds me, I have an overload of accounts wanting background checks. I don't have room to hire anyone else. How soon can you take them off my hands?"

"Houston and I were just talking about that. I can do them from here. All I need is the software."

"I'll lend you one of my laptops, already loaded, until you are set up. I'll bring it home with me tonight, with the applicant's applications."

"Thank you, Uncle Manny. That will help so much."

"Good, I need to get back to work. I'll drop this by David's house so the kids can start working on that postcard. They love this kind of stuff."

"Love you, Uncle Manny, and thanks for the work."

Sophie immediately called Houston and told him they had their first 'bread and butter' job.

CHAPTER TWENTY-SEVEN

Sophie worked in the living room on the laptop Manny brought over. He brought over one hundred applications with him that needed background checks. She made it through twenty-five names, cleared them, and fell asleep on the couch. Bully was lying on his bed in the living room.

Bully woke when he heard Sophie talking in her sleep. She was having a bad dream. He used all the strength he could muster and lifted himself from the bed. He gave a small yelp when he finally got on his feet and limped to the couch.

Bully put his front paws on the couch and licked her cheek. Sophie was startled awake.

"Oh, Bully, was I talking in my sleep again." She wrapped her arms around his neck and hugged him, rubbing behind his ears and kissing his forehead.

"I'm sorry I made you get up. Come on, let's see if you can walk to the bedroom. Maybe I can help you get up onto the bed. We will both be more comfortable."

Bully walked gingerly with a limp and made it to the bedroom. He put his front paws on the bed, and Sophie lifted his back end, trying to be careful of his injured hip. Bully yelped but managed to get on the bed with her help.

Sophie changed into her pajamas and slipped under the covers.

TUESDAY

Houston and Fons left Trenton early. They made it to DC by 10 am. They unlocked the gate to the backyard and unhitched the flatbed. Fons backed the U-Haul truck as close to the outside stairs as possible.

All the furniture and boxes from Fons' apartment were loaded four hours later. They left the flatbed and the U-Haul in the backyard and went downstairs.

"If I knew we would be done this early, I would have asked the broker to come today," Houston said.

"Do you need to go to Quantico to finish your separation papers?"

"No, I did that before I left," Fons said. "Why not call the broker and see if he is available today."

Houston called, and the broker showed up two hours later.

"Mr. Townsend, I did my due diligence. I looked up all the houses in the area and compared them to the county records of your home. There isn't another house with an incoming producing apartment upstairs close by. With that in mind, I determined your home's value, which will sell the property quickly and give you a nice profit."

"I'm not in a hurry. I would rather get the best possible price."

"I understand. Are you leaving the living room and dining room furniture here?"

"Yes."

"May I look upstairs?"

"Sure, it's not locked. And it has a separate entrance outside."

The broker walked around upstairs and down the apartment's back steps. He walked around the patio and backyard, taking pictures. When he came back into the living room, he asked.

"The stove, dishwasher, refrigerator, washer, and dryer on both levels are staying?"

"Yes."

"I will adjust my appraisal. I'm convinced we'll get the best results if we list the house for nine hundred fifty thousand. If we do that, we will get a bidding war for the property and end up with over a million dollars.

Houston liked what he heard. That was almost four hundred thousand dollars more than what they paid.

"I say bidding war because of the decline in crime in the three blocks surrounding your home. People check for that nowadays. It's one of the first things they ask about. Even though the comps don't account for that. Experience tells me it will create demand."

Houston looked at Fons. He knew that might change now that they were gone. Their home was constantly under FBI protection while they were on the task force. He couldn't pass that information on.

"Do you have a contract with you?"

"Yes. I will need a minute to fill it in. Do you mind if I sit at your kitchen table?" the broker asked. Houston nodded.

They watched as the broker pulled out his laptop and a small printer and filled out the contract. An hour later, the contract was signed. The broker's fee was 8%. That was higher than in Austin, but what could he do about that?

Houston handed him both sets of keys to the upstairs and one to the bottom level.

"I will lock up when we leave and mail this set of keys to you."

"Don't bother. We always suggest the new owners change the locks."

They shook hands. The broker handed Houston a copy of the contract, and he was out of there by four o'clock.

"Man, Fons, I want to head home, but I know we will get stuck in traffic and waste gas," he paused. "Are you feeling homesick about moving?"

"I thought I would feel sad about leaving this place. I loved the apartment. But I don't. I only feel excited about getting back to Austin and making our business successful. What about you?"

"I feel nothing. It's strange. I feel like we are finished here, and I can't get out of here fast enough. I can't explain it. Except in my spirit, I feel it was time for us to move on."

"That explains how I feel too. What do you say we lock this place up and get on the road." Fons put his hand on Houston's shoulder and smiled.

"Let's do it."

Sophie had fed Bully after helping him off the bed. She didn't put him in the wagon. He was moving slowly but moving. She removed his diaper and slowly walked him outside so he could do his business. Then she put his bed by the couch where she was working to finish the background checks.

She hadn't gotten very far into the names when her cell rang. "Hello?"

"Sophie, Emma here."

"Madam First Lady.'

"Oh, stop that. Call me Emma."

"Hello, Emma. I hope all is good with you and the President."

"Yes, we are fine. I'm calling because Aileen told me about that little boy you are trying to help."

"Yes, you met Dr. Lawson Cornett. He is the one who is trying to save him. Because the device he invented has to be redesigned to help Fabian, Lawson has to have FDA approval. His adult device is still in the final stages of approval. He can't do anything that would jeopardize that," Sophie explained.

"Yes, I remember. I called the office of the Commissioner of the FDA and made an appointment to see him tomorrow. Micheal appointed him. He didn't dare turn down my request to see him. But that doesn't mean he will push the application through."

"Thank you, Emma. I don't know how long this boy has to live. He's only five. His parents brought him here from Denver because of Dr. Cornett, hoping he could help their son.

"Lawson told me he has come up with an adaptation of his device that might work."

"Well, if Aileen and I have any clout in this town, we will get what you need."

"Thank you. You have always been there when we needed you. I appreciate that."

"Michael and I can say the same about you. I know the team at the task force miss you all."

"Thank you. You know I'm pregnant, but not many people know I'm having twins."

"Yes, that is so exciting. Aileen told me. Send me pictures as soon as they are born."

"I will. And thank you again."

"Goodbye, Sophie."

Sophie considered calling Tanni but felt the letdown would be too much if Emma couldn't pull it off. She went back to work on her background checks. She hoped to finish most of them before Carol came over with dinner.

Sophie didn't get far when the cottage door opened, and China, Drew, and Kato walked in. They would have knocked if Houston was home.

"Look, Sophie, we finished the postcard," Drew said. Bully got excited to see them and tried to get up, but he had overdone it already today. Kato went to him and stroked him to keep him down.

"Bring it here," Sophie patted the couch. They sat down next to her. She looked it over. The front of the postcard was the dark navy blue the police used. Bully's paw print covered a large portion of it in white. Underneath, it read, 'The Gentle Warrior'. On the back, where a message would go, it said, 'If you see someone in trouble, be a gentle warrior and get help for them. And remember, everyone needs a friend. Especially those others snub.' Then, a small paw print where a signature would be.

"This is awesome, guys. You came up with this?"

"Yes, we tried six other ideas, but we liked this the best," Drew said.

"And Liam is working on our website. He gave us the website address he paid for so we can print it on the back," Kato said from the other side of the room.

"You guys are amazing. Let me take a picture of both sides and send it to Houston."

Houston and Fons had just locked the back gate and pulled out on the street from the alley. Fons was driving. Houston's cell pinged. He checked his texts and saw the postcard front and back. He showed it to Fons.

"That's great, Houston."

"Yeah, and it doesn't give away anything." He texted her a thumbs-up emoji and wrote 'perfect'.

"Houston likes it," Sophie said. "I will go to the printer tomorrow to get them done. How many do you think we will need?"

"There were over a hundred letters in that first bag. And there will probably be that many in the second. We have to respond to them all. Hopefully, they will contact the site after that," China suggested.

"Ok, I'll have three hundred made up," Sophie said.

"We can start addressing them as soon as you get them from the printer," Kato volunteered.

"You can start addressing the postcards, but we can't send them out until the site is up," Sophie insisted.

"And remind me to pay Liam for the site."

"He'll never take your money, Sophie," Drew said.

"We should handwrite each kid's name on the message side. That way, they will feel like Bully is talking directly to them," Kato said.

"That's a nice touch, Kato," China said.

"Remember, you must be very careful with what you put on the site."

"We know, Sophie," China said.

"Stay for dinner. Carol should be bringing it over soon."

"Sure, but I need to call Mom," Drew said.

WEDNESDAY

After Sophie helped Bully off the bed, she fed him and removed his diaper. She walked outside with him in her pajamas. Bully was moving more and limping less, but doing so wore him out. Sophie moved his bed in front of the window so he could lie in the sun. Then she went and took a bubble bath and got dressed. She was determined to finish the background checks today.

A few hours into the background checks, she had only ten left to do. Sophie's reports showed that two applicants didn't reveal felonies on their applications. It was up to the business owner to decide if the felonies were egregious enough to not hire them.

Sophie worked the next application in line, as she looked it over, there was something off. She couldn't quite put her finger on it, it was just a feeling. Her name was June Duncan, and it showed she moved to Austin a few weeks ago from Des Moines, Iowa. She was applying for a bank teller position. The bank's application only asked for the past six years of employment. But something about the references made Sophie question them. Normally, the bank is the one who checks references. The background checks are mainly to see if the person is who they say and if they have any criminal record they might be hiding.

Sophie called the first number on the list. It was a bank in Iowa.

"Bank of Des Moines, how can I help you?" A voice came over the line.

"I need to speak with HR, please."

"One moment."

"No one is answering, perhaps I can help you."

"Ok. I am trying to verify employment for a June Duncan."

"One moment, please."

"Yes, I show she worked here for two years starting in 2018."

"Do you know why she left?" There was a lengthy pause at the other end.

"I'm sorry, I don't have that information."

Sophie tried the other two references and got similar versions of the first call. It didn't feel right, so she decided to look up the companies online. They were real companies, but when she called the numbers on the websites, no one by the name of June Duncan ever worked there.

The woman must have some serious money to pull this off. But why? Maybe she changed her name and is hiding from a violent husband. Sophie thought. Either way, she was going to have to get more information. The applications had no pictures, but Texas required a thumbprint to get a driver's license. Sissy could access that. Sophie gave her a call.

"Hello, Sophie."

"Hi, Sissy. Are you in the middle of something?"

"We're in Quantico at the command center. We have a new case."

"Oh, if you are busy, I'll let you go."

"No, Matt's handling it right now. What can I do for you?"

"I'm doing background checks. I have this one woman that I can't go back past six years. I don't have a picture, but Texas requires a thumbprint to get a driver's license if she has one. Can you get into the Department of Public Safety in Texas and see if you can find a thumbprint? Then run her through the federal system?"

"I can. I'll have to wait until I get home. I don't want to do anything personal on the command center system."

"Ok, I'll email her information to your secure email."

"Good. How are you feeling? Still lots of morning sickness?"

"No, haven't had any for a couple of weeks. Did I tell you we discovered the other twin is a boy?"

"That's awesome. I can't even imagine having two babies to deal with at one time. Lucky for you, you have tons of family and friends."

"You're right. I don't think we could do this on our own."

"I'll tell you what I find at the DPS."

"Thanks. Tell Matt hello for me."

"Will do."

Sophie was on her last background check when Houston called.

"Hello, love."

"Hello, sweetheart. How are things going at home?" Houston asked.

"Bully is walking and moving a little. He is still in pain. Where are you?"

"We had Fons' things loaded early in the day. So, I called to see if the broker was available. He came over and after that, we got back on the road. Leaving DC during rush hour was slow, but we wanted to get home. The broker thinks we can get close to a million for the property."

"Oh. That's outstanding. I bet it's because of the income-producing apartment you and Fons built."

"Yeah, that had a lot to do with it. But also, because the crime in that neighborhood dramatically dropped in the last few years."

"I hope that continues now that there won't be any protection detail."

"Me too."

"I ran across a situation with one of the background checks."

"What is it?"

"The history the woman put on her application is all bogus. I'm thinking she may have changed her name to hide from domestic violence. Sissy will get into the Texas Department of Public Safety to get her thumbprint from her driver's license. Then, she'll search the federal database to see what she finds. How long before you get home?"

"We were trying to drive straight through, but we need a room for tonight. It's not worth pushing it and getting in an accident."

"That's right. Get some rest. Will you be home tomorrow?"

"Yes, probably late."

"Are you going to load Fons' thing into the apartment?"

"Yes. I got a text from Jonathan; the papers are ready to sign. I asked if he'd call Akito to get permission for Fons and Carol to move in tomorrow."

"Good."

"Are you all done with your PI test so we can get your license," Houston asked.

"Yes. I'll go by tomorrow and pick it up."

"Ok…. I miss you, sweetheart. I hate being away for so long."

"I miss you too, just get home safe. Stay in a room tonight."

"We will."

Sophie headed to the printers to make up the postcards before they closed. Then, to the post office to pick up books of postcard stamps.

Sophie stopped by the law firm to talk to Manny. She went upstairs and found him in the command center. They were surveilling a suspect in a murder case for a different firm. Their client swore he was innocent and gave the attorneys names of others he thought could have committed the crime.

They let the rumor fly that a witness knew where the murder weapon was. When the story got out, they put three drones in the air. So far, the other two suspects were going through their regular daily routine.

The third suspect was driving out of town to an abandoned industrial area. Manny was on the phone with the police, giving directions to where the suspect was. The police were ten minutes out. The man went into the large metal warehouse. They debated whether the drone should follow him in. They were concerned it would be detected.

"What do you think, Sophie?" Manny asked.

"The suspect has no idea he's being followed. He hasn't looked back once. Does your drone have a noise reduction muffler?"

"Yes."

"Then I would. If you can capture him pulling the gun from its hiding place. That would seal the deal."

"Do it," Manny said. The pilot switched on the muffler and flew the drone through a large broken window, but the suspect was no longer in sight.

"We've lost him, Manny," the pilot said.

"No, he's there. Fly it into the rafters."

"There," one of Manny's operatives said, pointing at the screen.

"Ok, zoom in so we can see what he is doing," Manny said.

"It looks like he is moving a metal drum. It must be empty, or he couldn't move it," the pilot said.

Under the drum, there was a hole in the concrete floor. It looked like a pole had once been there and removed. He reached in and pulled out something wrapped in a rag. He stuck it in his pocket without looking inside. He put the drum back and headed toward the exit.

"Sherriff, where are your men? The suspect is leaving with the weapon," Manny asked.

"They are outside waiting for him to come out."

"Good. I'll send you a copy of the drone footage."

"Thanks for your help, Manny."

"Anytime, Sherriff."

When Manny finished with the sheriff, he turned to Sophie and gave her a hug. I received all the reports but one. Quick work. Thank you."

"That's what I came to talk to you about. June Duncan, there is something not right there. Her work history is all bogus. I'm wondering if she changed her name to hide from someone. I asked a friend to see if she could get her fingerprint off her Texas driver's license and send it through the federal system. I'll let you know what I find out. You saw that two others on the list had felonies they didn't put on their applications," Sophie pointed out.

"I saw that. It looks like the one man's felony was when he was nineteen. And his record has been clean since then. It's up to the client to decide. The other one is a repeat offender. I wouldn't recommend that company hire him."

"I brought the file with the applications back. I'll put them on your desk. If you have any more work. Just let me know. I'll finish up on June Duncan and send it to you."

"I do have another hundred names. If you are ready for them. I'll give you their applications now. And I can cut a check for your work," Manny walked Sophie to his office and picked up the file off his desk filled with the applications and handed it to her.

"Uncle Manny, wait until I finish these," she lifted the file he gave her. "When Houston returns, he can give you the business account information. You can direct deposit it. I'll be taking over the accounting when we get the office running. Right now, Houston is taking care of it. She looked down at the large file. "Uncle Manny, if Houston thinks you are giving us work that is taking money out of your pocket, he won't take it. And I will check to make sure you keep your ten percent."

"I'll handle Houston, Sophie," Manny smiled. "But truly, we have more work than we can manage. And rather than losing the business to someone else, I outsource it. To you or another firm. If something changes and we can do it ourselves, I will let you know."

"Thank you, Uncle Manny," Sophie got up and took the file with her after saying goodbye.

CHAPTER TWENTY-EIGHT

On the way home, Sophie's cell rang. "Hello?"

"Sophie, It's Emma."

"Emma. How did it go?"

"The commissioner located the application on the desk of a woman who is gone on emergency leave for two weeks. No one had picked up her cases. He apologized and realized a mistake like that could cost someone their life. He looked over the application while we waited. He said the change in the device's use and adaptation was not such a stretch when it came to saving a boy's life. He signed the approval and emailed it to Dr. Cornett. He should have it."

"That's wonderful news. Thank you, Emma. You are the best First Lady this country will ever have."

"I'm just doing what is right. There is no need to be thanked for that."

"I'll call Lawson right away. I'll keep you updated on how it goes."

"Please do."

As soon as Sophie said goodbye to Emma, she called Lawson.

Lawson stepped out of the surgical unit through the double doors. He removed his mask and reached behind him to untie his surgical gown and put it in the laundry bag, heading to his office.

Lawson was not sure if the surgery he performed would save the baby. It was touch and go. He planned to pray for her tonight and stay in his office if the baby got worse. As he walked into his office, he heard his cell phone ringing.

"Did you get it?"

"What, Sophie? Get what?"

"The approval in your email. The First Lady met with the Commissioner of the FDA today, and he approved it while she was there and emailed it to you."

"No, I just got out of surgery. Let me check my email," Lawson said. Sophie heard him tapping on his keyboard. "I got it! I'll see him tonight and talk to his parents. I'll reserve a surgical room and put my staff on standby."

"When will you go over?"

"In an hour."

"I'll meet you there with Bully and the kids," Sophie said.

"Alright, I'll see you there."

Sophie called China and told her the news. She asked if they would like to come with her and Bully to see Fabian."

The excitement on the other end of the line gave her the answer.

"Meet me at the cottage in half an hour."

When Sophie got to the cottage, Bully was outside, ambling around the yard. He was trying to chase a squirrel, mocking him by running a few steps and stopping. Then, he waited for Bully and ran away again. Poor Bully.

"Hi, Grandpa, how long has that been going on?" Sophie asked, referring to the squirrel.

"Ten minutes. I recorded the first few minutes. It's payback," Emmet laughed, sitting on the patio.

"I told you about the boy in the hospital waiting for surgery."

"Yes."

"The approval came through. I'm taking the kids and Bully to see him. Is Carol here?"

"Yes, she's finishing the vlog. We get to eat her creation for dinner. Can't wait, it smells wonderful."

"Grandpa, would you put the wagon in the back of my SUV? Bully may not be up to walking that far into the hospital."

"Sure," he got up and grabbed the wagon. Bully saw Sophie and abandoned the mean squirrel to greet her.

"Hello, my poor boy. That is a mean squirrel," Sophie rubbed his face, neck, and behind his ears. His tail wagged. "We are going to say hello to a friend at the hospital."

Carol heard Sophie's voice and came out. "What's going on?"

"The First Lady got the approval for the surgery. We are going to meet Lawson there. Do you want to come?"

"Yes. Let me clean up. I'll be right back."

"I'll call Lizzy to see if she wants to come."

Bully was in the back of the SUV, lying next to the wagon. Sophie had put his service vest on him and brought his leash. China, Kato, and Drew were in the back seat. Lizzy was working and wouldn't be off in time.

At the hospital, the boys helped Bully out of the back. He seemed strong enough to walk, so they left the wagon and put on the leash, slowly walking to Fabian's room.

The door to the room was closed. Sophie knocked. Tanni came to the door. Her face was ashen. She was surprised to see a dog and an entourage outside the room.

"What's happened?" Sophie asked. Tanni recognized her voice, realizing then who she was.

"Mrs. Townsend, Fabian has taken a turn for the worse."

"Don't give up. The First Lady went to see the Commissioner of the FDA today, and he approved the surgery. Dr. Cornett is on his way over now."

"Really. Fabian is going to get the surgery?"

"Yes. I thought we might cheer him up."

"Yes, please come in. Fabian is very weak," Tanni said, opening the door wider. Her husband Haan questioned who they were. Tanni introduced them and explained what had happened. He covered his mouth and cried, holding his wife.

Fabian's eyes were closed. Bully put his front paws on the bed and used his nose to nudge him. The boy opened his eyes.

"The hero dog! Mama, the hero dog, came to see me!" Fabian smiled and tried to get up but was too weak.

"Is it alright if we lift my dog on the bed?" Sophie asked. Tanni and Haan smiled and nodded. Drew and China carefully lifted Bully. He gave a small yelp.

"His injuries have not healed. But he wanted to spend time with you." Sophie leaned close to the boy. "I will tell you a secret. But you cannot tell anyone. Ok?" The boy nodded. Bully had snuggled up to him, and Fabian wrapped his arms around his neck.

"His name is Bully. But we can't let him do interviews or tell anyone his name because he is an undercover dog. Can you keep that secret, so he remains safe?"

"Yes," Fabian said, kissing Bully on the forehead and whispering his name into Bully's ear. Bully's tail wagged.

"Later, I will tell you of some of the other heroic things Bully has done."

"Really?" Fabian asked. Sophie nodded. She and Carol moved away so China, Drew, and Kato could get close to engage with him.

Lawson entered minutes later and saw Fabian smiling and hugging Bully.

"Mr. and Mrs. Herrmann, I have some news for you," Lawson said. He moved the parents over to the small table and chairs in the corner. He explained how he planned to use the device to help Fabian. Lawson emphasized his procedure had not been tested, and there was a possibility it might not fix the problem.

"You will have to sign liability waivers to protect the hospital. You must also contact your health insurance to ensure they cover an experimental procedure."

"I don't care what it cost, Dr. Lawson. I have money. Nothing matters except him," Haan said.

"I understand that, but you must remember this surgery may not save him," Lawson repeated.

"We don't care. We want you to do it. My son has no chance at all without it," Tanni said.

Carol and Sophie could hear the exchange and understood the parents' desperation.

"Alright. I will arrange for Fabian to be transported to the Heart Hospital tonight. After you get all the paperwork finished, contact your insurance. I will see if he is strong enough to undergo surgery tomorrow."

The three of them stood, and Tanni hugged the doctor. "Thank you, Doctor Cornett."

"It was Sophie's doing. She got ahold of the First Lady and asked for help."

Lawson went over and spoke to Sophie and Carol before he left.

They stayed with Fabian and his parents for over an hour. The energy in the room had changed, and Fabian was gaining strength from having the kids and Bully around.

"This is the happiest I have seen him in years. I can't thank you enough for bringing your dog in to see him."

"I would let him take a picture with him, but the chances are it would get out to the public, one way or another. We can't let that happen. Not since all the publicity surrounding the news of him capturing a criminal."

"Will you come back again once Fabian is out of surgery?"

"Yes. And I'll bring his entourage with him. Fabian seems to be enjoying their company."

"He's an only child. Because of his condition, he hasn't been able to play with any neighborhood kids, and we are homeschooling him," Tanni said.

"Oh, I know just the person who can encourage him. Xander Whiteing. He had a heart condition when he was young, and his mother never let him out of the house. She was so afraid that his immune deficiency would cause him to contract something and die.

"He had one last surgery that they said would fix his heart condition. A new experimental thing like this. His father finally insisted Xander be allowed to attend sixth grade in school. That's when I met him. You'd never know it now, but he was so pale and skinny," Sophie chuckled.

"You don't mean Xander Whiteing, the movie star and director."

"Yes, and I'm sure Xander will come to see Fabian. I'll call and talk to him. His mom and dad may want to come too."

"You mean Carmen Whiteing," Tanni gasped.

"Yes, she is the sweetest woman," Sophie said.

A nurse came in and saw Bully on the bed. She was not happy about it.

"I need to get Fabian ready for transport in an hour. I think it might be time for your company to leave," the nurse said.

"Noooo," Fabian pleaded.

China stood up, "don't you worry, Fabian. We'll come back to see you. And we will bring Bully," she whispered in his ear. Fabian clung to Bully a moment longer.

"Bully, I will pray for you every day that you feel better," Fabian whispered in his ear. Then Drew, China, and Kato helped Bully off the bed, being careful not to hurt him.

"Do you mind if we pray with Fabian before we go?" Sophie asked.

China, Drew, and Kato surrounded the bed with Sophie and Carol. They quietly prayed for him. Then Sophie kissed Fabian on the forehead.

"We'll be back," she said. And they left.

The ride home from the hospital was quiet. It was a hard thing to watch a five-year-old boy near death. Everyone felt it.

"Aunt Sophie, will Fabian live?" Kato asked.

"I trust the Lord that he will."

"Can we go back to see him after his surgery," Drew asked.

"I promised him we would."

Sophie drove the boys and China to David's house and headed home. Carol helped Sophie lift Bully from the back of the SUV. He was exhausted, and his limp was more pronounced. Sophie let him do his business outside, gave him a pain pill, and put a diaper on him. He went to his bed in the living room.

"I promised Emmett dinner. Want to eat with us?" Carol said.

"Yes. Then I want to check something out. Want to come with me."

Sophie went over to Emmett's to eat with them. She left the door to the cottage open in case Bully wanted to find her.

An hour later, Emmett said he would watch the game at the cottage, so Bully wouldn't be alone.

Sophie grabbed June Duncan's file and called Lizzy to see if she wanted to come. She had just gotten off work.

After Sophie picked up Lizzy, she told them she needed to verify something about a background application. The file said the woman was working as a waitress while she waited for her bank teller job.

Sophie drove to the address on the application. Her apartment was the last one on the first floor at the end of a block.

"We have to make sure she's not home," Sophie said.

"Why?"

"I want to go into her house and snoop," Sophie said.

"Sophie! Is that legal?" Carol asked.

"There is something going on with this woman, I think she is in trouble with no one to turn to," Sophie said. "But to answer your question, no, it's not legal."

"You can't go in by yourself. I'll go with you," Lizzy said.

"Ok, but first go to the door and knock. Then go around back and see if we would be seen getting in from there."

"Ok," Lizzy got out, and Sophie watched as she knocked on the door. When no one answered, Lizzy went to the back door. Moments later, she returned to the SUV and got in.

"The back of the property has a small patio for each downstairs apartment. A six-foot wooden fence encloses it. About twenty feet past the fence is a copse of trees. It separates them from another apartment complex," Lizzy said.

"Is there a gate in the fence?"

"Yes. The gate is five feet. We can't jump it."

"We'll figure it out. Carol, will you stay here and be our lookout?"

If you see someone, call me. I'll have my phone on vibrate."

"Sophie, how good an idea is this?" Carol asked.

"Not very. But are you in?" Sophie asked. Carol and Lizzy nodded.

Sophie looked at the file again to see if it said what shift she worked. It didn't.

"What are you doing?" Carol asked.

"I'm going to call the restaurant." Sophie dialed the number.

"Marketplace Diner."

"I'm sorry to bother you, but I've forgotten when June gets off her shift. I came to see her, but I can come back unless her shift is almost over," Sophie said.

"I'm sorry, but she didn't show up for her shift. She didn't call either. So, if you find her, tell her to call right away."

"Oh, thank you," Sophie said, then looked at Carol and Lizzy. She didn't show up for work."

"That's odd," Carol furrowed her brow.

"It is. June's file doesn't say what kind of car she drives. So we have no way of knowing if it's here. Let's go try to get into her apartment."

"Sophie, you don't have a key. How will you get in?" Carol asked.

"I'll pick the lock."

"How do you know how to do that?" Carol asked.

"Sissy and I sat in on a class taught at Quantico while the rest of the team set up command."

"Do you have the tools?" Lizzy asked.

"Yes," she reached across the car to the glove box and pulled out a small black pouch and two pairs of gloves.

"Do you have a flashlight?" Lizzy asked.

"Yeah, in the console." Sophie pulled out a small flashlight that fit in her pocket.

"Let's go."

Sophie looked for cameras but didn't see any. The apartment next to June's was dark, so Sophie felt they wouldn't get caught. She and Lizzy put on gloves and headed for the backyard.

"How are we going to unlock the gate?" Lizzy asked. "There is no handle on this side."

Sophie knelt on one knee, leaving the other bent. Then she interlocked her fingers and put them on her knee, palms up.

"I'll give you a boost. Reach over the gate and unlatch it."

Lizzy slipped off her shoe and put her foot in Sophie's hands. It lifted her high enough to reach over the gate and slip the small bolt over. Lizzy stepped down, slipping her foot back into her shoe, and opened the gate. They entered and shut the gate behind them.

Sophie squatted in front of the doorknob to pick the lock when Lizzy reached over.

"Why don't we see if it's open first," Lizzy said. The knob turned and the door opened.

"That's why you get paid the big bucks, Lizzy," They both chuckled and walked into the kitchen.

There was enough light coming through the windows to move around. Sophie knew it wouldn't last long.

"Lizzy, look for mail or pictures, anything that may tell us who she really is. Be sure you put everything back as you found it."

Sophie saw a picture on a bookshelf in the living room. It was a picture of a cabin by a lake, but there were no people in it. She took a picture of it and then opened the back to see if it had a name or date. When she opened the back of the frame, another picture fell out. It was a man, a young girl, and a woman in hiking clothes. She didn't know if it was June because she had no picture of her, but it was definitely at the cabin in the other picture. She took a picture of it, on the back was written 'Camping in the wild,' Ha ha,' like that was a joke.

Sophie looked but didn't find any other pictures. Lizzy came up behind her and said all the mail was in June's name. They went to the next room that was made into an office. One wall was set up like a murder board. They stopped and studied it.

"Sophie, what is this?"

"It looks like a murder board. June is tracking someone." Sophie stepped closer to look at one of the pictures. "It's the man in the hiking picture."

"Who?"

"The only picture in the living room was hiding another picture behind it. It was this man, a young girl, and a woman, I have to assume the woman is June."

"There is a lot of information on here. Do you want me to take pictures of all of it?" Lizzy asked.

"Yes. I'll check the rest of the house." Sophie checked the medicine cabinet in the guest bathroom. Nothing.

Sophie headed to the master bedroom and froze in her tracks. In the middle of the floor was a woman dressed in a waitress uniform lying on her back. Blood covered the carpet. *It must have happened before her shift*, she thought. Sophie covered her mouth to muffle a gasp. June wasn't the first murdered or dead body she had seen. The bodies of Duke, her dad, Nikko, the assassin who tried to kill her, all flashed through her mind. And now June.

They needed to leave, but first Sophie needed to check for a pulse. She maneuvered around the blood, and the gun lying next to her, to touch the artery in her neck. It startled her that the body was still warm. There was no pulse. Sophie stepped away and took pictures, then walked back to the office.

"Lizzy, we need to get out of here," Sophie said.

"I haven't checked the desk yet..."

"We need to go."

They went back out the kitchen door, then used the same technique as before to bolt the gate behind them.

When they got into the SUV, Lizzy asked. "Sophie, what's going on? You are pale as a ghost." Sophie pulled up the picture on her phone and handed it to Lizzy in the back seat.

"Oh, that's awful."

"What is it?" Carol asked.

"June is dead."

"How?"

"She was murdered," Lizzy said, returning the phone to Sophie.

"We need to call the police," Carol said.

"Yes, I'm just trying to figure out how to explain how we know," Sophie said.

"We can call in for a wellness check," Lizzy said.

"Yes. I can tell the truth. I needed to speak with June because I'm doing a background check for her job at the bank."

"That's good, but how do you explain us."

"I won't. You will stay in the car." Sophie dialed 911.

"911, what's your emergency?"

"I would like a wellness check done at 1611 Cinnamon Path, apt 101."

"Your name."

"Sophie Star Townsend."

"Are you there now?"

"Yes, I'll wait for the police."

"They are on the way. Do you want to stay on the line?"

"No," she said and hung up.

"You are going to have to explain why you wanted a wellness check," Carol said.

"I'll tell the truth. I came here because I am doing a background check on her for a bank position and I had some questions about her application. When she didn't answer the door, I called her work and they said she didn't show up or call. I started to worry she may have been injured."

Ten minutes later, two police officers arrived. One officer knocked on June's door. He called out her name and then went to get the manager. Sophie lowered her window in hopes of hearing what was being said. She listened to the manager tell him where her parking spot was. The officer sent his partner to check for her car.

The officer came back and said the car was there. That's when Sophie saw the manager unlock the door. He waited outside.

It didn't take long for the two officers to come back out. One of them was on his phone.

"Should we leave?" Carol asked.

"No. I need to tell them I was the one who called." Sophie knew it would take time for a detective, the ME, and evidence techs to show up.

Sophie stepped out of the car. "Stay here." She walked up to the officer.

"Officer, I am the one who called in the wellness check. Is Ms. Duncan alright?"

"I'm not at liberty to say." The officer asked her a few questions. He wanted to know why she was looking for Ms. Duncan in the first place. She explained. The officer accepted her response and asked for her address and phone number. Then told her she could leave.

Sophie got back in the car and headed home. "Carol, I'm sorry I got you into this. Are you alright?"

"Yes, I'm fine, how are you? You are the one who saw her."

"It's unsettling, but I'm fine. How about you, Lizzy?" Sophie asked.

"I never saw anything but the picture. But it is creepy we were in the house where someone was lying on the floor, murdered."

"I need to call Houston and tell him what I've done. He is not going to be happy."

CHAPTER TWENTY-NINE

Sophie told Emmett what happened. He made sure Carol was all right and called Lizzy. Hearing Sophie got herself into a risky situation was not new to him. CJ called to make sure Sophie wasn't traumatized. He didn't seem upset that Sophie got his wife involved.

"I'm glad you didn't go in alone," CJ said. "You need to call Houston."

"I will," Sophie said, dreading it. Emmett and Carol walked back to his house. Emmett had taken the diaper off Bully earlier and let him go outside to do his business. He put another one on him and lifted him to the bed for Sophie.

"Thanks, Grandpa," Sophie said and hugged him.

"Anytime, angel," he said. Sophie smiled. That was the name he always called her when she was young.

It was 9 pm. Sophie didn't know if Houston and Fons were still driving or if they had gotten a room. She decided to bite the bullet and call him.

"Hello, sweetheart."

"Hi, love. Are you driving?"

"No, we pulled into a Travel Lodge. We are asking for a room on the first floor to keep an eye on the truck.

"Good. Are you in the room?"

"Just walking in now. What's going on?"

"I told you about the woman's application I thought was sketchy. June Duncan. I was sure she was in trouble and had nowhere to turn."

"Yes."

"Well, Lizzy, Carol, and I checked her out. She didn't show up for work and didn't answer her door. So, I picked the lock, and Lizzy and I went in to see what we could find..."

"You did what?!"

"Houston, calm down. I'm a partner in this agency. I can make executive decisions," Sophie said.

"Sophie, that's not the point. We agreed that you would not do anything that would endanger you or our babies."

"I didn't. If this were a man, I would have waited for you, but it was a woman. And Lizzy and Carol were with me. I told you I would not go out on my own. And I didn't."

"I'm not crazy about this but go ahead. What did you find?"

"She was dead on her bedroom floor."

"What?!" Houston said. Sophie could hear Fons in the background asking what was going on. "I'm putting you on speaker. What did you do?'

"Lizzy and I got out of there and called in a wellness check for her. When the officers arrived, they found her dead. I went up to one of the officers to tell them I was the one who called in the wellness check. I explained I needed to talk to her about a background check for a bank job. When I found out she didn't show up for work or answer the door, I got concerned."

"What if you left fingerprints in there. They will find out you were inside."

"We wore gloves."

"Someone will eventually figure out one-on-ones aren't generally done for a background check."

"Who's we?" Fons asked.

"Carol and Lizzy came with me."

"How did she handle seeing a dead body?" Fons was concerned for his wife.

"She didn't go inside. She was our lookout."

"Carol said she was fine, and Emmett made sure she was alright," Sophie said. "Are you upset I took her along?"

"No, better that you didn't go by yourself. I'll call and check on her," Fons said. Houston took the phone off speaker.

"Sophie, you didn't expect to see a dead body; that's the point. You don't know what you'll find. Besides the fact it was breaking and entering. I wish you would wait for one of us to do something like that," Houston had calmed down.

"It was just a sneak and peek, like you did," Sophie said.

"That was for a client, and that wasn't exactly legal either. We have no client here. Your job was to do a background check."

"Is Fons upset at me for taking his wife?" Sophie asked.

"I don't think so."

"Houston, I don't want to keep fighting over this same issue. I am your partner in this agency. And I have task force experience too. I won't go headlong into something I know could be dangerous. But this wasn't that."

"I hear you, sweetheart. And I know I tend to overreact. But you did make promises to me. As long as you keep those promises, I can adjust," Houston compromised.

"Ok. Good. Houston, I'd like to see if we can help the police with this case. I want to know what happened to her and who she was."

"We can ask. But remember, we are supposed to be doing this for a paycheck. There is no one to hire us on this one. The woman is already dead," Houston changed the subject. "How's Bully doing?"

"I talked to the Vet today, to tell him Bully was moving around. I asked if it was all right to let him up. He said it was fine but now that he is moving around, we need to make sure Bully doesn't overdue it. He wants to see him next week.

"Oh, and I didn't tell you. Emma came through. The FDA approved Fabian's surgery. I took Bully to see him. China, Drew, Kato, and Carol came with me. You should have seen Fabian's face. It was so great to see him light up."

"I can imagine."

"That reminds me. I want to call Xander and ask him if he will see Fabian after his surgery."

"I love you, Sophie."

"I love you too. Get some rest."

Sophie called Xander to tell him about Fabian. It was after ten, but she knew he stayed up late.

"Hello, Sophie. Do you know what time it is? I could be in bed," he teased.

"Yeah, Yeah, how long have I known you?"

"Ok, so I'm not in bed. What's up?"

"You know about the boy with the heart condition, right?"

"Yes, Lawson was waiting on approval from the FDA."

"The First Lady intervened and pushed the approval through. Lawson is performing the surgery tomorrow. If his body can take it. I told Fabian and his parents that you were homebound until sixth grade," Sophie chuckled.

"Sophie, what did you volunteer me for?" Xander was smiling. Sophie could hear it in his voice.

"I didn't exactly volunteer you... well maybe I did. I told his parents you were skinny and pale. I just wanted them to know that how you start out is not how you need to end up," Sophie said half apologetically.

"The truth is the truth. I'll go to see him once Lawson says he can have visitors. I'll let Mom and Dad know too. They might want to visit."

"Thanks, scrawny boy," Sophie laughed.

"I was, but I'm not now, so you better watch out, Miss Tattletale," Xander laughed.

"Really, thanks, Xander."

"I'm always happy to be a pawn in one of your episodes. Just like when we were kids." They both laughed.

Sophie decided she needed to tell Manny what had happened.

"Hi, Sophie. Is everything all right?"

"Sorta, I know it's late, but I thought I better tell you what happened."

"Ok."

"It's about June Duncan, the woman who had the sketchy history. She's dead." Sophie went on to explain everything that happened."

"You better hope you didn't leave any trace of yourself in there. And I know you are no longer law enforcement, but that is still breaking and entering."

"I know, but there was something off about this woman, I was worried about her. And I didn't leave any traces, Uncle Manny. I asked Houston if we could offer to help the police with this investigation. I'd like to know what happened to her."

"They might. They must know by now that you were the ones who took down Agent Vogt's side business."

"Not to hear SAC Ramos talk about it," Sophie said.

"People see through guys like him."

"We'll see, I guess. I thought you should know. Are you going to tell her potential employer?"

"Yes. I need to report that to them. And next time, call me in a situation like that. I'll come with you."

"I will. Thanks, Uncle Manny. Goodnight."

"Goodnight."

Sophie hung up. Then it dawned on her she forgot to pick up her private investigator license.

THURSDAY

After getting ready for the day, she fed Bully and herself. Sophie gathered all of her cleaning supplies into a mob bucket. She had already called Lizzy, Piper, and Sienna and asked if they would help clean the apartment for Carol. All agreed. Sienna said she would be there after her last batch of cookies was made.

Sophie walked into Emmett's open back door. She saw him drinking coffee and eating eggs and bacon.

"Hi, Grandpa," she leaned over and kissed his cheek.

"Hi, angel," he said. Sophie wondered why he started using that endearment again. She liked it. It reminded her of happy times.

"I'm going with Carol to the apartment to clean it before the men bring her belongings. Do you know where we could get a carpet cleaner?"

"I have a shampooer. We use it when we buy back one of the homes in the subdivision. It's not a commercial grade but the best on the market. You are welcome to use it. It's in my shed. I'll run over and get it when I'm done eating. I might have rug shampoo, too."

"That's great, Grandpa. Thank you."

Sophie knocked on Carol's bedroom door. "Carol, can I come in."

"Sure, the door isn't locked."

Sophie walked over to the bathroom door; she was putting on makeup in the mirror. "Carol, are you sure you are alright?"

"I'm fine. I actually enjoyed doing the spy stuff. Knowing there was a dead body, not so much. I saw it bothered you."

"It did. The fact I didn't know her helped me not to obsess about it," she paused. "Is Fons mad at me for taking you along?" Sophie was worried she might have damaged their friendship.

"No. I told him I was a big girl and could have said no. I did tell him I wouldn't mind going on stakeouts and stuff like that with him. It's kinda fun."

"Yeah. I called Lizzy, Piper, and Sienna, we are going over to your apartment. We want to help you clean it before the men bring in your furniture and stuff."

"Oh, thank you. I was going to head over there myself, but with your help, it shouldn't take long," Carol said.

"Grandpa has a carpet shampooer. If we do the three bedrooms with carpets first and open the windows, they should be dry before the men arrive."

"That's perfect. I'm ready to go."

Sophie asked the kids to watch Bully. They agreed but wanted to stay at David's so they could keep working on the letters. Emmett loaded Bully, the shampooer, and the other cleaning materials in the SUV.

Piper had ridden with Lizzy and was waiting in the parking lot. Carol unlocked the door, and they hauled the cleaning supplies upstairs.

"I'll shampoo the carpets," Lizzy volunteered.

"Ok, but we should wash the walls first and clean the windows and bathroom. We won't want to walk on the carpet once wet."

"I'll clean the kitchen," Carol said.

"Ok, then. Piper, that leaves you and me to wash the walls and the windows," Sophie said.

"It's you and me, Soph," Piper smiled. They started in the master bedroom.

Two hours later, the three bedrooms were clean, and the carpets were shampooed. After cleaning the kitchen, Carol washed the living room walls and windows with Sienna's help. The living room and hallway had hardwood floors. The kitchen and bathroom had tile. Sienna went to her apartment to bring back hardwood floor cleaner. It was the last thing they were going to do before they left.

"Can we take a break before we do the hardwood floors?" Sophie asked.

"Sure, let's walk down to the bakery. I'll make us lunch," Sienna offered.

"Actually, I need to go by and pick up my private investigator license, and the printer texted me. The postcards are ready."

"Sure, Sophie, we'll wait for you at the bakery," Sienna said.

"I could really use the time to get groceries for the apartment. I'd like to stay here tonight," she turned to Sophie. "Do you think we can?"

"Houston already got permission for you to stay. We sign the papers tomorrow."

"I need groceries, too," Sienna said.

"I haven't picked up what I need for dinner yet," Lizzy added.

"Why don't you three go shopping. Piper can come with me. Unless you need groceries too." Sophie turned to Piper.

"No, I'm good."

"Ok. We'll meet back here and finish the floors. Then we can go out for a late lunch," Sophie suggested.

"Sounds good to me," Lizzy said, and the others agreed.

They were done with the apartment by four o'clock and decided to eat at Olive Garden.

Fons called and said they should be at the apartment at 11:30 that night. Carol and Sophie said they would return to the apartment to meet them.

"I'll text Xander. He said he wanted to help unload the U-Haul," Piper said. She took out her phone and texted when the men should be there.

"No, Piper, that's too late to expect anyone to help," Carol said.

"No, it's not. Not for a friend."

"I'll text Jean-Paul too. He wants to help."

Sophie and Carol pulled up to the apartment at 11:15 pm. Word had gotten around, and all the men were there to help unload the U-Haul.

"Oh," Carol said. "Everyone is here. Sophie I never expected this."

"Carol, it's how our family does things."

"How will I ever repay them?"

"You don't have to."

The U-Haul pulled in ten minutes later, and the men went to work. Fons unloaded his SUV off the flatbed trailer and unhooked it. Houston backed up the U-Haul close to the apartment door and pulled out the ramp.

Carol directed where each box or piece of furniture was to go. Sophie couldn't pack boxes, so when the men put the bed together, she found the box with the linens and made up the bed.

With all the help, the U-Haul was unloaded in less than an hour. Fons didn't know what to say.

"I can't thank you enough for coming down at this time of night to help us."

"I'm sure you would do the same for us," David said, patting him on the back. The other men agreed.

After the men left, Houston asked, "Can we leave the truck in the U-Haul parking lot even though they are closed?"

"They told me I could and showed me where to drop the keys."

"Good, then I'll come back and hook Emmett's flatbed to my SUV and take it home with me. I'm so glad we were able to bring your SUV back."

"I need to fill Emmett's vehicle with gas, wash, and detail it before I give him the keys back.

Please tell him I plan on doing that first thing in the morning."

"Carol, do you need help unpacking boxes tonight," Sophie asked.

"No, we are done for the night after Fons returns the U-Haul. Thank you for making our bed. I'm so excited to stay here tonight."

"Are you sure?" Sophie asked.

"Yes. I want to take my time and decide where I want things to go."

Carol choked up. "I've never had friends like this. It's overwhelming," she paused. "I'll have a dinner party for everyone as soon as I have my kitchen together.

Houston checked with Fons once they got back from dropping off the U-Haul to make sure he didn't need anything else. Fons and Carol said they were done for the night, stood at the downstairs door, thanked them for their help, and said goodnight.

Houston and Sophie headed to their vehicle. Houston was opening the door for her when he stopped and pulled her close, kissing her. It was his first chance since they made it back to Austin.

"I hated being away from you," Houston said.

"Me too, love," Sophie kissed him again. Houston put his hand on her tummy.

"I missed you guys too...oh, did you feel that?"

"Yes," Sophie smiled.

"How long have they been kicking?"

"This is the first time."

"I'm glad. I would have hated to miss it," Houston patted her tummy again, and she slipped into the vehicle.

On the way home, Sophie showed him her private investigator's license and the postcards from the printers.

"They look great," he said.

"Bully is at Uncle David's. We can drop off the postcards then. The kids will be asleep, but they can start addressing them in the morning. I think they started on the second bag of mail."

"I can't believe Bully went viral."

"Yeah, and I got a text from ASAC Berry. He has another bag at the office. The website should help stop the mail."

When they pulled into the driveway, they saw Bully in the window waiting for them. He started wiggling.

"He must be feeling better," Houston said.

"Yeah, but remember the Vet told us he will want to overdue and not take the time to heal."

They both went to the door. Anna opened it and invited them in. Bully came over to Houston, still limping, happy to see him. Houston squatted down and rubbed Bully's face and ruff. He ran his hands down the rest of his body using his fingers like a comb to see how Bully reacted when he hit the sore spots. He winced but didn't yelp.

Sophie handed the postcards to Anna, "Will you give these to the kids tomorrow."

"Oh, they turned out nice," David said, coming from the kitchen. "I don't think the kids realize how much work it will be addressing all those."

"Oh, they'll love it," Anna said. "Liam told them to put all the addresses on the website and then print them out on labels. He said they can keep track of everyone who contacted Bully that way."

"That's a great idea. Is the website ready?" Sophie asked.

"Yes, he needs you to approve it," Anna said. "I think he emailed it to you."

"We'll look at it in the morning," Houston said.

"Aunt Anna, I didn't realize how much work this is putting on you," Sophie said.

"This is a great experience for them, and it keeps the kids busy. School doesn't start for another month."

"Oh and tell them ASAC Berry said there is another bag at the office."

"Unbelievable," David said. "One thing about the website. China can help with it when she goes home when school starts."

They said goodbye, and Houston helped Bully into the back seat.

"I had no idea what a big production this was," Houston said.

CHAPTER THIRTY

FRIDAY

Houston put Bully's service vest on him, then called out, "Sophie, we have to be at the title company at 10 o'clock."

"I'm coming," Sophie walked out in tan color cotton cropped pants, a cotton top with raglan sleeves, and sandals. Houston was dressed casually in khaki pants, a summer cotton button-up shirt, and slip-on Dr. Martins.

They walked into the Title Company at precisely 10 o'clock. Akito Lam was there already. Reading the paperwork, signing, and transferring funds took over an hour. Outside the title company, Akito shook hands with them, and they said goodbye.

"We have to go to see Uncle David now. I asked Lizzy to meet me there at eleven. We're late," Sophie said. Houston helped Bully into the SUV.

Lizzy was sitting in CJ's office waiting for Sophie. "CJ, why would I need to meet Sophie in Uncle David's office?"

"I don't know, honey, but you'll find out soon enough. I just saw Houston's SUV pass by.

Houston and Sophie entered the law firm and headed to David's office.

"Hello, Uncle David," Sophie said, walking in. David looked up.

"Hello, Sophie. Lizzy's in CJ's office. I'll buzz him and let him know you're here. Should we have CJ come in?"

"I think so. Houston's here."

David brought over two more chairs from the table in his office. Bully was lying down next to Houston.

CJ was carrying Jett, and Coco was trailing behind them. When Jett saw Bully, he leaned down from CJ's arms to be let down. Bully's tail was thumping the ground when he saw Jett.

"Be careful, Jett, Bully still has owies," CJ said. Jett sat next to Bully, hugging his neck, and stroking him. Coco lay down next to him. Houston watched Jett pet and hug Bully, then do the same to Coco, back and forth, so he wouldn't hurt Coco's feelings. *Such a soft heart.* Houston thought.

"Hi, Uncle David," Lizzy said.

"Hi, Lizzy, CJ. Now that Sophie is home, I need to close out her mother's estate. And since that involves you, I thought we'd take care of it at the same time."

"What do I have to do with Clair's estate?"

"If you give me a second, I'll explain," David chuckled.

"Sorry."

"It should be no surprise that Clair considered you Sophie's sister. A second daughter. Two hundred fifty thousand dollars has been left to you from Clair's estate."

"What? No! That money belongs to Sophie," Lizzy turned to Sophie. "I can't take money that should go to you."

"Lizzy, you know my mother loved you. Why would it surprise you that she left you something?"

"But Sophie, it doesn't seem right," Lizzy dropped her head. Sophie hugged her.

"Lizzy, there is plenty left for me. Don't worry," Sophie laughed.

Lizzy turned to CJ. "Should I take it?"

"That's not up to me or you. That was Clair's choice," CJ took her hand.

"We can use it to start building our house, CJ."

"If that's what you want. It's your money," CJ said.

"No, it's our money," Lizzy turned back to Sophie. "Thank you, Sophie."

"Why are you thanking me. Just enjoy it." Sophie stood to hug Lizzy. Lizzy stood, and they hugged for a long time."

"Your mother was the most generous woman I ever met, next to you," Lizzy whispered in her ear. Sophie wondered if she knew she had something to do with this.

"Ok, back to business," David said. When the ladies were seated, he continued. "And, of course, the rest of the estate goes to you, Sophie."

After they left the room, Lizzy stopped Sophie. "Are you sure you are all right with this?"

"Lizzy, you know I am. Please don't feel bad. If you do, it will ruin the blessing."

"You're right. I am excited. This means we can start building our houses at the same time."

"I know, I can't wait," Sophie said. CJ and Houston were further down the hall.

"Houston, this is Sophie's doing. Isn't it?" CJ asked.

"She knows best what her mom would want. Wouldn't you think?"

"So, it is?"

"CJ..."

"All right... Sophie has always been the most generous person I've ever known. I'm sure Lizzy knows it too."

The small group went out to lunch, and then CJ had to return to work. He put Jett in his car seat and helped Coco get in. "See you in a few hours, honey," CJ said.

Sophie and Houston said goodbye to them and headed home. "I think she knows this was your doing, Sophie," Houston said.

"It doesn't matter. It's done now. And I know my mother would approve. You don't mind, do you, Houston?"

"No, of course not. It's your money, you can do what you want with it. And I know how much Lizzy means to you."

"Houston, I really want to help with the June Duncan case," Sophie put her hand up to stop Houston from saying it. "I know we don't have a client. But I want to."

"Ok. I will call Agent Berry to see if he will give you an introduction to the detective who caught the case. You can see if he is willing to work with our firm. I promised Fons we would get to work on remodeling the office as soon as we got back. We owe it to him to start bringing in a livable income. They dropped everything to join us."

"I understand. You and Fons need to get the office running. I don't mind working on it by myself."

"Just promise me, if it becomes dangerous, you will let me know. Then Fons and I will join you," Houston said.

"It's a deal. Can you call Agent Berry now?"

Houston pulled out his phone.

TO
BE
CONTINUED.

FROM THE AUTHOR

I hope you enjoyed the new characters in this book. At first, I planned on making Felix and Robin Wynne truly bad guys. But when I got into the story, I realized they were just dumb kids that made a very bad choice in a desperate situation. I couldn't put them in jail or let them be killed.

That's the thing, you can't look at someone and decide by their circumstance they have a bad heart.

The Bible says, "...Man looketh on the outward appearance, but the Lord looketh on the heart." 1 Samuel 16:7. KJV

L. J.

If you enjoyed this book, please write a review. It's the only way I can tell if I am writing something people want to read.

www.ingramcontent.com/pod-product-compliance
Lightning Source LLC
Chambersburg PA
CBHW070837260626
47170CB00007B/2404